DOCTOR · WHO

THE INSIDE STORY

GARY RUSSELL

BOOKS

Published by BBC Books, BBC Worldwide Ltd,
80 Wood Lane, London W12 0TT
First published 2006.

BBC Books would like to thank the following
for providing photographs and for permission to
reproduce copyright material. While every effort has
been made to trace and acknowledge all copyright
holders, we would like to apologise should there
have been any errors or omissions.
All images copyright © BBC, except:
pages 254 and 255 courtesy Russell T Davies
pages 33, 37, 98, 99, 100, 156 (top), 160 (top
right), 161 (top and centre), 174 (top right) and 206
courtesy Mike Tucker
pages 110, 113, 146 (top left), 152 (bottom left)
courtesy Lucinda Wright.
All production designs and storyboards are
reproduced courtesy of the *Doctor Who* Art
Department.
Images on pages 93, 96, 101, 106, 155 and 156
(bottom) courtesy of Millennium FX.
All Computer Generated Imagery courtesy of The
Mill, including images on pages 31, 38, 83, 103,
104, 105, 108, 109, 130 (top), 170 (bottom), and
210 (top) and design on page 31.

ISBN-13: 978 0 563 48649 7
ISBN-10: 0 563 48649 X

Commissioning Editor: Stuart Cooper
Project Editor: Steve Tribe
Design and original illustrations
by Lee Binding @ tea-lady
Production Controller: Peter Hunt

Colour origination and printing
by Butler & Tanner Ltd, Frome, England.

CONTENTS

ACKNOWLEDGEMENTS

A book of this size and scope is far more than just the writing done by the credited author. And the list of thanks may well resemble an Oscar actress's acceptance speech but, credit where credit's due, I couldn't have done this without:

Stuart Cooper at BBC Books, who offered me the task in the first place. You fool!

Steve Tribe, editor extraordinaire, who understands how to keep all the balls in the air and manages to ensure everyone is happy all the time.

Lee Binding, the only designer I ever wanted on this project, and I got 'im! Hooray for brilliant Lee!

Ian Farrington, Joseph Lidster and Stuart Manning, supportive best mates and top transcribers, whose fingers are numb now. And Stewart Sheargold who kept me vastly amused as we considered 'What If the *Doctor Who* incidental music had been by Bananarama rather than Murray Gold?'

Kari Speers, for more top transcribing and instant proofreading.

Every single person I interviewed for this book (all forty-plus of you, blimey), marvellous, the lot of you, particularly those who directly led me to other 'victims'. Please note: a handful of quotes have been unceremoniously reworked from (but with the full cooperation of) *Doctor Who Confidential*.

The handful of people who tried to help but couldn't for all sorts of good reasons, thank you anyway.

Everyone up at BBC Cardiff who made me so welcome, often at the busiest times – a list too long to run with here but including obviously Russell, Julie and Phil, Ian Grutchfield, Ross Southard, Matt Nicholls, Helen Raynor, Simon Winstone, Lindsey Alford, Jo Pearce, Brian Minchin, Matthew Bouch, Jan Arwyn Jones, Gillane Seaborne, Susie Liggat, Matt North, Jonathan Allison, Peter McKinstry and both Claire Joneses.

To a gang of folk who know why they're listed here – big hugs and thank yous: Clayton Hickman, Tom Spilsbury, John Ainsworth, David Darlington, Scott Handcock, Jason Haigh-Ellery, John Binns, James Goss, Justin Richards, Peter Griffiths, Allan Smith, Ken Ellington and Andrew Pixley (the most generous man in the world).

Finally, I want to dedicate this entire book to someone it simply couldn't have been done without – Edward Russell (no relation) whose tireless enthusiasm, dedication and friendship meant that the whole process was painless, smooth and above all, damn good fun. Cheers, mate, you're a star!

FOREWORD BY DAVID TENNANT

It's 30 June 2006, and yesterday we started work on the third series of *Doctor Who*. By the time this book reaches the printers, we will be right in the thick of it.

This year, just like last year, we will make a single hour-long Christmas special and thirteen forty-five-minute episodes. When filming begins in earnest next week, it will feel like we've started running and can't slow down for nine months. Each day blasts into the next, the scripts keep coming, the lines keep needing to be learnt; it is a relentless and unstoppable beast of a schedule. Friends and family get used to not hearing from you for months on end as the machine of production lurches back into life and steals the rest of your life away. Nothing can quite prepare you for the peculiar, delightful torture of working on this show.

I've been acting for quite a few years now, but nothing is like this. At yesterday's read-through of the Christmas episode, *The Runaway Bride*, the whole team was assembled,

milling round, drinking coffee, nibbling on pastries (it is a law of television that script readthroughs must always be accompanied by coffee and pastries) and greeting each other like long-lost siblings. It is only eleven weeks since we finished work on the last series, but everyone seems relieved to be back. Working on this show grips you with a fevered and slightly worrying all-consuming obsession and it's much easier to spend time in the company of fellow sufferers. Friends, family, even confidante pets don't appreciate the unique mania that *Doctor Who* fills one's soul with.

We assemble around a long table in a posh hotel in the centre of Cardiff and Jane Tranter, the BBC's Controller of Drama Commissioning, fixes us all with a wild grin (she only visits us every so often, but the madness has got to her too, you can just catch the glint in her eye every so often – oh, she hides it well, she's a big powerful TV executive, she has to sit in meetings with the sane, telling them how the licence fee is in safe hands, but here, amongst all of us, she can't pretend) and welcomes us back.

Next to her sits Julie Gardner, the Head of Drama for BBC Wales and executive producer of the show. She is the busiest woman on the planet. There hasn't been a single thirty-second period in the last four years when her mobile phone hasn't rung at least eight times, she hasn't slept for more than twenty minutes since 2004, and she is, at this very moment, double-booked for six meetings on another three projects, but her enthusiasm and glee at being back with this show is edible.

Next to her is producer Phil Collinson, fizzing and bubbling with it all, laughing his glorious, head-back laugh and beaming at his assembled team, who all grin back, the *Who*-madness glinting off their teeth.

Next to Phil sits Russell T Davies. Head writer, executive producer and the one who has infected this roomful of lunatics. It is his brilliant, fantastic, witty, mind-expanding

scripts that inspire the affection, commitment and absurdly long hours that everyone in this room is about to pour into the next nine months of filming. It was Russell who started it.

Except it wasn't, of course, because *Doctor Who* started years ago. In 1963 to be exact. This generation of children is not the first to be growing up captivated by the TARDIS. Russell himself was prompted to become a writer, in no small part, by a fascination with the Doctor. I was there too. Every Saturday night in front of the telly, gripped, enraptured and enthused by this odd, unquantifiable TV show.

There is something about the type of imagination that powers *Doctor Who* that sweeps up viewers and inspires them in unexpected ways. Something about its mix of the fantastic and the mundane, the far-flung with the domestic, that is unlike anything else. Something like that anyway. I won't claim to have identified what makes *Doctor Who* work, it is far too nebulous and ephemeral, and anyway once you can understand something magical it just becomes a trick. All I know is that everyone who was in that room yesterday is intent on keeping it going. For the next nine months we will have the time of our lives pushing ourselves, and each other, to make the best show we possibly can. Of course it's also the hardest work we've ever done. Who knows how long we can keep it up without killing ourselves but, for now, it is a huge privilege to be part of this big, bonkers and brilliant show.

Enjoy this book. It has been put together with great love and more man hours than can possibly be justified, but then... its author is one of us. You see I know that he grew up with this show too, he knows the madness, and more than that – as soon as he sends this off to the publisher, he's coming to Cardiff to be one of our script editors. Oh yes, look at his eyes. See the gleam...

And, as you have bought this book, then presumably you know at least a little bit about this madness of which I speak. There is probably already a corner of your soul that is dimensionally transcendental. I bet there is. Isn't it great? Isn't it? It's fine. You're among friends. Thank you for coming along with us. Thank you for watching. Enjoy.

David Tennant

AN ADVENTURE IN SPACE AND TIME

When *Doctor Who* began its current run on BBC Television in March 2005, everyone at the BBC, the long-term fans and followers, and the millions of 'casual' viewers who remembered it from their childhoods all held their breath, hoping it would be good, be successful and, above all, be fab!

Obviously, it was. The ratings were great, the audience appreciation figures were high, and the evening audience share was 'marvellous'. Forty per cent or more of the television audience (as much as twenty per cent of the population) was watching *Doctor Who*, and the show became a fixture in television's weekly top twenty, a chart generally dominated by innumerable soap operas and little else. The BBC bosses were ecstatic, the newspapers were supportive and ITV could only watch dumbstruck as whatever competition they put against the show during its first two series couldn't hold a candle to the good Doctor's success.

But two more important questions remained. Why was it so successful? And how had it brought in two demographics (oh yes, such meeja-speak is a necessary evil in today's television industry; you or I would probably just say 'types of people') that had certainly been lacking in the final years of the original version of *Doctor Who*, namely teenaged girls and under-tens of both sexes?

Before this book takes us behind the scenes of *Doctor Who* to find out how it was made, how it was brought, all shiny and gleaming, into the twenty-first century, and how every decision, and subsequent repercussion, was discussed, explored and deconstructed, we need to take a brief sojourn back in time to find out exactly what *Doctor Who* the TV series is, where it began and why it is held in such affection by millions of viewers around the globe. If you want a really expertly detailed look at the history of the show, the stories and their creators, allow me to point you towards Justin Richards' rather splendid book *Doctor Who: The Legend Continues* but, in the meantime, here are the basics.

Who is the Doctor? (He's never called 'Doctor Who', oh no, no, no.) He's a Time Lord. From the planet Gallifrey. He, like all his fellow Time Lords, is essentially immortal (barring accidents), having at least twelve 'regenerations', those magic moments when he can completely rebuild his body and personality. For millennia, the Time Lords inhabited their secluded world, observing other planets, other cultures, recording and filing away the information they gathered for purposes no one can quite figure out. Perhaps they were just nosey. But whatever the reason, the Doctor decided to opt out and he fled his home planet, stealing one of their dimensionally transcendental time ships (that means it's bigger inside than out – don't ask how that happens, it's a closely guarded Time Lord secret), and began his explorations. Accompanied over the years by a number of companions (a better word might be 'friends'), the Doctor went across time and space, righting wrongs, helping the underachievers, the undervalued and the downtrodden.

Along the way he made enemies – amongst which were the Daleks, the Cybermen, the Ice Warriors, the Nestenes, the Sontarans and even a fellow Time Lord in exile, the Master. But he always triumphed, using his wits, his skills and his sonic screwdriver to overcome the odds. He was rarely cowardly or unkind, only resorting to violence when

Above: The TARDIS, the most iconic and irreplaceable element of Doctor Who throughout its forty-three-year history.
Below: Matthew Savage's concept art for the Cyber Controller in The Age of Steel.

every other option had been tried at least three times. The Doctor abhorred guns, decried the obvious military solutions of bombing an enemy into extinction and was always willing to sacrifice himself to rescue his friends and sometimes to save a people or planet he'd only just encountered. That's the kind of man he was – he believed in the goodness of the universe. To all intents and purposes, he was a classic hero.

On the factual side, *Doctor Who* was a television series, devised in the optimistic, post-war expansion of the medium in the early 1960s. One 2006 episode, *The Idiot's Lantern*, showed us how, ten years before *Doctor Who* was created, television was still a primitive device, watched by very few, and rather starch and pompous in its delivery – very austere and somewhat patronising to its audience. Over the next ten years, television sets entered more and more homes and, after the advent of ITV's commercial competition in 1955, BBC Television developed a more populist approach. The BBC began to prioritise mass entertainment. Suddenly things like 'ratings', 'audience shares' and 'appreciation indexes' mattered to those BBC bosses. Thus *Doctor Who* was born out of a desire to create a Saturday evening teatime series aimed, unusually, at not just one part of the traditional viewing family (typically, a programme was made either for children or for adults). The BBC's new Head of Drama, Sydney Newman, wanted a serial that, for twenty-five minutes, the whole family – kids, mums, dads, grans and granddads – would watch together. Something fantastical, that would take them on a journey. Something to combine that old BBC adage: to inform, educate and entertain.

Doctor Who arrived on television on 23 November 1963, and there it stayed, changing lead actors, timeslots and sometimes even moving away from Saturdays altogether. It became a national institution, a show that most people in most places in the UK had watched at some time. And words such as 'Dalek', 'TARDIS', 'Cyberman' and 'Regeneration' were slowly but surely absorbed into the English language. Even those who didn't actually watch the show would know that if someone said his house was 'like a TARDIS', he meant it looked small but was actually larger than it appeared; it didn't matter that the house didn't resemble an old-fashioned police box. *Doctor Who* had become part of twentieth-century culture.

But all good things must come to an end and, by 1989, the longest-running television sci-fi series in the world had outstayed its welcome. No longer a groundbreaking leading light of television drama, it had become a victim of its own success. From 1963, clashes between the Daleks and William Hartnell's First Doctor could draw audiences of ten or twelve million; in the mid 1970s, Tom Baker's Fourth Doctor led *Doctor Who* to a regular place in television's top thirty. By the late 1980s, however, millions of people just assumed it was there, they didn't need to watch it, *Doctor Who* just, well, existed. Of course, the truth of the economics of television is that no programme survives if no one watches it. Saying it's a national institution is all very well, but if people forgo tuning in, it has to go. And so, on 6 December 1989, twenty-six years, one week and six days after the show began, the Seventh Doctor (Sylvester McCoy) and his companion walked off together into the English countryside, talking about burning skies, cities made from song, danger, injustice and tea getting cold. One of the best moments in the whole history of the show saw a television legend fade from our screens, and many thought it was gone for good.

In fact, it very nearly was. In 1996, a television movie made in Canada, co-produced by Universal Television and Fox – both in America – and the BBC was

made, featuring Paul McGann as a new Doctor (the eighth in fact). With over nine million viewers, the movie was very successful in the UK, but it fared poorly Stateside and, as that was where it had been made and where the money was mostly coming from, it marked the Eighth Doctor's only television outing. For many, the television movie was seen as the final nail in the coffin of *Doctor Who*.

Yet *Doctor Who* continued away from the television screens in many forms, before and after the broadcast of the movie. BBC Worldwide gradually released all of the classic series on video, DVD, audio cassette and CD, while a record-breaking run of over 250 original novels has been published since 1991, initially by Virgin Publishing in the form of *The New Adventures*, and latterly by BBC Books. *Doctor Who Magazine*, published by Panini, has continued uninterrupted since 1979, complete with a comic strip – which in itself holds a record as the longest-running continuous comic strip based on a television series in the world. Starting in *TV Comic* in 1964, brand new exploits for the Doctor have been drawn without a break ever since. In 1999, Big Finish Productions began a continuing monthly series of audio CD adventures starring the original TV series actors reprising their roles. These official and licensed continuations of the Doctor's story may have been seen by a smaller audience than can be gained by television, but the general public's fondness for the show was demonstrated in many surveys and awards, one highpoint coming during the BBC's celebrations for its sixtieth birthday in 1996. The viewers' vote on that occasion confirmed *Doctor Who* as the nation's Favourite Popular Drama. Seven years later, the show was still not forgotten and, in August 2003, *Radio Times* readers chose *Doctor Who* as the programme they would most like to see returned to their screens.

Meanwhile, never one to let a good thing die, the BBC waited and waited, until the right team of producers, writers, directors and actors could be brought together. On 26 September 2003, the BBC was finally ready to make an announcement to the world:

Doctor Who, one of the BBC's best-loved and most enduring characters, is set to return to BBC One, it was confirmed last night by Lorraine Heggessey, Controller of BBC One. Heggessey said that all rights issues regarding *Doctor Who* have been resolved and that she has green-lit scripts from award-winning writer Russell T Davies.

And, from that moment on, a legend was reborn…

Bringing Back the Series

'The extraordinary thing about the three people in charge of *Doctor Who* nowadays is that you can ask anything about the production, or bring up a problem, to any one of them and it gets resolved, because if you talk to Phil you're also talking to Russell and Julie. If you say something to Russell, then Phil and Julie will get to know about it straight away, because it's for all their ears, they are as one. Russell is the heart of that team, he keeps everything beating, everything is driven by him. I find Julie extraordinary – she's there for you, and is totally hands-on, as much as her time and her job will allow her to be. Phil's a terrific producer, he's a tremendous support – he's got an old head on young shoulders and I like the dreams he has. I found them extraordinary. It was a very, very happy team.'
Graeme Harper, director, Series Two and Three

BRINGING BACK THE SERIES

There's an old adage, 'There's many a slip twixt cup and lip,' which basically means that it's all very well having great ideas, but you have to be prepared for any number of things to go wrong before you get exactly what you wanted.

It is fairly standard in the world of television production that lots of things will indeed go wrong, often hideously so, before it all goes right. *Doctor Who*, however, seems to have been a bit of an exception to that rule — nearly everything went pretty much to plan. Yes, it was hard work, involved many sleepless nights, frayed tempers and occasional hiccups, but *Doctor Who*'s genesis between September 2003 and its first day before the cameras (a day that involved a Time Lord, some soldiers, a scientist destined for bigger things and a little piggy in the sweetest spacesuit ever) was pretty darn smooth.

Of course, all great ideas have to start somewhere and, although what we now have on our screens may well be the most perfect vision of *Doctor Who* for the twenty-first century, Russell T Davies wasn't the only person to have had thoughts about how to bring the show back. Apart from co-creating the BBC One drama *Life on Mars*, and writing *Fear Her* for *Doctor Who*'s second series, Matthew Graham had batted a few ideas around himself a handful of years ago.

'I wouldn't have made it as bubbly and fun as Russell has,' he laughs. 'I'd probably have made them all two- or three-parters, because cliffhangers are very much part of my memory of *Doctor Who*. I would probably have tinkered too much — been tempted to change the TARDIS a bit, to change the Daleks too much, modernise them, re-imagine them, which I can see now would have been a big mistake, because you don't need to. But they must have had those debates, sat there and said, "Is the TARDIS going to be a portaloo, or is it going to be a modern phone box? Are kids going to understand what a police box is?" So I think I would have kept the sense of invention that Russell did, but probably made it a bit more Gothic. And darker.'

And what of Matthew's idea for the Doctor — was he thinking darker in tone for his leading man as well? After all, the press were throwing up no shortage of names, including the downright bizarre, like magician Paul Daniels and even 1980s pop star Phil Oakey of the Human League. But amongst those nonsensical pieces of fluff were a few good, solid actors. People such as Richard E Grant, Bill Nighy and Ken Stott. 'I think, at the end of the day, a younger Doctor is more fun,' concedes Matthew. 'But I'd have probably gone older which, hindsight shows us, would have been a mistake.'

'DIDN'T THEY WANT TO SEE A DINOSAUR WALKING DOWN A LONDON STREET?'

So if that's a vision for the show that didn't materialise, what of the one that did? The one spearheaded by executive producer, head writer and all-round creative powerhouse Russell T Davies. With a career stretching back to 1987, Russell had become one of British television's leading writers, with such recent successes as *The Second Coming* and *Bob & Rose*, and a series of credits taking in the children's fantasy drama serials *Dark Season* and *Century Falls* and hotel drama *The Grand*. As what the Americans term a 'show-runner', Russell is the driving force behind today's *Doctor Who*. He had first put forward a proposal to revamp the show back in the late 1990s — 'so unfocused

The sequences with Jimmy Vee as the space pig in Aliens of London *were the very first ones shot for the new series* of Doctor Who.

and flimsy, it doesn't bear thinking about,' he says dismissively of it today. A meeting took place towards the end of 1999, with Patrick Spence, an executive at the BBC Drama Department, but nothing came of it. Then a couple of years later Russell found himself at another meeting, this time with an executive producer called Laura Mackie. They were discussing various projects with Russell, who had by then garnered a lot of acclaim for his Channel 4 drama series *Queer as Folk*. The BBC wanted Russell to join them, and used *Doctor Who* as a carrot, according to the man himself.

'They kept saying to me that they knew I really wanted to bring back *Doctor Who* but, having mentioned it for five seconds, they'd try to interest me in things like a new version of *A Tale of Two Cities*. Although they weren't particularly big *Doctor Who* pitches, the one with Laura was more detailed. I sat there and talked about *The Weakest Link*, suggesting we could use that in an episode, and I talked about dinosaurs because they'd just made *Walking with Dinosaurs*, which was everywhere. I said that, much as I liked those dinosaurs wandering round the plains of Africa, didn't they want to see a dinosaur walking down a twenty-first-century London street? Wouldn't that be a marvellous drama? I said that was what could be done with *Doctor Who*. I was pitching that sort of stuff, but nothing was ever written down – it was just twenty minutes of chat before they tried to get me to make something else.'

But even those brief meetings don't represent Russell's first written foray into the *Doctor Who* world. In 1991, he had written what he terms 'a kids' thriller' for BBC One, entitled *Dark Season*. 'That first brought me into contact with the sci-fi specialist world. I was interviewed by a lovely man, David Richardson, and he suggested I write a *Doctor Who* novel for Virgin, who were publishing *The New Doctor Who Adventures*. And I thought that was a good idea: I had been reading them on and off, I'd always wanted to do prose, and I thought it was a great opportunity.' And it was – the book was eventually commissioned and published in October 1996 to terribly positive reviews. Called *Damaged Goods*, Russell is justifiably very proud of it.

If you can find a copy of the novel, a quick flick through it will show that the nascent ideas within its pages would definitely shape what was to come to our screens less than a decade later: the urban settings to firmly place the show in the real world, and the monsters and menaces that affect real people with real emotions. And yet there are aspects of it that necessarily veer very definitely away from Russell's television show. The whole range of Virgin *New Adventures* books was aimed at readers aged seventeen-plus, and thrived on being very dark and very gritty. The readership that Russell was writing for in 1996 was appropriate – the eighteen-year-olds were *Doctor Who*'s audience by then, children and younger teenagers were far more excited by *Power Rangers* on TV, *Final Fantasy* on the PlayStation and the dying embers of Britpop on their CD players. *Doctor Who* was not cool, not 'retro' and certainly not watched by anyone who didn't have an emotional or, more truthfully, nostalgic attachment to the show. 'There were some adult themes in the book,' Russell concedes, 'with endless amounts of violence. I could introduce a character for one chapter just to kill them brilliantly. I loved to do that, and I wanted to put that into a novel, but you could never do that for *Doctor Who* on-screen, absolutely never. So, the influence of *Damaged Goods* really is half and half. That reality of "situation" and "character" is here in the TV show, but nothing else. Real characters are almost more important to me. If I was writing something called *Moonbase 67*, then the cook would be a main character and the man in charge of oiling the airlocks would be a very important character, rather than the bosses in their silver wigs.'

Having been a *Doctor Who* fan since seeing the First Doctor, William Hartnell, turn into the Second, Patrick Troughton, in 1966, Russell believed the series deserved a future. But the 1990s were clearly not a great time to announce to the world that your burning ambition was to make a new version of *Doctor Who*. 'I remember being at Granada TV in the early 1990s, when independent approaches were being talked about because the BBC was keen for an independent company to bid for the show. I mentioned this to David Liddiment, who was Granada's Head of Drama, and I was

Two aspects of the same ship. The new police box shell on the brand new TARDIS interior set.

practically blasted out of the room: "Why would we touch that piece of rubbish?" And I was saying, "Yes, you're absolutely right," and flinching.'

'THE BEST OF ALL WORLDS': THE TELEVISION EXECUTIVE

Strange the way things work out… Fast forward to 2003, and a huge, typically 1960s piece of architecture dominating the start of London's premiere thoroughfare, the A40 – Wood Lane to be specific. This is the BBC's main headquarters, Television Centre. Shaped like a question mark, it is home to BBC News 24, the *Blue Peter* garden and a tall plinth topped by a statue of Helios, the Greek god of the sun. With the exception of a four-week stint in Birmingham in 1977, and a number of expensive sojourns abroad in its later years, *Doctor Who* had always been recorded in and around the BBC studios in West London, from Hammersmith's famed Riverside Studios to the old 1940s movie studios Lime Grove in the heart of Shepherds Bush. But its main home was the BBC Television Centre in White City, containing six studios of varying sizes (the biggest, TC1, was for many years reckoned to be the largest studio in Europe and many a Dalek or Cybermen fell to the Doctor's cleverness in there). At TV Centre can be found one of the show's staunchest defenders and a prime mover in the twenty-first-century relaunch: the lady charged with commissioning the BBC's entire drama output, Jane Tranter. It was Jane who struck the deal with the then Controller of BBC One, Lorraine Heggessey, to return the show to our screens.

Russell T Davies informs an industry conference about his plans for the as-yet unbroadcast new series of Doctor Who.

'We wanted to bring *Doctor Who* back,' volunteers Jane, 'because it felt like something which potentially had the best of all worlds. If you consider that its historical baggage is a really good and positive thing – which I did – then it is a brilliant idea.'

It had been a long time since the BBC had shown home-grown drama on early Saturday evenings, least of all a supposedly niche programme like *Doctor Who*. Other fantasy-based output – such as *Strange* and the reworking of another old 1960s series, *Randall & Hopkirk (Deceased)* – had occupied a later timeslot. Both of those had, to some extent, failed, so why should the Saturday evening audience be crying out for another old show to be given a new lease of life?

'*Doctor Who* brings sci-fi to the screens in a very user-friendly way,' believes Jane, 'because, in fact, it's barely sci-fi. *Doctor Who* is bigger than that. We're talking the biggest universal themes, we're talking the essence of who we are and where we live and what we stand for. We're talking about the basic fight between good and evil. There isn't a bigger idea than *Doctor Who*. I think that, for anyone of my generation, the series is a big part of our television history – it's a big part of folk memory. I watched *Doctor Who* all the time as a kid and, when I first came to work at BBC Drama, I put up in the office an enormous black and white photograph of a Dalek, alongside one of Carol White in *Cathy Come Home* and one of *Dixon of Dock*

Green, to remind everyone working in BBC Drama of our roots and our history.'

If the programme was to return, however, there was a potential obstacle to overcome – the actual rights to *Doctor Who*, although it was a BBC show, were mired down as a result of the 1996 television movie. Universal and Fox Network's options had long since dropped, but the domestic rights were held by a subsidiary of the BBC, BBC Films. Over the years, there had been brief moments when BBC Films had looked into bringing *Doctor Who* back as a theatrical movie, but these had gone nowhere. Jane asked Alan Yentob, who was then the BBC's Director of Drama and Entertainment and a long-time supporter of the series, to help sort through the mess. Using his not-inconsiderable influence, Yentob did so and subsequently told Jane that the programme was now hers to relaunch. 'Then,' she says, 'all I needed to do was find the right person to make it – and there was only one name.'

Jane first met Russell in October 2001 at the Manchester launch of a BBC drama series called *Linda Green*, made by a production company called Red, which had also made *Queer as Folk* for Channel 4. *Linda Green*'s producer was Nicola Shindler. She had been the producer of a number of shows, including Russell's *Queer as Folk*, *The Second Coming* and *Bob & Rose*. Jane recalls that Nicola passed her a message, because Russell was allegedly too shy to tell Jane directly, that one thing he would absolutely love to do would be to bring back *Doctor Who*.

'And that was really the moment when, instead of just being an old photograph on a wall, *Doctor Who* suddenly made perfect sense. I'd never worked with Russell but I knew his work very well, and I had no hesitation asking him. Although his background isn't in family drama, he has terrific humanity, a brilliant sense of comedy, and is naturally witty, warm and irreverent. He has a very modern sensibility as a writer, and yet the themes of his stories – whether he's writing *Queer as Folk* or whether he's writing *The Second Coming* – are universal. And he is a terrific craftsman: he's got a very strong sense of structure; he knows how to hold a narrative; he has a brilliant sense of pace and velocity. And so I knew we'd have something with *Doctor Who* that would mean something, and that would be funny, and that would feel modern. I didn't know if the series itself was going to work, but I knew that as a piece of drama we would have something that would be worthwhile in many ways and on many different levels.'

Jane was admittedly anxious – would today's television audience buy into it? But she decided not to focus on that and instead to concentrate on producing the best piece of drama they could, and on marketing it as well as they could. It was felt that, whilst no one can make an audience watch a genre that they don't want to watch, they could ignore the genre pigeon-hole and just think about making a quality drama. 'Russell arrived for a meeting one day,' Jane smiles, 'and gave me a toy Dalek that still sits on my office window sill – I knew then that we could do it and it wouldn't fail.' Jane suspects that the most difficult thing for Russell was finding the 'voice' of the Doctor and getting the tone right for the twenty-first century. So they had discussion after discussion, meeting after meeting, and Jane saw Russell's confidence in the programme grow.

Initially, it was thought of as a six-part series, the standard for most BBC dramas. At the suggestion of BBC Worldwide, this quickly became thirteen episodes, more attractive to overseas buyers but far more than would normally have been commissioned by the BBC. 'That was a mild anxiety,' Jane suggests, 'simply because we're not used to running with that many. But each episode is a self-contained story, apart from the occasional two-parter, so it wasn't as if we were tackling a great big thirteen-part serial or something. And I knew that Steven Moffat was really keen to do *Doctor Who*, so having him on the writing team made us all feel very confident I think.'

'When I walked into our first meeting,' Russell adds, 'it was six episodes, forty-five minutes long, early Saturday nights. Jane just smiled and said, "Off you go, if you want to." It was confirmed as going out at seven o'clock right from the word go, and that's the genius of it: not eight o'clock, not six o'clock, so we knew exactly where we were pitching at. That was absolutely brilliant. Forty-five minutes was perfect too, we didn't even debate length for a second. I'm absolutely happy with that – it's the perfect time for modern drama. Fifty minutes? Doable, but I suspect that an extra five minutes would be five minutes of chat because, in terms of the practicalities of filming, of post-production, of effects work, we're already absolutely at the limit, so you'd have to slot five minutes of chat into an episode. That could be done

Right: Christopher Eccleston and Billie Piper rehearse the opening TARDIS scenes for The Empty Child.

– especially because they're my bosses, I'll do whatever they want. If they turn round and suddenly say, "We're doing hour-long episodes," somehow we'd make it work. We'd need significantly more money for that and more time, but we'd make it work. Anything works, as long as you write it properly.'

The only thing Russell was dubious about was that Jane Tranter and Mal Young, then the BBC's Controller of Continuing Drama Series and an executive producer alongside Russell on Series One, wanted every story to be a two-parter. Possibly they were thinking of story lengths in terms of traditional *Doctor Who*, which had utilised cliffhangers and continuous stories, often spread over four weeks. Russell knew he could argue that one down. 'I just pointed out that if they looked at all the American shows running, none of those did it that way. You might have a few two-parters, I said, halfway through and at the end, but I wouldn't start with one and I wouldn't make the majority of them like that. I wasn't keen either on that American thing of cliffhangers between seasons. End on a high, make people anxious for the next season yes, but stopping halfway through a story, with a banner saying "To be concluded" – no thanks. It just doesn't feel right to me. I'm not saying they're wrong, because it can create a buzz, but it's a buzz created just at the time. Six months later when you're back on air, where's your buzz then? That's a very hard thing to keep going, and it's very unfriendly. "Ooh, did you see that cliffhanger last year?" And if you didn't, you're not remotely interested in the new series. If you can anticipate an episode that's coming up – "Look, we've got great cast to come; look, we've got an old monster to come" – great. But if it's "Look, we're going to resolve that issue that was last broadcast six months ago", that's not good. There's no energy in that.'

'CARDIFF HAS BEEN USED MAGNIFICENTLY': BBC WALES AND JULIE GARDNER

With the basics sorted out, the next big question was where was it going to be made. The days of all major series being made at TV Centre were long gone – the majority of modern television drama is made well outside the confines of those old studios and

something as big as *Doctor Who* for a new millennium needed space to breath. Even the biggest studio at the BBC's HQ was never going to accommodate thirteen almost mini-movie productions. Enter BBC Wales…

Broadcasting House in Llandaff, a few minutes outside Cardiff city centre, is another piece of 1960s architecture. Built on the site of the famous Bayton House, and still overshadowed by two huge trees that overlooked that earlier building, BBC Cardiff's Broadcasting House might not seem the most obvious place to choose to recreate *Doctor Who*. But the BBC has a commitment within its Charter to assign a certain amount of its output to 'the regions'. As a publicly funded corporation, this means that a certain amount of work is guaranteed to those who pay for the BBC to function. Programmes that are transmitted locally ('regional') and throughout the UK ('networked') are made at a number of the BBC's many regional broadcast centres. So, why Cardiff for *Doctor Who*?

Jane Tranter suggests that one important reason for this choice of home for the TARDIS was the appointment in July 2003 of Julie Gardner to head Cardiff's drama output. 'This was around the time that we were sorting out the rights for *Doctor Who*. Julie knew Russell and she was very likely going to work with him in Wales, because they had been doing *Casanova* together, which was moving with Julie from ITV to BBC Three. I felt it would have been perverse not to have asked Julie to work on *Doctor Who* with Russell.' The only drawback, if it can be called that, was that Julie, unlike Russell and Jane, hadn't really watched *Doctor Who*. But Jane grins at this, pointing out that, within forty-eight hours, Julie was sat amidst a pile of tapes immersing herself in its rich history. 'She's become the world's leading expert!' Jane laughs. 'All of that aside, to make a show like *Doctor Who* as big and successful as we wanted it to be, you're going to have to build somewhere to film it. So it may as well be in Wales as anywhere else. And Cardiff has been used magnificently in *Doctor Who*. Julie has been so clever about that.'

And the object of this praise herself? When Julie Gardner was offered the job as Head of Drama, BBC Wales, she was unaware that there were plans to bring back *Doctor Who*, but she was well aware that one of the people the BBC wanted to convince to work for them was Russell. At their very first meeting, she and Jane Tranter discussed a number of projects – including the one Julie was then overseeing with Russell, *Casanova*. Also on the agenda was *Doctor Who* – and Julie immediately knew that this was the show they wanted Russell for. 'I knew he was a huge fan of the show because, throughout the year Russell and I worked together developing *Casanova*, we would talk about it in comparison to *Angel* and *Buffy the Vampire Slayer*. It was a really exciting time for those shows, and we talked about what we could learn from them, what we liked, and why Britain wasn't making things like that.' BBC Wales had not previously made very many dramas at all. Julie's predecessor was Matthew Robinson, who had actually directed two *Doctor Who* adventures in the mid 1980s and had subsequently made a lot of local Welsh programming, but he hadn't really had the opportunity to do much in terms of network programming. Julie's main brief was to build up that network programme-making, and she could see what was coming. 'There's no easier or better way to do something like bring back *Doctor Who* than with a creative genius like Russell at its head.'

Of course, Julie had never made a thirteen-part series before, hence for that first year her safety net was Mal Young, on hand as a co-executive producer. 'I knew Mal really well,' Julie says. 'I also knew that he had, for years and years, pitched the notion of bringing back *Doctor Who*, he really wanted it.' Mal was very experienced at overseeing long-running shows, but he did it from his base in London, which might have implied that Julie would receive a degree of interference from the eastern end of the M4. That didn't happen. 'We were,' Julie affirms, 'fully supported from the moment we started. It's been the easiest experience. The BBC is genuinely pursuing a policy of moving shows to the nations and regions, both independently produced series and in-house shows, and that's really important. Scotland had been flourishing; Ireland is now flourishing too. It was Wales's time at that point, and I think it was a very easy decision: it was a drama department that needed work; I was coming in new; Russell was coming in new; we were both from Wales. It made sense for us to go there, fixing two problems: find a home for *Doctor Who*, and kick-start BBC Wales drama.'

BBC Wales's Broadcasting House in Llandaff, the new home for *Doctor Who*.

It was good for local talent as well, although Julie also brought in a lot of people from outside Wales. 'First and foremost you're looking for the best possible people. For instance, our special effects work is done in London by The Mill. There were people in Bristol that we met, there were people nearby who could have done a great job for us, but there was something about The Mill — the quality of their work was extraordinary, and they had a well-established infrastructure, which a show like ours needed to rely on, so we wanted to utilise that. For other levels of the crew, we went locally — partly because people are there with the right experience, but also you don't want to spend most of your budget on accommodation, on hotels, overnights and travel costs. You want to put as much of your budget as you can on-screen. And inevitably, by basing something in Cardiff, a huge amount of money goes into the local economy.'

They also needed to find somewhere big enough to film it, and to allow the one main set to be permanently erected — termed a standing set, one used repeatedly and never taken down — the TARDIS interior. Cardiff's Broadcasting House drama studio is not huge, and it certainly couldn't cope with the needs of *Doctor Who*. Besides which, it already has standing sets, which belong to the BBC's longest-running soap opera, although few outside Wales have ever heard of it. The drama studio is home, as it has been since 1974, to *Pobol y Cwm* (*People of the Valley*), which has been the staple of BBC Wales's drama output for over thirty years. So once the decision had been made to go to Cardiff, it was obvious that *Doctor Who* was not going to be sharing studio space with the inhabitants of the fictional village of Cwmderi.

'First off, we needed a studio – there was nothing at the BBC's buildings in Cardiff that was even remotely big enough,' Julie confirms. 'So we looked around and found Q2, a warehouse near Newport. Choosing that was a very simple decision to make, mainly because it was within travelling distance of the BBC; again we didn't want to be wasting time getting somewhere.' Q2 had already been used for various local shows, so the BBC crews were used to working from there. Converting a warehouse to a film or television studio is not that uncommon these days. A number of major shows both in the UK and abroad have had to do so because few can afford purpose-built studios and, if these shows don't always need the most perfect sound or the ability to block out light, they can spend money on other things. Ultimately, Q2 proved to be *Doctor Who*'s new home for both of its first two years, and Julie believes it taught the production team a lot about what they do and don't need. As a result, for Series Three, and for the *Doctor Who* spin-off series *Torchwood*, they have moved to another, even larger warehouse, the charmingly named Upper Boat.

SECRET FILMING... IN PUBLIC: FINDING THE RIGHT LOCATIONS

Of course, there's a lot more to *Doctor Who* than the interior sets built at Q2 or Upper Boat. The show thrives on its extensive use of exteriors, or locations as they're usually called. Streets, fronts of buildings, moon surfaces, seasides and schools, anything and everything that a script may require must, if it can't be built cheaply or accurately, be tracked down. Scotland, Norway, even the planet Krop Tor – Wales has doubled for them all in the last two years. And it's not just a small plot of land with a cameraman, a sound-recordist and a handful of actors that go on location. The whole 150-plus crew must be fitted, safely, into these places. This often involves filming on private land, with permissions to be sought, and everything left in the pristine condition it was in when the crew arrived. If, after filming at a location has finished, you can tell a BBC team has been there, someone hasn't been doing their job properly.

South Wales, one of the UK's most beautiful areas, offers the *Doctor Who* production team first-class locations all the way. So much so that, bar the odd excursion to central London – always for specific London-based moments – all of the first twenty-seven episodes of new *Doctor Who* were shot in and around Wales.

One of the reasons for this is that it's easier to travel around Cardiff than London; there's less traffic, and parking is a great deal easier. Logistically, moving a film crew around is less problematic in South Wales. The production team also have access to a huge range of diverse locations. They can do urban wastelands, they can do Victorian, churches, inner-city council estates, beaches and glorious countryside – all within close proximity. 'The one difficulty, if you're doing a thirteen-part series year after year,' explains Julie 'is avoiding replication. Even though you can find locations that you love, and that you want to keep going back to because they're easy to get to or the owners are really accommodating, you have to be very sure that you're redressing them in a way that doesn't feel repetitive.' It is quite possible to reuse locations, provided The Mill can then matte-paint in extra bits and pieces – buildings, skies, all sorts of things have been added in post-production. By way of example, Julie cites a location that is part of Cardiff University, called the Temple of Peace. 'It's in the Civic Centre,' she explains further, 'and has these huge extraordinary white marble pillars. That was a brilliant location for *The End of the World*, because The Mill created the ceiling and the glass roof and covered

Facing page Top: Beaufort Arms Court doubles for a snow-swept Cardiff in The Unquiet Dead. *Bottom: Joe Ahearne points out something on the TARDIS, towered over by the Millennium Centre in Cardiff Bay during the making of* Boom Town.

one wall with green screens so they could superimpose the outside views of the sun exploding later. Now by mixing and matching, that one building gave us a location, plus the opportunity to utilise design and special effects work and so enabled us to maximise our on-screen value. We could never have built it; we could never really have afforded to build one end of that wall properly with that level of pillar and we certainly couldn't have coated a floor in marble. Those kinds of locations are really good in Cardiff – there's a range of great ones.

'Another is the Paper Mill in Sanatorium Road, Canton, where we shot the Nestene Consciousness sequence for the opening episode, *Rose*. To have something that urban, with height, and a staircase on three or four levels was extraordinary – it gave us a set that we couldn't have built, and we would have had problems finding anywhere else so convenient. We have used it a few times since, redressed, because it gives us so much freedom.'

Reusing places can offer up a few headaches for everyone, Julie says. 'I remember us all being very worried by one tiny section of *The Christmas Invasion*, which we filmed below the Millennium Stadium. We've done a lot of work at the stadium, particularly in the basement, because they've got spaces that we're able to build sets in, and because they've got concrete walls and very flat floors. So, we shot *Dalek* in there. We built the Dalek cell, and a lot of the running sequences were along these very flat corridors, which has a staircase at

Right: A selection of alien guests prepare to shoot a scene in Cardiff's Temple of Peace for The End of the World. *Below: The eponymous Dalek hovers around Van Statten's underground base; the platform it sits on was removed in post-production by The Mill.*

the end. There's a scene in the Christmas special where Penelope Wilton and Daniel Evans are realising their workforce is being turned into zombies, and there's one shot in that staircase. We reduced the number of times we saw that shot because we thought people would recognise it from *Dalek*, where the Dalek levitated.'

The Millennium Stadium is one example of the good relationship the team have built up with the inhabitants of Cardiff. Another is the Auton attack from *Rose*, which was filmed on the roads around St Mary Street in the city centre. 'Those streets have massive department stores in them. We shut off those streets for two whole nights – it's hard to think where in London you'd be able to do that! So many people have put themselves out to help us make the show, we've had extraordinary help.' The only downside comes with the legal paperwork, it seems. 'We were shooting on a weekday and, on the previous Friday, the council issued paperwork, explaining that St Mary Street would be shut off to traffic between the hours of two am and eight am. Which was fine except they added that it was due to filming *Doctor Who*. Suddenly everybody in the world knew,' Julie laughs. 'In many ways that was lovely, because we saw first hand the excitement the show generated really early on in our schedule. You can say "Doctor Who" and get access to things that normal drama productions don't. But at the same time, that information was on the Internet and the television news within half

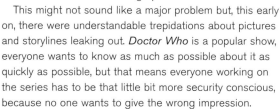

an hour. And on the filming nights, we did have more than a few *Doctor Who* fans turning up.'

This might not sound like a major problem but, this early on, there were understandable trepidations about pictures and storylines leaking out. *Doctor Who* is a popular show, everyone wants to know as much as possible about it as quickly as possible, but that means everyone working on the series has to be that little bit more security conscious, because no one wants to give the wrong impression.

One particular cause for concern was the TARDIS which appeared briefly in those scenes filmed in St Mary Street. At that time, no images of it had yet been made available, simply because it hadn't been finished. Edward Thomas, the series' production designer, was still trying to work out precisely what shade of blue the TARDIS should be and how pristine it should look. In fact, when Julie first saw the TARDIS on location, she asked Edward to repaint it because he'd done too good a job on it! 'I felt it looked really too weather-beaten,' she explains. 'It was a good call by Edward; he wanted to give a sense of it really flying through time and space. The TARDIS is a very physical thing: it crash-lands; things break down – it wasn't going to just be the little safe capsule. He wanted to imply a sense of danger for the Doctor and Rose as they travelled. And part of that was interpreted as it looking quite battered, but when I saw the first paint coat, I thought it looked a bit unfinished. I knew it wasn't supposed to be pristine, but I was worried that, if we weren't careful, on TV it could have looked like a cheap prop – if you come in looking a bit shoddy, however deliberate, people will say "nothing's changed". And Edward's too good a designer to deserve that. And with a lot of fans arriving at the location, what I didn't want was that first paint job being beamed across the net.'

Julie had similar concerns about the costumes of the two leads. 'I didn't want the first pictures of them being seen through mobile phone cameras. When it came to Series Two, I suggested we do a proper, quick photo shoot with David and Billie in their new costumes; we'd get it out; we'd control the image; maybe it would take the pressure off us. Of course, it didn't take any pressure off us at all because although it meant we had a better photo out that we were all happy with, what that photo also showed everyone was the Powell estate, and so everyone guessed we were filming in London. People knew where the Powell estate was. And turned up en masse...'

'THE MAN WITH HIS FINGER ON THE PULSE': ENTER PHIL COLLINSON

After the September 2003 announcement that Russell T Davies and Julie Gardner would be bringing back *Doctor Who* in Cardiff, it was actually another three months before BBC Wales would really begin work on the new series. The first task was to assemble the core production team.

A curious Jackie Tyler (Camille Coduri) emerges from the Powell Estate in *The Christmas Invasion*.

'When we started all this,' Russell explains, 'it was just six episodes. Then suddenly it was thirteen – that might have been my fault, I may have been a bit confident: "Oh, we can do thirteen as easily as we can do eight," I probably said. So many stories to tell, so little time… Anyway, by early 2004, we knew we had to find a producer, the man with his finger on the pulse.'

So enter the next member of the team of producers on *Doctor Who.* With Russell writing and overseeing the stories, Julie sorting out the tone and structure of the show and seeking out money from the BBC, BBC Worldwide and outside investors, it would fall to the newest team member to keep an eye on budgets and coordinate the various departments that came together to physically make the show. Basically to be on set, on location, in the production office and in the editing suites. Preferably simultaneously. But who was going to fill this nigh-on impossible task?

Julie, Russell and Mal Young met up with three producers, early in 2004, all of whom were considered good, and they chose to go with Phil Collinson. Russell had known Phil for many years, and knew he had a great deal of experience in setting up new series, such as *Born and Bred* and *Sea of Souls*. Julie remembers him as being immediately likeable, someone who would throw himself into the show, in the same way that Russell and Julie already had. 'There's not a terribly formal structure between us,' Julie says, 'so if Phil misses a viewing of an edit but Russell and I are there, that's fine; it's very fluid.'

Russell agrees with this. 'He was the script editor on a show I worked on called *Springhill*. I knew he was a *Doctor Who* fan. Not that that matters, but it does help if you speak the language. He was dying to do it – the moment he heard it was coming back, he phoned me up. He'd done *Linda Green* for the BBC, so Jane Tranter and Mal Young already knew him. He was always top of my list.'

Having 'lobbied quite hard for the job', as he puts it, Phil Collinson found himself moving to Cardiff to join Julie and Russell in getting the show under way. 'It was daunting, but daunting in a good way,' he smiles. 'I love a challenge, and this has been one hell of a challenge – right from the word go, really. I was thrilled. I still have moments of disbelief – there are at least one or two of them every week about something, whether it be some monster that you remember watching as a kid, a press launch, viewing a new episode, or just the sheer joy of doing *Doctor Who*. I've never made any secret that I was a big fan of the show when I was younger, and for me, now, to be in this position is amazing on so many different levels.'

'QUITE A RADICAL MOVE': RE-IMAGINING DOCTOR WHO

With the core team in place, it fell to Russell to re-imagine the whole story of *Doctor Who*. But this wasn't an arbitrary reworking of it; however different it would look and, more importantly, feel, this version was still tied to the past of the show. *Doctor Who* in 2005 was a definite continuation of what had run between 1963 and 1989 on the BBC and been reborn so fleetingly in May 1996. This was actually quite a daring idea, because there was an entire generation of television viewers out there who had no idea what *Doctor Who* was and to bring it back, with forty-odd years of history in its wake, might surely have been more of a hindrance than an advantage when trying to inspire the children of 2005 to watch it.

'I wanted the Doctor to be a loner,' explains Russell. 'The opposite of Rose, because we were making quite a radical move, in *Doctor Who* terms, by giving her a family, giving her a mum and a dad and a boyfriend. You want them to be polar opposites. So you give him nothing. But key to that is – instead of giving him a High Council and a planet and big collars, all that stuff – you strip it all away so, the more opposite these two people can be, the more they've got to talk about, the more they connect. That's why the Time Lords had to go, it was a programme coming back with an awful lot of mythology and back story, and I wanted to give it a background in which fans and brand new viewers would be on a level playing field. You didn't have to know about the Death Zone on Gallifrey and the Master and the Rani, Rassilon, the Hand of Omega, all that sort of stuff. Time Lords: strip them away, clear the decks. Very simple decision, really. It put some emotion into him so, rather than saying, "I come from a great big planet full of powerful people," he says, "I am alone." Which statement is going to connect with you more? It's an easy decision. And so every viewer just started from scratch without it being a reboot, which would have upset the viewers that did know all that Time Lord stuff.'

Producer Phil Collinson has always been a fan of K-9 and actually supplied his voice during the café scene rehearsals for School Reunion.

This was also the reason he was referred to as the Ninth Doctor right away – the team knew that's what the newspapers would always call him anyway. And, more importantly, it was how they felt mums and dads would refer to him. Oh, they might not know the right number, but every parent was hopefully going to sit down and explain to their offspring that there had been lots of other Doctors. 'After all,' Russell suggests, 'I doubt that many kids sat down with absolutely no idea at all what *Doctor Who* was. I mean, it's a thing they've seen on DVD, or on UK Gold. Simply because of that, a reboot was never possible. It was, far more importantly, never what I wanted. There was no way I wanted to write a new *Doctor Who*. I wanted him to be the same man who had fought the Macra and the Sea Devils and who was in that junkyard in 1963 and who was in Perivale in 1989. The same man I saw change from Sylvester McCoy into Paul McGann. I wouldn't have been interested in saying this is a different person. Absolutely not!'

Jane Tranter also felt that the history of *Doctor Who*, the whole legacy, needed to be treated with respect and needed to be continued. 'I don't think Russell could have done anything but build on it because he was so interested and embroiled in all of the *Doctor Who* folklore. We always talked about it being twenty-first-century *Doctor Who*, and about the fact that a seven-year-old had to be able to grab hold of it and, as each generation of children had before, claim this Doctor for themselves. We knew that, while there would be a lot of parents who would sit down and say, "My Doctor is Jon Pertwee," we still needed to create *Doctor Who* for the new generation.'

Clearly, moving away from the past yet embracing it as well would always be a difficult tightrope for Russell to walk. He believes he had to find a way of not repeating what had gone before, and indeed of moving on so far that falling into the trap of trying to emulate the show that had gone before wasn't an issue. By 1989, many felt that *Doctor Who* was slightly tired, slightly drained, still telling great stories but no longer relevant to the times they were transmitted in. 'In today's television, you can get to the tired and clichéd point far more quickly than the twenty-six years it had taken them. So we had to revamp the whole thing and I think we set that tone and mood in concrete right from the opening moments of that first episode. That whole Rose story, that whole family environment, that emotional base. Which is a really weird thing to be saying about drama because I can't think of any other programme where you'd consciously have to say, "Let's add some emotion in there," because most drama is already about emotions. *Doctor Who* really wasn't before, but I wasn't just going to write spaceships and robots and stuff like that.'

Rose (Billie Piper) and
Mickey (Noel Clarke)
get reacquainted outside
the TARDIS.

Russell considers that a lot of people would disagree with him about the emotional moments, but suggests that a lot of classic *Doctor Who* gets defined by little moments of emotion between the Doctor and Sarah Jane Smith, or by an event like Jo Grant's departure. However, he insists they are so memorable simply because they are the only tiny emotional moments in the entire output. 'Moments like those,' he explains 'really were few and far between in the programme's history. I have to write contemporary *Doctor Who* differently, with the freedom to be funny and then sad and very modern and in big pictures. I was dying to work with CGI properly. I've got a very good instinct for what looks tacky and what doesn't – I watch stuff like *Buffy* and *Angel* and *Star Trek*, and get a taste of what can be achieved. And I don't just mean in terms of spaceships, I mean in terms of the size of the frame and the amount of action you can contain within it.' But Russell also believes that a lot of the American shows, ones that the press frequently compare *Doctor Who* to, are terribly tame and that they could go much further. The scope, that level of storytelling that can be done in the modern series is, for Russell, a magnificent chance to further the show's legacy. 'I dread the day I leave the programme, because then I'll have to go back to writing bedrooms and offices and pubs. And maybe a field, if I'm lucky.'

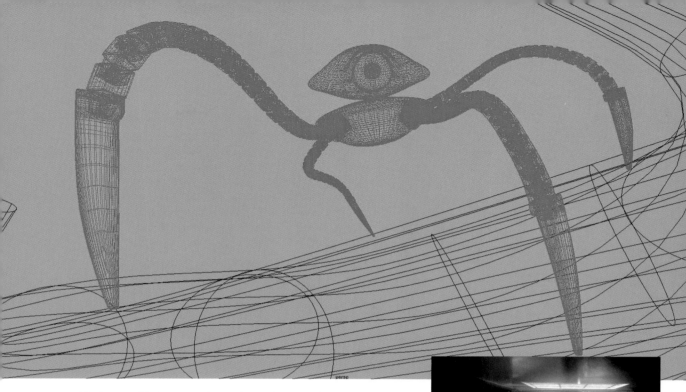

The legacy did throw up a few problems for Julie Gardner, however. After over forty years, there is a huge amount of subsidiary material that's linked to *Doctor Who*, unlike almost any other show in the world – probably on a par with the multi-formatted *Star Trek* shows from America. What this means is that *Doctor Who* is not just a television programme. Indeed, having had the best part of a decade away from its parent medium, the show has grown and developed in several other ways. Since 1989, there have been hundreds of novels, audio adventures, magazines and comic strips; add to this toys, games, clothing and a massive online presence, and *Doctor Who* has become an extraordinarily complex and multi-layered franchise.

As soon as it was announced that the show was coming back, the first question Julie had to face in regard to the subsidiary stuff was what, if anything, needed to be shut down to protect the integrity of the series. 'By this point,' remembers Julie, 'I'd educated myself in the world of *Doctor Who* as much as I could, but Russell was already a huge fan of all the extra stuff – like the Big Finish audios, the novels, the magazine, the list is endless. We wanted to make sure that those groups still had space to do what they were doing, because they'd kept *Doctor Who* alive across a number of years – it was very important that they continued to flourish. At the same time, we had to look long and hard at the kinds of things that might damage the core show. Not damage because they're bad – nothing was bad – but because the messages were different, the tone was different, the age level that they were aimed at was inconsistent. My first problem was an endless deluge of emails from people working in these areas, being anxious about what the series coming back meant for them. In the end, I think the only thing that was hard to shut down – very sad but the right thing to do – was our own website's latest venture: webcasts of new animated adventures with Richard E. Grant playing the Ninth Doctor. It was difficult because Richard E. Grant's a great actor; it was made by the BBC, and those people really loved what they were doing, and really believed in it. There were more

Top: An animatic created by The Mill of one of Cassandra's spiders from The End of the World. *Above: Its positioning in the finished scene.*

The clapperboard was traditionally used to synchronise sound and picture during editing. Here it's marking a shot for The Girl in the Fireplace.

in development, but we felt it would have been very confusing for that to continue. I knew people who were very confused about the search for our first Doctor. They kept saying, "Haven't you cast Richard E. Grant? Isn't he doing it?" and "Aren't you doing that in animation?" And so we had to stop that. We needed to create enough space, so that when we announced our Ninth Doctor, Christopher Eccleston, there was a gap between all that had gone before and Chris. This being the main show; everything now has to feed from this.'

'PEOPLE THAT KNEW THE LANGUAGE': SELECTING THE WRITERS

One of the potential curses of *Doctor Who* is that, prior to Russell T Davies, no one person had ever overseen the show so completely. Different producers, directors and writers had come and gone, but very little coherence or, to use a popular word in Cardiff circles, tone had been adhered to. Russell and Julie were determined to correct that but, across thirteen episodes, it was going to be near impossible for one man to write *and* produce everything. Jane Tranter earlier referred to Scots writer Steven Moffat, who has contributed scripts to both series so far. At what point did it become necessary to involve writers other than Russell on the show?

'When it was just six or even eight episodes,' answers Russell, 'I could have done them all. The moment that was bumped up to thirteen, there was no way that I could. Which, to be honest, was good; it's what I wanted as well, it let me get a team in. I thought it would be very difficult to convince Jane and Lorraine and everyone, they'd all stressed how this was going to be led by me but, when I asked for other writers, it was no problem, so long as they were writing under my guidance, to keep that same tone and feel.' Assembling that team of writers took a while. Steven Moffat, writer of *The Empty Child*, *The Doctor Dances* and *The Girl in the Fireplace*, was obvious; *Coupling*, Steven's comedy-drama for BBC Two, had been a huge success, so he was a given. Mark Gatiss was also an easy pitch for Russell, thanks to the success of his BBC Two comedy *The League of Gentlemen*, and Mark contributed *The Unquiet Dead* and *The Idiot's Lantern* to the first two series. Paul Cornell and Robert Shearman were the 'unknowns'. With Paul, Russell just explained that he wanted him because he, like Russell, had written *Doctor Who* novels, great stories which had just the emotional material that the series needed. Mal Young had worked with Cornell before – on both *Casualty* and *Holby City*, two of BBC One's most popular drama series, and Russell knew that Mal liked him a lot. Robert Shearman was the only writer relatively new to television – he had penned one episode of the TV series *Born and Bred* and he had a number of award-winning theatrical and BBC Radio plays to his name. However, as Russell wanted to adapt a previously existing *Doctor Who* story of Robert's, the Big Finish audio play *Jubilee*, no one could really question Robert rewriting his own work for the television series.

'Maybe it wasn't so important with hindsight,' Russell believes, 'but at the time it felt important for the first series to get people who knew the language, the shorthand of the original series. Not in a fannish way, not in a way that's going to reference the planet Vortis and the evil Menoptra and thus exclude everyone that wasn't watching in 1965, but people who would understand when I said to them that they could use the sonic screwdriver, but not to save the world; they were people who instantly understood that. If writers don't get *Doctor Who*, if they've never watched it, if they don't know the shorthand, it's a very tricky thing to write. So it had to be people who could write it without having seen our new series. In contrast, when people came along for Series Two, we could play them tapes and say, "This is our show." Once people have got something to work with it's much easier to get different writers in.'

Steven Moffat and Mark Gatiss returned for Series Two, this time joined, for *The Impossible Planet* and *The Satan Pit*, by Matt Jones, who had been Russell's script editor on *Queer as Folk* and who had, as a producer in his own right, overseen Paul Abbott's hugely successful series *Shameless*. Tom MacRae, writer of *Rise of the Cybermen* and *The Age of Steel*, was someone whose work Russell had followed enthusiastically, believing that being very young and very ambitious he'd most likely meet that other requirement, being very fast. Contributing *Fear Her* and *School Reunion* respectively, Matthew Graham and Toby Whithouse were not Russell's choices, but suggestions from his fellow executive producer, Julie Gardner. Julie had executive produced Matthew's BBC One series *Life on Mars*, while Toby had created a very popular and gritty Channel 4 drama about nurses called *No Angels*, and Russell felt that both of them had the kind of sensibility and 'voice' he wanted for the second series. One of the more interesting choices was in selecting Toby to write *School Reunion*, the most continuity-reliant story so far, which not only referenced the original BBC series, it actually brought back two former travelling companions of the Doctor's from the 1970s, Sarah Jane Smith and the robot dog K-9. Russell didn't want to do that story: 'I knew I might get too bogged down in minutiae, debating whether to mention *The Five*

Writer Robert Shearman and friend, on set for Dalek.

Right: The Doctor (David Tennant) surrounded by friends old and new, Rose (Billie Piper) and Sarah Jane (Elisabeth Sladen). Below: The refurbished K-9 prepares to accompany Sarah Jane on her future adventures.

Doctors [1983's twentieth-anniversary special] or *K-9 and Company* [a 1981 spin-off show]. I just wanted nice, honest, sexy, modern dialogue between the two women.'

'OUR DOCTOR WHO IS VERY, VERY, VERY SATURDAY NIGHT'

If sorting out the script writers was reasonably easy, what about assigning the next important person, the director – the individual with responsibility for making each episode, from the first meeting right through the filming, the editing and the final mix, ready to be shown on Saturday night.

'It's been harder finding directors with the amount of experience in green-screen work, prosthetics, CGI, all the extra stuff that goes with *Doctor Who*,' says Russell. 'They've really got to come on the show to learn.' Indeed, one thing the team realised quickly was that, because of the show's technical requirements, they were unlikely to attract interest from the top-level directors within the industry – Adrian Sheargold and Charles McDougal, people like that. 'They're not going to fit in,' explains the executive producer, 'because we have to make so many decisions in advance: designs and the amount of effects, indeed the type of effects, are decided almost a year in advance – with a lot of leeway, but actually that's decided for them. It's not an auteur's show, the director is not God here. The strength really comes from the writing, the authorship of something comes from the script and not from the camera, to be honest. So, we find ourselves in the exciting position, I think, of finding up-and-coming talent; people who will be great directors for years to come. Someone like Euros Lyn, one of the finest directors I've ever worked with, and we're just very, very lucky that he lives on our doorstep in Cardiff. And in three years he will be the person we're begging to work with, but who won't be free because he'll be off doing great big prestigious productions. So, you catch those people at the right time – grab them as they're coming off *Holby City* and *Casualty*, coming off those fast-turnaround shows, use them and work very closely with them. It's easier to get rising talent in terms of directors than it is in terms of writers, to be honest.

'I also love to expose that complete fallacy that writers just write the dialogue but then directors do the pictures and the CGI people create the effects and so on. We're a team, but it has to all be there on the page first. No one can make the show without the story. People say, "Oh, that's really well directed because the pictures are big and huge and a spaceship flew into Big Ben." And I'm thinking, yes it is beautifully directed but I described that scene, that concept, every single word of it. Dialogue's the least important thing in a script really.'

Something Russell feels the writing can only benefit from refers back to an observation he made earlier – the timeslot. When Jane Tranter told him *Doctor Who* would go out at seven o'clock on a Saturday night, it became the various writers' greatest weapon. 'Having been given it on *Doctor Who*, I would beg any subsequent commissioner to give me that information up front.' Usually, people in television are far less firm about broadcast times, even the day, as these often have to be scheduled almost at the last minute. When Jane Tranter set that time and day in stone, it enabled Russell to get a grip on what the show had to do for that specific audience. 'There's a huge difference between drama on a Monday at nine o'clock and a drama on a Friday at six o'clock. Knowing right from the word go that we were up against Ant and Dec on ITV1, with that scope, that format and that vitality, enabled us to make sure people didn't channel hop over to them. Our *Doctor Who* is very, very, very Saturday night.

'What I still think is fascinating is the amount of consultation, the amount of marketing we *didn't* do. Julie and I knew each other's likes and dislikes from the start, because we'd spent time together watching television: loving *Angel* but preferring *Buffy*; seeing elements of both in *Smallville*. So I knew we'd be in sync. I never thought I would write a *Doctor Who* that was radically different to what Julie liked. I just delivered an initial script, and then that was the template. *Rose* was a nice introduction, but *The End of the World* sealed it, really. That was saying that's how funny we can be, that's how mad we can be, oh, and that's how expensive we can be.

'Actually, that script is a nightmare. Anyone with any sense would have thrown it back and told me to cut it in half and then maybe we could afford to make it. I was very quick to follow that up with the first two Slitheen scripts, which are more filmable. Yes, they have great big effects in them, they've got Big Ben being destroyed and Downing Street blowing up, monsters on the loose – nonetheless, they're very filmable. *World War Three* is effectively set in one room.' So, having gone cinematic and huge and expensive, Russell quickly followed up with another pair of scripts saying exactly the opposite – hence *The Unquiet Dead* and *Father's Day*. And with those first six scripts, Russell showed Julie Gardner, Jane Tranter and everyone else that he understood not only how to make radically different *Doctor Who* on a weekly basis, but also how to make it practical. 'Julie could have turned round and said the BBC couldn't afford all of that, and I certainly wouldn't have blamed The Mill if they'd said that what I'd asked for couldn't be done. But they didn't, and in fact Julie convinced everyone across the teams to rise to the challenge and take it even further.'

'The scripting tone was predominantly governed by Russell,' Julie says, citing this as an example of the enormous amount of trust the BBC commissioners put in both executive producers. Normally on a show of this complexity, detailed documents – colloquially termed a series bible – listing every story, every character, would have to be written. The whole series is plotted out in minute detail and then approved by an army of other executives, followed up by many long hours of discussion about who does what, and why. On *Doctor Who*, that simply never happened. Indeed, Russell wrote – possibly for the first time in his career – a slim bible, about twelve pages long, as opposed to the fifty-plus most bibles have to be. It simply mapped out the thirteen stories and set out who the Doctor was, who Rose was – but none of it in huge detail. On the front page he outlined the tone of the series.

And the tone of the series was optimistic, it was romantic, it was about adventure and, most importantly, the show was about what it is to be human. 'I can vividly remember a paragraph on that front page,' Julie says. 'It was something along the lines of Russell stating he was not interested in going to the planet Zog because the people on Zog weren't human and he wanted to see a human's reaction to the incredible, not a Zoggian's.'

The result of this was that our human character, the person that we, the audience, watch the adventures alongside, had to be very average, terribly normal. Hence Rose Tyler – a normal girl who worked in a normal shop, who's got an on-off relationship with her boyfriend, and a mother who worries about her. And we were going to see our first monster through her eyes. 'There was a lot of discussion about what that first monster would be,' Julie explains. 'Russell wanted it to be the Autons because the following day they were going to be something that school kids could be walking past in shop windows, and they would look at them in a different way. He never wanted it to be about Rose Tyler going into the basement of the store and being confronted by a green, million-tentacled lump of fat. It had to be something from our everyday life. That was one of the key things for the tone of the series: recognition.

'I think anyone else would probably have put the Daleks in episode one. "Oh, my God, we're bringing back the big series, we've got to bring back all the big icons – of course it's got to be the Daleks." It takes someone of Russell's confidence and experience to know you build towards that and, even then, you don't reintroduce them with twenty-five million Daleks in spaceships in the first episode; you've got to remind the audience why they're scary. We didn't want to make something that was cold and detached. I'm not interested in that very macho, conquering kind of sci-fi; I've never really watched *Star Trek* – I've enjoyed it occasionally, but it doesn't emotionally engage with me. *Doctor Who* had to be full-blooded drama. That was our tone.'

For Russell, there was one other important word to remember while people were putting the show together. 'Fun, that's the word I keep on using. That's the word I worry about when other writers' scripts get too dark. Optimistic. Fun. And to be optimistic and have fun there's got to be a darkness there. I think that's a very British attitude.' As an example of this attitude towards comedy and drama, he cites the third episode of *Queer as Folk*. 'It's the biggest comedy episode you could possibly ever see, and then one of them drops dead in the middle of it. I think that's what drama should be. I think drama should never settle into "ooh, this is serious" and "ooh, this is funny". The greatest surprise of my life was winning the most ridiculous award – the comedy

writer of the year for *Bob & Rose*, which isn't funny. I mean, I won that in the same year as *The Office* was shown. I don't know what happened that year. That's just weird. But I suppose it's just the tone in which I write, which can swing from being funny to being dark in a second, as life can. Modern animation movies like *Toy Story* and *Shrek* and *The Incredibles* have paved the way for my take on life – they have a very similar attitude towards fun and sentiment to my *Doctor Who*. They have the emotion, they have the modern jokes and the adult references for the parents. I think they were the best template you could possibly use.'

'IF YOU DO NOTHING, YOU'RE WRONG, YOU'RE A COWARD'

Of course, Russell has rules he won't break, boundaries he won't cross, and doesn't even seem interested in pushing the limits. He cites *Tooth and Claw* as a story that perhaps tested the boundary, but it still followed his self-imposed basic rules: no blood and no human doing violence to another human. That's something he will not allow. He mentions a *Doctor Who* story from 1971, *The Mind of Evil*. In that, there's a prison riot and characters good and bad are gunning one another down, something you will not see modern *Doctor Who* undertaking. 'I won't have a human picking up a gun, especially a revolver,' Russell is adamant, 'and aiming a bullet at another human. I think we have a moral responsibility to be careful. I live in the middle of Manchester, where if I wandered down the road and walked for ten minutes there would probably be a twelve-year-old with a gun somewhere. So I choose to present what I hope is an optimistic, fun programme, and that makes putting a realistic gun in someone's hand impossible. If we were telling a gritty, urban-decay drama then it would actually seem odd not to see guns in people's hands; and I would happily do it. But since the whole ethos of *Doctor Who* is optimism, the Doctor leading the moral way, then taking care with guns becomes even more important. I mean it set my teeth on edge in *Rise of the Cybermen* when the Preachers used modern guns. We talked for a long time about that and I accepted that it wouldn't, frankly, be credible if the Preachers didn't have guns. But still, we trimmed that back and the only time they open fire is against a fantasy element, the Cybermen. I used to work in children's television and had a brilliant boss called Martin Hughes, who was very, very strict about this sort of stuff. I'd always write comedy sketches with someone getting hit over the head with a frying pan and he'd say, "No, you don't hit people on the head because that's the worse thing you could possibly do. That's genuinely violent. If you do it, it's got to be with a big, soft comedy mallet and not a frying pan." He taught me very good rules that weren't in the official guidelines as such; they were his personal guidelines. And I've always agreed with them. It's very hard to do that in an adventure series, where you're fighting monsters, but that's the challenge built into the format about a man who doesn't carry a gun but nonetheless he's got to blow up the Daleks or Cybermen at the end.'

Jane Tranter offers her opinion of *Doctor Who*'s level of scariness from the point of view of someone who has to strike this balance across all the BBC's drama output, and is ultimately responsible for deciding what is and isn't too scary. She will ask any production team to cut anything she feels goes too far but, so far, this hasn't cropped up on *Doctor Who*. 'There have been a couple of sequences or moments that we've discussed, particularly in the second series, where I felt that we'd gone to the edge of what I think we can do in that timeslot. There are certain things we've done that have felt scary not in a scary-monster way, but scary in a sense-of-dread way. Some of the things that we do can be very, very frightening, particularly for young children because Rose is us, if you like. Rose is the point of entry for younger children, so if she's in danger, that gets very frightening for them.

'I think *Tooth and Claw* is the scariest that *Doctor Who* should be. There are things that we have done in the second series that we would not have done in the first. Part of the reason *Fear Her* is scary is because its world is very real. It's a kid, with paper and a pencil, which anybody can get hold of. A lot of the time the fear comes from the dread of what's going to happen. Of course, you want a bit of hiding behind the sofa, that's what we all love but, on the other hand, you can't go too far, because *Doctor Who* is not horror. In some ways, one of the scariest things we've done is regenerating the Doctor; effectively, for a seven-year-old, we killed him. And now, with Christopher gone, the children have seen him turn into David. His Doctor has such humanity, he seems to understand us and he's very warm, so he's a comforting Doctor to be with, and he enables us to be slightly scarier than we had been.'

Created entirely by The Mill, this iconic shot shows the Tooth and Claw werewolf howling at the moon. As all good werewolves should...

While Russell's background of working in children's television provides one measure, Julie Gardner also has all the BBC's own guidelines on how far a programme-maker can go. However, the *Doctor Who* team are not making a children's TV, they're making family drama. And Julie believes that children want to be scared; they want to feel emotional; they want to be able to question their world. But she knows it has to be done responsibly. 'We don't show blood, or graphic death; if humans die, we're really careful about it, and there's always a context for it. For example, when we reintroduced the Dalek we had to remind people why it was the scariest thing in the universe. As well as that, we challenged the Doctor and so I think that's one of the darkest episodes for the Doctor in Series One – it's about what he is truly like when he confronts the great villain who has destroyed his race. His first instinct is to torture it, which makes it a pivotal moment when Rose asks him what he has become and the realisation hits him that he's gone too far. We wanted the younger audience to be able to ask questions about those stories, and one of the nicest things anyone said to me came from a dad who described *Doctor Who* as the one show he could watch with his kids and it stayed with them for a week; they kept talking about it; with that particular episode, they kept talking about the Dalek being alone and how sad that was, and that he'd done a bad thing but should he be forgiven? These are big questions that very young kids were asking.'

Were there are other questions that young kids could ask which parents might be less relaxed about? For instance, did anyone within the BBC question the appropriateness of introducing Captain Jack Harkness, to all intents and purposes, a bisexual (he'd probably say *any*sexual) companion?

'We did get a couple of complaints,' confesses Julie, 'about *The Parting of the Ways*, when Jack kisses Rose and the Doctor on the lips. But not from within the BBC – they were very supportive of Captain Jack. I have talked to John Barrowman about how he and the director, Joe Ahearne, had decided to play that scene: it was really important to John that he kiss both the Doctor and Rose in exactly the same way. It's a beautiful moment, about a man knowing he's going to face his own death, saying goodbye to the

Pete Tyler (Shaun Dingwall), the Doctor (David Tennant) and Rose (Billie Piper) flee the Cyber attack at the end of Rise of the Cybermen.

two people he loves most. It's a really amazing scene, but I don't think that's been done at seven o'clock before. I think we're now considered a liberal show that is very, very moral. We want people to discuss and question after they've watched an episode. I think if there's one absolute truth it's that if you do nothing, you're wrong, you're a coward. And you can't be a coward in life; you have to live your life. There's an extraordinary speech at the end of *Love & Monsters* where Elton says that when he was a kid he used to think it was all about growing up, getting married, having a job, and a mortgage. But what he learns is that there's so much more to life than that. It's so much darker, much more complicated, much harder, but also full of possibility. And I think that's the message of the whole series. You have to live a life that has to be good and you must be as moral as you can in the choices you make. You know, some of the choices Rose and the Doctor have to make are extraordinary and complicated and hard.'

'That's the optimistic aspect of *Doctor Who*,' responds Russell. 'We don't want loads of angst and bitterness – why would he explore the universe if it was difficult? Because frankly by now he could actually afford to buy a house and settle down and live in the country and have a very nice time. So he must love what he does – travelling is not his job; he's not paid; he doesn't have a boss; he doesn't have taxes to pay. It must be the most marvellous life, yet with a strange loneliness about it. So you take the tone from the Doctor; you take the tone from the fact he lives in a police box. It's not a high-tech, missile-laden, flashing spaceship; it's a police box. We're not here as adult drama like *State of Play* or *Edge of Darkness*. You could do *Doctor Who* like that, and I've always maintained that if the BBC had said it was for nine o'clock on BBC Three, then that's what you'd now have. Although I would have thought twice about working on it, because what's the point of doing something so mundane with such a great original concept?'

Julie Gardner understands exactly where Russell is coming from with this – it's an ideal they both share. But, as always, she acknowledges that the ultimate vision for the show has to come from just one place – Russell. She believes he is the heart of everything they do. In every single way: from the writing through to the look of it, to the tone, absolutely everything, it is his vision that she, Phil and everyone else are trying to sustain, honour and fulfil. 'I think he writes with enormous heart,' she says. 'Take *New Earth*. It's a really big episode, it's got a huge scale to it, lots going on, a new Doctor, and underneath the fun of Cassandra being Rose and all of that, it says a huge amount about the modern world with drug testing and cloning and whether humans have the right to immortality. A very big thematic episode, but all done within the context of *Doctor Who*. I think Russell's greatest strength as a writer, and very few people have it, is the shift he makes between comedy and fun into something dark and serious. He makes sure every character has a life of their own, even if they're just saying a couple of lines. I think he writes with the most enormous generosity to his characters. He's a man writing at the very, very top of his game.'

John Barrowman and Noel Clarke enjoying the location filming for Boom Town.

Julie acknowledges that there have been a couple of questions raised about whether the show has allowed the writers to vent their own personal opinions, their own agendas. But she says not, suggesting that the writers of the show are too good, and their primary objective in everything they do is to tell the best possible story. At the same time, she says that any good writer has a view of the world and that's what is wanted of them; a different view on the world. Julie recalls David Tennant saying during an interview that Russell is the least cynical man in a very cynical age. 'I think that's the key thing about *Doctor Who*,' she says. 'It's never cynical; it's never casual; it's very full-blooded; full of adventure; it's romantic; it's all about what it is to be human.' Julie promises that it's never going to be snide or knowing, or smug. Even the odd, slightly disparaging reference to the royal family is not intended to be anti-them – it's part of the fun. Since they're part of our establishment, part of the UK landscape, it could seem odd not to have cultural references to them. She reckons all the references are full of affection: 'The Camilla and the Princess Anne references aren't in any way left-wing or political. They're part of our lives, like *Pop Idol*, so Rose is bound to refer to cultural icons in that way, because that's what they are.'

'THE TOP NOTE IS SHEER ENTERTAINMENT': EXPLAINING THE SUCCESS

Everyone involved in the creation of the series has obviously been overjoyed by the huge success it has become, no one more so than Jane Tranter, who took that big gamble in the first place in deciding to bring back what was, to all intents and purposes, a dead

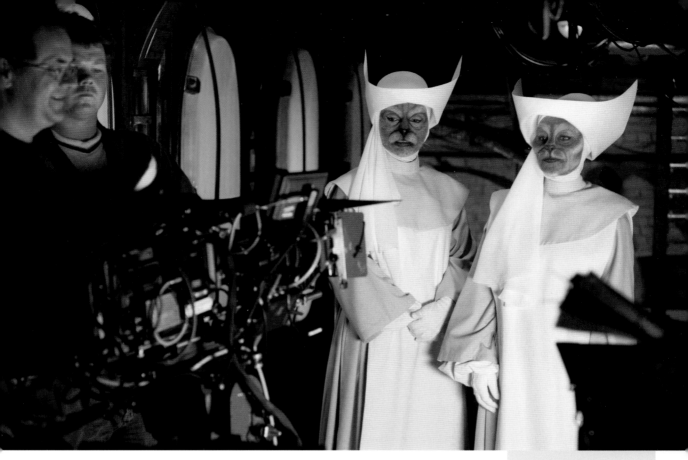

Sister Jatt (Adjoa Andoh) and
Matron Casp (Dona Croll) are
lined up for a shot for New
Earth *by camera operator*
Julian Barber *and focus puller*
Steve Rees.

programme that, according to one of her predecessors at the BBC, had seen 'a battle-weary Time Lord languishing in the backwaters of audience popularity'.

'I think getting an audience to watch it in the first place wasn't so hard, because it's such a new thing to put drama on at that time of night, and it's clearly something that anyone with a family can really appreciate. And certainly a lot of Saturday evening shows – like *The X Factor* or *Strictly Come Dancing* – are watched by families. So to convince them to watch drama is but a hair's breadth away. And I do think there's an appetite for drama which is slightly "other". If families are going to the cinema to see things which venture through space and time, then how brilliant to have that for forty-five minutes once a week on your TV set.

'I think the reason people have stuck with *Doctor Who* is to do with – and I don't use this word lightly – the genius of Russell T Davies. I think there are very few people who can save the world via a council flat and Number 10 Downing Street. Every single episode, whether he's storylined it, talked to the writer about it, or worked on it himself, exists on many different levels, and the top note is sheer entertainment. Below that, you get various levels of thought, of contemporary relevance, of emotional truth, of complexity of theme, of looking at the whole mystery that is *Doctor Who*. There are so many different levels on which you can enjoy it. And that means you've got forty-five minutes of time really brilliantly spent, every Saturday evening. Plus Russell's characterisation is absolutely fantastic. I mean, he just took Christopher Eccleston's Doctor and, in big, broad, iconic strokes, gave him a really big boot with which to push open the door for *Doctor Who* into the twenty-first century. Having achieved that, in David Tennant's Tenth Doctor you've then got a Doctor who's much nimbler, who can turn on a sixpence more,

Above: An early design drawing by Ben Austin showing the devastated 10 Downing Street. Below: The final shot after the Prime Minister's residence has been obliterated in World War Three.

who is more overtly compassionate, and empathetic and burdened with the responsibility of looking after all humanity. And Rose, clearly, is the most empathetic of the Doctor's companions that you could get. These characters, complete with their Shakespearean flaws and everything, feel ordinary in certain ways and on certain levels, week after week. It's forty-five minutes of drama that open doors onto different worlds whilst at the same time holding a mirror up to ours.'

So why has this British television icon struck a chord with the viewing public all over again? One of the truisms of the show's original run was that no one could ever completely pinpoint the reason for its success, and the same is undeniably true today. James Hawes, who has directed a number of episodes, says that he can't offer an explanation, but that he's quite glad of that. 'I don't think anybody has yet fully computed the impact of *Doctor Who* on our television habits. Focus groups – and I spit at this point – had said family TV-watching was dead. Granny was going to watch the videos and DVDs of 1950s movies with Cary Grant, kids were on the PlayStation or out rollerblading. Everybody was doing different stuff. Somehow this has proved the focus groups wrong, because *Doctor Who* made families sit down and share a storytelling experience all over again. That is human culture reinvented. That sounds massive, but I think it's that strong, it's the campfire tradition reinvented. It is a coincidence of factors because the essence of *Doctor Who* – and I don't mean its history, I mean its ability, its design as a format – is to tell fantasy stories that say something significant about now with a mixture of fear and laughter. Added to that format – and its potential for longevity and invention – is not just Russell, but the whole team of creative forces who have combined their love of the original series to make it fresh enough for now.'

Christopher Eccleston suggests its success may go back to the past, likening it to the European fairy tales of Hans Christian Andersen and the Brothers Grimm. 'They have the same quality, and *Doctor Who*'s really just a fairy tale with one advantage – that whole central idea of time travel. It means you are always dealing with matters of life and death because you have that device, that ability to move forward and see what's going to happen or move backward and see what has happened. So consequently you're never really dealing with purely domestic emotions. It's never just kitchen-sink drama.'

Camille Coduri, who plays Rose's mum, Jackie Tyler, believes that the biggest impact the series has had is on the kids because she gets recognised an awful lot by children. 'I really love the fact that kids are so transfixed by the show, for some of them it's a huge part of their lives. How fantastic to have a life-changing thing happen to you through television and through the brilliant writing and the visuals and so on. Kids get so excited and they can't believe that they're talking to you. I love that moment when the children come up and say, "You're Jackie, look there's Jackie." It's great.' Camille's

daughter's favourite story was *Father's Day*, and it was her friends' favourite too. Camille reckons this is because they all love their fathers, and they all put themselves in Rose's position. 'She's quite a role model, isn't she, Rose?' Her son, who's younger, was really upset whenever the Doctor and Rose left Jackie alone in the flat at the end of a story, rather than by anything in the story itself. Nevertheless, he loves to play *Doctor Who* in the playground at school. And Camille recalls stopping her car near his school to let two classes across the road: 'It took about half an hour, because they were all like, "Oh!! Jackie Tyler!" Sixty-two kids, it was great. Not many television shows can make kids happy so easily.'

For Jane Tranter, this just proves that her faith in the show and her belief in Russell T Davies and Julie Gardner were well founded. 'I think the easiest thing to have done for this whole twenty-first-century version of *Doctor Who* was making the decision to bring it back, and that was the bit that I did. The hardest thing was the making of it and the casting of it and all those sorts of things, and if I have been associated with any of that, in any way, I'm very proud.'

Casting

With everything now in place to begin production of *Doctor Who*, with the tone set, the number of episodes agreed, where they were to be filmed, and who was writing and directing, just one, rather important, consideration remained. Who was going to star in them?

When the series had last been in production, casting was decided by the producer, maybe his script editor (as they were the only two full-time production staffers on every episode) and individual directors. Modern BBC programmes have expanded this process and the board seeing potential lead actors for *Doctor Who* consisted of the executive producers, the producer, Jane Tranter and Lorraine Heggessey. It's indicative of how important the series was going to be to BBC Television that so many people had to be involved. To coordinate the whole, they utilised a casting director, in this case, a gentleman very highly regarded in media circles, Andy Pryor.

CASTING

Andy Pryor receives each script at a fairly early stage, reads it thoroughly and makes notes about the characters. He then draws up a list of possible actors for everyone to consider, before meeting with the individual director and Phil Collinson to discuss the kind of actors they want, both in terms of profile, in order to bring an audience to the show, and in terms of giving it an interesting mix of people. The reason Andy tries to find good 'guest artists' such as Pauline Collins, Simon Callow, Catherine Tate, or Tracy-Ann Oberman is that it helps to create an interest in the show, not just among viewers but also in the papers. It's largely the press that keeps the programme in the public eye, and it is always of interest to them when casting is done 'against type' – in other words, when well-known actors appear in roles that viewers are not used to seeing them playing. Some good examples of this can be seen in *Rise of the Cybermen* and *The Age of Steel*: Roger Lloyd Pack, who plays the villainous John Lumic, is best known for his comedic roles in *Only Fools and Horses* and *The Vicar of Dibley*; and Andrew Hayden-Smith, better known as a children's TV presenter, has the chance to play the gritty leader of the gun-toting Preachers.

Andy considers it a great strength that *Doctor Who* 'can combine a cast in a way that you often can't on other dramas – you very often have an extraordinary mix of acting styles within one episode on *Doctor Who*. Most actors find the idea of playing an alien or something that's completely new and fresh and different quite attractive,' he explains. 'Rather than doing a run-of-the-mill cop show or a medical drama, *Doctor Who* stretches them. Look at the CVs of any actors who work regularly and they'll usually have played several policemen or doctors or nurses or whatever. But I believe they will also be able to play a cat-nun or a Sycorax leader, and that's appealing to most actors.'

'THE NAME WE KEPT COMING BACK TO WAS CHRISTOPHER ECCLESTON'

'Our obvious priority,' states series producer Phil Collinson, 'was finding our Doctor.' Part of the problem, very soon after production was announced, was that the British press began throwing around names like TV magician Paul Daniels and quiz show presenter Carol Vorderman. This caused a few headaches for the production team, leaving them wondering if that was how far the image of *Doctor Who* had sunk over the years. The perception was that it was a light entertainment show and that, although it was coming back, it was always going to be a bit shoddy and silly. 'We all very quickly realised that whoever we were going to cast needed to be an actor with gravitas and stature and somebody who was primarily known for their drama work. We wanted people to see that this was a drama. So Russell, Julie, Andy and I talked for quite a while and knocked ideas and thoughts and names around, but the name we kept coming back to was Christopher Eccleston.'

They began by drawing up a list: 'one of the craziest most bonkers lists I think I've ever drawn up – hundreds and hundreds of names of all kinds of people, all shapes and sizes,' says Andy Pryor. 'It was really just an exercise in thinking of alternative ways of approaching the character and of what kind of actor we wanted. Julie and Russell certainly didn't come to me and say we need somebody who had starred in an ITV prime-time show. They didn't say it's got to be a film star or it's got to be a comedy person. They just wanted to explore what the possibilities might be far more organically. So we got together with this big master list and very quickly whittled it down to a group of favourites and the clear top of the list was Christopher.'

Julie knew Christopher because they had worked together in 2001 on a modern version of *Othello*, where he'd played Iago. For her, 'he was someone with credibility. Someone who was undeniably a brilliant actor.' One of the most recent things Russell had done before starting on *Doctor Who* had been *The Second Coming* in 2003,

which Christopher Eccleston had starred in. Russell recalls receiving an email out of the blue from Christopher, enquiring about *Doctor Who*. Phil Collinson remembers being very excited by this idea, as were people like Jane Tranter and Mal Young. 'Russell, Julie, Chris and I met up in the bar of the Malmaison in Manchester, had a drink and a chat and a talk about him coming and making *Doctor Who*. We were quite straightforward about what a challenge we knew it was going to be for any actor to take on, but we obviously didn't scare him and he was still up for it, so then we talked about a screen test. Actually, he put it into our minds, because he reckoned people would think he might be a bit too dour for the Doctor.'

Ten days later, in BBC Manchester, a screen test was duly shot – a process by which a few short scenes are recorded so they can be shown to the various BBC executives. Christopher read three scenes from the first episode, with Julie Gardner playing Rose. Julie winces at this memory: 'I'm absolutely terrible at reading in. And he was absolutely wonderful; he had that balance of intensity and presence and emotion. It started to feel very real when he was there.' The rest is history: the screen test went off to Jane Tranter and to Lorraine Heggessey. They both watched it; they both loved it. 'And so,' says Phil, 'we asked him to play it. He thought about it for a couple of days, and then he said yes.'

'The Doctor is a tremendous optimist and he sees the positive,' explains the man himself, Christopher Eccleston. 'You'll see him confront a bad situation, and he'll make a joke about it, he'll lighten the mood; the nicest thing about playing him is that he cares. He believes himself to be the last of the Time Lords, a man with no home, and that gives him a sadness, a loneliness that's key to his relationship with Rose. He's basically saying he's lonely, he wants somebody to travel with him. He seems very fond of the human race for some reason but, equally, if the human race behaves unpleasantly towards an alien he takes it very personally, calls them stupid apes and gets frustrated with their cruelties and negativity. He wishes they'd open their minds. The Doctor is

The Doctor (Christopher Eccleston) considers his opinions on humanity.

tremendously open minded, which again is a good quality for a television hero to have, and yet there's another side to him, which is a ruthless, brutal, pragmatist: if something or somebody body is threatening the human race or existence, he'll kill it. I like the idea of a writer as intelligent and rigorous as Russell writing for children because I think, if you can get them young with good stuff, as they grow older they're going to demand even better stuff from television.'

It was Christopher's down-to-Earth approach that appealed to Russell. He didn't want to follow the previous 'tradition' of casting an 'eccentric' Doctor – it simply would not have fitted the format of this version of *Doctor Who*, because Russell believes the Doctor to be fascinating already. 'He travels in time and space, he's got two hearts, he's a Time Lord – that's eccentric enough to be getting on with.' Russell was determined to write him as a proper, real character, and having made the decision to rid the series of the Time Lords, this made him a survivor, and a great loner. 'I think all the exaggerated eccentricity that had accrued around the character before,' he adds, 'is actually stuff that fills in for bad writing, it's a lazy shorthand. Being eccentric, wearing a costume rather than clothes, that's not drama. Drama is an interesting character in a situation doing fascinating things. I think there's all sorts of areas you can take the character that aren't "eccentricity", but which are fascinating: his glee in the face of danger; the darkness of the loneliness; his awkwardness in domestic situations. That's fascinating. There's more than enough to be going on with. You don't need eccentricity on top of that. Eccentricity's

a very forced thing, it's very hard to write. I don't think any good writer has ever sat down and thought, "Let's write an eccentric character." It's just fake. I think you can spend too long giving characters adjectives, saying she's this and he's that. Most of us just get up in the morning, go to work and are already fascinating. We are all twenty-seven different people every day. You're one thing to your boss; you're one thing to your lover; you're one thing if you're out boozing; you're a completely different thing when you're sitting in on your own, just thinking away to yourself or watching television; you're a completely different person that no one ever sees. The worst day of your life must be your funeral, when all those different people come together. Surely funerals should be great big rows between everyone: "No, he was this," and "No, he was that." I think, the most happy character can be miserable one day. And I learnt that on *Coronation Street*, where – especially when they had fewer episodes every week – they'd write characters very differently depending on which person was doing that twenty-five-minute script. It was the same actor on the same sets, but she was just written to be in different moods on different days. And that was a great eye-opener for realising you can't decide a character is one fixed thing because real people aren't one fixed thing. So, with the people at the centre of a drama, I think you should be careful to give them potential to go anywhere and do anything, and don't define them too rigidly. No guaranteed reactions. Just keep it alive.'

Joe Ahearne, director of five first-series episodes, including *Dalek* and *The Parting of the Ways*, was surprised by the casting of Christopher Eccleston because he was considered to be primarily a terribly serious actor. 'I didn't imagine they would get someone who was so well established in his own right. I think most of the Doctors in the past have come to prominence through playing the Doctor, so it was different with Christopher because he had a huge body of film and acclaimed TV work behind him before he took on the role. What he brought to the role was that real weight which played off against the comedy – it was a huge surprise to me that he was funny. I hadn't seen him do comedy before in his TV stuff and I thought that he did it brilliantly.'

'WE ALL KNEW WE'D FOUND OUR ROSE': BILLIE PIPER

If, instead of Christopher, the team had opted for a more traditional London-based actor with that neutral non-regional voice, would it have informed the casting of Rose Tyler? Would the Tyler family have become Northerners, from an estate in Withinshaw, or Grimsby or Sunderland? Julie Gardner is quick to dismiss that possibility.

A rare moment for the Ninth Doctor out of his regular costume, as Christopher Eccleston poses for pictures collected by Clive in Rose. *This is the 'Edwardian' Doctor, photographed shortly before the RMS* Titanic *set sail for America.*

'We were talking about the show having universal appeal but being very British, and part of that universal appeal was about iconic London.' She does reveal that the team met actresses from outside London, and a few of them got high up the list, but the bottom line was that they needed the right actor, whatever her accent. 'There was something wonderful about Rose being from London though. So you could do those iconic shots, you could do Trafalgar Square, those Parliament buildings, a tourist's idea of London, a London little kids get excited by.'

Russell had written *Rose* before casting began, so Andy Pryor knew from the script that he needed to find someone who was going to appeal to adults and children, someone who was strong, who was an individual rather than a generic pretty sidekick. 'I drew up a list of possibilities, both well known and unknown. We auditioned quite a few people but Billie was the one we were all quite excited about. She came in and just blew us all away immediately.'

In 2003, Billie Piper had appeared on BBC One in an updated version of *The Canterbury Tales*, a performance Andy Pryor describes as 'fantastic'. She was the first girl auditioned for the part of Rose, although the casting process took rather longer than it had for Christopher Eccleston. Phil Collinson takes up the story: 'It is fair to say that from the minute she came through the door we all knew we'd found our Rose, but we couldn't quite believe it. And so we went through a process of seeing lots of other people. I think we saw about forty different girls over three days, but we kept coming back to her.' A second round of auditions followed, where Phil and company asked five of them back, Billie Piper included. The five girls read scenes with Christopher, and Billie and Christopher got on well, and that was that.

In the middle of all this was something that the production team found a bit alarming. Before they had even asked Billie Piper to audition, some British newspapers were running stories about her having been cast already. This worried Russell because stories like that can annoy actors and their agents – they might feel they're being blackmailed into taking a job. Although he now sees the press speculation as perfectly natural – 'Looking to cast a young woman? Billie Piper! Simple as that!' – at the time, Russell actually knew very little about his future star other than that he had seen her in *The Canterbury Tales*, which he thought she was lovely in. 'She came and did the most marvellous audition, very down to earth. After she left the room, I was sat there convinced that she was busy, her career was taking off, she was married and settled into London life, so she'd never agree to come to Cardiff for nine months. We did that second audition with Christopher and that was absolutely brilliant, but I was actually looking at the other girls, thinking we had to keep an eye on them because Billie Piper was bound to say no or that she'd only do six episodes. But then she said yes. Gobsmacking, absolutely gobsmacking. And, despite auditioning her, knowing she was good, I never ever dreamt she was going to be that good. She brought Rose to life exactly as I'd imagined her. By the time she was cast, I must have written loads of stuff and everything else was planned, right up to knowing exactly what was going to happen in *The Parting of the Ways*. I always knew that ending from the moment I started writing the series. So there wasn't much in the way of conversation with Billie about how Rose's story would progress, it was already sorted.'

Indeed, as a general rule of thumb, Russell doesn't talk a great deal to actors he works with on a long series about their characters' journeys. He believes that writers do one

job, actors do another and it is when the two combine that the real synthesis occurs and you end up with great television. 'I just hand in the scripts, and then watch the results. But obviously you pick up on stuff, strengths, weaknesses, moments where you realise a particular actor could take something a bit further next time because they have a skill you hadn't been aware of. *New Earth*, for instance, is very funny for Billie. It's a big comedy script because I was aware we hadn't really done big comedy for her. Similarly, that's why *The Satan Pit* started looking at the Doctor's beliefs, so we start stripping him down a bit because that's a mode that David Tennant had never had a chance to shine in. I'd much rather go to areas that they're not filling, but let it grow naturally as they settle into the roles rather than artificially decide beforehand which episode is their scared episode, which is their tortured-soul episode and so on.'

Julie Gardner believes Billie was exactly what was needed for Saturday evening family drama. 'It's about glamour on a Saturday night; it's about stardust; it's about being colourful at seven o'clock. And she has the combination of being an extraordinary actress and having a smile which makes everyone else smile at the same time. It means your audience is always going to look at Rose and say, "Okay, Saturday night's safe. Or it's a bit safer than it was." That's the thing that really swung it for me. There was a moment between readings where Billie was talking about her love of pork pies. And I remember thinking, "God, that's so Rose Tyler, it's just how she is." And then I noticed that I was smiling with her. That's the magic that Billie Piper has, unlike like any other woman I've worked with. On or off camera, she's smiling; you look around and everyone is smiling back. It's some absolutely indefinable, indescribable piece of stardust that she has, and we were very, very lucky to have her.'

If any eyebrows were raised at her casting due to her earlier pop stardom – which actually interrupted the acting career she had started some years before – they were quickly lowered once the series was transmitted. Like so many people, Joe Ahearne had read stuff about her and wondered about the consequences of casting someone primarily known for having had a brief pop career. 'Then, after five minutes of screen-time, I realised that she's a really brilliant actress. So whatever preconceptions I had were washed out of my brain after take one! One shouldn't need to be reminded, I suppose, that Russell is very clever, he doesn't cast people that can't do it. He obviously spent time casting those two roles, and getting them to read together and making sure the chemistry was right. They worked brilliantly together.'

Rose and Mickey's travels with the Doctor eventually saw them parted, apparently forever, at the end of The Age of Steel.

'NOEL MADE IT SPARKLE': NOEL CLARKE AS MICKEY SMITH

In contrast with earlier versions of *Doctor Who*, the Doctor's companion this time around came with baggage, albeit good baggage, in the form of her on/off boyfriend Mickey Smith (called Mobbsy in Russell's original series document), and her mobile-hairdresser mum Jackie (originally Judy) Tyler. These important roles were part of the casting process for the first three episodes of Series One to enter production, *Rose*, *Aliens of London* and *World War Three*, which were directed by Keith Boak. According to Keith, 'Christopher was cast before I was on board, Billie just at the same time – so I wasn't around for their casting. But I was involved with casting both Noel Clarke and Camille Coduri, alongside Julie, Phil and Russell.'

'We did about six days of casting,' explains Phil Collinson, 'so various Jackies and Mickeys were mixed in there with people we were seeing for Joe Green or Indra Ganesh. Russell was keen for Mickey to be black, and Andy Pryor brought in probably half a dozen different guys, but Noel was the first we saw and was the person we wanted. That caused Keith Boak some headaches because Noel was filming *Auf Wiedersehen, Pet*, and so we had to bend our schedule a bit to fit around him. He couldn't be with us for the first four weeks of filming. But eventually we made it work. We were also working around Penelope Wilton (Harriet Jones), who was off filming with Woody Allen.'

Russell recalls Noel's commitments outside *Doctor Who* as quite a challenge for all concerned. 'Noel was the only man who could possibly do that part, and so we turned our schedule upside down to accommodate his work on *Auf Wiedersehen, Pet*. We wanted him, but the dates clashed and so we thought that was it.' Mal Young spoke to the BBC's Head of Drama Serials, Laura Mackie, and they discussed ways around it. Neither *Doctor Who* nor *Auf Wiedersehen, Pet* changed any filming dates, but each production made efforts to coordinate their schedules, which meant that Noel was flown in from Thailand where he was filming *Auf Wiedersehen, Pet* and came straight to the *Doctor Who* location. He didn't attend any readthroughs or rehearsals for the first block. Instead he had to fly back and forth, dropping into his two very different characters at the drop of a hat. This was difficult for Keith Boak and his team, because no one wants a major cast member to miss rehearsals, but everyone feels that ultimately it was worth it.

'Noel Clarke was the only person who read the audition scripts with enough lightness,' remembers Russell. 'Everyone else delivered Mickey as a very hard, a very angry character.' For the auditions,

Russell had elected to use the scenes in *Aliens of London* where Mickey talks about being accused of Rose's murder, because they involved a lot of heavy dramatic material. 'What Noel did was to make it sparkle. With most actors, it doesn't matter what they're doing, it doesn't matter how tragic the script is, what you're looking for is comic timing, because that gives you a sign of intelligence. And he was brilliant. I knew then that we could eventually make Mickey stronger, and put him aboard the TARDIS as a full-time companion during the second series.'

'As it's gone on, they've written to Noel's strengths,' agrees Andy Pryor. 'By the end of his time on the show, Mickey was a much more complex individual than the guy we saw in the first episode. This is the thing about the regular characters in a series like *Doctor Who* – you don't want them to be just playing the same thing all the way through because it's boring for them, it's boring for the writers and it's boring for the audience. I needed to offer Russell and his team actors who I knew would to be able to take the characters and run, to flesh out their relationships and make something of the opportunities *Doctor Who* was presenting them with.'

'SHE'S GOT FIRE': CAMILLE CODURI AS JACKIE TYLER

Next up was Jackie Tyler and, again, Andy Pryor supplied someone everyone immediately fell in love with. Mal Young was a supporter of Camille Coduri's, and he had mentioned her to Andy. Phil Collinson had already seen Camille in a couple of things but had never met or auditioned her before. Andy brought her in and, Phil believes, 'She was instantly Jackie. I think if you put her and Billie together, they look alike. That's the first thing that I thought when Camille came in: she felt like the kind of mother Rose would have. She immediately understood what Jackie was, from the very first scene she ever read really. Often you'll ask actors and actresses to read stuff again and again and again and you'll give them notes but, with Camille, we just laughed from the first time she opened her mouth. In one scene, she hits the Doctor and says "Stitch this" – at least that was the scripted line, but in the audition she added a "mate" to the end of it, and that was perfect: "Stitch this, mate." And belted him. And I thought, "She's brilliant. She's got fire." And I think she really grew during Series Two, she went through the mill. Whenever we have screenings for the press or crew, the minute Jackie walks on-screen there's a palpable feeling in the room, people love that character. There's a real glee about her and a joy to her, and I think that is absolutely down to Camille.'

Julie agrees with this enthusiastically, recalling that they were down to two people

for Jackie – two strong favourites. 'It was really tough, because the other person was also incredibly good, and there was lots of discussion about who to go with. Camille looked so much like Billie, such a perfect fit for a mother and daughter. And she was so grounded and funny. You wanted to be with her, you know, Camille's got a kind of cuddliness about her. And I think she's grown in performance, episode by episode. There's so much warmth and Camille's got such a generous spirit, such a big heart. She's just this presence that glues people together and I think that comes across on-screen.'

'I was very familiar with Russell's work,' says Camille herself, 'so I was very excited, and quite terrified, because I respect him so much. When I read the scenes that I was to go in and do, I thought the script was amazing. I

Two sides of Jackie Tyler…
Above: Terrified by the
Autons in Rose. Below: By
the time she meets the new
Doctor and the Sycorax
in The Christmas Invasion,
she's chilled out a bit.

met Keith Boak and lovely Andy Pryor, first time around.
Andy played Rose and the other characters, and I sat
in front of a camera and mugged away. And they were
really nice, and then I went off and thought I had to find
something else to do for a living, because I thought I was
pants. But I got a call a while later to say they wanted to
see me again. Phil Collinson met me at the door, and told
me they thought I was so crap last time, that they were
giving me another go. And I just fell about laughing, but
totally agreeing with him. Of course, he didn't really mean
that, but they wanted me to play the scenes a bit lighter,
as I'd made Jackie quite cross first time round. She was
totally real, an ordinary mum waiting for her daughter, not
knowing where she'd been for a year, so anything could
have happened to her. Just that – a solid human being.'

'Hooray for Camille!' exclaims Russell. 'Nicest woman
in the world. How lovely is she? When she did that scene
from *Aliens of London*, adding in the "mate" I went back and wrote that into the script.
I thought it was so nice. There was something very real about Camille, so it was a very
easy choice in the end.' Andy Pryor believes that Russell and the other writers saw
something in Camille that they could use. 'Some of what Jackie Tyler did in the second
series was incredibly moving – because Camille had that range.'

'THAT MATINEE IDOL FEEL': JOHN BARROWMAN AS CAPTAIN JACK HARKNESS

The final regular, for the first series at least, was the character of Captain Jack Harkness,
played by John Barrowman. Though he didn't turn up on-screen until the ninth episode,
The Empty Child, John's casting was announced very early on. Indeed, one of the
earliest conversations Russell and Phil had about casting was with regard to Captain
Jack, or Jax as he was in Russell's initial notes. They thought he might be American, and
both knew of John Barrowman, realising he'd be able to play the part easily. They asked
him to come in and read and do a screen test. 'It was the fastest casting I've ever done,'
says Phil. 'He came in and saw Russell and me, I think, at two o'clock in the afternoon

Captain Jack Harkness inside
his spaceship. Well, maybe
not his, strictly speaking…

and we taped him reading a couple of scenes. Later that afternoon, we had a meeting with Julie Gardner, Jane Tranter and Mal Young to talk about the outline of the series, because it was that early on, and we just stuck the tape in Jane's VHS. She loved him, and so we cast him that afternoon.' If John Barrowman was to play Captain Jack, he needed to be cast quickly because, as a musical-theatre performer, John gets booked up for long stretches quite quickly. With confirmation that they needed him for a particular period of time, his schedule could be arranged accordingly.

'There aren't that many parts for American leading men in this country,' adds Andy Pryor. 'We wanted someone who had that kind of matinee idol feel but again had the dramatic range to be able to take the character elsewhere.'

'I'd love to take the credit for John Barrowman,' laughs Julie, 'because I adore him, I love being with him, so I'd like to say he owes everything to me! He actually owes me nothing at all, because I had absolutely no idea who he was! But Russell, Phil and Mal Young all knew him from theatre, from his musical work, and his presenting work on kids' TV shows. They played us the tape and everyone loved him, because he's so sexy, has so much charm, and he was perfect for the character that Russell was creating. I mean, absolutely perfect. So that was one of the easiest bits of casting we ever did.'

'CAN I HAVE A LONG COAT?' DAVID TENNANT

Having forged this excellent team of players for the first series, it became necessary to start the search for a new Doctor. Enter a young Scots actor called David McDonald, better known these days as David Tennant.

'David's always been one of my favourite actors,' says Andy Pryor. 'I've seen a lot of his theatre work and he's really got one of the most expansive ranges of any British actor I know – he can do almost anything and, although it's often said, that isn't really true of that many actors. David can do strength, vulnerability, he can be sexy, funny; he can do pretty much anything you ask him to do. It was a brilliant piece of timing really, because *Casanova* and *Blackpool* had just happened, so he was becoming a household name. Not that we felt it absolutely necessary for the Doctor to be a household name, but the fact that he was in people's consciousness and had recently demonstrated that he could carry a drama on his own and be a strong leading man was perfect timing. There was no competition and no discussion about who else it might be. We all agreed one hundred per cent that it should be David right from the word go. No one else was ever seen or thought about.'

The first time anyone mentioned it to David Tennant himself was at Russell's house where, along with Julie Gardner, they were watching an episode of *Casanova* shortly before its transmission. Julie whispered the words 'Doctor Who' to the actor. He just laughed. 'It seemed so surreal, and absurd that this show which I loved so much was even back at all, and it was back so robustly and being cared for so deeply by Russell and Julie and everyone in their team. So to be asked not to have a little part in it, which was what I had been angling for, but to take over from Christopher Eccleston... it seemed absurd. And very funny. I remember laughing a lot that day.'

David didn't say yes straight away. Although it was a scenario that had played in his mind many times during his career as an actor because it was a show he loved, actually being faced with the possibility provoked an entirely different reaction to the one he had anticipated. It was mainly shock, a reaction Russell told David was not entirely unexpected. 'Russell very astutely told me not to respond straight away. Because Russell loved the show like I did, when he'd been asked to produce it, he'd also had to think about what it meant. And he told me he knew I was not reacting as I thought I would have. It was a slightly more mixed sensation. Part of me was very excited at the prospect and part of me was a bit scared. It has all this history, all this baggage and, on purely practical terms, it's something that takes up nine months of the year to film. There's a big undertaking in going into a long-running TV series, just because of the nature of what they are, and the bigger the series the bigger that undertaking is. I could do *Doctor Who* for nine months and then be on stage at the Royal Shakespeare Company for twenty-five years but my obituary's still going to talk about *Doctor Who*.' So David went off to consider his options, and it took him a while. Indeed, he clearly recalls there being a point when he decided to say no because it would take his career and life in a direction that he hadn't intended. 'And then, I woke up the day after I'd made that decision and just told myself not to be so silly. How could I have walked away from this? This is so unique and so individual and the things that were frightening me off were precisely the reasons why it was an experience I had to have. And anyway, what would I have done if I hadn't done

Above: Filming in freezing cold Tremorfa in winter, pretending it's boiling hot London in the summer, David Tennant and first assistant director Peter Bennett share a joke. Right: Sad and lonely – the Tenth Doctor at Bad Wolf Bay in Doomsday.

it and then John Simm from *Life on Mars* or someone else brilliant had; I'd have been sitting at home, watching the series thinking, "Damn, it could have been me."

'I only had one question. In fact I asked this on that first night in Manchester, before agreeing. "Can I have a long coat?" There were a hundred sensible, practical questions I could have asked, but all I wanted was a long coat. Which, I'm happy to say, I got! The only other question of any importance to me was whether Billie Piper was staying on, because she'd been so good. They assured me that, contrary to what was being reported in some corners, she was there, for the whole second series, which was great news.'

One question that did occur to a number of people, David included, concerned his voice. Being from Paisley, David has a soft but very pronounced West Coast Scots accent. His predecessor had been very broadly Mancunian, hence that famous line in *Rose* where he responded to his new companion's query with 'Lots of planets have a North.' Did this mean that, at some point, Russell was going to be adding a line into *The Christmas Invasion* along the lines of 'Well, every planet has a Scotland'? As it turned out, Russell wanted David not to use his natural accent, but to adopt a more London, more rakish tone. 'I never thought to query it,' David admits. 'I'd just been working with him on *Casanova* doing a similar accent. As Christopher had done something which was so robustly and very effectively anti-South East, maybe it would have seemed a bit gimmicky to then go to Scotland for the next one. I never thought about it until other people started mentioning it, because I do non-Scots accents all the time – I spend half my life not using my own voice, so it doesn't bother me at all.'

Working on *Casanova* was the first time Russell had ever encountered his new leading man. It was as a result of an audition tape arriving at his home that the two met. *Casanova* was, according to Russell, a nightmare to cast, because the character has to be a beautiful man in all sorts of ways, and so he and Julie were auditioning what Russell refers to as 'every handsome hunk in the world. But, oh my God, they always turned out to be boring. Now, strictly speaking, in some financier's terms, David wasn't famous enough for a major BBC drama. Even though we already had Peter O'Toole in it, some people were saying David wasn't a big enough name. But we argued our case, because he just fitted my dialogue. Not everyone does; not everyone gets the rhythm of it and the speed of it, and has the nerve to play the comedy of it. It takes a lot of nerve in a "Serious

58 ◀ DOCTOR WHO: THE INSIDE STORY

Drama" to pitch that level of comedy, and David just did. I'd never even met the man but there I was, arguing for using him. And then the first time I met him, I suppose, was the rehearsals for *Casanova* in London in some godforsaken hall near Soho. And what a lovely man, I loved him immediately. He and I quickly went through twenty-seven *Doctor Who* conversations because we both loved it so much.'

For *Doctor Who*, this turned out to be an equally lucky meeting because, although

the team had always known that Christopher Eccleston was only making a one-series commitment, they were nervous. They hit January knowing that the last script was written and he was off, so they would soon have to sort out a new Doctor, but desperately wanting to keep that Series One ending secret. 'If we'd announced to agents that we were looking, the secret would have been out and in the papers,' explains Russell. 'You see, there was no way we wanted to be launching that first series, while simultaneously letting it be known that the lead actor was going – that would have been a disastrous start. Of course the whole thing went wrong anyway, because it leaked in the press. We had been secretive but, truth be told, we were too secretive, because the papers were then full of all sorts of stories, not one of which was true. It was awful. But Christopher carried on promoting the show, and he did so with dignity and enthusiasm, and we are so grateful to him.'

David Tennant had in fact been on Andy Pryor's list of potential Doctors for the first series, alongside Christopher Eccleston but, back then, no one really knew of him. Russell continues: 'I hadn't seen *He Knew He Was Right*, and *Blackpool* hadn't been transmitted. So I only knew him from a couple of Big Finish *Doctor Who* CDs, but I do remember people saying what a lovely man he was. People like Jane Tranter had already seen *Blackpool* by that stage – she was telling me that he was marvellous, but he wasn't famous enough for *Doctor Who*. By the time we needed to cast again to replace Christopher Eccleston, David had had a year of *Blackpool* and *Casanova*, and it was weird how all that fitted neatly into place. God knows what we would have done if he'd turned it down!' A matter of weeks after Julie Gardner had first whispered the idea to him, David Tennant was announced as the Tenth Doctor on 16 April, and five days later he was recording his first few lines in the role.

'With David, no one ever has a bad day or a cross word,' says Russell. 'Another series under way, and still nothing. He's forever happy, and brings such energy to work. He is the engine of the show, welcoming the guest stars in, welcoming the directors in. It's very hard — especially taking on that mantle from Christopher, who'd been so successful, big shoes to fill. The actor playing the Doctor is the one constant thing on set, which makes it very hard work — the maddest job in the world — and he is utterly brilliant.'

'WE SIT THERE LIKE SIMON COWELL': CHOOSING THE SUPPORTING CAST

Even with all the leads in place, there are always countless other parts to cast, so Andy Pryor's job just keeps going. Essentially, his job is to cast anybody who speaks. 'I strongly believe that productions can be let down by bad casting in the small parts,' says Andy. 'It only takes one person to deliver a line in a fairly dodgy fashion and a whole scene can come crashing down, particularly when you're putting them in scenes with the very accomplished actors who play the big parts. So it's both important and enjoyable casting those supporting parts, particularly when the writing's good. In Russell's series, the small parts are still good, it's never just Cop Number One, Cop Number Two. In *Doctor Who*, they're always there with a purpose and they have a character.'

Andy has to work closely not just with the directors and with Phil Collinson — sometimes the scriptwriters will have come up with a suggestion, or a good, strong pointer to the kind of actor they were thinking of. For the majority of parts, Andy brings in a selection of people for the director to meet, although sometimes he auditions them on his own and the director will just cast from the tapes Andy has made. 'The director, Phil, Russell and Julie will have a look at the choices that I've brought to the table, then we'll debate who we think is the best. Usually it's so we can bring down the list of possibles from seven or eight people to just a few which I'll then audition again, either on my own or with the director. It's quite rare for us all to disagree, strangely. It doesn't always happen like that on other productions, but I think everybody on *Doctor Who* seems to know a good thing when they see it.'

Above: Charles Dickens (Simon Callow) finds his enthusiasm for living renewed by meeting the Doctor and Rose. Left: Queen Victoria (Pauline Collins), one of the few members of the Great British monarchy that the Doctor's charms failed to impress. So much so that she established the Torchwood Institute to help overcome alien threats such as him...

This way of working is important on a series with *Doctor Who*'s fast turnaround, according to Phil Collinson. After viewing the tapes, the team all have a conference call with the director and Andy, and work out who they want to cast in what role. 'We just sit there, like Simon Cowell on *The X Factor*, while Andy wheels people's tapes in and out. Julie, Russell and I are very hands-on with the casting because the three of us have an overview across the series, we know the tone and stylistic approach, whereas a director will just do one or two episodes.' After decisions have been made, Andy will deal with the actor's agent; this sometimes requires a quick call to Phil because one actor may want a chauffeur-driven car to Cardiff or another wants at least a first-class train ticket. And Phil, his mind firmly on a rapidly vanishing budget, usually says no. Or yes. Sometimes...

DOCTOR WHO

ROLL 87B	SLATE	TAKE
SCENE 18 13/20	527	3
DIRECTOR		PANAVISION
DOP: ERNIE VINCZE BSC		
DATE: 01	VFX N°	B DAY

Behind the Scenes

On 19 July 2004, *BBC News* reported:

'Shoppers in Cardiff will have a sneak preview of life in the fourth dimension as filming of the new *Doctor Who* series starts this week. The science fiction show, starring Christopher Eccleston as the latest reincarnation of the timelord, is being made by BBC Wales. Singer and actress Billie Piper is appearing as the Doctor's sidekick. City centre streets are being closed off for filming on Tuesday and Wednesday for location work. The new series, written by *Queer as Folk* creator Russell T Davies, will hit TV screens in 2005.'

For the first time since 1989, the BBC's cameras were about to begin filming a new series of *Doctor Who*...

GETTING UP AND RUNNING

With BBC Wales commissioned to make the new series, Russell and the team of writers gearing up to write it, and the main elements of the cast in place, attention quickly switched to the day-to-day practicalities of actually making a modern television drama series. Two people are important here, and we'll turn first to Phil Collinson. Phil is *Doctor Who*'s full-time producer, and is central to the process of keeping everything running smoothly, on time and – most importantly – on budget.

Phil Collinson, like many of the people working on the series today, has a self-evident love of the show, its history and its place in our culture. He joined the *Doctor Who* production team in January 2004, soon after starting up BBC One's *Sea of Souls*, and he describes himself as the series' 'project manager'.

'I'm probably the only person on the team to go through every single process, or to be involved in every single decision. *Doctor Who* was commissioned as a thirteen-part series, so my first job was to sit down with an accountant and work out a basic budget. The budget for the series is about twenty A4 pages of minute detail, because we had to work out what every single thing was going to cost. Having done that, I then had to manage it, make sure we brought the show in for what I said we could do it for. Or I made people above me aware if things were going slightly awry and took direction from them about what we should do. Do we pull scripts back? Or do they smile and give us a little bit more money? Usually, of course, it's the former.'

Producer Phil Collinson keeps out of reach of a Cyberman.

Russell, Julie and Phil work closely together at every stage, with the producer's involvement commencing at the scripting stage, alongside writers and script editors. If it's not Russell or Julie wondering aloud how on earth an effect or a stunt can be realised on-screen, it's Phil. The director for each production block is chosen by the three, but it's Phil who works with the director during the period of preparation for making the episodes, ensuring coordination with the various design departments, and helping in the hunt for suitable locations. Phil is also present, 'at the beginning and end of every day at least', on location or in the studio once recording starts. 'As much as anything, I'm a support for the directors; a liaison between Russell and Julie and the production as a whole, ensuring that what's going in front of the camera is what they want. I sit behind the directors and whisper a lot in their ears.'

Phil also has to work very closely with the Art Department. One significant and sometimes problematic difference between *Doctor Who* and more generic TV drama is that the TARDIS can and does go anywhere in time and space. 'On *Born and Bred*, for instance, at the beginning we built six sets: a hospital, three wards, a pub, two houses. And they stood as our sets for every episode of two or three series. On *Doctor Who*, we can have new sets going up – and being torn down again – two or three times a week, and every single one of those has to look right and feel right. Other than the TARDIS interior, we don't build any sets that stand for the whole series, which eats energy and time and money, and it's a very challenging show because of that.'

The challenges continue, endlessly it seems. Phil had set up three other series from scratch before joining *Doctor Who*, and so had some experience and know-how in most of the areas that the new series so relentlessly demands: green screen, physical effects,

Members of Graeme Harper's team (and bronze chum) on the Sphere Room set during Doomsday.

burning things down, blowing things up, stunts, special effects… The list goes on. 'I never thought it was going to be an easy job,' says Phil. 'On a normal programme you might plan two stunts; on *Doctor Who*, you're planning four stunts every single block. The complexity of our shoot is guided by what The Mill will need to achieve the special effects we want, which I didn't know anything about before doing this series and have effectively taken a crash course in! Luckily, I already had a relationship with Will Cohen and Dave Houghton at The Mill, because they'd done *Sea of Souls* with me. So they talked me through lots of different things, and I realised quickly that we had to set up tone meetings, which we did right from our very first block.'

At the tone meeting, the entire team is gathered around one table: Edward Thomas's design team, the people from model effects, The Mill, the stunt coordinator, Millennium FX, costume and make-up people, writers, director, assistant directors. With all the experts assembled, everyone goes through the script, page by page, line by line, blow by blow, discussing each scene, throwing up alternatives, suggesting all sorts of ways to create the magic that will end up on-screen. Rarely does the script that's read at the

start of the day remain intact by the end of the meeting — forty-odd highly creative people working together en masse cannot help but find new ways to tweak scenes, or request changes to enable something that seemed innocuous on the page to come to life in a practical way and within the budget Phil has set. Phil sees this approach as beneficial both to the show and to the creative teams behind it:

'I think it continues to be a very collaborative show. Everything's a learning curve, even after two series of it, we're all still learning or refining our knowledge. Now, when I pick up a script and the Doctor's got a confrontation with a guy at the top of Alexandra Palace mast — I don't freak out any more. I did at first: I kind of sat there

Above: The Doctor on top of the Alexandra Palace mast, shooting the climax for The Idiot's Lantern. *Below: The effects team transmit an image of the Connolly's Gran (Margaret John) to the Bakelite TV prop.*

and felt that it ought to be something I should know how to do, and now I do. I'm able to run those meetings more efficiently now, and pre-empt problems and know when we can achieve something and when I don't think we can.

'I think people are happy in their work. People never get the chance to be bored by it or frustrated by it, because it chucks different challenges at you every day — the crew are turning up at a different place two or three times a week, working different shifts and different hours, and there's a lot of joy there, a lot of fun in making it. Series Two was certainly more cheerful, more relaxed. Every single person was less nervous, simply because we knew how to make it. We weren't worrying about how the audience were going to take to it, because the first series had been such a phenomenal hit and that feeling of pride runs through everyone, every single technician, runner, the guy dishing the chips up from the catering van. We certainly have, I believe, the happiest crew that I've ever worked with.'

'HANDHOLDING, SUPPORTING AND CHIVVYING': THE SCRIPT EDITOR'S ROLE

There is one other member of the full-time production staff who is integral to the daily running of the show — the script editor. In the early days of *Doctor Who*, the story/script editors were responsible for commissioning writers, working with them, polishing their ideas and, as a last resort if it still wasn't quite working, they would sit down and do a polish themselves, crafting it so it suited whichever period of the show was being worked on. For its original run, the programme's first ever story editor was David Whitaker, the fifteenth and last script editor was Andrew Cartmel. Joining them on that long list have been three people over *Doctor Who*'s first two series in the twenty-first century: Elwen Rowlands on the first series, Simon Winstone on the second and, working across both series, Helen Raynor. But the script editor's job in 2005–2006 bears scant resemblance to the role the Whitakers and Cartmels of yesteryear filled.

'The script editor is absolutely vital,' Julie Gardner assures us. 'On the first series, Elwen and Helen were already script editors in the BBC Wales Drama Department. They forged fantastic relationships with the writers and we needed that backbone so much.'

An aspect of the job that might have been a bit daunting for the script editors was that Russell had been a script editor in the past, as had Julie and Phil. They had three bosses from a script-editing background and, as Russell concedes, that can be very tough 'because we're very opinionated and had a lot to say. However, there's an awful lot of day-to-day stuff that script editors dealt with, lots of handholding and supporting the writers, chivvying and stuff like that, which I backed away from. I probably spoke to the writers once a month; Helen and her team were on the phone to them daily. If a writer genuinely has a problem, and wants to speak to me, I'm always open to it, but I am also busy, so writers will tend to deal with the script editor in the first place. Of course, that means there's a lot going on that I don't know about but, curiously, I'm very grateful for it. And that means that when there's a meeting, and we're sitting in a room, hurling ideas around, it's a democracy. Anyone can say anything about the scripts – that's the script editor's chance to pipe up and weigh in with stuff.' However, at times, especially mid series, when everything is really manic as opposed to the very mildly manic it is the rest of the time, meetings tend to fall by the wayside. That means Russell, Phil and Julie will have read the scripts but passed notes back to the writers, via the script editors – and Russell admits these are often very contradictory notes, which the script editors need to filter and work out which bits to take back to the writer that will still ensure the executives get the script they're looking for.

Filming the Ood attack on Sanctuary Base.

Script editors Helen Raynor and Elwen Rowlands and (right) Simon Winstone.

So it seems obvious that the one person to guide us through exactly what the job is must be Helen Raynor, simply because she's been across every aspect of both series since Day One. 'Lovely Helen Raynor', everyone calls her. Which, frankly, when dealing with the mixed messages from the execs, the bruised ego of a writer – who wanted the scene to be as he wrote it, not as ten other people ultimately wrote it – and the bewilderment of the writers' agents, is terribly important. Apart from doing a highly pressured job, Helen is rather like one of those marvellous nurses in a busy A&E department: nothing winds her up, she's both totally unflappable and a very calming influence. Ideal then to be a script editor. Assuming she can actually define what a modern script editor actually is…

'Back in the Olden Days on *Doctor Who*, the script editors drove the show to a large extent, I gather,' she laughs, imagining those halcyon days when script editors ruled the world. 'I read things about script editors commissioning storylines and co-writing episodes and deciding what stories were going to play across a season, and I think how lovely that would be. But that's not something that comes within today's script editor role at all. My role, and the role now of Simon Winstone, is to bring to Russell and Julie's attention the people that we think would be fabulous to write for the show and try to get them to agree. And, of course, they've got writers that they have their eye on as well, so there are quite a lot of names brought to the table. If I go in, passionately convinced that Writer A has got something amazing, then they will have a look at their work, and they will want to meet them. But *Doctor Who* is very pressured and really that means they're going to have to go with people with a track record in telly, which automatically rules a lot of people out.'

One difference between *Doctor Who* and most other television drama series is that there isn't a huge hierarchical structure. On a traditional show, a script editor might be working upwards to an assistant producer, a producer, an exec with whom they probably don't have any direct contact or might see at readthroughs once or twice a year. This means that, for many script editors, the whole of the editorial process is about second-guessing the person above them, which is probably somewhat frustrating. An editor might spend months working with a writer taking their script in one direction and just one set of notes can come back from someone they've never met, telling them everything is wrong and they need to start again, or do something completely different.

On *Doctor Who* this trauma is lessened because Russell T Davies has what Helen describes as a 'god-like plan' of where he wants the series to go overall. 'I'm convinced that it's planned out in his head in much more meticulous detail than he lets on. Occasionally, you say to him things like, "We should do a story about X" or "Wouldn't it be fabulous to do a story set in Y." And he'll say, "Oh yes, absolutely, but we need to keep that for Series Four." He's got an incredible instinct about what story can play where – there are stories in Series Two which would have seemed odd in Series One, because it was all a lot newer, but he had them all planned.'

A *Doctor Who* script editor's basic day has to be very fluid – it can start with anything from mapping out the series and where it's going to dealing with a specific script and asking a writer to write a particular episode, the brief of which might be as simple as 'Pigs in space' – something which is essentially a concept or event in a sentence – or a very detailed outline, because Russell needs that particular story to set up something for a major event or revelation later in the series. With work on the series split between two script editors, it is Russell and Julie who decide which one works with which writer. The editor then talks the concept through with the writers and waits for them to deliver an outline or a treatment, and that's when the fun starts! Or the trauma, depending on your outlook. 'This,' Helen says, 'is the moment at which you actually start thrashing out with the writer what the story is going to be. From whatever that small premise was that you worked out together, now you're deciding what happens in the actual story. As script editor, I work with the writer on getting that outline up to showroom quality. Not every draft of every outline goes to Russell and Julie, simply because they're too busy and there would be no point. And it's nice for a writer to have the script editor as someone

that they can show their workings to, knowing it won't be pre-judged or emailed to seven million other people. We provide quite a nice, private space, where they can make mistakes, and try out ideas which might sound brilliant but actually be complete codswallop.'

The actual process of agreeing an outline, however, can take absolutely ages. 'I think that seventy per cent of the effort goes into working out the important things: what the story is about; why you want to tell it; where you want to get to at the end – everything crucial is worked out at outline stage. Outlines are very difficult to write and really unrewarding, because you have none of the fizz of character or the fun of dialogue; it can feel like absolute drudgery, for everyone involved.' Once Helen has a reasonable-looking outline, she'll take it to Russell and Julie, and they will give feedback, requests and criticisms back to the writer through Helen, or she'll bring the writer in and have a meeting with everyone together. Helen prefers the latter because, no matter how tactful and emotive she can be in an email to the writer, 'Nothing can really replicate Russell. So much of what he wants is conveyed not by his words but by his body language. His huge infectiousness and cheekiness and audacity with ideas come across best when you meet him.'

When work first began on the series, Julie Gardner had to learn about and take on board the spin-off merchandise which the series generates, something which subsequently fell under Helen's purview. Now the *Doctor Who* office has two people working full-time on what is termed Brand Management. Their job is to inspect, approve and generally manage every single aspect of anything outside the actual television show that carries the *Doctor Who* logo, literally or metaphorically. This isn't just toys and books – it's also events, studio visits, organising Design-a-Monster competitions with *Blue Peter*. Helen's job crossed into theirs in one specific area because she had to approve anything written, fictional or factual: comic strips, novels, audio CD adventures, even the blurbs for DVD packaging. Helen cannot think of another programme on British television where the script editor has to get so involved in extracurricular activities like this. Indeed, it only started to become apparent that the job needed doing halfway through the first series' pre-production period.

'I had absolutely no idea that that was going to be a part of my job: publicity, toys, other merchandise, additional fiction – I now use phrases like "additional fiction" as if I'm discussing the weather or what restaurant to eat in. For an insane couple of months, I was writing copy for DVD boxes, reading outlines for new audio plays featuring the Eighth Doctor and signing off lists of things it was acceptable for a talking Dalek pen to say. It was absolutely bizarre. However, it would be impossible to do this job and say that you only wanted to do the scripts and be involved in nothing else. For a start, you've got Russell, someone who is very aware of what's going on commercially. He absolutely knows what feels like the right amount to be offering people, and when it suddenly feels that we might be looking too cynical about it. He's always genuinely concerned that we don't have merchandise out there that looks in any way like we're trying to cash in and make a fast buck from people who love the show. He gets terribly excited about the magazines and comic strips, and when new toys arrive

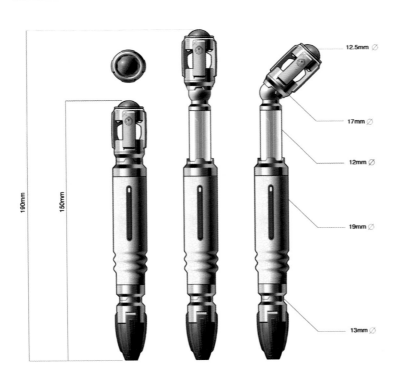

Concept designs by Dan Walker for the sonic screwdriver.

190mm

150mm

12.5mm ⌀

17mm ⌀

12mm ⌀

19mm ⌀

13mm ⌀

he gets all enthused by them. That's the kind of kid he was, he loved the show, got everything to do with it, probably bought the T-shirts but didn't wear them, kept them nice, that sort of thing! So he's protective of the brand.'

Agreeing that 'brand', like 'additional fiction', is a phrase unused by script editors generally, Helen explains that, on a traditional show, all the script editor does is work with the writers but on *Doctor Who* she's been lucky in having that greater variation, although the writers remain the primary concern. She also notes that different writers have very different ways of working. Some, while they're writing, will be remarkably quiet, take however many weeks it takes for them to do what they've been asked and she won't hear from them and must just assume that they're OK, haven't left the country, and one day there'll be a first draft arriving on her desk. Other writers will be on the phone almost every day, asking every question imaginable, and a few that previously weren't. And then there are Russell's own scripts, which still need to go through the script-editing process, even though he's the show-runner. Although, unsurprisingly, Helen feels that there is a difference working with him on his own material, not least because he takes on even more pressure. 'Because the whole thematic slant of the show comes from him, he's sort of editing himself before he even gets properly under way. I don't think as a writer his editorial judgement takes a holiday when he writes a script, I think it's rather the reverse. Because Russell's got a very strong production background, more experience in more different kinds of telly than virtually anyone else on the show, he tends to be very good about knowing what we can and can't do in production terms. He always pushes it, he's always at the brink of what we can achieve, but he knows that. That's the challenge he throws down for production.'

Even for Russell though, some things occasionally need a rethink. Not just moments where two people go running out of a door which they've already gone running out of – these sorts of things crop up in every writer's script, and usually they're the shadow of an earlier draft, a rewrite that hasn't quite been sorted out. But there are times when that extra pair of eyes is invaluable to him. Helen cites working with him on *New Earth* – quite a dark story, about using human beings as lab rats. It was intended to feel very contemporary and very in tune with what's going on out in the real world. At the same time, there were cat-nuns and Cassandra and and high-comedy body-swapping amidst all this darkness. 'In the first draft of that script,' Helen explains, 'the Doctor managed to leap into the lift and get the disinfectant going and then everyone died. There was no passing on of the healing touch. What was necessary to save everybody and save the world was to kill all these poor people. And it felt incredibly harsh – I remember getting to that bit and realising they were all going to die. As a viewer you feel repulsed by them, but you also feel terribly sorry for them. They're more like children than adults, just strange, caged people who don't know what to do with themselves. And so killing them off felt extraordinarily brutal and really caught me by surprise. We had a conversation about it, and Russell must have been thinking along similar lines, because I didn't have to convince him. He couldn't believe he'd written that they would all die, couldn't believe he'd written an episode which ended with this pile of corpses everywhere.'

Nonetheless, a version of the script does exist where that happened, so Russell does revisit his own work editorially. Helen says if there's something that she doesn't quite

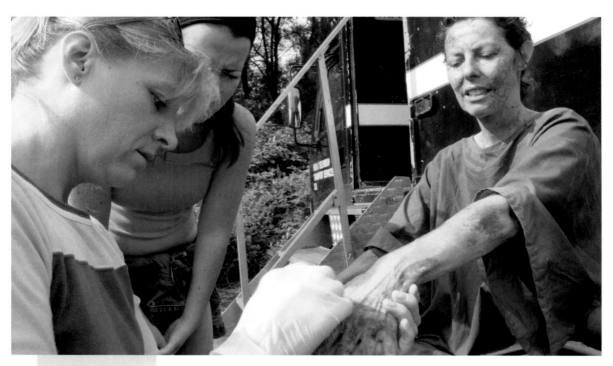

Working closely with the Millennium FX prosthetics team, the make-up artists apply diseases to the arm of one of the unfortunate patients bred in New Earth's *New New York hospital.*

think is working in a script or she doesn't quite get, she'll email him with a question or say, 'That wasn't what I was expecting' or 'Are we supposed to feel this way about this character?' And they always discuss it. 'I think I'd have been very worried if I'd ever been in a position where I got a Russell script that I felt really didn't work or that I had a huge number of questions about – that would have been a profoundly unsettling experience, because then I'd have felt that we'd lost our editorial motor.'

So script editing the boss isn't the most awkward job on the series, as one might have assumed. Helen suggests that more awkward is the period at the start of a series when there are a lot of writers writing at the same time, everything's roughly at the same stage, and it can be difficult to keep an eye on what's happening on one script and to make sure there's no repetition – a situation that arose early in Series Two. Helen recalls that Steven Moffat had an idea for *The Girl in the Fireplace* about clockwork droids essentially stealing body parts in order to rebuild themselves and rebuild their ship. 'We hung on to some of that idea – they repair the ship with body parts, which is beautifully gruesome – but he had the idea that the droids actually repair *themselves* by stealing bits of people. He told me about it and I thought it was a brilliant idea. I think he'd already gone some way down the path with that idea, but of course it clashed massively with Tom MacRae's two-part Cybermen story, about where human beings end up, having enhanced themselves artificially. At that stage, Tom's script was going to be very body-part-based, spare bits of arms and legs everywhere, so I had to warn Steven off and explain that it was such an integral part of Tom's episodes that it might have to be dropped from his episode. Steven did that with very good grace although, ironically, *Rise of the Cybermen* ended up not really being about spare parts – instead it involved taking the brain out a human being and putting it into a Cyber casing. So now, part of my brain's thinking that there's still a story idea going begging really, isn't there, about people repairing themselves with bits of other people…'

Once the team have read the first drafts and shared their thoughts, concerns and ideas, and notes have been given to the writer, the script editors make sure that the writer is happy to go along with what has come out of those conversations, is clear about the direction that the next draft is taking and is ready to go off and do it. While Helen said that seventy per cent of the work is in the storyline, occasionally things that seem amazing in an outline just don't work once the script arrives. While outlines function as a sort of editorial safety net, everyone has to be prepared to allow themselves to deviate from that agreed starting point. Other things will come together in the script that weren't in the treatment, especially characters. When Mark Gatiss delivered his first draft of *The Unquiet Dead*, the story included a maid called Gwyneth, a minor character that the team liked. Over subsequent drafts, Gwyneth gained psychic powers and a place at the heart of the story. 'Often, a character who seemed fairly minor and peripheral to the narrative,' Helen suggests, 'actually comes off the page so well that everybody falls in love with them, and then the note from the execs is that they love this character, and want to see more of them, want them more active in the story. So a lot of the time I think the second draft is about getting rid of the people we don't like and having more of the people that we do. Which sounds very unscientific, but actually isn't a bad way to go about writing a story.'

So it would appear that a *Doctor Who* script editor is a bit of a human buffer, having to convey the clarity of the message from the execs without upsetting the writer, yet without softening that message to such a point that it becomes impossible to understand. Writers will discover that there are some notes which are optional, there are some notes which are suggestions, there are some notes where people are happy to be convinced either way, and there are some notes which are absolutes and imperatives. The script editor is the person who has to work out which is which. The more

A selection of concept artwork by Peter McKinstry for the mechanical apparatus containing a human eye found by Mickey aboard the SS Madame de Pompadour.

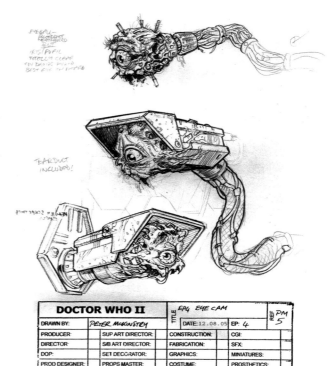

DOCTOR WHO II		TITLE	EP4 EYE CAM	REF PM 5	
DRAWN BY:	PETER MCKINSTRY		DATE: 12.08.05 EP: 4		
PRODUCER:	SUP ART DIRECTOR:	CONSTRUCTION:		CGI:	
DIRECTOR:	S/B ART DIRECTOR:	FABRICATION:		SFX:	
DOP:	SET DECORATOR:	GRAPHICS:		MINIATURES:	
PROD DESIGNER:	PROPS MASTER:	COSTUME:		PROSTHETICS:	
© BBC CYMRU WALES 2005		OTHER:			

they work with a producer, the more they learn what does and doesn't work for them. 'A lesson we learned on Series One was that we hardly ever have a red herring, in an Agatha Christie way – we never take the viewer up a story cul-de-sac in order to make them think something's happening when in fact it's something else. But there's a big difference there between your red-herring-story-cul-de-sac and actually having a story which takes you in unexpected directions. And I know that's because Russell feels that very deliberate red herrings somehow make you distrust the show and the storyteller – they feel as if they're putting a joke over on the viewers rather than taking them on an exciting story journey. So I think one of the tricks with a *Doctor Who* script is to constantly allow it to go in exciting and surprising and unexpected directions, but not by simply stopping the story for twenty minutes while you do a bit of a tap-dance routine and try to dazzle the viewer into thinking something else is going on. It's useful to spot

Above: Rose and the Tenth Doctor shortly after his regeneration. Above right: Queen Victoria (Pauline Collins) is menaced by… well, a big green screen, although The Mill will replace that with the werewolf eventually!

that in advance and to steer writers away from it. I think it was less of an issue for the Series Two writers, because they'd seen that first series and absorbed the new DNA of the show.'

One of the biggest problems that can crop up is if the well-planned running order for a series suddenly has to change. All those carefully laid plans where a nice quiet, character-led story follows a couple of epic bangs 'n' flashes episodes to allow the series to breathe, and the viewers to relax, can go right out of the window if a script is delayed or an actor is unavailable. Viewers will tend to remember what Helen calls the 'boys-with-toys' stories, though it's not always the case. Children especially will remember an event, a spooky threat or a dark psychological thrill rather than the overall episode it is from. 'I think the thing to accept is they are very different episodes but the imperative is still exactly the same, which is to tell a gripping story. When we say that one episode is more "character driven" or more "psychological", there probably still needs to be a monster; there still needs to be something of a chase, there needs to be fear, and anticipation. A quieter episode still needs a story that stands up in its own right, a story which looks at the nature of good and evil and looks at the moral dilemmas inherent in dealing with another species. So we never say, "This is the one where Jimmy goes to meet his mum and they have a nice chat about holidays they had as a kid." That's not a *Doctor Who* story. We do schedule as carefully as possible, while knowing there has to be flexibility built in, because something could go wrong or change. The episode order for Series Two got shaken up a few times, for example, because BBC One asked us for a Christmas special.'

That particular change resulted in all the production team's preliminary ideas about how the second series was going to play suddenly being thrown in the air – it wasn't simply a case of bumping all the others down one and adding another one at the end. *Tooth and Claw* was eventually broadcast as episode two, but for a while there was some discussion about whether it might be episode one, or even three, because the tone of *The Christmas Invasion* might have affected the tone of *New Earth* – were they sufficiently different? *The Girl in the Fireplace* was initially going to be broadcast later in the series, as was *School Reunion* which was originally going to be episode ten. 'There

are lots of different reasons why things move,' Helen explains. 'Everything from artist availability to the speed at which people write. We knew that we were going to get an absolute gem off Toby Whithouse very quickly so it made sense to put *School Reunion* in the first half of Series Two. We knew *Love & Monsters* was going to be double-banked with the *Satan Pit* two-parter and so it needed to be a Doctor- and companion-lite episode. Russell's philosophy of the series is that every story should be something transformative and something which involves and engages you, leaving you a slightly different person. In that sense, even when you have an episode in which the Doctor and Rose or Martha don't feature enormously as characters, thematically the episode is still very close to the heart of the show's concept.'

Because they have to fit the mood and tone of the series, as well as fitting into the ongoing story of Martha Jones or another character, Russell will often give scripts, even the ones that aren't his, a 'Russell T Davies polish'. 'I think everybody involved in that, Russell especially, can feel very uncomfortable,' says Helen. 'One writer rewriting another writer's work is a very odd process, I imagine. I've never done it, that's not the script editor's job, thankfully. But it's always for a reason, to make the show work not just for that forty-five minutes but as a whole thirteen-part series. I've been told off by writers for tweaking their punctuation, and I know exactly why they feel iffy about it, because it's something that they feel very protective of and so it's never particularly comfortable. We learnt from Series One exactly how much input Russell did and didn't need to bring to other writers' scripts but, to cover ourselves in Series Two, virtually every writer was approached on the proviso that they would only take the job if they were happy that there was a possibility – not a probability – that Russell would do a last-minute once-over, a polish.' There are exceptions – Matthew Graham and Steven Moffat, for example, are both very established names and the question of rewriting their work wouldn't even arise. In reality, of course, no writer on any TV series, unless they are also the producer, has complete control over how their episode ends up, because what goes on in the cutting room is entirely down to producers, directors and others.

'As a script editor, my ideal is always that the writer, aided and abetted by me, should be able to deliver a script which is immaculate and needs no changes, so everyone's happy – and frankly it's less work for Russell. The practical aim is to get the script as far as you can and for Russell to rewrite as little as possible. That then is the situation of least damage and discomfort for all concerned. I don't think I've encountered it on *Doctor Who*, but the downside of that can be that, if writers assume that somebody's always going to be there as a safety net, or as an interfering busybody, that can teach them to *not* be responsible for their own script. There's a law of diminishing returns with a telly writer: you quite often find writers who don't seem to be pushing their work or seem uninvolved in it. You'll find out that, for the last five projects they worked on, somebody took over and the script editor rewrote their script or sorted things out. All that's teaching writers is not to be adult, mature artists. There will be hundreds of script editors who disagree with that, but then they tend to be the kind of people who do feel rewarded when they get editorially stuck into a script. I think editorially fiddling away and rewriting are very, very different processes. The script editor is the person best placed to think ahead. A director can be on location, running out of time and thinking he's just going to have to lose three pages, not caring how, just that he's got to do it. The script editor will be the one sitting out in the cold realising that you can't lose those three pages because they need to happen here, but looking to see if anything can be lost from somewhere else. So I think we offer a very valuable perspective in those situations. My personal feeling is that script editors are a structural necessity of the industry – useful in all sorts of ways to smooth the path between commissioning and production, to smooth the path between producer and writer, and to keep track of copyright and legality.'

The legal question is yet another example of the different kinds of jobs the script editors must undertake on a series such as *Doctor Who*. The BBC has a department called Negative Checks. If a script is delivered and it features, for example, 'Billy Bone's Fish & Chip Shop', that department will simply check whether or not Billy Bone's Fish & Chip Shop exists. If it doesn't exist, the script writer can use it; if it does exist, things become a tad more complicated. The first thing the script editor must do is consider how the name is being used. If it's simply a character saying, 'See you in Billy Bone's tonight', it couldn't be more innocuous, nothing particularly significant happens – indeed, the final shot on television might not even show the shop front or the name. If, however, the script implies that Billy Bone's is an incredibly incompetent alien chip shop dedicated to trying to wipe people out by poisoning the chips, the script editor has to consider whether a

On this page: A selection of graphics put together by Peter McKinstry for use in Rise of the Cybermen *and* The Age of Steel.

real Billy Bone's Fish & Chip Shop might have any legitimate basis for a complaint. The grounds for a challenge are always whether there could be any confusion between the fictional use of the name and its actual existence in the real world. If so, would it be to their detriment?

Helen laughs at this. 'Now, as this is *Doctor Who*, my first line of defence would be: "Well, there was a great big green monster running through it and somebody was opening a door with a sonic screwdriver and then they all dematerialised and went off to another planet, so personally I think the grounds for confusion are fairly slim." But it's always better safe than sorry. I'm always in favour of finding another name, one that doesn't already exist, because it's easier. And then we've got it, we can do what we want with it, and if somebody subsequently wants to write a later episode set in a fish and chip shop and wants something terrible to happen there, we don't suddenly have to worry about whether or not we can use it. This goes for character names as well, especially police or murder victims. A writer will come up with a really great name, Commander Simon Winstone of MI5, say. And then somebody will find out that there is a Commander Simon Winstone, and there's a faint possibility, because you're using the police force, that people might be confused. Since there's then a risk of litigation, you find that realistic names end up becoming more and more diluted, and at some point you're looking at Commander Zebediah Bungalow, who actually doesn't exist, but then nobody's going to be called that, are they?'

Helen has to check the name of every character, unless they're known only by first names. It's only when they get very specific, a character with a real rank, title, job, in a real-world situation that there's a possibility of confusion or that families might find it distressing. That's one level of clearances for the script editor to undertake. Another occurs every time the team want to film somewhere real, such as at the London Eye, or Canary Wharf or some other big landmark. The people who own, run or license that landmark will want to know how it's being used in the episode. Does the story paint it in an unflattering light? So Helen will talk them through the story, make sure that everyone is happy and no one has been antagonised. 'There's always a huge demand for newspapers, shop fronts, company names, things like that. The Art Department will tend to come to the script editors and ask for two company names or a newspaper headline and some text. Just when I think I've finished a script, I'll get a call from someone very nice in the Art Department saying, "Hi, only twenty things, don't worry about it."

'And I just sigh, and tell them to go ahead…'

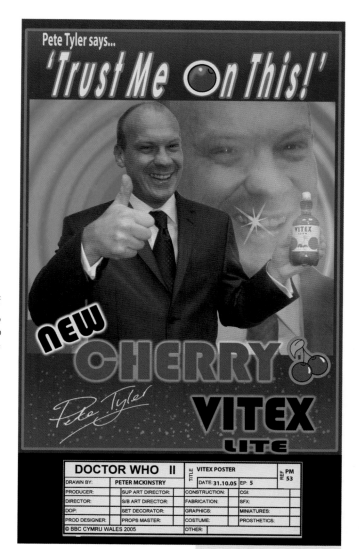

Would you buy a drink from this man? Of course you would – he's Gemini, he'll save the world!

CRAFTING THE NEW SERIES

Hooray! The programme was commissioned, the scripts written and the lead actors cast. Cardiff was gearing itself up to be the Hollywood of South Wales. Every possible square inch of land was being scouted out for possible locations, letters went back and forth from Phil Collinson's team at the BBC HQ in Llandaff to the city council. With the studio space at Q2 getting up and running, what else could possibly need doing?

Crucially, the series needed to be designed. That didn't just involve someone putting up a few fake TARDIS walls in Dyffren, it required an entire 'look' for the series, a 'tone' (yes, that word again) that would always say on-screen: 'The stories may be different, the characters may come and go but this is *Doctor Who*, be in no doubt.' Charged with masterminding this new image for modern *Doctor Who* was Edward Thomas, the production designer, who assembled around him a team of staff and freelance designers, each with their own department head, but ultimately all taking their lead from him. So to find out how all these, often disparate, segments of design all came together, let's turn our attention to the man in charge.

Edward Thomas's design background goes back to his days at technical college, studying Theatre Studies – alongside Julie Gardner – and Art. Julie and Edward were part of a college theatre group, and he went on to design for a number of stage productions before working on a BBC Wales drama, *The Importance of Being Jones*. More than thirty film and television jobs later, he joined the *Doctor Who* production team in Cardiff. He is now based at Upper Boat, the new studio space acquired for Series Three and the first series of *Torchwood*. Upper Boat seems, from the outside, to be a fairly unassuming building, a typically modern warehouse, albeit a great deal larger than most, in a huge industrial estate known as the Treforest Business Park. Only as you make the final approach into the cul-de-sac it's situated in do you realise that the blue and white frontage you can see from the main road hides two very important facts. Firstly, the building stretches back a long, long way and, secondly, behind it is another identical warehouse.

The front one is the actual studio – on the floors above are the *Torchwood* and *Doctor Who* productions offices. The main studio is split in two – one half houses the permanent *Torchwood* set known as the Hub, the other half is the new home to the TARDIS interior which, as is revealed later, has been slightly modified since its move from Newport. The secondary studio holds the other semi-permanent *Torchwood* sets and has ample room to build more, for both shows, as and when they're needed. Unlike Q2, Upper Boat appears not to be on any major flight paths, has no roar of heavy industrial traffic from outside, and has huge doors that can let in copious amounts of natural light if required.

Behind the second building are two car parks (both full of lorries and trailers – the latter for costume, make-up and little mobile homes for the lead actors to relax in when they're not on set. The building itself has had its downstairs converted into a massive building space where sets can be assembled and, if necessary, monsters stored. Above this is the Art Department, and this is where Edward Thomas and his team of artists work, beavering away, if one believes what they say, 24/7.

Below: An initial concept for the new Cyberman headpiece by Matthew Savage. Facing page: Concept artwork for a Cyberman by Peter McKinstry.

cyber industries

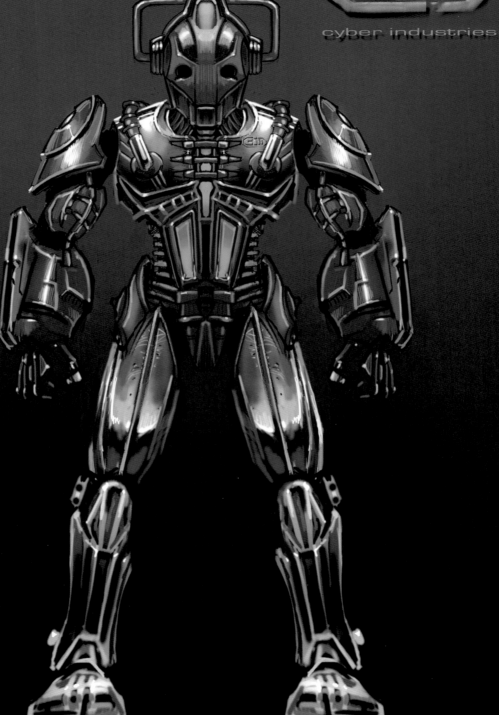

Concept artwork by Matthew Savage
(above) the Dalek renewing itself fr[...]
Dalek and (right) the Dalek saucers fr[...]
Bad Wo[...]

RECORDING BLOCKS

Doctor Who is made not just episode by episode but in what are termed recording blocks (since television programmes are rarely made in the order that we see them on-screen), with a differing set of support staff for each block, although the respective heads of departments will work across all of them. This means manpower is spread more easily and work can go ahead on a variety of different stories simultaneously because the first assistant director on Block Two is a different one to Block Three, and the unit manager for Block One might also do Block Five but won't do Two or Three. And so on…

For ease of reference, listed here are how the blocks broke down over the first two series. It's important to have this information to hand at this point in this book, because occasionally scenes involving characters and/or locations/sets from different episodes were actually shot at the same

time, so that things did not have to be pulled down then rebuilt later, or to ensure the availability of actors. Many of the people contributing to this book refer to their work in terms of what was needed for a block rather than just a specific episode. In Series One, this is especially prevalent in Block One; in Series Two, it happened a few times with Block Three. Russell T Davies explains: 'Very early on I made the decision, given how busy the whole production was turning out to be, that episodes one, four and five were all written to be shot together. It made sense in that Rose, Aliens of London and World War Three all required, to a certain extent, the same sets – the exteriors of the Powell estate where the Tylers lived, all the Central London filming and so on. I thought they'd make a very good block because Keith Boak could go to London for a week and shoot scenes for all three episodes, and then off to the Tylers' estate and shoot scenes for all three episodes. And we could only have Noel and Camille for a limited amount of time, so doing their stuff in one chunk was easier for them.' >>

'YOU GO TO BED THINKING ABOUT DALEKS'

Edward heads up this team of concept designers, art directors, graphic designers and model-makers, and oversees all the visual aspects of the scripts. He has to ensure firstly that the vision of the executive producers and the directors gets carried out in the way that a script requires it to be and secondly that there's a visual continuity throughout the series. 'We usually get each script, or an early draft at least,' Edward explains, 'somewhere between ten and eight weeks in advance of when we shoot. Now, as I oversee every episode, I'm always on board from the beginning, before the director's even there. Obviously the directors, when they arrive, still have a huge influence, but I have to start the ball rolling and get certain concepts down visually. A trust, I suppose, developed between me, the writers and the directors and the producers.

'To pick one example, we knew very early on that there was a Dalek spaceship coming up at the end of the first series, so we started designing that on day one. By the time *Bad Wolf* came around, we had been thinking hard about it and so could present it to both Russell and Joe Ahearne and say, "This is your ship, these are your corridors, this is the layout, this is the best way to use it." That was an easy one – others can be less so, because you often go through five or six drafts of scripts before you get the final shooting script.'

Over time a lot will change as a result of meetings, discussions and practicalities. Edward suggests a variety of reasons for these changes, budget being the most common one. A script may require the interiors of a family house to be built but, while a script might require five bedrooms, Edward's team can't always afford to do that. They might be able to stretch the money to provide two though, so, at the beginning of a block, the scripts may have to be fluid. Sometimes Edward's team will have designed something that isn't actually used in the end, but this is *Doctor Who*, so it's never a real waste of time, because the Art Department can just utilise those ideas elsewhere down the line.

Edward cites the work done on *Dalek* as an example of his department's efforts not to waste any ideas. 'The process of designing a Dalek and the Dalek spaceships was a long one. We knew that Daleks were going to crop up twice in that first series, so we started by designing a Dalek that was much more complicated than what was actually seen on the screen, then worked backwards to the Dalek that we finally went with. We had all done an incredible amount of work on the Daleks when Julie Gardner suddenly rang and said they weren't sure if they had the rights to use the Daleks after all.

So, we stopped and began working on ideas for something new. Then we heard that maybe there was a chance, so we started again. And then it was definitely off. We stopped again. When we finally got the go ahead and it was all systems go, we went back and picked up all the designs again. That's the great thing about the concept of *Doctor Who*: you go to bed one night thinking about Daleks and you wake up the next morning and you're thinking about Queen Victoria or the Ood. When you start researching reference material, you have to keep an open mind, because often something you think

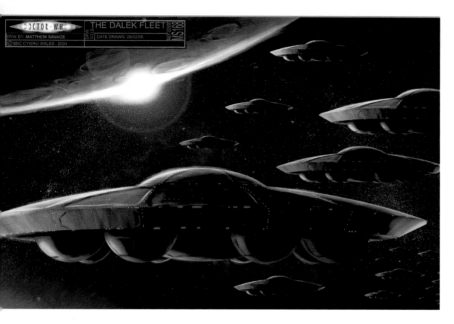

could work for one episode actually ends up being used in a completely different episode.'

As initial storylines are formulated, Edward and Russell's discussions begin, with one of the most important aspects of each episode's design being the choice of locations. 'I'm always driving past buildings in and around Cardiff and thinking, "That could be a really good exterior courtroom in New York in the Forties," or whatever. Location hunting is always a good time, the real start of a particular episode.'

In those early weeks, Edward will read the script, make notes about props, vehicles, settings – anything that jumps out of the page for him. He also makes notes about locations that he thinks might work. It is Edward's job to brief the location managers on the kind of place required for the script, whether for its look or as somewhere that the Art Department could adapt. While a dedicated location scout goes out and finds interesting locations, the location managers will deal with whoever owns or manages those locations. Edward often gives the location managers a handful of conceptual drawings so they can explain to the people with whom they are dealing exactly what will

Above: Edward Thomas prepares to flick the switch that Chip will use to execute Cassandra's Plan B in *New Earth*. Above right: the honeycomb-like pods that the Sisters of Plenitude grow their human Patient Zeros in.

be needed, and why. Or he might explain to the location scout, via the drawings, what he wants the interior of a space station to look like. The Art Department often builds only a partial set – The Mill adding the rest via CGI – so the scout might have to find something that provides Edward's team with a nice shiny floor, plus the first three metres of some walls. In the case of an episode that requires some vast interiors that simply couldn't be built – usually thanks to budget constraints – a lot can hinge on finding the right location.

'COLOUR SHAPES EVERYTHING AROUND US'

'I wait until they find the location,' Edward says, 'because often that will then provide me with the architecture for all the small auxiliary sets. For *The End of the World*, we waited until we'd found a place called the Temple of Peace, a marble building, in Cardiff. The existing interior designs and colours gave us the paint finishes and the architectural style for the rest of the episode. That even influenced the colour we painted the exterior of the space station – everything came from that one location.'

Colour is a theme that crops up in all of Edward's conversation. Along with 'tone', 'hooray' and 'marvellous', it seems to be one of the catchwords of the entire production team, all of which will, most probably, be etched onto everyone's tombstones one day.

'I talk about the use of colour a lot, because it shapes everything around us. Whatever we learn through life experience, whether watching TV, reading books, or just living day to day, I find that is represented by a certain colour for me. A particular moment in my life may come to mind, and it immediately evokes a colour palette in my memory. Historical periods are the same. So, when I'm reading a script for the first time, I immediately think of a colour palette that we could use in that particular episode. What I do then is sit down with the decorators, the concept artists, and the costume and make-up designers and present them with that colour palette and explain the colour boundaries I want them to stay within – the greens that I want to use, the blues, the tones and shades of each. That way, when we get to the final imagery, the decorators haven't gone off using one colour green, while the Costume Department has used another. When The Mill come to the grade, which is where they darken or lighten the images on-screen and tweak the colours, we ask them to enhance those greens, ensuring that they all go the same way, as opposed to one going a bit yellow, one going lime, one going olive. It's important to me that we get all of that established straight away. I think it comes from my background of working on film as opposed to video.'

Doctor Who is recorded on video, which has several important effects on the look of the show, as Edward explains. 'When you break it down, a piece of film is literally layers of colour, and some colours work very well on it, some don't work. You have to learn the tricks of the trade, in reference to the differences in colour. The colour themes are most noticeable when you watch, for example, *Tooth and Claw*. As a Victorian-set episode, it was all the dark colours, strong reds and blacks, and then all of a sudden, at the end of that episode, there's the trailer for *School Reunion* and you see greens and blues and pastels and everything's much lighter and airier because it was a modern-day episode. Knowing the transmission sequence of the episodes, I would sit down and work out what would look good in the throw forward for the next episode, what would really show that the TARDIS had shot through time. Where it wasn't quite so obvious a choice was when the next episode was a futuristic one. The past, the present, we had things to draw upon but the future is an open book. And that means we can have some fun! Very early on, we decided we wanted the Dalek to be to be bronze and copper because they're very strong, very regal colours, and they age very nicely, so we could get some depth into them: we could oil them up and put verdigris on them to age them, so they would look a bit more solid. Once we'd decided that, we then had to decide which contrasting colours showed the Daleks off in the best light, made them feel evil, made them stand out against everything else. An obvious colour is black, and straight away we thought of black spaceships; that all Dalek environments should be black − interior spaceship: black; exterior spaceship: bronze and coppers. We also knew that one day the Daleks were

Below left: David Tennant on the set of Tooth and Claw. *Below: The Mill's beautifully rendered CG werewolf.*

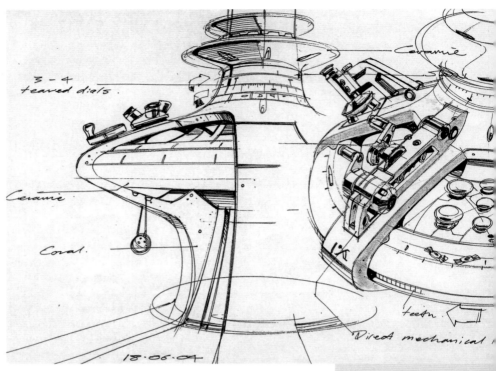

Handwritten annotations on sketch:
3 - 4
teared dials.

Ceramie

Coral.

18·06·04

Ceramie

teeth

Direct mechanical

going to come up against the Cybermen, and the Cybermen were
going to be silver, so we were going to have silver enemy versus
bronze enemy. Which looks brilliant on-screen.'

'YOU'VE GOT TO HAVE A SHELL': THE TEAM WORKING TOGETHER

Assembling a good team of designers, people who can think along the same lines as
Edward, who understood his colour themes and ideas, took some time. Not only did they
need to be brilliant in their own right, but they had to be brought together to work as part
of a team, and learn to draw upon each other's strengths and weaknesses. Not always
easy when, for a lot of people, art and design is often a fairly solitary role, but it seemed
that there was no end to the people eagerly lining up to work on the show.

'Doctor Who has such a pull that we were able to get the very best people for the job:
The Mill and Millennium FX for starters. We couldn't ask them to just up sticks and move
to Cardiff, because of their hardware and everything else. Despite the distances involved,
what I found incredible working with those guys was that everybody was so open, no
egos, everyone was willing to pull together, and feed off each other's ideas. No one
ever dismissed another person's suggestion or input – and that's very rare in television.
I remember discussing The Christmas Invasion in the tone meeting, and we knew that
the Sycorax ship was going to be a CG effect, so that was ultimately down to Will Cohen
and Dave Houghton at The Mill to create. However, we all had differing ideas as to what
it should look like. We needed to nail it down at the tone meeting because I had to get
the interiors designed or, in this case, adapted because it was a location. And Costume

and Make-Up needed to know what the look was, what the colours were. We needed a starting point, and I used the phrase "You've got to have a shell", meaning the basic idea. Then I pulled an actual shell out of my pocket and said, "There's your Sycorax spaceship." It was a shell I'd found whilst on holiday and I meant it sort of as a joke, but it *was* the right shape. No one had intended it to be a stone spaceship, but The Mill then took the shell idea and ran with it. The shape and texture made them think about the architecture, about the location, about how it was all going to come together. Then from those discussions, I went back to my team and we all started to conceptualise things.'

'YOU DON'T BUILD A TARDIS, YOU GROW ONE'

The Art Department that Edward assembled comprised fifty full-time staff, including three conceptual artists, two set designers and a team of set decorators. An important early responsibility for the department was redesigning one of the visual icons of *Doctor Who*.

Each person who had a go at it came up with something different and, although everyone was adamant that they would retain the police box look, some adaptation was going to be necessary.

'The final design came from Colin Richmond, who is now designing sets for the Royal Shakespeare Company – he has a fantastic, theatrical vision. The real working Metropolitan police boxes came in various shapes and sizes, ranging from timber ones to concrete ones. Colin changed the shape from the TARDIS last seen on TV; we made it much bigger and beefier; gave it what we called a British Bulldog look. I really wanted people to think, "Yeah, that could actually be safe in outer space", when they saw it. Some of the TARDISes in the past have been very tall and thin, which I felt looked a bit brittle. We went to great pains to make sure that it looked wooden, taking blow-torches to all the timber, to burn away all the soft grain, leaving a hard grain. Then we coated the whole police box with Idenden, which is a sealant that left a tough-looking sheen on it.'

Having developed a new take on the familiar old police box exterior, attention turned to a more radical evolution of the inside of the TARDIS. 'That grew from a conversation between myself and Bryan Hitch, a comic-book artist who helped us out at the start of the first series. He and I sat down, had a long lunch and a couple of bottles of wine and went through all his books and all my books, and we just looked at everything: architecture, plants, space, nature, everything that we could. We stockpiled a huge store of ideas, not all relevant to the TARDIS, but all interesting.'

DOCTOR WHO | DRW TITLE: Visual 2 tardis interior | DW
DRW BY: Dan Walker | DATE DRAWN: 15/06/04

Best known for his work on comic book series such as *The Authority*, Bryan is a superb illustrator who has in the past actually drawn *Doctor Who* comic strips for the UK division of Marvel Comics. It was from some of his sketches that Edward was able to form a new version of the TARDIS walls. It had an organic look although, at that stage, none of these ideas was transmitted to the console and flooring – all that came later. Edward took Bryan's ideas back to his team to further the concepts. Edward chose his concept artists very carefully, utilising their individual skills. During Series One, the main artist was Matthew Savage, who knows his *Doctor Who*, and sci-fi in general. Matthew was joined on Series Two by Peter McKinstry, who had previously been a concept

More art department designs for the TARDIS by (above) Dan Walker and (below) Matthew Savage.

designer for a video games company – and, as a sideline, was also inside a Cyberman costume for both two-part Cyberman adventures. The main person working on all aspects of the TARDIS interior was Dan Walker, who was mainly an automotive concept designer and had recently helped design the Batmobile for the *Batman Begins* movie. He was a very focused concept artist, Edward says, who understood functionality, which was an essential requirement for the TARDIS. 'Dan took the TARDIS interior to the next stage,' Edward says. 'He also added new elements to it, which meant that the console itself flowed into the curved walls, floor and ceiling. Then Matthew Savage started work on the roundels which, like the hat stand, were part of the show's history and something I was keen to keep.

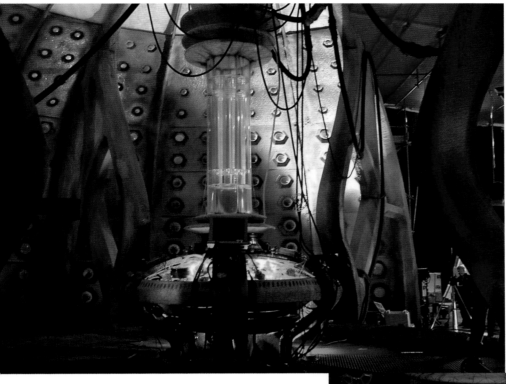

'The brief I gave the guys was that you don't build a TARDIS, you grow one — a phrase that actually turned up in a script, but I'm not sure whether I got the line from Russell or vice versa. I wanted to be able to say to the public that the TARDIS had changed so much because it travelled through time — it was nine hundred years old; it had developed; it's organic. That will also give whoever comes after me the chance to change it again, and take it further. I wanted everything that said "the Doctor" to reflect where he came from: his sonic screwdriver, his TARDIS, Gallifreyan architecture, all those things, everything had to have the same look, feel and origin. I kept coming back to coral, glass and timber — all natural products — and we started layering in those textures. I didn't want flashing lights on the console; this thing is nine hundred years old, the Doctor can't just nip into Halfords and buy a new bulb. The various switches and controls are made from all sorts of things. We imagined the Doctor as a great collector. He finds, say, a chess piece and thinks it would make a great switch because, over the years, the originals have probably been lost and so he finds odd things that fit and in they go.'

Construction begins on the components for the TARDIS interior.

It was important to Edward's design team that the TARDIS didn't seem in any way 'sci-fi' because they felt that would detract from the organic feel the ship now had. 'Sci-fi' implied metal and cold, and Edward wanted the TARDIS to reflect the Doctor's nomadic existence. It represented his only home, not just because he travelled in it but because it was all that remained of his home world. So, to add to that lived-in feel, he wanted the interior to be an amalgamation of different sciences, from across the universe, not just Gallifrey or Earth.

'I imagined Gallifrey to have been a beautiful place with lots of water – not exactly Atlantis, but a place of tranquil beauty and lots of flowing water and lush forests, so we made sure that there was a nautical element to the ship; indeed, the whole thing feels a little bit like a submarine. Taking a spark plug for inspiration, we also gave the console a lovely great big ceramic surround because the Doctor's always leaning against it and, if there's electricity coming out of it, he doesn't want to get an electric shock. I also wanted to be able to control the light that occupied the TARDIS interior, because one of the biggest things about production design is how you harness the light, and so a glass ceiling seemed to make sense. I wanted to be able to show whether it was day or night inside the TARDIS. If there was a police car outside, I wanted to make sure that we had flashing lights flickering through into the TARDIS, so it had to have a semi-translucency to it that you didn't see from the outside; but on the inside you knew that you were just a membrane away from reality.'

Of course, having built this massive standing set, and used it in almost every episode of the show so far, a problem arose when it came to shifting the TARDIS set from its old Q2 home to the new studio at Upper Boat. For Edward, this meant making the immoveable moveable.

'If you build anything, there is a certain way that it goes together, and, if it goes together then logically it can come apart. But when we built the TARDIS interior, we built it to stay put. It was assembled as an exoskeleton of steelwork, which was constructed for us by a company called Cardiff Theatrical Services, who build all the sets for the Royal Opera House. The vacuum-form elements – the roundels, and all the glass parts – were fixed in position, and we joined it all together with a spray foam. Now, that's the sort of stuff that you don't get a second chance with – once it attaches itself to something it really sticks. CTS came back in to move it and they've done an incredible job. They treated it so delicately, to them it wasn't just about moving a piece of scenery; it was about moving *the TARDIS*. It moves through time easily enough but moving it twenty-five miles up the road – that's a nightmare. But it was done, with minimal fuss and minimal damage, so we could relax.'

Edward also took the opportunity to make some changes, taking advantage of the larger space available at Upper Boat and reviving some of his original intentions for the TARDIS console room. For Series Three, the console level will be higher off the floor, made possible by the higher roof at Upper Boat. This is so that cameras can get underneath the flooring to shoot upwards, giving more angles for the directors to work from. It's something Edward had wanted to do since the beginning, but the lack of available height at Q2 had made it impossible – and although at Upper Boat it isn't as far off the ground as he'd ideally like, Edward is still very pleased with the space the new studio does supply.

'We've also been able to make the front floor section removable, so that we can actually go in and follow the Doctor down underneath the console a bit more. When I conceived this TARDIS, I saw it as basically an elliptical shape and we're in the top half of the ellipsis, the reverse of that is basically underneath; it's probably some sort of big engine room, that looks like a heart, because it would never be as mundane as an engine. It would have to be something that really was pumping, the best oil valve in the universe. Russell's always known that and I'm sure one day he will write a script where he takes us down into that.'

So far, viewers have seen only the console room and, in *The Christmas Invasion*, the TARDIS wardrobe. The classic series established quite early on that there were more 'rooms' beyond the main console room – bedrooms, laboratories, art galleries and even an Olympic-sized swimming pool (which leaked). Edward sees his version of the console room as 'just one cell within the TARDIS, almost like a honeycomb. Then you have a million other cells – a wardrobe, a gym, a swimming pool, a mortuary – all held in time and a relative dimension. So when the Doctor calls for one, it's like he's opened a suitcase and there it is. The rooms come to him rather than vice versa.'

More shots of the TARDIS console under construction.

'HIGH HEELS ON A WIRE MESH FLOOR': COORDINATING WITH COSTUME AND MAKE-UP

Edward has mentioned the way he works with The Mill, but what about costume? Where exactly is a line drawn between what Edward's team will design and what the Costume Department – headed by Lucinda Wright on Series One and by Louise Page on Series Two and Three – will design. Also, what would happen if the needs of set design and costume design came into conflict?

'It's one of those things that comes out of the tone meetings. A good example of that would be a scene featuring a woman in high heels on a wire-mesh floor. Now, that could happen but it never has, because at the tone meetings we have the concept drawings, we have the technical drawings, we have the models; we all sit down and iron out most of those problems straight away. Where exactly our work divides is a rather blurred line that is established at the meetings. Logos on shirts, those sorts of things, all come to us, but the shirt will come from Costume, so we meet in the middle. If somebody's got a gun, does it need a holster? As we do the guns, we'd do the holsters. We usually do name badges, sometimes we even do bags, if a character is carrying a rucksack, or a handbag. If there's a story-relevant piece of jewellery, Costume will get it, but we might need to adapt it to place, say, an insignia on it that might be relevant to an episode. I was very worried when Louise came to me and said that David had asked

Reinette (Sophia Myles) in The Girl in the Fireplace, in an example of the lavish costumes seen on Doctor Who.

if he could wear light-coloured trainers because, having done Series One, I had seen what Christopher's big pair of black boots went through. I was concerned that, when we take him to a quarry in the middle of the night and it's raining and he's there for twelve hours, plimsolls might not hold up for one episode, let alone a whole series. As production designer, I have to think about the practicalities as well as about the visual side of things. That said, I knew Louise wouldn't have mentioned it if she hadn't been confident that it would be all right.

'Louise is a very practical person. When we were preparing for *The Girl in the Fireplace*, we discussed nylon. Now, obviously, a costume designer isn't going to make Regency costumes from nylon, but she might have used it in part of the minute detailing; and some actors were going to be very close to that fire. We had to be very careful that, when Sophia Myles was kneeling down next to the fire, there was no nylon in her costume, because obviously that's very flammable. Louise and I – and before that Lucinda and I – always talked over our choice of colours and textiles to match curtains and dress fabrics. We wanted them to match tonally so that people weren't jarring – the choice of blues, the choice of reds: this is our period red, this is the fabrics they'd use, that sort of two-way discussion. Louise gave us samples of fabrics for the French episode so that we could then go off and match the wallpapers, the curtains, the paint finishes, and so on.'

This kind of close cooperation followed through into make-up, both straight and prosthetic. Edward would present Neill Gorton of Millennium FX and the Make-Up Department with the design elements of, say, a spaceship – colours, structure, environments. They would then work out who was doing what within the confines he had given them, and would pick the colours and the textures. 'With the Sycorax,' Edward recalls, 'Millennium FX brought most of the suggestions to the table and, as their sculpt

Left: Prosthetic make-up being applied to Sean Gilder as the Sycorax Leader. Above: An early sculpt of a potential Sycorax head.

progressed, I started to approve things, also taking part of the exoskeletal bone concept they had come up with and adding it to our interior. Louise would similarly work it into her fabric colours and stuff. We saw Louise's fabric colours for the Sycorax coats and we then made huge banners in similar fabrics, so it all tied in.'

SCARY MONSTERS

The series' many monsters are the results of the same collaboration. In the case of the Cybermen, for example, Edward asked for input from as many different people as possible, so everybody across all the different design departments had a go and came back with vastly different images. The closest to what Edward wanted was by Alex Fort, the digital matte painter from The Mill, who does all the big backgrounds of alien planets, star systems and so forth. Without even seeing the scripts, Alex had done a series of beautiful art deco-looking Cybermen and, since Edward knew the direction Tom MacRae's storyline was going in from conversations with Russell, he could see some promise in Alex's work.

Following pages: Three concept paintings for The Satan Pit. Peter McKinstry's underground Valley of the Kings-style passageway; Peter's take on the Beast lunging out for the Doctor; Ian Bunting's painting of Sanctuary Base.

Rocket design
unresolved.

DOCTOR WHO II		TITLE	BEAST CAVERN		REF	PM 102
DRAWN BY:	PETER MCKINSTRY		DATE: 1.02.06	EP: 9		
PRODUCER:	SUP ART DIRECTOR:	CONSTRUCTION:		CGI:		
DIRECTOR:	S/B ART DIRECTOR:	FABRICATION:		SFX:		
DOP:	SET DECORATOR:	GRAPHICS:		MINIATURES:		
PROD DESIGNER:	PROPS MASTER:	COSTUME:		PROSTHETICS:		
© BBC CYMRU WALES 2005		OTHER:				

DOCTOR WHO II		TITLE	BASE EXTERIOR		REF	IB 012
DRAWN BY:	IAN BUNTING		DATE: 13/02/06	EP: 08/09		
PRODUCER:	SUP ART DIRECTOR:	CONSTRUCTION:		CGI:		
DIRECTOR:	S/B ART DIRECTOR:	FABRICATION:		SFX:		
DOP:	SET DECORATOR:	GRAPHICS:		MINIATURES:		
PROD DESIGNER:	PROPS MASTER:	COSTUME:		PROSTHETICS:		
© BBC CYMRU WALES 2005		OTHER:				

LOCKED
13/02/06

A selection of views of sculpted Cyberdesigns by Millennium FX.

'Some of the other guys were way off – just too scary; they were more like *Hellraiser* and that sort of stuff,' Edward laughs. 'After seeing Alex's ideas, though, I was able to tell everybody to concentrate on art deco. More designs turned up and we finally had it – and my Art Department could then step back, and wait for Neill Gorton's guys at Millennium FX to start showing us sculpts in clay. This meant we could see what a Cyberman looked like in three dimensions, with twelve-inch maquettes to begin with, although I think they made a full-size helmet straight away because that was obviously quite an important aspect. As Millennium FX sent us pictures of these through, we picked up on their ideas and decided we could follow various lines through from the sculpted head into the body armour. And so I then sent Neill revised drawings of the body but he pointed out that there were some things we had designed which an actor wouldn't be able to walk in, which my concept guys hadn't thought of. Neill broke the whole body armour down into separate elements, retaining as much of the original concept as he could, but ensuring it was practical. Millennium FX did an incredible job on the Cybermen, and everyone was happy.'

An early pass at a Sycorax helmet by Millennium FX.

If the Cybermen represent a collaboration between Edward's concept teams and Millennium's sculpting teams, how about something different? Take the werewolf from *Tooth and Claw*, which The Mill created entirely in computer graphics, who contributed what to that design?

'We did a few early concepts,' Edward says. 'Some had too much hair, some not enough hair – those got thrown back and forth at us because although there are certain computer programmes that deal very well with hair, there are some that don't. Obviously everyone wanted this to look as realistic as possible, but having decided it would be created by The Mill, it had to be designed within their parameters. On the other hand, devising the Krillitanes for *School Reunion* was a much more collaborative job. We all got round the table and drew some sketches, made some changes, adding and removing things. Then The Mill made them as CGI. It was a similar process to creating the Reapers for *Father's Day*.'

Doctor Who has always been about collaboration between so many departments, and nowhere is that more obvious than among the various design teams. 'We mesh together really well and, regardless of who actually did what, very, very rarely are the producers disappointed by what we give them to put on-screen.'

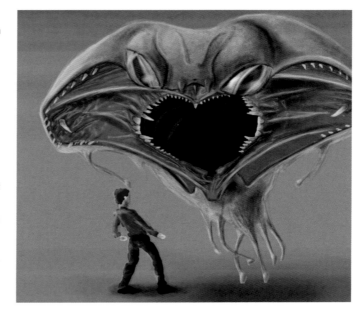

Matthew Savage's painting of a very early Reaper concept.

MODELS AND MINIATURES

Another important aspect of the design work, and one thing not handled by any permutation of Millennium FX, The Mill or Edward's Cardiff-based teams, is model work. Twenty years ago, amidst big-budget movies and American science fiction shows, *Doctor Who* often came in for a fair amount of unfair comparison and criticism for its model work. Models are used when it would be impractical to build a set or a prop because of its size or shape, or maybe because it needs to be blown to pieces at the end of a story – places like the Temple of Peace in Cardiff were unlikely to be overly positive if Edward's team had detonated the place at the end of the filming day.

In recent years, model work in science fiction or fantasy shows has lessened as computer-generated imagery has become *de rigueur*. Indeed, compared to when he worked on the series in the 1980s, today's *Doctor Who* rarely impacts upon designer Mike Tucker's schedule. A BAFTA award-winner for his recent work on projects such as the BBC's recreation of the eruption of Krakatoa (yes, it was all a model), and also a big *Doctor Who* aficionado, Mike is delighted to be one of a very select group of people (make-up designer Sheelagh Wells, director Graeme Harper, and a small number of actors, such as Gabriel Woolf from *The Satan Pit* or William Thomas from *Boom Town*) to have worked on both the original and the new series. Back in the 1980s, Mike was part of the Visual Effects Department at the BBC, responsible not just for blowing up models, but also for any other pyrotechnics (Auton wrist guns firing or Cyber heads exploding would have been under their remit back then) or CGI work or monster building.

When it was first announced that *Doctor Who* was returning, Mike immediately put in a bid to supply model work – it was a foregone conclusion that CGI, pyrotechnics and prosthetics would these days go to separate companies.

Mike first met up with Russell and Julie and Phil in December 2003, and they had a very long chat about the state of the effects industry, what had changed since *Doctor Who* had last been on air and what was available to them as a production team. The old BBC Visual Effects Department had closed during 2003, but it had reformed as a kind of post-production workshop, doing 3D and digital effects and Mike was running a model unit alongside them. However, the wheels were in motion to start closing even that down because the BBC wanted to outsource more and more work.

'Nevertheless,' Mike smiles, 'there was no way on Earth I was going to let *Doctor Who* slip through my fingers without at least giving it a try. So, at that point, I was pitching for it to be done within the BBC framework. The guys from BBC Digital Effects and I went in for a more formal meeting, putting budgets and proposals forward, as did a number of other companies, including, of course, The Mill. The BBC was pitching for the entire package, both CG and model work. We weren't successful; The Mill were. Not being one to give up, I trotted down to see the now-successful competition with my portfolio – although they were well known for their CG work, they didn't have a miniatures department. So I asked if they were going to need miniatures and they were pretty certain they were. They were directly responsible for saying to Phil that they wanted me at the first tone meeting – they believed it would be useful to have someone there with a sort of miniatures hat on. So, having failed through a BBC pitch, I circuitously came aboard via The Mill. At that first tone meeting, a few things were raised which The Mill

Above: Mike Tucker's team proudly disp[lay]
their scale model of the Dalek Empe[ror]
Right: Millennium FX prepare the fac[e of]
Sister Jatt for New Ea[rth]

thought would be best done in miniature and from that point I was sort of on board, not as a freelancer though, but still as a member of the BBC. It was a bit naughty, I suppose, because I had secured the model work by working with the people who had beaten my own department to get the CG contract! While this was going on, and seeing clearly that the writing was on the wall for the BBC Post-Production Department, I made a decision that, when the inevitable happened and I was made redundant by the BBC, I'd be ready to set up my own company, which I did. I left the BBC in September 2005 and immediately formed the Model Unit, and carried on doing *Doctor Who* smoothly.'

Mike's new company also has a degree of historical connection with the old series – the Model Unit's home is at the old Ealing Film Studios in West London. The very first scene ever shot for the very first episode of *Doctor Who* was filmed there on 19 September 1963, and the studios continued to be used for *Doctor Who* right up until *The Five Doctors*, twenty years later. These links to the past are not lost on Mike, who smiles as he finds himself directly involved with another piece of epoch-making history. 'The last job ever done by the BBC in-house effects people was blowing up the school in *School Reunion*, the first thing done by the Model Unit was the telescope for *Tooth and Claw*, despite them being broadcast the other way around. That was a bit of history ending, doing *School Reunion*. The BBC Effects team had handled *Doctor Who* on and off since 1963, and a story that featured two major elements from the old series, Sarah and K-9, brought it all to a conclusion.'

'RUSSELL LIKES TO PUSH US PAST OUR BOUNDARIES': MILLENNIUM FX

The next cog in the machine expanding on Edward Thomas's design concepts is Millennium FX, who make all the prosthetic costumes for the series, such as Cybermen, Slitheen and the Sisters of Plenitude. Millennium FX was set up by Neill Gorton in the mid 1990s after he had made the majority of the masks for the Gerry Anderson fantasy show *Space Precinct*, which mixed humans and life-sized aliens. The company moved into movies, doing all the relevant work on blockbusters such as *Saving Private Ryan*, *Gladiator* and *From Hell*. Millennium FX has now cornered the lucrative market in TV – *Doctor Who* is just one of countless shows they work on. A quick glance around their workshop in Buckinghamshire reveals everything from pregnant women for the medical drama *Bodies* through to the ageing make-up that transforms Catherine Tate into Nan Taylor each week in her eponymous comedy show. Apart from creating the many masks, bodies and other pieces of fleshy scariness, Neill and his business partner Rob Mayor also oversee anything animatronic, from Clockwork Android heads to murderous Christmas Trees.

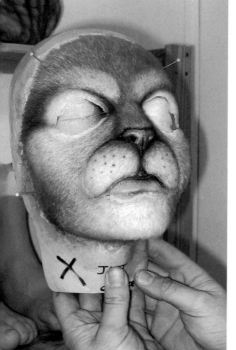

'I was aware of *Doctor Who* coming back,' begins Neill, 'and wondered if we might hear from them, because there's not many places they could go to in the UK for a job like this. I got a call from Phil Collinson asking me to come down and have a chat. I hadn't met either him or Russell T Davies before, but I knew Davy Jones, who was doing make-up. I had assumed he was going to do everything, but in fact Davy had kindly recommended me. So Phil, Russell and I chatted, they asked me to come aboard, and that was it.'

Thus Millennium FX were formally in charge of prosthetics – which means if it's a creature and will have an actor, dancer or performer of any kind wearing it, Millennium FX will design it, because they will also have to build it. 'It's great if a guy sat in the Art Department in Cardiff, who doesn't do anything but drawing, can design what he wants,' Neill explains, 'but if we can't fit it round a human being, if we can't make it function, it's a waste of time doing that drawing.' As Edward Thomas mentioned, Neill had important input into the ultimate design of the Cybermen. 'You can draw a Cyberman any way you like and it might look great on paper or even as a three-dimensional sculpt,' Neill points out, 'but if it doesn't bend when an actor is wearing it because there's something in the way, it's useless.'

Neill, like many members of the production team, describes the first production block in 2004 as 'a learning curve for all of us. At the first tone meeting in Cardiff, we were all preparing for the fact that in four weeks we would be filming with Autons and Slitheen – and that was our first problem, right there. We had more experience than anyone else at that meeting of how to make big lumbering creatures — we also knew that when a script required a Slitheen to run down a corridor, a man in a rubber suit, who can't see anything in front of him and has a ten-kilo animatronic head on, isn't going to do it very well. So we suggested The Mill did it as CGI. Unfortunately, the director, Keith Boak, still wanted it to be a man in a suit, but we could foresee that asking three Slitheen to run down a corridor just wasn't going to work. In the end, we convinced Keith to split the difference: sometimes the Slitheen were men in suits, but the running stuff was CGI. As a result I actually designed the Slitheen because I knew how to get a man inside it.'

'That was where I think we made some headway, with people who were unfamiliar with us realising that we really did know what we were talking about,' explains Rob Mayor. 'As time's gone on, every story has given us the chance to do bigger, better, scarier monsters. It's all about problem solving within the parameters that you're given and, after two series, I think we can pretty much accomplish anything they ask for. Russell is a fantastic writer and when we go to the tone meetings we can see that he writes knowing how much money he's got to spend on each episode — not that it dictates what he writes or doesn't

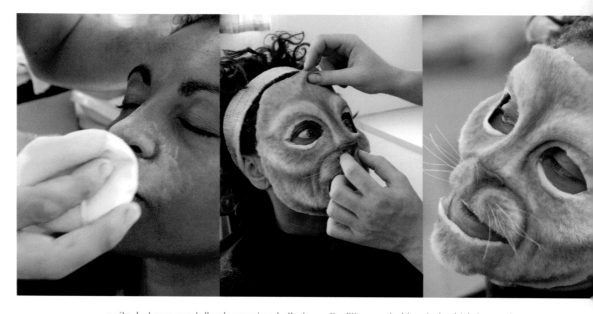

Actress Adjoa Andoh has the appliance attached to her face that will transform her into Sister Jatt.

write, but you can tell subconsciously that practicalities are in his mind, which is rare in a writer. Anyone could sit down and write a blow-away script if cash wasn't a problem, but he knows how to write around things. I think he's got a handle on the effects now and how they can be done. So, between The Mill and us, we can give him pretty much anything really. And he's very adaptable — if in the meetings we suggest something might not be one hundred per cent perfect, he'll happily lose it rather than compromise. He likes to push us past our boundaries though, and that's great. That's what we live for!'

'MYSTERIOUS BLACK MAGIC PEOPLE': THE MILL

If that's the physical creatures and designs taken care of, what about the ones that aren't present during actual filming, the oft-discussed CGI — computer-generated images.

Everything from armies of Cybermen to flying Krillitanes, from scrabbling Reapers to exterminated soldiers are all courtesy of The Mill's artistic endeavours. So too are the backgrounds that are added into sequences where actors have been filmed in front of what is called 'green screen' – a process by which The Mill's computers can be programmed to ignore the colour green and a whole new background can be dropped in. This is how Christopher Eccleston faces whizzing fan blades in *The End of the World*, or David Tennant comes up against the Beast in *The Satan Pit*. Ships in space, black holes, flames, alien landscapes, metallic spiders, night skies and exploding department stores, even Alexandra Palace at Muswell Hill – all have been brought to the screen via the work of The Mill.

Established in the early 1990s, visual effects company The Mill has provided award-winning effects for a huge number of films, television programmes, commercials and music videos. These include work with Kylie Minogue and Busted, and on the BBC's 2004 D-Day coverage, as well as blockbuster movies like *K-19: The Widow Maker*. The Mill's *Doctor Who* team is led by Will Cohen and Dave Houghton, based in their Central London building which, once you are inside, resembles the swish modernity of Yvonne Hartman's Torchwood Institute in *Army of Ghosts*. People mill around (pun intended) on many levels, in and out of glass-fronted mezzanine offices aided by a series of runners and assistants wearing green 'The Mill' T-shirts. On the ground level are a series of suites where huge, almost cinema-sized screens can display to Phil, Russell or Julie the latest episodes of *Doctor Who* in various stages of completion. And almost casually nestled away in a recessed cabinet is the Oscar™ they won for *Gladiator* – an irony as the company has in fact opted not to continue supplying effects for the movie industry, choosing to be the industry leader in British television.

Dave Houghton and The Mill first worked with producer Phil Collinson on BBC One's fantasy drama *Sea of Souls*. When Phil Collinson moved on to *Doctor Who*, explains Dave Houghton, 'I realised I actually had a chance of working on my favourite television show. I badgered him to let us bid for it – I wrote a pitch and put together a small tape of 3D animations we based loosely on the scripts for *Rose* and *The End of the World*. We

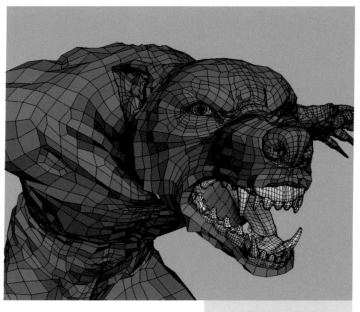

did little animations of characters and the sun exploding – just test pieces for Phil and Russell to look at. I also knew that the Autons were in the first episode but there was no clear idea of what the Nestene Consciousness looked like at the end. I got one of the guys here to build on his computer the Nestene from the cover of an old *Doctor Who* novelisation called *Terror of the Autons*, and then I animated it into a very dark scene in *Sea of Souls*. I showed that to Phil and Russell and we got the job. They phoned us up and told us how much money they didn't have and asked if we could do it for that, and we said yes.'

The Mill are given a budget by Phil Collinson that is then spread across an entire series. Because The Mill provide material for every episode, and because the scripts are still being written when they start work on the series, they have to allocate a certain amount of schedule time through guesswork.

Facing page: The Cybus Industries Zeppelin flies through the London skyline, courtesy of The Mill's CGI wizards. Above: Before skin texture and fur is added, this wireframe version of Tooth and Claw's *werewolf is prepared, to show the movement the CG creature will be capable of.*

This is loosely based on Will and Dave going through a series synopsis (usually just a paragraph on what each episode is about) and theorising how much work they believe there's going to be – there might be some Daleks in one, or another is going to be a big one for creatures and explosions, or the landscapes in another will need additional backgrounds – matte paintings – added. Then, when they get the script for an episode, Dave reads through it and prepares a breakdown of what effects he reckons The Mill will end up doing.

At this point, they can get down to the specifics of what will be required of them for that forty-five-minute show. And anything can go their way: if a script has a throwaway comment about a sun (or a moon) rising on a beautiful landscape, they know immediately that they will need to create that, even if it's a case of adapting something that gets shot during the filming. This is because, even when the director shoots something like that, it is rarely going to be exactly what the script required. By way of example, Dave cites a shot in the movie *The English Patient*. 'There's a lovely shot of a bay with ships, and the moon's out – it looks perfect. And no one ever watches that film thinking what a beautiful visual effects shot it is, but in fact a lot of people have spent a lot of time making it look real and beautiful just so you *don't* notice. You think, how lucky they were to have got such great weather, the moon's in exactly the right place above the bay. That's very satisfying for an effects team because, if people don't realise it's an effect, the job is done.'

Above: An early maquette of a Slitheen. Below: Paul Kasey inside the Slitheen costume in Aliens of London.

'Russell's got better and better as we've gone on,' adds Dave. 'He now tries to write into the scripts a description of exactly what the effect is, he's very visual in the way he writes. Most people write a script and they say the scene is set in an interior room here or an exterior place there, and they don't tend to say there's a post-production effect – they leave that up to you to try and guess. But Russell tries to point it out to make life easier for everybody.'

'Invariably, stuff ends up being simplified too,' adds Will Cohen. 'At the start of a tone meeting, there's always more in a script than can practically be done. Russell might start writing an episode requiring fifteen or sixteen creatures but, once it's realised that each one needs to be animated, we get it down to six or seven. We're all refining the creative process because of the cash and the time – schedule and budget are the two big enemies for us, and for every department in fact. If this was a movie, time would be less of an issue, but this is television, so they're forced to think about what's really necessary and really important to tell the story, instead of just getting the chequebook out and demanding to see the creature all the time. Which makes it a better show, I think.'

Dave agrees with this, but says there have been moments where the learning curve has been to the show's possible detriment. Normally, when he and Will go to the tone meeting and the work is divided up, it generally becomes obvious whether a monster is going to be CG or prosthetic. 'If it's talking a lot, it's a prosthetic,' Dave says. However, that was not always a hard-and-fast rule and he looks to exactly the same guilty party as Neill Gorton did when discussing Millennium's prosthetics – the dreaded Slitheen family.

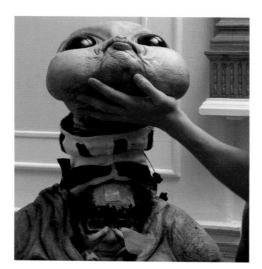

In fact, Dave believes it would have been so much better if, as Neill Gorton had proposed, the creatures had been created entirely as CGI. 'The job of the various design teams is to support the narrative and get the story told in as effortless a way as possible,' he adds. 'And sometimes that works against the amount of time we'd like to add the polish. That's always the way with visual effects: the less you have to do, the better you can make it. But when you're faced with the stories that we're faced with on *Doctor Who*, it's a tug of war – somewhere in the middle you end up with what you get. Which I think was the situation with the Slitheen in *Aliens of London*.'

Will is keen, however, to point out that the Slitheen were everyone's first pass at what could or couldn't be done for *Doctor Who*. 'I think by the end of the first series we had exceeded their expectations of what

Above: Adjusting the Slitheen before the voicebox is added to ensure the actor can see out through the neck.

could be done and how good it could be. Of course, that raised the bar because we wanted to make the best-looking television programme out there. An episodic drama with this volume of visual effects is a very rare thing in Britain, it didn't really exist outside of dinosaur documentaries. We will make a spaceship for six shots, and blow it up. That'll take months of work, but we just move on to the next thing. So in Series One they were cooing with delight when they saw the work, and during the second series we hopefully surpassed their expectations, but it gets harder and harder. Even after doing twenty-seven episodes, we're still these mysterious black magic people to a lot of them – CG's a bit like voodoo, nobody really understands the lengths of time and the techniques involved. When we're on set, people may not realise the value of what we ask for. Everyone can instantly see the value in watching an actor in costume, speaking lines, getting it right in four takes. But if we beg for a wind machine to disturb an actor's hair, they can't always see the value in it because they're short of time. In fact, it's essential because, when we put the background in, if the viewer can see the actor's hair moving if they're high up, or falling from a barrage balloon, or sitting in an open-topped spaceship, it's going to help sell the shot! These are the little things that help add the polish and make it work on-screen.'

Dave remembers a typical incident when The Mill were creating an army of Sycorax warriors for *The Christmas Invasion*. 'We needed a big group of them against a green screen so we could make hundreds of them, by grouping them up and shooting them a few times. When I arrived, we had two Sycorax warriors available because the rest were on set. And we ended up waiting for the others to be free, and then had an hour and a

Right: An animatic showing the intended positioning of the CG TARDIS in the pre-filmed sequence at the Powell Estate for the start of The Christmas Invasion. *Below right: The final matte shot.*

half to do a day's work in. By the love and hard work of the technical people and some very understanding Sycorax warriors, we got what we needed. But that's television – you want twelve Sycorax all day, and you end up with twelve Sycorax for ninety minutes, if you're lucky.'

Although it often depends on the director, the value in The Mill's requests is now understood, but it was a bit touch and go in the first few episodes. Every director is different, Will says, and reckons that those who do it again and again get better and better at it. 'Joe Ahearne was an exceptionally good director who really had the episode in his head when he sat down and talked to us about it. He meticulously planned everything and knew exactly what he wanted. But then Joe had worked on effects before. Each director has a different background: some have been cameramen before; some have been theatre directors.'

Dave says this is also true of the team they got in at The Mill to work on the show. 'We knew the shoot would go over schedule, just by looking at the script and the number of shooting days, so we knew we'd end up needing extra people. We went into Series

One with too few people and, when we were hiring people, we told them they'd each have to do the work of two. We hand-picked a team of people that we knew were good, with their own specific strengths, although those who had been working in movies had to be un-trained a bit, because movie people can be a bit too precious, and keep refining and refining because they still think that we have the time and budget that they're used to from the movies.'

One thing the team had to do very early on was the title sequence. Dave explains that this developed when The Mill were asked to pitch for it; it didn't come automatically just because they were doing the CGI for the rest of the series. 'We had two basic approaches. The first was more akin to *The Avengers* – lots of graphics with images that were related to time travel and distortion. It was an interesting kind of idea, but absolutely not what they wanted. Our second idea was a much more traditional route based heavily on *Doctor Who*'s 1970s title sequences. We had to develop the vortex anyway, because we were doing shots of the TARDIS travelling through it in the actual episodes, so the title sequence grew from that work. We wanted the vortex to make sense as well, it wasn't just a pretty effect for the sake of it: if the TARDIS is travelling forwards in time, the vortex is red, but it's blue for travelling back in time. We wanted to show both directions in the title sequence, but if the TARDIS came forward, twisted and went straight back in, it looked very two-dimensional, so we added in a couple of beats of it hanging in normal space before shooting back down the vortex. Originally we were going to have the shape of the vortex slightly distorted by the TARDIS as it flew

down it, as happened in the old Jon Pertwee and Tom Baker sequences in the 1970s where the vortex briefly matches the outline of the TARDIS. We didn't have time to do that, unfortunately.

'We were then given the logo to incorporate into the whole thing, so we made that reflective and that enabled us to use the textures that the logo designers had put on it reflected from our vortex, so the two things kind of come together. I'd quite like another go at the whole thing now, give it an overhaul, make the logo work better in it. We've done odd tweaks like putting David Tennant's name into it, and will do so again with Freema Agyeman for Series Three, but it'd be nice to strip the whole thing down and jazz it up a bit.'

Edward Thomas explained how important it is to him to get the colours right throughout the visual design of the series. Each episode has a different visual feel, a distinct set of colours, which helps to convey the mood of the story being told – the very bright and vibrant look of *Fear Her* is in stark contrast with the much darker tone of *The Impossible Planet*; the gas lamp and candlelight of *The Unquiet Dead* contributes to its Dickensian feel, while *Tooth and Claw* is much greyer in tone. Much of this is achieved by The Mill in a process Edward mentioned called 'grading'. Dave Houghton explains that 'what you see on your television, the beautiful, coherent, cohesive whole, where there are colours on every shot and they blend together and everything works together is all done in the grading. Grading is essentially colouring each shot, balancing them, then adding a general tone and look to the whole thing. *Tooth and Claw*, which is very contrasting, got

"The Doctor"
Simple, stylish costume,
-help character, not
dominate;
Tough, sleek.

DOCTOR WHO
DRW BY: Lucinda Wright
© BBC CYMRU WALES 2004
DRW TITLE: "The Doctor"
DATE DRAWN: May 2004
REF CODE: D

Lucinda Wright's
costume design for
the Ninth Doctor.

Battered leather 3/4
jkt - (900 yrs old).

V-neck jumper
(ep 6' Green).

Black trousers - jeans -
long + lean for costume

Colours -
Dark palette -
Deep Reds, mauve, blues,
dark green; - reflect
the Galaxy + stars.

Tough, Black leather
boots - good for running
Action look.

a blue wash over it, to give it atmosphere. You don't get that consistently when you're filming over a long period. Increasing the contrast to actually retain a consistent look to everything means you have to use lots of filters, you have to mess around with the contrasts during shooting, which would have disastrous results if you got it wrong and had nothing to refer to. But when everything's finished, all the effects are done, and the pictures are all edited and conformed into a whole show, our main colourist here, Mick Vincent, will go through and balance and colour grade all the shots so that you have a consistent look to the whole show, and give everything a look that suits that episode. It's a long process, but is actually terribly important because, without it, an episode would look very incoherent.'

'A SILHOUETTE YOU COULD INSTANTLY RECOGNISE': LUCINDA WRIGHT'S COSTUMES

Costume and make-up are two staples of the film-making process that have been around since its earliest days. When *Doctor Who* was relaunched in 2005, it was the responsibility of costume designer Lucinda Wright to oversee the first series.

'I was doing a BBC film called *Dirty War*,' Lucinda explains, 'and was asked if I wanted to go along for an interview for *Doctor Who*. I met up with Phil and later Russell, who then offered me the job. It's one of the best costume jobs you can get, you have futuristic, period, contemporary – things that you've always wanted to design, and an excuse to get away with it. That said, I always treated it like a contemporary drama, it had to be very realistic and not go too far into make-believe because, if you did, you lost the realism in it, and you couldn't relate to the clothes – you'd just think, "Oh come on, even in the future, no one would wear that!" So we were trying to keep it as a contemporary drama but still have fun with it, like having a little pig in a spacesuit!'

Lucinda's biggest task was undoubtedly coming up with a 'look' for the Ninth Doctor, working from Russell's 'no eccentricity' brief. 'I thought about Christopher Eccleston and what you get with him is that he's rather raw, isn't he? There's no kind of layers to him, really, he's slim, tall and angular. Because I wanted him to be a Doctor with a silhouette you could instantly recognise, I could see we needed something simple that would suit his shape, which led me towards the leather jacket, complemented by hard boots and black trousers. He was looking very dark and moody already, so all his jumpers were muted colours, ranging from dark greys and dark greens to burgundy reds. We must have gone through hundreds of jackets and, as well as Russell and Phil and Julie seeing each stage of the design, I really wanted Chris to have input, because he needed to be comfortable, able to run in it, and also have something he could throw off. We decided the jacket needed to look as though it had been lived in for a long time, because the Doctor was meant to be 900 years old and so too was the jacket.'

Christopher Eccleston adds: 'It wasn't something I'd wear personally but I think it was perfect for the Doctor. Lucinda did a fantastic job.'

'When we started the conversations about Chris's costume,' puts in Julie Gardner, 'we were determined it was never going to be silly. Before Lucinda joined us, we met lots of costume designers and production designers who had brilliant ideas, but they were thinking in a sci-fi way. We came across suggestions such as the colour of the costume changing every time he's in oxygen – nonsense things that you really didn't need. What we needed to work at was making him someone we wanted to spend time with. That's the key thinking behind his clothes not being overly, knowingly eccentric.'

Lucinda found working with Edward Thomas on colour palettes for the tone of each episode especially interesting, particularly if he was doing sets and other design work in brighter colours. 'I wanted to keep the Doctor as a dark silhouette, so that he would never clash or distract from the other aliens or people. At the tone meetings, Edward would say what the mood would be. For instance, in *The End of the World*, with the sun exploding, I wanted to use reds and yellows, and so I tied in my ideas with Edward on the set colours. Then we'd check with Ernie Vincze, the director of photography, how he was going to light it, and with Davy Jones for his make-up plans of course, so we'd all be working to a colour palette, and that made each episode very distinctive. And Chris would be a dark silhouette against everything.

'Rose was different altogether, she went on a huge character journey. When she started off, she was an average shop girl but, as she gets more confident and becomes an equal with the Doctor, I wanted her clothes to go from quite muted colours to quite

"Rose" - Billie Piper.

EP1-4. "Soft colours, lilac,
blues, colours, baggy relaxed -
-EP6 - Tougher, stronger
Reds, blks. more into character.

DOCTOR WHO | ROSE EP.1 —
DRW BY: Lucinda Wright | DATE DRAWN: June 2004 | REF CODE: 9
© BBC CYMRU WALES 2004

strong ones. By the time we get to *The Parting of the Ways*, she's very bold, the jeans have changed to tight black trousers, giving her a sharper look. So at the beginning she was all pinks and dull reds and purples and baggy jeans, but at the end she's in a bright scarlet, a very tight top, black trousers, hard boots, and so her look actually progresses with the storyline. It was the same with her mum, Jackie. She was like an older version of Rose, so sometimes they would mirror one another – they might both have differently shaded pink zip-up tops on or Jackie would have an older pair of the same brand of jeans that Rose was wearing.'

Actress Camille Coduri had some thoughts on Jackie's attire as well, thoughts that echo her costume designer. 'Jackie is bargain-bucket stores in the high street, and reduced-to-clear stuff. Sometimes the naffest top was just superb. It was something that Lucinda and I would both think of separately then, when we came together, she would suggest it and I knew that we were on the same wavelength.'

And Lucinda found designing for Mickey Smith even easier, 'because he just had to look attractive, which isn't hard with Noel Clarke – a kid of today, someone you could see Rose falling for, but also quite vulnerable because he was caught up in a kind of triangle with the Doctor.

'At the end of the first series, Phil asked me to come back for the second and, although I was very honoured and thrilled, I decided that I'd done all I could do. I had done everything from creating the look of a new Doctor to watching Chris running down a corridor chasing a piggie in a spacesuit I had designed. Then I won a BAFTA for *Doctor Who* – well, it doesn't get any better than that, really, does it? But I knew it was time to move on.'

'SEXY AND FUNKY AND CONTEMPORARY': LOUISE PAGE'S COSTUMES

With Lucinda departing, Louise Page joined in time to oversee *The Christmas Invasion* and then the whole of Series Two. Like Lucinda before her, Louise was immediately confronted with the task of devising a look for a new Doctor. Unlike Lucinda, Louise faced this challenge during her interview for the costume designer's job… 'It was actually a bit of a weird request,' explains Louise, 'because I didn't know how far to go. I knew it was going to be David Tennant, and that I thought he should be sexy and funky and

hair up or down?

mac, grey hooded top,
hant grey 'mambo'
slashed t-shirt u/neath.

Jewellery.
Mac, silver
beaded bracelets.
Rings - (thumb).
Simple silver
hoop earrings

Faded baggy jeans - EP 1-4.

Converse trainers
to be able to run, fight,

One of Lucinda Wright's design sketches for Rose Tyler's outfit in Rose.

contemporary, quirky and slightly eccentric. And those were the key words. I'd seen David doing *Casanova* and I felt that perhaps that would be the way to go.'

Phil Collinson, James Hawes, who was directing the Christmas special, and Louise met David Tennant to discuss the new Doctor's costume. The actor was quite keen on the idea of a suit, right from the beginning, thinking that it would look quirky without being OTT.

'It would be wrong,' believes David Tennant, 'to go back to the frock coats and Victoriana of the classic series, because Chris had done something almost aggressively modern, which I think worked brilliantly to bring the show back. It still had to be something of now, but different from the leather jacket and the jeans because that had been done. We also had to think about what I'd actually like to wear every day, and the practical considerations: it's got to be comfortable and it's got to be reasonable to look at. I don't think you want an audience asking, "What on earth is he wearing?" So we wanted something vaguely… fashionable would be the wrong word, but at least stylish, and we just tried to balance all those different elements and also look for something that's a bit special, without being self-consciously quirky or gimmicky. It had to look like clothes that somebody would wear, but we also just wanted it to have a bit of *je ne sais quoi* about it.'

Above: David Tennant, windswept in Gower.
Right: Indoors and in coat, the Tenth Doctor.

'I'd initially done a lot of research on long coats,' Louise continues, 'and then I discovered David was equally keen on a long coat, so we were already thinking along the same lines. We went to Selfridges and had a wander round, trying a couple of jackets on, and looking at shapes. You see, I needed to get on and do stuff without him as he was going on holiday, but I couldn't unless I'd seen a few things on him. We chatted about colours, I'd been looking at greys, and David said browns really suited him. The next time I saw him was about a week later. We went to Angels, a big costume supply house, and we had about three hours of trying on 1930s-style suits and coats, just to find the right silhouette for him. We wanted the Doctor to have a modern feel – there should still be something about him that appealed to kids, something cutting edge and contemporary.'

As well as getting different suits from Angels – different periods and different coats – Louise dashed around and bought a few other jackets from High Street shops, and it became obvious when they were trying them on that the narrower shape suited David. The actor had quite strong opinions as well – how he wanted it to be, and what he felt would be right. David told Louise that he wanted the Doctor to be dressed quite messily.

'The suit that we ended up with is only thin cotton,' Louise adds. 'It's not a heavy suiting fabric, it's not a traditional tailored suit in that way. It buttons up the front but he wanted it to crease, he wanted one button to be undone, and to have quite a haphazard feel to it. Even in the fitting room, he was leaping up on chairs: because he's so physical, he wanted to make sure he would be comfortable with whatever he wore and it could cope with whatever he had to do physically in the show, and it went on from there.'

Louise explains that the long brown coat originally had much bigger lapels, giving it what she calls a swashbuckling feel, and it was much more period because it flared out at the bottom and had big cuffs on it – almost a seventeenth-century highwayman feel. Phil Collinson felt that that was too much and asked Louise to pare it down a bit. She took the big cuffs off and then, when Russell said he felt the lapels were too wide,

Louise began to worry that the coat was going to lose all its charm and use as a silhouette. 'I was worried that he'd look like something out of Duran Duran if we carried on trimming the bulk out of the coat. The way they were going, David was going to end up looking like a long pencil. And then Russell said, "I love that idea. A long pencil sounds marvellous!" Somewhere along the line, Phil said he thought the coat was too long as well, but David didn't agree, he felt it was perfect. Nevertheless Phil made us cut it five inches shorter and then Russell said he thought it was too short. Great – we'd just cut five inches off the bottom of it! Of course we changed it again, and Phil apologised and agreed it was better longer.'

The coat was also something Russell thought might be a tad overused if they weren't careful. 'I do keep on niggling about the coat, to both Louise and David. I try to make them take the coat off as much as I can, because we want to treat it as a real coat. When you go indoors, you take your coat off, so should the Doctor. I started putting that in scripts: "He takes his coat off." No one wears an overcoat that much.'

Louise, meanwhile, was still battling to find the suit, but then had half a victory because she discovered a pair of trousers she liked, with a thin electric blue pinstripe threaded through them. David liked them too. A lot in fact. But they were to lead to more unforeseen problems.

'David said they were perfect for him because they were lean and narrow and after this long search, that was enough for me. He loved them, I loved them. And, once the

fabric and style had been approved by Phil, Russell and Julie, those became the trousers he actually wore in the series. Now, I liked the cut, style and shape of a completely different jacket, but it didn't exist in the specific pattern and fabric of the trousers – indeed the trousers were just that, trousers, not part of a suit at all. So I used the jacket I had found, with weird pockets and strap on the back and everything, as a template and designed the jacket from scratch. I designed it knowing that David wanted to do a lot of "pocket acting" – he was going to put his hands in the pockets a lot – so we put the pocket flaps on the outside, which meant that they wouldn't keep flapping up. But I needed material to make these jackets from, so that it looked like a suit and therefore went out and bought up every pair of trousers in the style that David had chosen. Size wasn't a problem, I just bought every single pair I could find and unstitched them. Just over thirty pairs, all unstitched by hand. Now I had loads of this fabric and had the jackets made by hand – roughly one jacket from three-and-a-half pairs of trousers! We also had to save some of

the trousers for David to wear, plus we needed pairs for the stuntmen, a couple of pairs that were up a size, for David to wear with padding, and so now I can't make more suits – we may need to come up with some alternative idea for Series Three because David has worn them all out during Series Two – it didn't take a lot to wreck them, because they were only thin cotton.'

Louise assumed that the Doctor would have quite relaxed layers under this suit – that maybe he'd just wear T-shirts. But in the final fitting, when the coat and suit was finished, David came in to try it on and suggested trying a collar a tie. So Louise went off, found a tie, he put it on and loved it. However, this fact leads Louise to make a confession. And an apology. '*Doctor Who Confidential* wanted to come down that day and film the fitting, and I'd agreed originally. At the last minute, because I'd had a whole lot of stuff going on to do with the coat and the length and the Sycorax and everything else, I said I was really sorry, I just didn't think I wanted

them to film – it was another stress I could see getting on top of what was bound to be a stressful session. And then David put this tie on, and leapt up and down in the fitting room and said, "Oh my God, I'm the Doctor!" And that was it. Costume decided on in five seconds. *Confidential* could have come after all because there was no stress. Sorry, *Confidential*...'

The final piece in the jigsaw that was the Tenth Doctor's image was footwear. Louise had seen some fantastic boots that she wanted him to wear, Japanese army boots which she considered beautiful, very unusual, made of fabric and leather and really quite quirky, just as David had originally mooted he wanted to be. But Mr Tennant had other ideas, because he'd been wearing his favourite plimsolls all summer and suggested he wore those instead. Louise's only reservation about them was what would happen when it came to December and it was cold and snowing on location? His feet would freeze and he'd regret his decision then. David promised her he wouldn't. 'But then, he also promised me he'd never want thermals, and that was a lie! I think he ended up wearing five layers of thermals under his spacesuit in *The*

Above: Louise Page models the custom-built spacesuit she needed for The Impossible Planet. *Below: A green mark on the carpet in Versailles shows David Tennant exactly where to stand in* The Girl in the Fireplace.

Impossible Planet! Anyway, we did use his own shoes for *The Christmas Invasion* and then I bought another five identical pairs. I've got about nine now, but we used his own initially because they were already very broken down, very distressed, ripped and torn. David liked the idea that the Doctor's shoes were worn in. He didn't want him being this neat, perfect character. I think that's why he wanted to wear big horn-rimmed glasses, all a bit Jarvis Cocker I suppose.'

'The glasses,' says David, 'were one of those things that just kind of arose. As we put together the look, it was becoming this sort of geek-chic thing, it seemed to make sense to add a pair of specs to that. There was one point where I was thinking about

having them on all the time, but that got a bit of resistance from some people, and maybe they were right; I don't know. I quite like the idea of there being a speccy hero; I mean it certainly hasn't done Harry Potter any harm. And maybe because I grew up "speccy four-eyes" in school, I would have quite liked to have had support from the Doctor on that. It just seemed right.'

'I love that look,' concludes Russell. 'I was worried about a suit; I thought it might look a bit "posh". But it's beautiful: so creased, and how thin is it? I love it when David takes the overcoat off and reveals he's a little streak of nothing, that's brilliant. That's such a different image, and it gives him such an energy.'

'SHE'S BEEN AROUND A BIT NOW': ROSE MARK II

Next on Louise's list was the Series Two version of Rose, a bit older, a bit wiser perhaps. Time was again working against Louise, just as it had been with David, and for much the same reason: Billie Piper was taking a well-earned holiday, which meant she only spoke briefly to her new costume designer on the phone, from the airport. They quickly agreed on one thing, it was time for Rose to move on from her appearance in the first series.

'Billie felt quite strongly that Rose was much more clued up, much more savvy, much more sophisticated, and she's been around a bit now — she knows what she's doing in Series Two. I think she was aware that David was quite tall and that perhaps she might want to be a bit taller, and didn't want to spend the whole series in trainers. We had one day to do some shopping and get to know each other, and we bought quite a lot of stuff that day. After the start of *The Christmas Invasion*, I didn't use a single thing from the first series, not one. We bought new jeans, new boots, loads of tops. The little denim dungaree dress, which we used in *Tooth and Claw*, we bought that day.

'Billie's very aware of her own body and what looks good on her and what doesn't. She's very opinionated about what she likes and what she doesn't like, and she's not frightened to say so, which is great, because you know where you stand. She's a good shopper, has a very good eye, so we only went to about three shops and bought a whole pile of stuff. We knew that we didn't need that much for the Christmas episode, although we found that hooded top which had ribbons on, which gave it a sort of Christmas feel.

And although I gradually wanted to get away from hooded tops and jeans, there had to be some sort of continuity from the first series.'

Obviously Louise did have to inherit one costume from the previous year, the one worn by Rose during the regeneration sequence at the end of *The Parting of the Ways*. That was unavoidable direct continuity, and she wears it in the scene where the TARDIS crashes in the Powell Estate on Christmas Eve (she also had to wear it for the specially recorded sequence for *Children in Need*).

Billie's hair was shorter for Series Two and Louise was keen for this to affect the types of clothes Rose would wear. She looked more mature with the short hair, so the clothes needed to reflect that.

'In *New Earth*, because Cassandra was going in and out of her body, she had an opportunity to be a bit more shapely, and Billie had a Wonderbra on underneath and a top she could unbutton to put the perfume bottle down her cleavage. We then decided that we'd get trousers that were much leaner for her, they were much more flattering on her, and she felt much better being in those black trousers – it immediately gave her a more sophisticated look. She had high-heeled boots on but I bought her lifts, which gave her about three extra inches in total.

In *Tooth and Claw*, various characters refer to 'the nakedness of the girl', but Louise says that it was pure fluke that she'd bought Rose's dungaree dress for the episode.

Rose (Billie Piper) is made up by artist Moira Thomson for The Girl in the Fireplace*'s spaceship sequences.*

'It was very short, and we thought it was quite funky and quite cute, and by chance I happened to have a T-shirt with a crown on the front of it. I asked Russell if I could use it and he loved the idea. In *School Reunion*, she's a bit more action girly, so she wore jeans and a different jacket. She's got lots of different jackets – she never wears the same one twice, ever. In fact, she never wears the same outfit twice, in the whole series. In *The Girl in the Fireplace*, she was coming up against a woman who was a lot more sophisticated than her, so I made her very much the girl next door. There's a shot where you see Rose's reflection in the mirror and Madame de Pompadour is standing there – this other woman in a rich fabulous dress, looking very sophisticated and Rose should feel slightly intimidated. Later on, when she was tied up, her jeans were tighter ones than she'd ever worn before and so was the T-shirt, and I remember Phil laughing his head off, because the T-shirt sort of moulded to her body and he said, "The boys are going to go mad when they see this." The camera panned straight from her boots to her boobs! She looked really sexy and very straightforward – I think that's why kids liked her; in fact, the boys love her, but girls want to be her. Billie has such amazing appeal, and I don't think I've ever worked with an actress who's had such broad appeal, from boys and girls to adult male and female. It's extraordinary.

'In *Rise of the Cybermen* and *The Age of Steel*, she's in a red jacket, bright red looks good on her. The only note I ever had from Julie Gardner about Rose's costumes was that she liked her in bright colours, and indeed she does look good in bright colours. I liked that red jacket quite a lot, although it was the only costume that Julie and Russell were concerned about. They thought that Billie looked too bulky in it. But Billie and I loved it, and when I saw it on television she didn't look bulky at all. And then Russell rang me and said, "I'm talking rubbish, ignore me." For *The Idiot's Lantern*, Mark Gatiss wrote that Rose came out of the TARDIS in a big pink dress. Now Billie's not really a pink girl, ever – it's the one colour she would say Rose isn't – Rose is a tomboy. So, if we were going to do it, it had to have a slightly funky edge to it. I found the shoes first, so most of the colour sampling I did for fabrics was based around the shoes. Billie has got the perfect shape to do the Fifties, because she's got a great waist and boobs. Billie wanted the net to be poking out the bottom of the dress, because she wanted to have a slightly *Sex and the City* feel about it.

'Raspberry was Rose's colour for *The Impossible Planet*, and it looked fantastic on her. Everybody else in the space station is wearing muted, earthy tones and I wanted her to stand out. James Strong, the director, told me he was going to use a lot of red light in the

episodes, so I knew that having the raspberry would help. She's not in *Love & Monsters* much, so we used a couple of things we'd used before, but when we get to *Fear Her*, she's wearing a denim jacket which again was Billie's idea. She'd worn it on *The Friday Night Project*, a sort of Channel 4 chat show, and loved it to pieces. They said they'd give it to her, but not quite yet, because it wasn't in the shops but I pleaded, and in the end they gave it to us, and so we used it.

In her final story, Rose starts off in a turquoise zip-up hooded sweater, a look determined by practical considerations arising from *Doomsday*'s climactic scenes in the lever room at Torchwood. 'Billie said to me that Rose wasn't really a sweater person, but I knew they were going to use a full-body harness for that scene, so we needed something that would stretch enough

and wouldn't show. You needed something that could go over the top of the harness and be flexible. She's wearing a leather jacket at the end of the episode at Bad Wolf Bay, because here she's a much more grown-up Rose. The mood is much darker, and we should feel that she's matured. She's been on a journey, really, and this represented the end of it.'

'LIKE TRYING TO GET A WHIPPET READY!': MAKE-UP

If that's the frocks 'n' socks, then what about hair, blusher and eyebrow pencils? As with costume, each series of *Doctor Who* featured different make-up designers and, for the first, it was a Scouser called Davy Jones who, alongside his wife Linda Davie, runs MakeupSFX. Together they had worked for Russell T Davies before on *The Second Coming*, and were also known for being the main contractors for prosthetics in the north of England, a role they almost filled on *Doctor Who*, before opting for straight make-up only. Davy recommended Millennium FX for the prosthetics side of things – he knew Neill Gorton as they were both from Liverpool and doing the same kind of work.

However, they very nearly didn't do *Doctor Who* in any capacity – feeling that what the production team would require was impossible on the budget. In many ways, they could see it turning more into a labour of love, which is fine on a short job, but not on one that would require both Davy and Linda to be fully involved for nearly a year. 'I had actually pulled out,' Davy explains, 'until I got a phone call from Chris Eccleston who said "Keep it under your hat but I'm Doctor Who, do you want to do it?" So I thought that I could look after him, Linda could look after Billie, and maybe it might be fun after all. I'd done *The Second Coming* and *Flesh and Blood* with Chris, and before that we'd worked together on a thing called *Hearts and Minds*, a school drama that Jimmy McGovern had written, so we knew each other really well. I like his company and he likes mine, because I don't fuss – he does like a non-fussing make-up person – he's a big hairy northerner, he doesn't want you going in and faffing with his hair, and I completely understand that,

because I don't like that myself. He only wants five minutes in the chair – it's like trying to get a whippet ready!'

Some time prior to filming, Chris had been on holiday somewhere exotic, gained a very healthy tan and had his hair cut to the bone. Davy liked the tan, but had to keep it artificially topped up with make-up because, on the first production block, everything was being shot out of sequence. All that really changed during the series was that Chris's hair was allowed to grow a little bit because Davy felt it made the Doctor look too hard. 'So apart from the tan and a bit of hair growing, Chris really stayed the same throughout the year,' Davy laughs. 'I don't think Chris Eccleston had been that polished in his whole life.'

Davy opted not to stay on for the second series. 'Having said to the production team that we'd just come and do Chris and Billie, before we knew it we were doing everything! It was a murderous, crazy shoot but, before long, it settled into a routine. Nevertheless, after that first year, Chris was moving on, we'd shared a BAFTA with Neill Gorton for our achievements, and Linda and I thought we'd drop out too and let someone new come in.'

MAKE-UP: SHEELAGH WELLS

That someone new was Sheelagh Wells and, as with Davy, there's a connection with Neill Gorton. 'Neill and I were friends from way back,' Sheelagh acknowledges, 'and he recommended me to do the straight make-up on *Doctor Who*. I had worked on the classic series in 1983 and, although production methods have changed, there was still

the same sort of craziness that had always been there. The main difference was that back then make-up heads and costume heads were the designers for just one story: we did four episodes, and then somebody took over for the next four. Now, however, you do the whole series, one script after another, so there's a certain amount of preparation needed for one story while the previous one is actually in production. That continuous pre-production meant there was a constant flow of meetings to go to, actors to meet, costume fittings to attend if the job in hand required it – it was often easier for Louise and I to see the same actor at the same time because nine times out of ten it was in London. This all meant that I couldn't be anywhere near as hands-on as I would have liked to be.'

But Sheelagh was confident that she had a really good team of make-up artists, and once the stories were set up and the actors were all established, she had the confidence to leave them and go away and work on the next script. Sheelagh also had to coordinate her straight Make-Up Department with Neill Gorton's prosthetics team, to ensure that the integration between what each of the two departments were doing was seamless. For example, Sheelagh's people did the hair work for Millennium FX that was necessary, such as the wigs that were required to be fitted to the prosthetic faceless people in *The Idiot's Lantern*, and on the clockwork droids in *The Girl in the Fireplace*.

'SPANGLY AND NEW': SOUND

With the sets built and actors clad in costume and made-up, the easy bit seems to have been actually shooting the episodes. Well, maybe not, but we'll take a look at that in more detail in the next section of the book. Jumping ahead to when the cameras have stopped rolling, the next thing that needs to be added is sound. Now, during filming, a majority of the actors' dialogue is safely recorded there and then, but sometimes a shot simply won't allow for a microphone to get close enough and, if the actors cannot wear tiny throat microphones, the sound won't be good enough for broadcast. Often on location, and indeed at Q2 which wasn't the most sound-proofed of buildings, the odd aeroplane or police siren or the trundle

Above left: Neil Gorton's face mask is adjusted on the female Droid in The Girl in the Fireplace. *Below: Another Millennium FX prosthetic, this time for one of the faceless ones seen in* The Idiot's Lantern.

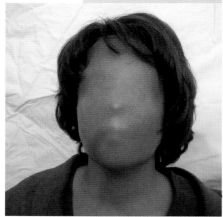

of a Dalek's wheels could ruin the sound for a take. If the pictures are perfect, a decision will be made that, rather than having to reshoot the scene, the dialogue can be dubbed in later. This is a process called Additional Dialogue Recording (ADR), and it is usually done either in the sound studios in the basement of the BBC in Cardiff or, if London is easier for the actors to reach, a studio such as Sir George Martin's Air Studios will be hired. Paul McFadden is the sound editor on *Doctor Who*, buried deep within the bowels of BBC Cardiff, overseeing both the ADR work and the actual creation of entirely new sounds, noises, roars, bleeps and gun blasts for the series. Or even the sound of the Sonic Screwdriver…

'You know,' says an enthusiastic Paul, 'not a lot of people realise, but it's the same sound effect from the 1980s, the Peter Davison one. We just sampled that, and we play it on a keyboard and change the pitch whenever the Doctor does anything with it. It's one of the sounds you don't mess around with, it's gospel. It works, and people will hate it if you invent a new sound for something so iconic.'

But, aside from that, the vast majority of sounds in *Doctor Who* are all bright, spangly and new. Those that aren't come from a massive library of sound effects stored on hundreds of CDs. However, it is when the CD library fails to have Track 8: 'Krillitane Screeching' or Track 23 'Adherents Memeing' that Paul's work begins in earnest. 'Basically, if it isn't on an effects CD, we create it here, from scratch. Slitheen voices, the Jagrafess, the voice of Chloe's Dad, some of the Ood, basically any alien crowd voices – that sort of thing. Rather than dragging some poor actor down here to go "Grrrrr" as

Rose Tyler (Billie Piper) absorbs The Mill's CG Vortex effect in The Parting of the Ways.

the werewolf in *Tooth and Claw*, or "I'm coming to get you" as the Dad in *Fear Her*, it falls to me to give myself a sore throat doing it over and over again, then mixing and remixing, layering and layering it until it sounds right. I don't do certain monsters though – Nicholas Briggs does all the Daleks and Cybermen but I get to do pretty much all the other voices.'

As well as his role as a kind of chief vocalist, Paul has to check over all the dialogue and then make sure all the ADR that's needed gets done. 'We needed to redo a lot of dialogue in *Tooth and Claw* because of all the wind machines, but I think the biggest problem came in *The Parting of the Ways*, when Rose absorbs the time vortex. Her hair was being blown about by a very noisy wind machine. She had given a fantastic performance, but we had to redo all her lines in ADR.'

As Paul suggests, noisy recording conditions on set can often make redubbing dialogue necessary. With the series often filming in power stations, quarries, stately homes or on beaches, sometimes the sound recording isn't good enough, and lines or phrases can be lost. These replacement lines are performed in a dubbing suite during what's known as 'post-sync'. The actors watch the screen and speak the lines, their lip movements in ADR matching their lip movements on-screen.

ADR can also offer an opportunity to add something extra to the recorded scenes. 'Sometimes you look at an episode and you might not be getting an important piece of plot information,' says producer Phil Collinson. 'When you cut to the scene you may start on a close-up of David over Billie's shoulder, so you can't see her mouth isn't moving, and then Russell will write a new line where Billie says, "Oh, what does that do?" and then he's able to explain. Whereas when it was filmed, no one thought the question would be necessary so it wasn't scripted.'

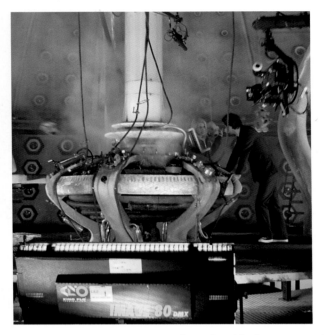

Director James Hawes, who had a huge job with wind and weather problems on *New Earth*, agrees that ADR is a necessary evil at times. 'It varies so much from person to person. There are actors, Chris Eccleston among them, who abhor it, but *Doctor Who* is so effects heavy, in scenes with snow machines or wind machines it's not a question for debate. If you want the effect then you have to do the sound afterwards, end of story. David and Billie happen to be incredibly adept at achieving it, and I don't think we've lost much if any performance in their repetition. There are actors though who cannot reproduce the same soul in their performance, when they are in an ADR suite, sat on their own.'

Paul McFadden is keen to point out that ADR is always a last resort – he and the other sound editors always try to clean up the original recordings as much as possible. Sometimes – if there's a bang over a line, for example – they try to find another way around it. The editors usually have everything that was originally recorded, the sound files from every single shot, so that a single word drowned out by a bang in an otherwise perfect take can be replaced by the same word cut from an alternative take. 'That way, everything is as clean and as precise as we can get it.' There are, of course, also scheduling problems to take into account: 'If I know an actor is going to be unavailable, perhaps because they're going straight to another job, I've been known to go out to the set with my laptop and record the ADR there.'

Another thing the sound editors oversee is the 'Foley' – the natural effects like crowd sounds, footsteps, wind, sea crashing on beaches, bird twittering etc. That involves going through every single frame of the picture, and seeing what sounds are needed. If a character is talking on the telephone whilst typing at a computer, that will require two separate tracks. Firstly they have to have the dialogue clean on one track, and the keyboard tapping cleanly on another – this is so that an overseas broadcaster can easily replace the dialogue track but keep the sound effects. But Paul says that, with *Doctor Who*'s hectic turnaround, that can often be forgotten during shooting the scene. 'It would be a lot easier for us if actors just waved their hands over a keyboard while talking but didn't actually punch the keys, then nothing would have to be re-recorded because it's going across their dialogue.

'That said, we do a lot of cleaning up and we have noise reduction programmes on our computers. Doug Sinclair, one of my fellow editors here, can load the sound files in and, if there's a clean bit of the noise with no dialogue, he can just take a footprint of that sound file and get rid of everything over it, which removes the background noise from the dialogue as well. One problem we had on the series was the main TARDIS console, specifically the cylinder that goes up and down. Over the months, it actually got hotter and hotter under the studio lights and melted. So now it's very slightly out of alignment but makes this really horrible whine, so we have to try and take out as much of that as we can – and we do most of the time.

'We also multi-track a lot of stuff, so a sound is made once but then laid over itself lots of times to sound like more than one thing. Cyberman footsteps, for instance, were made by hitting various surfaces with sledgehammers. We ended up with maybe fourteen tracks and then we added some sort of hydraulic sounds as well, some air hiss. So there are about fifteen tracks there just for the footsteps.'

'WAYS INTO THE NARRATIVE': MURRAY GOLD

Before the show is finished, there's one other, important and notable ingredient yet to go in – the music. Different directors and producers in film and television have ventured all sorts of different opinions on incidental music, its use, worthiness and general placement in the final version of a film or episode. But whatever you want from music, it has to be composed. Every second of original music for this new version of *Doctor Who* has been scored by Murray Gold, a young composer who had worked with Russell before but who never expected to get the gig. Let alone to do every episode. And the theme tune. And to orchestrate it with the BBC National Orchestra of Wales. Quite an honour, and a great deal of pressure, to place on just one man.

'Russell offered me the job – just like that. An email and it was done. I didn't consult my manager. I didn't even consult the person with whom I was already doing a feature-

Above: The TARDIS in the Vortex, an image created by The Mill. Above right: Blon Fel Fotch Passameer-Day Slitheen gradually shedding her human disguise as Margaret Blaine (Annette Badland) in Boom Town.

length drama. I just rang my dad and said that they'd asked me to do *Doctor Who*. Deep down, I wanted the job because I loved *Doctor Who*. I started watching it with the Third Doctor, Jon Pertwee, and I loved his final story, seeing him turn into Tom Baker.'

Murray believes it would be a great mistake to think the style of music from the old series would have worked for this one. 'Any idea that what you want with a farting Slitheen is old synthesized music is misplaced – it would clash with the modern writing style, that intimate, less obvious kind of writing. I'd also like to take what I do a stage further – it would be nice to work on a more sculpted chamber type of sound although one potential drawback to any chamber music is that you hear the strings on the bows, and the breath in the instruments, and it sounds intimate and ever-so-slightly alone, which might not be in keeping with the new series – one step too far perhaps. But I've had quite a good spread of styles already, because there's the haunting little *Bad Wolf* tune, sung by Melanie Pappenheim, and those odd little moments, like the cor anglais in *Boom Town*. The composer Adrian Johnson wrote to me and said he's not been able to use a cor anglais since; every time he does he imagines a Slitheen on the toilet.'

'YOU'VE GOT TO HAVE THAT THEME': THE THEME MUSIC

Of course, loving the old series doesn't mean being slavish to the past, but it seemed fairly inevitable that the *Doctor Who* theme tune would still be recognisable as the piece of music that Ron Grainer composed back in 1963. However, with everything else getting a makeover for the new series, it did at least accord Murray the chance to put his own stamp on it. And what a stamp…

'I didn't really consider doing a new theme – if I had done so, it wouldn't have been *Doctor Who* – you've got to have that theme. But when they said they wanted it updated, I didn't particularly know what they were after. I thought it might be a novelty to try a different sort of counterpoint to the melody – a string ostinato, a repeated pattern. There is this attitude that *Doctor Who* music should be sombre and serious. That's quite difficult when you've got Russell at the helm, because the whole flavour of the show is different – it's not going to be sombre or serious. So I didn't want to go for a great achievement or development in avant-garde music, as Delia Derbyshire did in her original arrangement of the theme in 1963.' Murray also opted to drop the middle eight from Grainer's original theme, comparing it to Band Aid's 'Do They Know It's Christmas' from 1984. 'I did initially drop the middle eight but, for the second series, I rethought that thanks to the BBC National Orchestra of Wales's input, which made reincorporating it practical. When *Doctor Who* was first trailed on television, they used bits of the new version of the theme, and people stopped me to say they thought it sounded good. Of course they also asked what on Earth I'd done to it, but they liked it, and that was the important thing.'

'I WRITE THE MUSIC, I DON'T IMPOSE THE AESTHETIC': INCIDENTAL MUSIC

One of the staples of film and television music seems to be that the musician will create a little theme, or even a musical stab, that tells you who a character is, and that particular piece will be used time and time again when they appear on-screen, or even off it, but are in the vicinity. Murray made a conscious decision to avoid this, and instead used his themes for mood rather than relating to one specific character.

'I don't really set out to create "themes" for characters throughout the episodes, but I think the odd "hook" gets repeated a bit. And much as I'd like to do more of the series with voice, solo viola, cor anglais, and smaller set-ups, it's not what's being asked of me. That stretches me, to work within those confines — I think I'm always looking for ways into the narrative, to explore what music can add to it. I'm quite a philosophical person — so I do look into these scripts in quite a lot of detail to find analogies. I think when something is as good as these scripts have been, I like to try and see why something is moving me. I find it easier to write music for things that are moving me — and when some haven't, it can be a bit of a struggle, and maybe my best work isn't done on those ones.'

One of the biggest changes in Murray's music occurred between the first two series — indeed, literally in between because *The Christmas Invasion* not only bridged the two series, it also bridged the crossover from Murray using sampled music to full orchestral sounds thanks to the integration of the BBC National Orchestra of Wales into his sound, most notably on the revised theme tune. But their contribution seemed to go far beyond just the closing bars. 'I always felt that if *Doctor Who* was going to use orchestral music, I'd prefer to use a real orchestra, but practically speaking that hadn't been possible. Once we knew the Christmas special was coming up I could see an opportunity. It was cut off from everything else — a one-off. Also a *Doctor Who* Christmas special sounded like event television, so it needed to be approached as event television — that extra something. I'd been nagging Julie about what we could do, and basically Julie used her connections with Tim Thorn, the manager there, to get the National Orchestra of Wales for a good price.

'So we did the whole of the Christmas special in one afternoon, and I suggested that, as they were willing, why didn't we come back later that evening and do a bunch of things from Series One that I was going to reuse as well?

The Pilot Fish's disguise — as a Robot Santa — is fitted over an actor's head for The Christmas Invasion.

So I selected a few – we were limited by the amount you can get done in such a short amount of time.'

Ultimately, Murray had two three-hour sessions with the National Orchestra of Wales, recording twenty-five minutes for the Christmas special in one session, and another twenty-five in the second. 'Doing that with an eighty-piece orchestra is really unusual, getting that amount of music completed – it might not sound a lot, but if I were scoring a Hollywood movie, I'd expect to get maybe two-and-a-half minutes of music recorded in that amount of time. If you were doing a British movie, you'd get maybe ten, fifteen. Ten on top of that is really going some, and I was just grateful for everything we got. *The Christmas Invasion* came out really well – and we did cheat a little there. That piece at the end, as the Sycorax ship was falling like snowflakes, is an orchestrated reworking of the "I can smell chips" music in *The End of the World*.

'Ironically, after that, trying to fit the other stuff into Series Two was quite a dilemma, as there wasn't very much I could use in a way that satisfied me that I was giving the Series

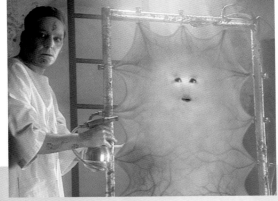

Below: Chip and the Lady Cassandra await the arrival of the Doctor in New Earth. *Bottom: Billie Piper and David Tennant coping with the inclement weather at the Gower Peninsula where they filmed the opening shots for* New Earth.

Two scripts all that they deserved. There's a whole sense of *The End of the World* linking to *New Earth*, but all orchestrated, so it sounded nicer, because *New Earth* had a repeated villain, so I could re-use Cassandra's stuff, and we did this fully orchestrated space waltz at the beginning of the episode, plus Rose's theme and more of Cassandra's theme, as the nuns are walking through the hospital. There's thirty-five minutes of new music in *New Earth*, and what themes were repeats were there because a character returned, and that music was now played by an orchestra, as opposed to the version of it that had been done in my studio, with samples.'

Towards the end of production on Series Two, Murray and the National Orchestra of Wales reconvened for another recording session. Murray was just starting work on the music for *The Impossible Planet*. 'I had one week to compose, and get down to Wales and actually record – the turnaround time for episodes eight and nine was ridiculous. It was the most demanding of the episodes, yet I had the least time to do it in. I geared a lot of what I was writing towards the Orchestra and was able to also get some music for *Love & Monsters*, *Fear Her* and the Dalek/Cyberman two-parter at the end of the series, so yes, I threw everything in. There were three episodes in Series Two – *The Impossible Planet*, *The Satan Pit* and *Love & Monsters* – which needed to be done in two weeks. I had five days on each of those episodes and when I saw that coming in the schedule, I sent a memo round asking the relevant directors if they could kindly try and find fifteen minutes of space in each episode that could remain music free. But I don't think my memo was ever circulated by the production team. In fact, the director James Strong was told to use as much music as possible throughout *The Impossible Planet* and *The Satan Pit*.'

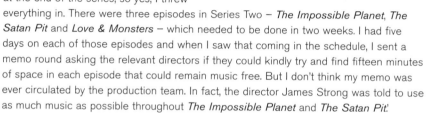

On set for The Impossible Planet, *David Tennant records Billie Piper for his video diary, destined to end up as a DVD extra…*

Different directors have different ideas on music – there are some directors who want more, some who want less and some who aren't too bothered. Murray cites Graeme Harper, director of all four of Series Two's Cyberman episodes, as an example of a director who was very interested in the music. 'Graeme Harper was really positive about my stuff, had done his research and knew exactly which pieces from earlier shows he wanted to reuse, or at least echo. I don't generally like to repeat things, but occasionally I've had to – such as the Sycorax "blood control" music. I needed a piece of emotive, slow music played by an orchestra in a later episode, and I thought of that one – so I just stripped the piano and bells away from it. I find that if a piece of music works for a scene that it wasn't actually composed for, and there's no other obvious thematic tie such as a returning villain or a specific person's emotional state, that suggests to me that, beneath the surface, there's something else about a piece, and what it says to the viewer, that had passed me by when composing it. So although I didn't realise it myself at the time, "blood control" isn't actually about Sycorax technology, it's about the separation of families. So Graeme requested it at the end of *The Age of Steel*, when Pete and Rose are separated. And then I used it in *Love & Monsters*, for the sequence when Elton and his mother are separating.'

The amount of control any musician has over the way his music is used in a programme has long been a source of arguments – film history is littered with angry composers who scored a film one way, only for a studio or even a director to strip it away, use the music in different places or, sometimes, throw the whole score away and use something else. Stanley Kubrick did it to Alex North in *2001: A Space Odyssey* and, in the mid 1980s, The Eurythmics found themselves in the same boat when their score for

1984 was replaced by Dominic Muldowney's. It's one of those things that happens on a collaborative show like *Doctor Who*, and Murray is adamant no one can be too precious about their individual contribution, because it's the end result that is more important.

'Just because I write the music, I don't impose the aesthetic. A decision about how *Doctor Who* is going to sound is too big a decision to be left to the composer, it really must rest in the hands of the executive producers. You hear people talking about the terrible contemporary phenomenon of wall-to-wall music. Well, sorry, but the phenomenon of wall-to-wall music dates to the origins of film, with the pianist sitting playing alongside it. Personally, I feel that we are much more in that sort of style than anything contemporary. There's a good old-fashioned sense of fun, and I feel that a lot of our music is very old-fashioned, and unashamedly so. I like to invoke a sense of the golden age of entertainment, when people used to watch the newsreels before the main feature at the cinema. There are aspects of *Doctor Who* which have that sort of Saturday morning *Flash Gordon* feel – there's that kind of melodramatic hook that you climax a scene with. The weight you give a scene ending, whether it's a big shuddering brass climax, or whether it's a more tasteful musical gesture, which would have something very creepy and spooky there. Whether you make the former gesture or the latter one is just a matter of taste and style, but it makes a big difference. And a lot of the time, the stylistic decisions we make do go for the big and the brash. I hold my hands up.'

'AN INFINITE CIRCLE YOU CAN'T SQUARE': SOUND MIXING

The final, final absolutely final oh-no-that's-it-guys-it's-locked-off-and-unchangeable part of the process belongs to sound mixer Tim Ricketts. Tim's job is to take the final, graded visual version delivered by The Mill, and the final sound version delivered by Paul McFadden and fellow sound FX editor Paul Jefferies, add in the music soundtrack delivered by Murray Gold and then, Jamie Oliver-style, whisk the whole lot together and so create a final mix of everything. This will then be played to Julie, Russell, Phil and the director for them to say 'oh the music's too loud' or 'the music's not loud enough' or 'that explosion isn't reverberating enough' or 'that line of dialogue has been drowned out by that door effect' or… well, you get the idea.

Left: A row of Ood lining up for a static shot that The Mill will then replicate to create a whole army for The Impossible Planet.
Above and facing page: Rose and the Doctor in The Idiot's Lantern.

'It's just an infinite circle that you can't square,' sighs Tim, with a slight exaggeration. 'You start with a big bang and then somebody says they can't hear the dialogue, so you turn the dialogue up and they say the bang doesn't sound as loud any more.' Unlike everyone else involved with *Doctor Who*, the sound guys are all buried away deep in the bowels of BBC Cardiff's headquarters, with no light, no sense of time passing and no one volunteering to go get them a bacon sandwich when deadlines are pressing. 'The bottom line is, I'm at the end of the food chain; when I've done my bit, there really isn't anything else they can do. Sometimes it can be a headache, especially during the second series, because it was shot and edited out of transmission order. Each episode has got next week's trail – or "throw forward" as we call them – on the end, put together by Matt Scarff. To make life simple for everybody concerned, he will only cut the throw forward from material taken from the finished version of the next episode, but this can actually cause problems. In Series Two, for example, *The Impossible Planet* and *The Satan Pit* were the last episodes to be worked up in post-production. In order of transmission, the preceding episode was episode seven, *The Idiot's Lantern*, which was ready to go a long time before the following two-parter, but it couldn't, because we had to put the throw forward together from episodes which, at that point, simply didn't exist. It also meant that, once *The Impossible Planet* was finished, we had to go back and finish *The Idiot's Lantern* by putting the clips into it, before we could start on *The Satan Pit*. We were close to the wire on those episodes – *The Satan Pit* was only finally finished on the Friday before its Saturday transmission. But we're used to that on *Doctor Who* – I think we'd be alarmed if everything wasn't close to the wire.'

Above right: Christopher Eccleston and Alan Ruscoe rehearse the struggle between the Doctor and an Auton (above) at the Paper Mill in Rose.

As has become apparent from everyone's comments, the series has always had fairly tight delivery dates. Indeed, right back at the start of the first series, the team were within a fortnight of transmission of the first episode, *Rose*, and the episode had not been finished. 'It didn't have the credits or the theme ready until very, very late on,' Tim recalls. 'At one point I was worried we'd have nothing fit for transmission. I can't remember exactly when we finished *Rose* but it was less than forty-eight hours before the Saturday night. When I finally mixed that episode, Julie, Russell and Phil came in, joined by Murray Gold and the director, Keith Boak – they were all here. So there was a roomful of people saying "try and find the style" and "lots of explosions" and "I can't hear what Chris is saying" and ultimately it just became everyone saying "louder, louder, louder" about their own favourite bits. The big scene at the end with the Nestene Consciousness was very complicated because I was trying to balance Nick Briggs's Nestene voice, the Doctor, music and sound effects of the Autons going through the windows, with everybody throwing ideas at me. They all wanted everything louder than everything else and it got later and later and later. That was the moment in that dub which set the tone for the next two years – we were wrestling with the Nestene Consciousness, with lava and bubbles and stuff and Murray said, "It's all in the music. Just get everything out and turn the music up," which we did and that was right thing to do. Because he writes such a big operatic score, we always go for the music – if there's a big sequence where there's explosions and fires and gunfire, we'll always favour the music. It got to about ten o'clock at night and I thought we weren't going to finish – my view being that if you get to eight o'clock you might as well go home because by that time you're all brain dead anyway. If you do carry on, what you do tends to be rubbish. The following day, you look at it afresh, and ask yourself, "Why did I do that, it's a terrible mix." But on that occasion, there was such a mindset with the execs, I could tell my suggestion to quit was going to fall on deaf ears. Julie went out for fish and chips – I can see it now – the executive producer of *Doctor Who* goes down Llandaff village for fish and chips. They just had to tick the box that they'd finished the first episode of *Doctor Who*. That was slaying the beast.'

Whilst it's always good to hear that everyone works until the last possible minute on these things, 'perfecting them' seems to be the preferred phrase rather than 'yes I know you wanted another six weeks, but there are only fifty-two weeks in a year!' The constituent parts of each episode are delivered separately to Tim, who typically takes about four days to build up the finished episode, layer by layer. 'I'll often start in sound only, just going through and mixing the dialogue and then the FX. Then I stick the

pictures in and I start fine tuning the rest of it. Murray's music doesn't normally turn up until the second day of the dub so on the first day I have the chance to do the dialogue, a first run at the sound effects, the Foley effects. The glue for the show is the music, so when that turns up you really start getting stuck in. Of course, no one yet uses the same sound systems: Paul McFadden and Doug Sinclair's stuff comes in as pro-tools sessions, Paul Jefferies gives me his stuff as audio files, Murray's music is downloaded from his i-disk as WAVs. On a full-on *Doctor Who* we'll have upwards of eighty sound tracks. And once I've got everything together, I mix it all up.

'When it's all done, I play it back twice. I'm working in a huge environment with massive speakers, full stereo, cinematic really. So I listen to it on that because then I know exactly what is and isn't there, which channel it's coming from and that everything is perfect. And then I play it back on a normal telly. With Series One there was this big quest for loudness from the execs, all explosions had to be bigger than everything else bar the music. The problem is that we're not mixing for a cinema with set volume levels – on a telly at home, people have a volume control. The only way you can make explosions loud on their telly is to get them to turn the volume up, and the only way you can get them to turn the volume up is to turn the dialogue down. Then, when the music and the explosions come in, you get a bit more of a kick out of it. For Series One, the execs heard all the final mixes through the massive speakers but, on the second series, I actually dragged a telly in and it was interesting to see the change in their attitudes. Now they watch it once through on the big screen with full sound and I get whatever notes there are and fix it. They come back later that day and see it again, but the second time they see it is always on the domestic telly and it just isn't as loud on the telly – it can't be. That way, we all get a truer representation of how the viewers will hear it. When they're enjoying it, which they nearly always do, you get a fantastic sight – you get a big scene and something will happen and six arms will fly up and they'll all cheer. They always do that now, as soon as we get the pre-titles and we hit the *Doctor Who* theme tune, there's a chorus of hoorays.'

For the DVD boxed-set releases, Tim prepares a full 5.1 cinema mix. 'That's the way I mix it in the first place. I can make the bangs louder, it has a much more dynamic range and it's more fun.' Some of these new sound mixes have included reinstated material, including a sound effect in an episode in Series One that was notable for its absence on broadcast, attracting some press comment at the time. 'Nobody's ever rung me up and said, "You shouldn't have put that back in, I didn't ask for that." So I don't know if directors watch the DVDs! For instance, with *The Empty Child*, when the gas mask comes out of Constantine's face, there's this fantastic bone-crunching noise. When we played it, Julie said she thought that was a step too far for the telly, so we took it out. And she was absolutely right, because while DVDs have certificates to guide you, TV doesn't, so you have to err on the side of caution. But for the DVD I put it back in.'

As with the incidental music, different directors want different things from the sound mix. Tim found that Euros Lyn, James Strong and Graeme Harper were all especially attuned to what sound can achieve. 'Graeme can hear things in the music that I'll never hear. When I was mixing *Rise of the Cybermen*, Graeme asked me to turn a bell up. I told him there wasn't a bell in it, but he was convinced it was there, in the music. I listened to the music and, sure enough, I could just hear it. I couldn't turn it up because it

Dr Constantine (played here by a supporting artist) faces death by gas mask in The Empty Child.

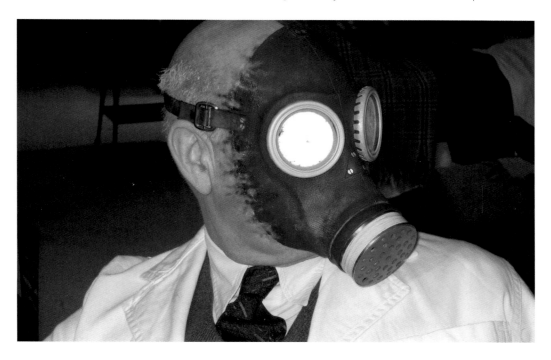

was part of the music, but what I could do was tweak it up and fiddle the sound effects down and there was this bell. Graeme could hear a lot of things in the music that I would never have spotted.

'Russell is also quite clever and will often spot things that I haven't noticed. At the end of a session, he'll tell me to move a particular sound effect or drop a line of dialogue. I don't know how he remembers it all – he doesn't seem to take notes, it's always in his head. He's the reason doing *Doctor Who* is such fun, he makes us want to go that extra mile for him. We work on the best show on television.'

'WE WERE IN THE BIG TOP AND EVERYBODY WAS LOOKING AT US'

Tim Ricketts' endorsement of the show is echoed by so many of the people who have pulled the series together. But the success of the show was never assured, and Phil Collinson remembers worrying that *Rose* might be seen by only two or three million viewers. It would have been a very public failure.

'There was so much attention on us, it felt like we were in the Big Top and everybody was looking at us, walking across the high wire. The minute we began filming, the press were there, the attention was there, all the absolute scrutiny that people gave it meant that it was terrifying. I think people were ready for us to fail, to have made a show no one wanted or needed. I thank God that they did watch, and I thank God that the kids in particular liked it. One thing that we always remember: we've got to make this appeal right across the board to so many people. It could have been a disaster. It wasn't.

'It's an enduring and brilliant idea; something that can capture people's imaginations in a particularly unique way. I don't think people should ever imagine it'll run for ever, because I don't think it will. Television doesn't work like that, unless you're making a soap. And in many ways the time it had off between 1989 and now, even with the 1996 TV movie, has been good for it. Lots of people have kept faith with it, lots of fans were always going to keep faith with it, with the magazines, the CDs, the books. And that faith allowed us to bring it back, with a bang, and with all the technology that's at our fingertips, and make it a show that feels very modern. I often wonder, if it had kept going on the television through all those years, whether it would still have the same affection it holds now in people's hearts.'

Series One

1.1 ROSE

The first work done in Block One was for *Aliens of London*, but *Rose* was the story designed to introduce the Doctor, as seen through the eyes of his new companion, Rose Tyler. It was a deliberate move by Russell T Davies to start the series off with a low-key menace so that the two characters were at the forefront of the storytelling.

Russell wanted the Autons as the new series' first monster because, although they're scary, they would also work as something that could be kept in the background of the story, supporting rather than driving it. There were fears that using a monster from the original series might be too nostalgic for a first episode, but Russell felt that they were easy monsters to understand. 'I can't, to this day, look at a shop-window dummy without thinking of the Autons… That level of recognition for kids, something so mundane being so frightening, is great. Why have something new when the best is there waiting to be reused.'

Rose Tyler (Billie Piper) prepares for the first day of the rest of her life.

The first episode would set the tone for the series as a whole. The production team toyed with the idea of giving the first block to a big-name director, but Russell was not keen. He knew that, however good it might be for publicity, a famous director would be used to working in a certain way that might not allow for the flexibility necessary to make a show like *Doctor Who*. 'On something as disciplined and as strictly budgeted and effects-driven as this, you need someone who will arrive on set and just do what we've already agreed in twenty-seven meetings.' He and Julie Gardner knew a young director called Keith Boak, whose work on series such as *Holby City* and *The Royal* had impressed them.

Eager to make a mark on the show, Keith's initial ideas were markedly different from those of his executive producers. 'I originally thought of filming it in a comic-book style, akin to the movie adaptations of *Sin City* or *Dick Tracy*. It had to be real yet stunning and stylish − a slightly heightened, powerfully visual world but not one that removed you from total reality. However, *Doctor Who* is not a comic, and it would have been too static. The show is about pace and energy and letting the style of the scene suit Russell's writing.'

Russell wanted the series to look so strong that any channel hopper would feel compelled to stop and watch. The look of a show like *Doctor Who* is of course dependent on a variety of factors and contributors − Edward Thomas's designs and Ernie Vincze's lighting mattered as much as Keith's direction.

Searching for the location to house the Nestene Consciousness for the episode's climax was a major task for the design team. Having considered railway yards and aircraft hangers, because of their size, Edward realised that, as it was fictionally situated under London's River Thames, the lair would need to be built from London-like red brick. The location scouts tracked down an old disused paper mill built around the long-demolished Canton Sanatorium. The building had great potential, with high ceilings and walkways. The size of the area below the walkways also determined the size of the Nestene Consciousness. Edward's next headache was to make Cardiff look like London

wherever possible. With Keith Boak, Edward hit upon a colour scheme that would serve as identification for London-based stories in subsequent adventures. 'In London you see lots of buses, pillar boxes, telephone boxes – a big red influence. And so we made London red. That was Keith's idea. It's a little visual shortcut so, even when we shoot scenes in Cardiff, rubbish bags are red, which subliminally helps to tell the viewer where we are all the time.'

A recurring element established in the first episode was the Powell Estate, where Jackie Tyler lives with her daughter. Brandon, a North Peckham estate in South East London, was selected. 'I couldn't believe my luck when we found it,' says Edward. 'These tower blocks were split into four sections, like the four TARDIS walls. They've got a semi-circular air-conditioning unit on the top, which looks like the TARDIS light. I was sold on it straight away.' The series would subsequently return to Brandon only occasionally, such as in *The Christmas Invasion*. For the rest of the time, similar-looking estates in Cardiff would suffice, redressed again to resemble London, complete with red rubbish bags. Edward was adamant that this could only be done for close shooting, because nowhere in Cardiff was designed or constructed in the same way as the Brandon estate. Edward also ensured that the interior set for Jackie's flat kept to the parameters that the London exteriors had. It was a particular bugbear for the production team that interior sets on television rarely match their exterior's proportions, simply because directors need to move their cameras around. Appropriate set dressing also concerned Edward: 'Often set decorators see in a script that there's bread on a table. They put out a loaf with four neatly sliced pieces of bread beside it – who on Earth leaves bread out, sliced and ready? People don't have matching mug sets and unchipped plates. We tried to keep all that real in Jackie's world.'

A number of discussions took place about blowing up Henriks department store. Keith Boak wanted to see the roof blow out and debris rain down onto the people in the street below, so model unit supervisor Mike Tucker was asked to build a model of the top two storeys of the store – but no one knew which store was going to be used (possible

Directed by KEITH BOAK

CAST

Christopher Eccleston *The Doctor*
and Billie Piper *Rose Tyler*
with Camille Coduri *Jackie Tyler*
Noel Clarke *Mickey Smith*
Mark Benton *Clive*
Elli Garnett *Caroline*
Adam McCoy *Clive's Son*
Nicholas Briggs *Nestene Voice*
Alan Ruscoe, Paul Kasey, David Sant,
Elizabeth Fost, Helen Otway, Catherine Capelin,
Michael Humphries, Jason Jones, Saul Murphy,
Paul Newbolt, Catrin O'Neil, Sean Palmer,
Ellen Thomas, JP Kingdom, M Couchman,
Alan Wadlan, Steph Grant, Glyn Page,
Louise Vincent, David Matthews, Rachel Chambers,
Maurice Lee, Richard Dwyer *Autons*

RECORDED AT

Q2 Studio, Newport
St Mary Street, Cardiff
Working Street, Cardiff
Queens Arcade, Cardiff
Trafalgar Square, London
Westminster Bridge, London
Victoria Embankment, London
Belvedere Road, London
London Eye, London
Brandon Estate, Kennington, London
University Hospital of Wales, Cardiff
La Fosse Restaurant, The Hayes, Cardiff
The Paper Mill, Sanatorium Road, Cardiff
Taff Terrace, Grangetown, Cardiff
Channel View Flats, Cardiff
Cardiff Royal Infirmary, Cardiff
Marks & Spencer, Skinner Street, Newport
Lydstep Flats, Gabalfa
Studio 1, Culverhouse Cross, Cardiff

locations in London included Harrods, Oxford Street's John Lewis or the Peter Jones store in Sloane Square). Howells department store in Cardiff's St Mary Street was finally chosen, but too late for a model to be built. Mike Tucker filmed an explosion at high speed against a black cloth, and gave this to The Mill, who then composited that back onto the shot of the top of the building.

The script required girders and beams to fall from the ceiling as the explosions go off in the Nestene lair at the story's climax. Mike Tucker photographed the Paper Mill then built a one-sixth-scale model of its ceiling, shooting all the rubble falling and the pyrotechnics going off. 'We really went for it in terms of nice big explosions and rubble dropping. They used almost every shot we gave them, and most people didn't realise it was a model.'

The sounds of the Auton wrist guns, both the noise as the hinged hand drops away and the actual sound of the gun going off, were the same ones used in the early 1970s during the monsters' previous appearances, sourced for sound editor Paul McFadden by *Doctor Who* audio expert Mark Ayres. Paul created the creaky sounds as the living plastic moved by recording the inner tube of a tyre being stretched and twisted. Nicholas Briggs voiced the Nestene Consciousness, which Paul then processed, adding what he terms 'lots of slop to make it sound a bit weird and more lava-like'.

Working on two stories in a block isn't unusual for television but, because this was everyone's first time as a team on *Doctor Who*, things took longer to come together. When The Mill's Dave Houghton worked out how many scripted effects shots could realistically be achieved, a number of moments had to be dropped. A planned shot of Rose walking into the TARDIS from outside would have started off outside the ship, following Rose walking round the TARDIS and then in through the door. This shot would then have been repeated move for move on the TARDIS set back at the Q2 studios, with The Mill morphing Rose from one shot to another – the camera would seem to have smoothly followed her from the exterior location into the TARDIS. It was quickly realised that this was far too ambitious for the schedule and that they couldn't physically shoot the elements in the time available.

An Auton lands on a specially constructed green-screen safety mattress, which The Mill will later replace with the bubbling, melting Consciousness.

Auton Mickey Smith (Noel Clarke) in front of the green screen with his chisel hand.

According to producer Phil Collinson, this very first block of *Doctor Who* shooting was terribly fractured and difficult for everyone concerned: one minute they were filming scenes for *Rose*, then back to something for the Slitheen two-parter being made alongside it. One reason for this was to accommodate Noel Clarke, who was abroad shooting *Auf Wiedersehen, Pet*. Indeed, they only had Noel for a handful of days, and had to shoot all his scenes for all three episodes. 'We couldn't really get a sense of making just one complete episode,' Phil explains, 'and we didn't know until three weeks after we'd finished principal photography on that first block and edited everything together that all three episodes were significantly short. We had to go back and do some second-unit shooting with Euros Lyn – Keith had moved on by then – and add some new dialogue to existing scenes from *Rose*. It was easier to reshoot whole scenes for *Rose* during *The Unquiet Dead* than to tack bits on.'

The main reshoot was the scene where the Doctor and Rose come down the stairs from Jackie's flat. Euros Lyn explains: 'There's a walking-talking tracking shot that develops into the Doctor's whole-world-revolves-and-I-can-feel-every-beat speech, which we had half a day to shoot. It was getting dark at about five-thirty but I thought that it would be easy because they already knew the words. For various reasons, the shots I'd planned just didn't work out. Chris's speech had to be rushed, but he pulled it off fantastically. Keith had shot the original conversation on a Steadicam and, at the point where the Doctor talks about the Earth revolving, he'd cantered the angle, which meant the tower blocks behind them went skewed and it was a really nice idea. But I felt that might distract from what the Doctor was saying and didn't work with the new stuff that had been written, the long walking-talking two-shot that was the point of the reshoot.'

Another thing that came out of the need to fill *Rose* up a bit was the trailer, or throw forward, for the next episode. 'We weren't originally going to do those,' Phil Collinson says, 'but we needed things that would save us expensive additional shooting, so we came up with an idea to fill forty seconds. It stuck, and we've had them ever since.'

1.2 THE END OF THE WORLD

Having started the series in a contemporary setting, Russell's second episode took Rose far, far into the future to witness the natural destruction of Earth. Made as part of Block Two, it was directed by Euros Lyn. Euros had discovered *Doctor Who* was coming back to television in an internet café in Siberia. As you do. As a fan of Russell's work and of the show, and discovering the series was being made by BBC Wales for whom he'd done a successful series called *Belonging*, Euros sent emails to Russell, Julie and Phil asking to meet them. Russell knew of his work on a series called *Jane Hall*, but had actually turned Euros down for a job on an earlier series, *Mine All Mine*. 'I can't believe I did that, because he's brilliant. It was his idea to reuse the shot of Rose running into the TARDIS from the end of *Rose*. The script started a few minutes after *Rose* ended, but Euros thought it would be better if the action was continuous.'

Euros had some experience of CGI, and understood the need to schedule a lot of time for The Mill to get what they needed for sequences such as the fan room to work properly. It was early days for the whole production team, though, and a few things still caught everyone off guard. For this episode, it was actually in the editing suite rather than in the studio that Euros wondered if he'd bitten off more than he could chew. The two big problems here were the final version of Cassandra, with Zoë Wanamaker's facial expressions (pre-recorded at Air Studios in London) CGed into it, and the spiders. At this point, BBC Wales was still setting itself up to deal with the level of work *Doctor Who* was going to involve, and among the last areas to receive an upgrade were the editing suites themselves. This meant that the episode was being put together on fairly old machines, which made dealing with the beautifully animated spiders a much lengthier process than Euros could really afford.

Both Cassandra's face and the spiders did make the final cut, but one adventurous sequence in Russell's script didn't. 'When Rose is trapped in the viewing gallery,' Euros explains, 'the whole axis of the space station was originally intended to tilt through ninety degrees, so Rose was going to be tipped over – not only were these killer rays streaming in, but Rose was going to be hanging off one of the balustrades from the gallery, suspended ninety feet above the glass window, which was shattering beneath her.' The sequence was to end with Rose lying flat on the glass itself, which cracks and splinters as the beams smash through it. Unfortunately, the required revolving set simply wasn't practical at this early stage of the series.

One aspect of *The End of the World* that all concerned seemed to love was its vast panoply of aliens. Costume designer Lucinda Wright cites the story as her favourite, because of its scope and variety. Among the dozen races aboard Platform One were the Adherents of the Repeated Meme. 'I thought there's nothing creepier,' says Lucinda, 'than black cassocks with no faces, and then just a bit of bling with the gold Tudor chain on the collar.'

Then there were the blue-faced aliens who administered the station. There were stories in the British press that the team had wanted to employ midget actors, but couldn't because they were all working on Tim Burton's *Charlie and the Chocolate Factory*. In fact, most of the Oompa Loompas in that film were played by one actor, but

The Steward (Simon Day) has his make-up adjusted prior to shooting a scene.

Platform One did end up staffed by some very excited children. A number of these children were relatives of sound editor Paul McFadden – Paul's nephew handed the Doctor the ticket for the TARDIS. Lucinda Wright's costume design included visored helmets for the children, so only the lower parts of their faces needed making up, but turning their faces blue still posed problems for make-up designer Davy Jones, since children are permitted to work in a television studio for only a short amount of time per day. To ensure a full supply, the children were called in at different times of the day but, because the make-up and costume took quite some time to apply, the children would often spend more time getting ready than actually being used. A child might get on set and go through a rehearsal, but his allotted time would be over before the final take. A lot of tears and tantrums ensued.

The tree people were originally less ornate – the script describes them as wearing long white cloaks – but Lucinda opted to make them more detailed. Since Jabe needed to be on-screen a lot, Lucinda chose to make her more regal. This look influenced the design of Lute and Coffa, her consorts. 'I'd always assumed that they were women, but Russell saw them as men, so I made them into bodyguards with metal breastplates. I tried to give them a fifteenth-century flavour.' Jabe is a perfect example of the coordination and cooperation between costume, make-up and prosthetic design, according to Rob Mayor at Millennium FX. 'I stuck all the prosthetic appliances to her face and hands, make-up did the hair, and Lucinda dressed her. She had sent over some samples of the fabrics she was using, and we adjusted the colour scheme because she was using lots of reds and golds to tie in with the sun exploding. Our initial idea had been for Jabe to resemble a silver birch, so we browned that up to make it more autumnal.'

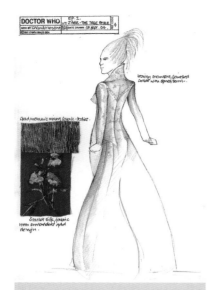

Lucinda Wright's costume design drawing for Jabe from the Forest of Cheem.

Having helped out with Jabe and her tree folk, Millennium FX contributed a couple of other things to the episode. For the recording days, they supplied a hardboard version of Cassandra's skin, with eyes and a carved mouth for the actors to use as an eyeline guide, plus the brain in the jar that sat at the bottom of the frame. They also built the Face of Boe ('he kind of bounces up and down and not much else, but has become this cult figure') complete with dreadlocks, which Neill Gorton designed from a couple of doodles he emailed to Russell. 'Some things can go through a hundred drawings, but if Russell thinks you're on the right track straight off, he'll say yes, that'll do it.'

Neill also designed the Moxx of Balhoon. In the original drafts, the Moxx was a bowl of blue jelly with eyeballs that floated around, which suggested to everyone that it would be a CG effect but, when The Mill pointed out that they already had enough to do on this episode, he became a full character. Building an animatronic puppet was briefly considered, but Neill felt time wasn't on their side and came up with the idea of putting Jimmy Vee into a suit and chair. Millennium FX already had a body cast of Jimmy, who had played the pig in *Aliens of London*.

For Euros Lyn, all these aliens presented a fresh challenge. 'I knew there had been problems on *Rose* with the Autons,' he says, 'because actors tend to feel a tad unwell when encased in heavy prosthetics under hot lights or on a warm location.' Euros therefore scheduled all the aliens' scenes in a block, so they could record and then get out of their make-up, rather than sitting around in it for hours. Euros also had to contend with the delightful Face of Boe ('he broke down every now and then') and the Moxx ('another example of me trying to save money by suggesting we don't give him a mechanised chair, thinking it would be easier to pull him along on fish gut, which kept snapping and he'd veer off in weird directions'), and a location that looked beautiful but was too small for what he wanted ('we shot it with some very wide-angle lenses to give the illusion of it being vast'). As if that wasn't enough, the episode also came up short in the edit. The sequence where Rose encounters the plumber, Raffalo, was written and

Below left: An early design sketch by Matthew Savage of the Moxx of Balhoon. Below right: Jimmy Vee gets comfortable inside the costume outside the Q2 studios.

THE MOXX OF BALHOON

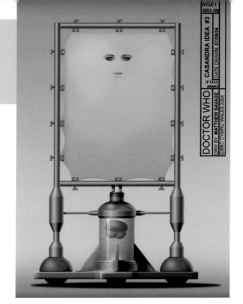

Right: Matthew Savage's concept art for Cassandra O'Brien Dot Delta Seventeen. Below: Christopher Eccleston and director Euros Lyn prepare for a complicated shot in the Manchester Suite.

DOCTOR WHO CASANDRA IDEA #3
DRW BY MATTHEW SAVAGE
DATE DRAWN: 07/09/04
©BBC CYMRU WALES 2004
MS61

shot towards the end of the editing sessions to make up the length.

Camille Coduri's availability led to the scenes of Jackie taking Rose's phone call being filmed by Euros on the set for *Aliens of London*.

Script editor Helen Raynor feels that the story of *The End of the World* needed to be told early in the new run, to demonstrate to Rose that there's more to the universe than her life back on Earth and that she's made the right decision to travel, even if she was slightly overwhelmed by it all. Having a gallery of weird and colourful aliens was also a good way to go: 'You still get kids talking about the Moxx and Boe and the Adherents. We could see it in the quizzes in *Totally Doctor Who*, kids know all their history, they know their names, they've got bits of biographical information about them, and to give kids characters they can own in that way is very valuable.' Helen feels the episode gets to the real heart of *Doctor Who*, and underscores the humanity that Russell imbued the series with. 'From the bit where Rose phones her mum just to say hello to the end of that episode, where the Doctor takes Rose back to her world, we watch as she learns to value everything differently. At the heart of this series is a journey that transforms Rose, and therefore the viewer, and makes you look at things in a different way. They come back and stand in a busy street and look around and contemplate the fact that one day it won't be there, which is an extraordinary existential moment in a family drama. And then they go off and have chips!'

'Chips' seems to be everyone's watchword for this episode – Julie Gardner seizes upon it as well. 'If I had to pick one scene that sums up the tone of the show, it's that. After all the explosions and the majesty of the end of the world, and the excitement as Rose has nearly died, there's this moment where the Doctor reveals something very personal about himself: "I am the last of my kind." They're walking through an ordinary street, and they've gone back to see what life is, and they're best friends. Russell at his best – from epic to domestic.'

Directed by EUROS LYN

CAST
Christopher Eccleston *The Doctor*
and Billie Piper *Rose Tyler*
with Camille Coduri *Jackie Tyler*
Zoë Wanamaker *Cassandra*
Yasmin Bannerman *Jabe*
Simon Day *Steward*
Jimmy Vee *Moxx of Balhoon*
Beccy Armory *Raffalo*
Sara Stewart *Computer Voice*
Silas Carson *Alien Voices*
Paul Kasey *Coffa*
Alan Ruscoe *Lute*
Von Pearce, John Collins *Cassandra's Surgeons*
Michael Humphries, Paul Newbolt, Saul Murphy, Dean Cummins, Jason Jones *Adherents*

RECORDED AT
Q2 Studio, Newport
Temple of Peace, College Road, Cardiff
BBC Broadcasting House, Llandaff, Cardiff
Headlands School, St Augustines Road, Penarth
Helmont House, Churchill Way, Cardiff
Queen Street, Cardiff

1.3 THE UNQUIET DEAD

Mark Gatiss wasn't the first writer to be contacted by the production team about writing for the series (that was Steven Moffat), but he was the first to be commissioned. Although Mark had an impressive *Doctor Who* back catalogue of novels and audio scripts, Russell T Davies was drawn to him not just because he knew the Tyneside-born writer was a fan, but also because of his darkly comic work as a writer and performer in *The League of Gentlemen*. Mark's flair for the Grand Guignol, mixed with a passion for that very British sensibility of horror and drama borne from the likes of the Hammer and Amicus film studios, made him ideal.

The director and stars on the TARDIS set.

On reading Russell's series outline, Mark was immediately drawn to the third story, then just a tagline 'The Name is Dickens', itself a parody of James Bond's famous introductory line. Russell wanted a story with the nineteenth-century novelist Charles Dickens, set in a haunted house in Cardiff, featuring a medium, and monsters made of gas. This was an interesting challenge for Mark: he knew that previous *Doctor Who* stories had often made references to historical figures, but they had rarely played leading roles in the stories. 'I was worried that having to explain who he was, why he was like he was, would get in the way. I thought it should be someone else, someone Dickens-like. Then I became very interested in the idea – it just worked, as it did the next year with Queen Victoria.' The story was originally intended to be set earlier in the writer's life – 1860 in fact, when Dickens actually visited Cardiff – but the production team soon realised that placing Dickens in a narrative shortly before he died provided better character opportunities. 'He was a disappointed man, he was in love with a much younger girl, and had fallen out of favour with his public,' notes Mark. 'What I saw initially was a Scrooge parallel, and realised it had to be set at Christmas. The whole thing became about the redemption of Dickens. He finds his *joie de vivre* once again, thanks to the Doctor.'

One of the challenges facing Mark was to match the tone of the new series. He was used to pitching *Doctor Who* at an older audience and, as a result, his first draft was, according to the writer, 'really rather grim. Gwyneth had lost a little brother to diphtheria, the house was adjacent to the cemetery, and the boy comes back and taps on the window like Danny Glick in *Salem's Lot*. I remember having a script conference after the second draft and Russell asking what the story was about and I said "grief". As soon as the word tumbled out of my mouth, I thought, "Ah yes, Saturday night. Wrong".'

Simon Callow, who played Dickens, is very knowledgeable on the subject and has for some years presented a hugely successful one-man show about the writer, but Mark felt that Callow might well be bored of constantly being asked to play him. 'He was delighted with the script,' says a happy Mark. 'He responded to the whole idea of this weary man, seeing fantastical things. I thought he was marvellous – I really love the séance when he's watching as the Tribune of the Gelth appear, and you completely believe what he's seeing; his eyes are full of wonder. Brilliant.'

Originally Sneed was the medium, but a much younger character ('written for David Tennant, would you believe? How strange the world is!') living in a house of mystics and charlatans. He was to be the only genuine one amongst them, believing that in the Gelth he's found real spirits. Mark was pleased to age Sneed up; indeed, a lot of the characters in the story are older than the average *Doctor Who* characters. 'I don't think children look at older people on the telly and say they can't relate to them, and switch off,' Mark says. 'If you make them likeable, the audience goes along with them.' Euros Lyn, the director of this story, agrees. 'There was pressure to cast young on the show, because it's aimed at a younger audience. There was discussion about casting a younger Sneed, but I'm really glad that we didn't.'

The very unquiet dead.

Once again, the story under-ran, although this was addressed during production rather than in a later reshoot. Eve Myles was terribly popular with the production team (she had also been on hand during certain days of *The End of the World* recordings, reading in Cassandra's lines) and, when it was decided to extend the episode, Russell extended the sequence where Gwyneth talks to Rose and mentions the big bad wolf.

The CGI work on this episode was light in comparison to the first block – mostly additional snow, including a tricky shot of snow falling off the TARDIS as it dematerialises, and duplicating the audience in the theatre. The biggest job here was the Gelth. 'At one point,' says Euros Lyn, 'we were going to use just Zoë Thorne's face, then we considered using a ghostly version of her entire body. There were a number of discussions as to how much was it going to be Zoë and how far was it going to animated. In the end, it was an animation of her face, so casting someone who looked right was really important. Zoë has an incredibly young look – she's in her early twenties – and she conveyed both the innocence and the evil that the Gelth required.'

Edward Thomas explains that Swansea doubled for Cardiff because there's very little Victoriana left in the Welsh capital, whereas Swansea offered a small, enclosed area of

Zoë Thorne as the Gelth is placed before the green screen, with a portable wind machine blowing on her for added effect.

Directed by EUROS LYN

CAST

Christopher Eccleston *The Doctor*
and Billie Piper *Rose Tyler*
with Alan David *Gabriel Sneed*
Huw Rhys *Redpath*
Jennifer Hill *Mrs Peace*
Eve Myles *Gwyneth*
Simon Callow *Charles Dickens*
Wayne Cater *Stage Manager*
Meic Povey *Driver*
Zoë Thorne *The Gelth*

RECORDED AT

Q2 Studio, Newport
New Theatre, Park Place, Cardiff
Cambrian Place, Maritime Quarter, Swansea Marina
Beaufort Arms Court, Monmouth
Church Street/St Mary's Street, Monmouth
Headlands School, St Augustines Road, Penarth

streets of listed buildings – ('even the lamp-posts are listed!'). For Edward, there's an important distinction between making *Doctor Who*-style historical stories and making other period programmes. 'We try to make everything look as accurate as possible, but *Doctor Who* isn't about total accuracy, it's a fantasy show. We do get letters about how in 1869 they didn't have such and such, but I'm concerned with setting a mood, building up a visual image of what the audience will appreciate as period. We're making a programme that will be seen around the world, not just in Britain, and I want that worldwide audience to recognise it as being Victorian Wales. It's not cartoon-like in any way, and I keep very tight control of the look and the colours, but we're not making a documentary; we're making a beautiful piece of television.'

One moment of disappointment for Edward was that budgetary considerations meant Charles Dickens's theatre engagement was played against a curtain. 'I imagined Dickens giving his performance in the middle of an opera run, and I would have loved to put up a set from *La Bohème* – irrelevant to his reading, but it would have been a beautiful visual background. We couldn't afford it, so we ended up with a red curtain, which is probably how they would have done it on the day, but it doesn't provide that extra layer, that additional texture to the shots on stage.'

Lucinda Wright enjoyed the period setting of *The Unquiet Dead*, as it provided her with a chance for what she terms 'lush costuming. The old velvets were such a contrast to the first two blocks and, as it was the first time Rose could be dressed up, I gave her a Victorian theme, but kept the reds and blacks, which made her look gorgeous. I had that dress made, because there were a lot of Victorian productions going on at that time and the costume houses were running out of good stuff. As Rose had to run, I gave her some black fishnet tights, so you would see them with the boots, which were actually Edwardian, though I adapted the laces.'

Mike Tucker was briefly involved with the story, when it was thought that the explosion of Sneed's house would be a practical exploding model. 'How nice it would have been to see all the windows blow out and all the debris come crashing onto the snow. But it was not an option to build a huge, expensive, detailed model and blow it apart for just one shot.'

Something that script editor Helen Raynor kept an eye on with stories involving real historical figures was representation. 'If we were making an explicitly revisionist programme asserting that Dickens never wrote any of his works and was in fact a violent criminal, I'm sure there would be some objections. I don't think anybody watching would think that we're saying that he really was haunted by strange aliens, which completely changed his outlook on life.' Helen admits that there is 'a seductive cheekiness' to fitting real-life facts around a story of complete fiction and invention: 'I think that reflects a natural curiosity and naughtiness in everyone's nature. To suggest Dickens started writing *Edwin Drood* because he'd seen some strange spectral aliens is a very cheeky idea. We have absolutely no evidence that that was the case. Nor do we have any that it wasn't. We'd only have to be careful if we implied something malicious or scurrilous.' And in the context of a family show like *Doctor Who*, it is very unlikely that Russell or Julie Gardner are going to stray into areas that bring that risk.

For Russell, the episode represents what he terms the received memory of what *Doctor Who* was – 'except, actually, it wasn't. People believe that figures like Dickens used to pop up all the time in the old series, but they didn't. In the very early days you'd have Napoleon or Marco Polo, but *The Unquiet Dead* was the start of what I call the "celebrity historical" – getting a famous actor in to play someone important to us all. I love the size of the story, the romance of it, the comedy of it, and the ability to attract an actor like Simon Callow, because the writing is so good that Dickens becomes a real character.'

This story also marked the moment when Russell knew that a good production team had been assembled, singling out Phil Collinson for particular praise in the way that the producer allocated and distributed the budget, ensuring that shooting could take place at night, in Swansea rather than Cardiff, complete with 'all those horses, all those extras, all those costumes, all that snow and that exterior street and the theatre. I really began to feel confident in what we were achieving.'

Charles Dickens (Simon Callow) surveys the devastation left by the Gelth.

Christopher Eccleston and Simon Callow rehearse the sequence inside the coach, recorded not on location but inside the Q2 studios, hence the TARDIS set in the background.

1.4/1.5 ALIENS OF LONDON and WORLD WAR THREE

If any story exemplifies the production team's initial intentions for their new version of *Doctor Who*, it is the show's first two-part story. 'I've always wanted to tell that story,' Russell T Davies explains. 'It's modern, it's got elements of thrillers – police cars, Number 10, council estate kitchens under siege, hospitals, soldiers, a real *Edge of Darkness* feel to it,' he says, citing the award-winning BBC thriller from 1985. But amidst all that are a space pig and the Slitheen. '*Doctor Who* is all about great big green monsters, I wanted them to be big and green. I love the Slitheen. A creature kids will relate to because it's big and it farts. Mind you, I remember worrying, thinking that come Monday morning, every fat schoolkid's life might be even worse. Then I realised it would be better, because all he had to do was put his hand to his forehead and pull on a zip. We heard very quickly that kids were doing this. Hooray, we had captured the young audience completely.'

Julie Gardner agrees with this assessment, feeling particularly happy that Jane Tranter's original decision to commission the show had been proven correct. 'This story offers you the end of the world, with humanity in the greatest danger, Rose and the Doctor are locked in Downing Street, him being a genius on the phone, and the world is saved from a council flat by Mickey and Jackie mucking around. That's where you see that *Doctor Who* can put epic danger alongside very real humanity, and be very truthful. We did have lots of discussions with Jane about whether the Slitheen farting was a step too far, but frankly if the world's ending you want a few laughs.'

The story was recorded as part of the first production block, mingling its shooting days with those for *Rose*, and director Keith Boak quickly saw how tricky it was going to be. 'I think in retrospect everyone would say that it was over burdened as a first block – no one knew what to expect and inevitably there were some minefields – but it is rare on British TV to get the chance to do so much and so varied a show, so I have no regrets. I wouldn't have preferred it to be any different – this was *Doctor Who*!'

Above: The space pig (Jimmy Vee) and below: Lucinda Wright's design artwork.

Once again, the episodes ran a bit short – a problem on the first couple of blocks as people began to find their feet, and learn how long scripts could and couldn't run. As he had for *Rose*, Euros Lyn shot some new scenes during Block Two, including the one with Mickey inside the TARDIS, where the Doctor insists on calling him Ricky. Also shot were new scenes at Jackie Tyler's flat, as Camille Coduri recalls: 'We're in the kitchen, Rose is very upset and so is Jackie – and Euros was terrific, because he just pushed us, and took us so far. We thought we'd hit our best, but no, he made us realise we could go so much further. I loved that about him and I thought it had been a long time since anyone asked me to really push myself so I thought for him, all right, I would. Some of my favourite scenes ever as a result!'

Lovely as the finished result may have been, it wasn't all plain sailing, as Russell admits. 'That was our first time building a prosthetic creature and mixing it with CGI, which is tricky. We didn't get it quite right.' Less sanguine about the challenges the story offered, particularly in regard to the Slitheen, are the people charged with bringing them to the screen. Much discussion was had at the tone meetings as to whether the monsters should be a prosthetic build, in other

words, a costume an actor can get inside, or a full CG creation built by The Mill and placed in during post-production.

Both the Autons in *Rose* and the Slitheen entailed similar challenges – trying to make heads that actors could see out of; making the costumes easier to wear as time went on so the actors didn't faint. The Slitheen were the biggest creatures Millennium FX had built, and trying to make Autons and Slitheen simultaneously was an enormous drain on the company's time and manpower. As everyone was very new, Keith Boak wasn't entirely sure where he wanted the prosthetics to end and the CG to begin, and tempers did get frayed. 'It's all about trust,' says Millennium's Neill Gorton. 'The first time you start out on any job, people aren't sure how much to trust you, because they've never worked with effects, they've never worked with you, and so you've got to build that trust up.' The problem for Neill and Rob Mayor was that the pressure and sheer volume of work during that first block didn't allow much time for trust-building and a lot of decisions were being made and changed on a daily basis. And although Millennium FX were familiar with what they were doing, a director and crew who hadn't worked on an effects-based show like *Doctor Who* before were bound to be finding their feet at a pace that was really too slow for such an adventurous story.

Millennium FX made one kind of mask for the wide shots, with good visibility for the actor inside it. For mid-ground shots, they made much smaller eye holes, so the performers' visibility was less, but the audience still wouldn't see the holes. For close-up shots, the people inside had to be really good performers – the mask effectively blinded them, so their movement had to be rehearsed. They couldn't walk along and pick something up, because they couldn't see it. The masks were to be switched as necessary throughout the shoot. All of which works fine in theory, if everyone is agreed on how to do things. For Neill and Rob, the greatest difficulty was not the building, but getting decisions made about exactly what was needed. 'We spent a lot of time in meetings, with everyone agreed on how do things,' Neill points out. 'There were things, on the night, that people wanted to change, but you can't. You can't change your mind with effects. A

The Slitheen performers are given much-needed air during a recording break.

director's job is to decide how to shoot something — if one of us comes along and says they can't shoot something the way they want to, they get understandably upset. But the fact is we knew what could and couldn't be done with the Slitheen. We'll always try our best to give directors and producers whatever we can, but we don't have a bottomless pit of money, so the way to get the best out of the show is to keep a tight rein on the pre-production process so everyone builds what is needed.'

A popular misconception is that one way out of problems is to ask The Mill to change things in post-production, but Neill Gorton says this is the worst attitude for a TV crew to have. It's also an expensive way out because The Mill won't have budgeted for it. 'Budget aside,' agrees Dave Houghton of The Mill, 'our problem was working out what we could salvage for Neill. Keith Boak was determined that the Slitheen needed to be real, but Neill had concentrated on building excellent prosthetics for close-ups, with moving eyes, translator units, all that. He hadn't realised that his Slitheen suits would need to run and chase people. From our work on *Jurassic Park*, we knew that we could match the prosthetic in terms of the look of the creature, but there were a few things that we specified in the initial meetings — the lighting had to be slightly dark, just to cover the joins and also the prosthetics shouldn't be allowed to run around or move too much. Needless to say, we saw what had been shot, and there's Neill's Slitheen running around in full-on light. We tried to help, we redid bits in CG but we'd created them to be dark, to be underlit, so it didn't really match the prosthetic versions on set. Poor Keith Boak was under a lot of pressure to get a lot done in a very short space of time. And that reflected onto us — we didn't have time either. We had them running quite fast because we thought they would only be seen running as CG elements but, in the finished programme, it's mix and match. In suits, they lumber, their heads bounce but in CG they're Olympic runners!'

Phil Collinson also asked The Mill to do some additional work on the appearance of the Slitheen, Dave notes. 'Every time you felt your eye had lingered on a Slitheen prosthetic for too long, we added digital blink to distract the viewer. It wasn't anybody's fault particularly, it was just the nature of that first block. When we came to *Boom Town*, director Joe Ahearne must have looked at what did and didn't work in *Aliens of London* and he shot his story accordingly. In *Attack of the Graske*, the Slitheen are purely CG and they look fantastic – a great example of how the Slitheen can look.'

Block One's problems led to a swift decision that future monsters on the series would be designed as either wholly CG from The Mill or wholly prosthetic from Millennium FX.

Other designs Millennium created included the body suits for the people replaced by the Slitheen family and for the space pig, but even that wasn't smooth running. For the body suits, they needed to take body casts of the Slitheen's victims, but one of the actors was on holiday and only returned the day before he was needed on set. The pig, whose sequences were the very first thing ever filmed for the new *Doctor Who* series, was only put into the story at the last minute, so Millennium had to turn it around very quickly. They recommended Jimmy Vee to play the pig because he had worked with the company before and they already had a body cast of him – which means they had previously covered him from head to foot in plaster to make an exact replica of his body which could then be used to create a skin or suit or something else that fitted him perfectly. Having kept his body cast, they were able to sculpt a pig head and trotters very fast, before handing the body cast over to

Above: Neill Gorton adjusts the mouth of an early Slitheen head.
Below: A Slitheen head mould.

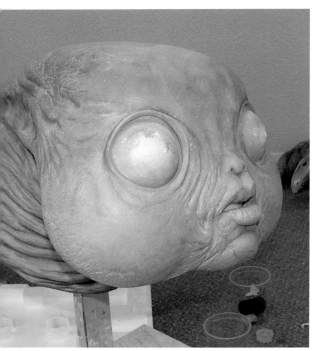

the Costume Department so they could make the spacesuit quickly and easily.

'He was originally described as a pig in a cloak,' says costume designer Lucinda Wright. 'But I said I wanted a spacesuit. Russell just said not to make it a silly sci-fi shiny suit, so I researched 1950s spacesuits. He's the thing I'm proudest of, my little piggy. Bless him.'

One of the most notable and successful elements of the story was the destruction of part of the Palace of Westminster – the clock face of St Stephen's Tower or, as it's inaccurately known, Big Ben (Big Ben is actually just the bell, which, thanks to Paul McFadden, you do hear

Right: Mike Tucker's model effects unit destroying the Big Ben clock face.
Below: Annette Badland's head sculpt in the Millennium FX studio.
Facing page: The unzipped body of General Asquith.

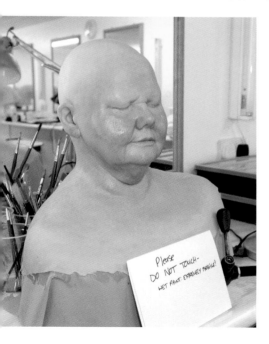

clanging rather amusingly as the tower falls apart). Mike Tucker's team at BBC Visual Effects were given the task of doing this model work. They only built two fascias of the clock tower, the tower itself and one wing of the Slitheen space craft. It is a spectacular sequence, and one everyone concerned is justifiably proud of but there is one little thing that niggles Mike.

'When I left the tone meeting, it was with the understanding that the spacecraft would be approaching Big Ben from a particular direction, and that the left-hand wing of the ship would slice through. The editing of that sequence and the digital effects were months down the line, and during those months it changed direction, but unfortunately we didn't have an option of going back and redoing the model shot, so it got flipped digitally in the editing. Unfortunately, this means that the clock face is clearly back to front, although it is such a fast shot nobody notices until it's pointed out to them. I'm immensely proud of the work our team did on that one shot – all the trailers for the first series used both that and the Dalek – both creations of ours. I was absolutely chuffed by that.'

The production team quickly decided that the 10 Downing Street interiors should not be exact replicas of the real thing. 'We wanted it to be a more idealised version of the place,' says Edward Thomas. 'You can go on virtual tours on the Downing Street website, so it's easy to find out what the Cabinet Room really looks like. But it comes back to what Keith Boak and I worked out for Block One – red for London. We wanted every room in our Downing Street to be red, apart the State Room, which was a slightly yellow colour, because that wasn't part of the Government. Some people probably thought that we'd got it wrong, but it was deliberate. We kept iconic things like the black and white tiles in the hallway but it's not a documentary about Downing Street; it's about Slitheens unzipping their heads in the Cabinet Office.

'When it came to filming the exterior, we phoned 10 Downing Street and asked if we could film outside. They were very positive and very pleasant but said no. I think it was the wrong time for them, lots going on when we wanted to film, so it was impractical. We looked around Cardiff but there was nothing that close, so I rang up the people who make *Little Britain* and asked where they shoot their Downing Street exteriors. They use a little mews close to Charing Cross station, so we went there. We put our own front door on, painted the arched bit and then blew it up!'

Much of the 'blowing up' was done by Mike Tucker's team at BBC Visual Effects. 'At one point,' laughs Mike, 'we looked seriously at building the entire frontage of Number 10 and Number 11 and blowing them to pieces, but costs started to spiral because we'd have needed at least two attempts at it. In the end we built a one-third-scale model of the door, and shot that being blown out, against black. The Mill were then able to composite that over the plate photography of their Downing Street set. For the sequence where the building starts to collapse, we built a large miniature with a breakable ceiling, added a load of pyrotechnics and dropped the model of the steel bunker that the Doctor, Rose and Harriet are inside through it. Everyone thought that worked very well, which was nice.'

Despite it being the most problematic production of the first two series, Rob Mayor looks back now with a certain nostalgia. 'Funny isn't it — we had no end of problems on that first block, a lot of people got cross with a lot of other people but, despite all that, I'm now very glad that it happened. It taught everyone so much straight away, and so many mistakes were never repeated again. Poor Phil Collinson, trying to balance his budgets and everything, he learned more than he thought he ever would on that one block.' .

Directed by KEITH BOAK

CAST

Christopher Eccleston *The Doctor*
and Billie Piper *Rose Tyler*
with Camille Coduri *Jackie Tyler*
Noel Clarke *Mickey Smith*
Penelope Wilton *Harriet Jones*
Annette Badland *Margaret Blaine*
Naoko Mori *Doctor Toshiko Sato*
Rupert Vansittart *General Asquith*
David Verrey *Joseph Green*
Eric Potts *Oliver Charles*
Navin Chowdhry *Indra Ganesh*
Steve Speirs *Strickland*
Corey Doabe *Spray Painter*
Ceris Jones *Policeman*
Jack Tarlton, Lachele Carl *Reporters*
Fiesta Mei Ling *Ru*
Basil Chung *Bau*
Matt Baker *Himself*
Andrew Marr *Himself*
Morgan Hopkins *Sergeant Price*
Jimmy Vee *Space Pig*
Elizabeth Fost, Paul Kasey, Alan Ruscoe *Slitheen*
Roderick Mair *Dead Prime Minister*

RECORDED AT

Q2 Studio, Newport
Cardiff Royal Infirmary, Cardiff
John Adams Street, London
Victoria Embankment, London
Brandon Estate, Kennington, London
University Hospital of Wales, Cardiff
Lower Dock Street, Newport
Hensol Castle, Hensol
BBC Broadcasting House, Cardiff, Studio C2
Channel View Flats, Cardiff
BBC Television Centre, Studio 4
Studio 1, Culverhouse Cross, Cardiff
West Bute Street, Cardiff
Loudoun Square, Butetown, Cardiff

1.6 DALEK

Episode six actually started life in a very different form – as a licensed audio drama called *Jubilee*, written by Robert Shearman and produced by the independent company Big Finish. Russell T Davies liked its central premise of a lone Dalek kept prisoner and the Doctor discovering it but being unsure how to deal with it, whilst his companion instinctively feels sympathy for its predicament. Russell had always intended ending the first season as a climactic battle between the two survivors of the Time War leading to the Doctor's regeneration, but he wanted a prelude to all this and the idea of a solitary Dalek faced by a solitary Time Lord fitted the bill perfectly.

Billie Piper watches voice artist Nicholas Briggs at work as the Dalek.

'I was trying to write a story for an audience who only knew about Daleks because their parents had mentioned them,' says Robert Shearman. 'My early drafts had some nice funny ideas but were a bit too slow: it took ages for the Dalek to get out of the cell; the Dalek gun was sentient and broke through glass in the museum cases, exterminating people. I took a long time on that and Russell's and Julie's very politely worded comments were about really needing to have things happen more quickly. I was trying too hard to make all the human characters stand out. And they would remind me, quite rightly, that what people wanted to see was the Dalek – I was trying to be a bit too clever too often.

'I was keen to make the Dalek into a communicable character, and Russell urged me to go much further with that. He looked at the scene when the Doctor first meets the Dalek, which was closely based on the audio version, full of traditional *Doctor Who* stuff about the Doctor never being cruel or cowardly. Russell pointed out how boring that is – he suggested we just have the Doctor go mad. Once he had given me that freedom to explore the Doctor and the Dalek, those scenes became an absolute blast to write. At one point, Russell and I had a very long chat, emails back and forth at about three in the morning. He wasn't speaking as my boss, which was lovely; he was speaking to me as a fellow writer sympathising and suggesting ways of approaching it. I loved that – you don't normally get that sort of approach.'

One of the most public and well-documented problems during this first series was encountered during *Dalek*'s pre-production. Robert had already written a number of draft scripts, when a contractual disagreement arose between the BBC and the Estate of the late Terry Nation, the writer who had created the Daleks back in 1963. This cast doubt on whether the Doctor's rematch with his oldest foe could happen. For a short time, Robert worked on a replacement script, which he cheekily called 'Absence of the Daleks' in lieu of any other working title. Then executive producer Julie Gardner wove her magic with all parties and, before long, work had resumed on Rob's original *Dalek* story.

Losing the Daleks, however briefly, put a lot of additional strain on Rob, who had to come up with a replacement story reasonably quickly, but one that kept the same characters, locations and settings. 'I was very proud of what I came up with for "Absence of the Daleks", because the best writing exercise you can have is, halfway through your

Matthew Savage's original idea for the Dalek creature being tortured by Van Statten's men.

drafting process, take out everything you've relied upon as a prop, then bring it back later on. The story's stronger for it. Early on, *Dalek* was more about Van Statten and his wife. She was the lead character, trying to break through the Dalek's casing and make it talk, to ask it one simple question, which was, "Did my Dalek-obsessed husband ever love me?" Adam was Van Statten's son. The biggest problem for me was Rose fancying Adam, which I found very hard to do and Russell made it work by making it clear that what Rose fancied in Adam was a Doctorish element, which is why Adam says "fantastic", which is such a great shorthand. I originally wrote Van Statten as an elderly man, but was asked to make him a lot younger – I heard rumours that they were thinking along the lines of Christian Slater, but no one ever confirmed that to me. I put in jokes about curing the common cold and things like that, and he became more of a threat once the Dalek wasn't there – the idea was that the Doctor would now be the prize of his collection. That gave the story more of a twist, but when the Dalek came back later, that stuff still survived.'

One of the integral things that Russell T Davies wanted to see successfully achieved was breaking that old adage that Daleks cannot get up steps (even though one classic series story, *Remembrance of the Daleks* in 1988, had shown a Dalek following the Doctor up a flight of stairs). For forty years, the newspapers had been making fun of the Daleks' apparent design flaw, and Russell was adamant they would be shown the error of their ways. So one of the first series' truly iconic moments was born in a stairwell deep down in Van Statten's Utah base. 'Flying Daleks How marvellous is that?

I know they've done it before, but not to the level we have, and not with "Elevate" as the catchphrase! When I was young and watching the Daleks, I never sat there thinking they couldn't go upstairs because I knew they could. It hadn't been on television, but there were comics strips and books, those marvellous old *TV21* strips with Daleks flying about on their little hoverbout things. But I wanted them to fly independently, to be able to just rise up, gracefully. What is so brilliant is our design team, and especially The Mill, were brought up on that stuff, so when I said I wanted the Daleks to fly like they did back then, they knew how to bring that whole idea to life. Oh, what a brilliant moment – I love that whole episode. It's probably the episode I've watched more than any other, as a fan – a flying Dalek on the loose, I just love it.'

Although the Dalek design was worked on by Edward Thomas's Art Department, charged with actually building the thing was model unit supervisor Mike Tucker, who reckons he got the gig through 'sheer bloody-mindedness on my part'. Mike acknowledges his debt to a memo from Russell telling the production team that he wanted Mike to build the Daleks, because he had worked with them on the old series and understood the problems and pitfalls. Russell was also sharp enough to know that if the design of the Dalek changed too much, was too radically different to what had gone before, it might end up looking more like a toy and less like the most fearsome thing in the universe. 'To prove the point,' says Mike, 'he brought to the tone meeting a toy Dalek from the 1980s and explained that this toy demonstrated what went wrong if you get the proportions wrong.' Mike had one of the Daleks seen during the Sylvester McCoy-era story *Remembrance of the Daleks* in his workshop and went over it inch by inch with Edward Thomas's team, deciding what stayed and what needed changing. 'Russell actually had some input too – he really didn't like the flatter frontage of the 1980s Dalek bases, he wanted a more 1960s look, with the front coming to more of a point. That did give me a budget problem, because I was having to build a base from scratch rather than using my existing moulds. In fact, I borrowed a fan-built one, because the proportions were so exact but, I have to say, it went back to the fan very badly damaged. Anyway, I was able to cast a new mould from that base, while Matthew Savage at the Art Department implemented all his redesigns

to make the Dalek look powerful and armoured. The shoulder section is a completely new build, but the head is my old one from *Remembrance* with the new grooves put into it. Eventually we had two completed versions, the broken-up one and the brand-spanking new one for when it rejuvenates itself.'

Matthew Savage's work on redesigning the Dalek was his most satisfying job on *Doctor Who*. Matthew's brief was to keep the basic silhouette of a Dalek, but 'beef it up, make it credible, make it look like a tank. And that's what we did; we added rivets and machine elements, but we made sure it still looked like a Dalek because if it hadn't we might as well have had a new enemy. The only thing I wish we could have had the time to expand on was the detailing around the eye-stalk, the imprinted patterning. I'd like to have taken that onto the bodywork too.' Another new feature was the electric blue glow in the Dalek's eye and from under its skirt. This was added by Edward Thomas, because he wanted to give a visual clue to a Dalek dying and then coming back to life again. 'Originally,' adds Mike, 'the ear lights were blue as well but, during the tests we did, Joe Ahearne thought it looked like a police car.'

Nicholas Briggs, who supplied the Dalek voices and is now the production team's resident expert on all things Dalek, noticed their resemblance to the Daleks seen in two Dalek cinema movies in the 1960s. 'I've always loved those movie Daleks, and these certainly have a flavour of those, with their big ears and bumpers, so I instantly accepted the new design. I thought the design team and Mike Tucker did a fantastic job, making it look armoured, upgraded and chunky, while keeping it essentially a Dalek. People not as anorak-y as me simply thought they hadn't been changed!' Over the years, a number of talented actors and voice-artists have provided the Dalek's vocals, and Nicholas is the latest in that line. 'I wanted to make it sound like an authentic Dalek, but at the same time give it more expression. That was essential for the story. The Dalek had to work as a character, not just a "speak-your-weight" machine. My favourite Dalek voices were done by Peter Hawkins in the 1960s, so when the tonal quality of my Dalek voice sounded nearest to his Dalek, I was happy.'

Inside every Dalek casing is a Kaled mutant and, in the original series, this ranged from a squashy mutated hand to a thing like a brain with thrashing tentacles. Neill Gorton's Millennium FX team, charged with creating the new version of the mutant, deliberately avoided looking at old tapes and focused on its description in Robert Shearman's script, although that in itself was certainly informed by what had gone before.

Top left: Mike Tucker with the team who built the brand new Dalek.
Bottom left: The Dalek encounters the Millennium hawk – owned by the Stadium to stop gulls getting in.

Below: The Cyberman head displayed in Van Statten's museum was modelled on one from a 1975 story, Revenge of the Cybermen.

'I'd always imagined that there was a little man inside a Dalek,' says Neill. 'A version of a little man, like Davros, the scientist who originally invented them. Russell on the other hand wanted an octopus with a big eye in the middle. Russell sent me a drawing of this octopus thing with an eye in the middle that looked like it came from a 1950s B-movie – I think this was the first time he ever sent us a design, suggesting this was what he wanted from a monster. I responded by making it more of an eye hovering in a shrivelled face, one eye decayed away and the suggestion of a mouth all sealed over. I was concerned that the viewer needs to feel compassion for it at the end of the episode, and I wasn't sure how much compassion the audience were going to feel for a turd with tentacles. I therefore erred on the side of making it more human-looking. Russell, however, said that the sheer inhumanity of it was the thing that would work and, of course, he was right. As he usually is, the swine.'

For studio purposes, of course, Neill was right: there *was* a 'little man' inside the Dalek – the poor soul who actually operated it. In *Dalek*, this fell to actor Barnaby Edwards, who had previously operated one of the beasts in the 1993 BBC One documentary *30 Years in the TARDIS*. Operating a Dalek is a tricky business, and isn't something actors get preparation for at drama school! 'It's cramped, dark and airless in there,' says Barnaby of his polycarbide prison. 'You have to strain to hear, your vision is limited to an envelope-sized piece of mesh at head height, and there are wires and batteries and projecting metal bolts all waiting to garrotte, electrocute or impale you. In addition to this, you have to be dressed from the neck down in black and wear a stocking on your head so that your face isn't visible through the mesh. The Dalek itself weighs about ten stone, so add that to your own body weight and that's how much you have to trundle around the studio using only your knees and calf muscles.' It's not the world's most glamorous job, by the sound of it, and Barnaby

Shortly before it electrocuted the lot of them, these foolish employees of Van Statten chose to pose with their enemy!

agrees with that, adding 'but I wouldn't have missed it for anything!' As an operator, Barnaby's main tasks are to move the Dalek around, operate the gun and the sucker, and 'do that sexy little Dalek wiggle when it's speaking'.

A Dalek requires one person to do the voice (Nicholas Briggs), one person to operate the remote-controlled head (Mike Tucker or Colin Newman), and one person inside doing all the other movements (Barnaby). In the original series, the actor inside the Dalek learnt the dialogue and flashed the lights. Because Daleks have a very particular rhythm, it's relatively easy to know how to flash them to suggest a Dalek-like pace and tempo. In 2005, however, Nicholas Briggs was doing the voice live on set. 'The initial idea,' says Mike Tucker, 'had been to use a radio-controlled device with a trigger on it that Nicholas could simply hold, clicking the trigger in time with his dialogue. It put everything in Nicholas's lap and, in theory, that seemed ideal. In practice, the device Nicholas uses to make that particular Dalek vocal effect is a frequency modulator, and our radio-control device also has a frequency to allow it to work. When we got to Cardiff, one affected the other: when Nicholas had the transmitter next to his microphone, the Dalek voice shot up about three octaves. It turned out that we couldn't have the light-flasher less than two metres away from Nicholas – the whole point of giving it over to him, so that he wouldn't have to worry about the timing, backfired on us completely.'

With the voice-activated ear lights yet to be perfected, a fourth member of the gestalt of operators (Melvyn Friend) was required. Barnaby recalls that Melvyn would 'click a button and flash the lights FOR… EV… ER… Y… SY… LLA… BLE uttered by Nicholas. Initially we all thought it was going to be impossible to coordinate a coherent performance from so many disparate elements but, within a few hours – and much to our own surprise – we all fell into a mutually agreeable rhythm. So much so in fact that, when Nick stumbled over his lines during one of the prison cell scenes and berated himself with a Dalek-intoned "BUG… GER", Melvyn flashed the lights, Mike moved the head and I did the Dalek wiggle, all in perfect unison!'

1.7 THE LONG GAME

'It's based on a story I thought of years ago,' explains Russell T Davies. 'I submitted it to the *Doctor Who* office in the late 1980s and got a reply from the script editor, Andrew Cartmel. It was very different, a more traditional four-part story as they did in those days, but the space station was always there. It's been in my head for years…'

The Long Game picks up where *Dalek* leaves off, with Adam Mitchell onboard the TARDIS. Originally dreamt up by Russell T Davies under the self-explanatory title 'The Companion Who Couldn't', *The Long Game* also worked as a set-up piece for the two-part adventure which would close the first series, via the introduction of Satellite Five. For script editor Helen Raynor, the most memorable aspect of the episode was Adam's inability to work alongside the Doctor and Rose. 'In a way it answers all of those questions which people ask: if you went to the future and discovered that they had a cure for cancer, why not just take it back home and give it to a hospital? It always sounds terribly prissy to say you can't mess about with the Laws of Time because we do all the time in the series. And so we have someone who is just like a child in a sweetshop: he has no responsibility; he is totally self-motivated, and he's clever and informed in a way that Rose isn't (not that she's not intelligent, but she's not a technological genius or a gadget wizard like Adam was). That gives us the opportunity

Currency in the year 200,000 – Matthew Savage's concept artwork for the metal 'money pencils'.

to show the viewer what could happen with advanced knowledge in less capable hands. I think leaving Adam with doors in his head is a comedic punctuation to the story and in a sense he's got what he wanted – he wanted to be ahead of the game, he wanted to be more advanced, but was too greedy about it, and now he's got doors in his head! Let that be a lesson! The Doctor and Rose are a team and Adam just didn't live up to the Doctor's expectations. He realises Rose is unique, is irreplaceable and that's a valuable lesson at the end of the day.'

Russell was very pleased to have Bruno Langley in the cast to play Adam. 'Once we'd cast Bruno, I was thinking it was a shame he couldn't have been given a bit more because he's so very good, but the story's more important. I always wanted to do a show with someone who was a rubbish companion and I think it's quite terrifying when the Doctor tells him to lead a quiet life and it'll never get noticed that he's got doors in his head!' And thus Adam's story came to a close. 'It's over and done with,' Russell confirms.

For production designer Edward Thomas, the most interesting challenge for his team was that this was the only story to feature no location work, everything was shot inside the Q2 studios. There were a lot of ideas about what kind of space station Satellite Five should be, whether to go for the minimalist cleanliness of *2001: A Space Odyssey*, or the military functionality of *Star Wars*, or simply a very 1960s impression of what 'the future' should look like. 'It was written as a tugboat in space, downtrodden, beaten-up, an industrial unit in space – very functional, full of steam and smoke. Because we knew it was also going to come back as a futuristic glitzy version run by the Daleks, we made it look very dark and shadowy. The lighting elements were practical lights, often in shot and therefore not as bright as a lot of studio stuff.' Where that changed was in the Spike Room, where characters such as Cathica, and later Adam, downloaded information into

their minds. 'That could have been out of the old series of *Doctor Who*: the set was basically an entire light box, which contrasted so well with the rest of the station below.'

This story caused a little bit of friction between Edward Thomas and producer Phil Collinson. 'It was a straightforward misunderstanding,' explains Edward, 'between what I wanted and what he thought I wanted. The two main sets, the main floor and the frozen floor at the top where the Jagrafess lived, were the same one redressed. To distinguish between the two, we wrapped the Floor 500 set in clear polythene, sprayed it with frost and so made the place look as if it had been vacuum-packed, with these icy membranes hanging from ceiling to floor. Phil walked on set on the morning of the shoot, just before we started filming, and said no. What Phil felt was that the plastic element took it too far away from what was written, which was that it was meant to look identical to the floors below but frozen. He asked us to take it all down and so we had to dismantle in minutes something that had taken us a week to build, because we were holding up the entire shooting crew. Now, sometimes when we discuss sets, he'll often joke that I'm not going to wrap it in plastic. But, bottom line, Phil's the producer, and he was right to ask us to do it, because it wasn't right for his show.'

The Long Game was a particularly busy show for Davy Jones in make-up. He dyed guest star Simon Pegg's hair and beard white, gave him blue contacts lenses and airbrushed his face with a small amount of white powder. For the corpses and Drones in the Editor's control room on Floor 500, 'we got them all in a big room and mottled them all up and paled them all out simultaneously, then frogmarched them onto the set.'

Lucinda Wright's costume team spent most of their time on the large number of extras on the main level around the shops and restaurants. 'It was a mixture of *Total Recall* and *Blade Runner*, really, with loads of very exotic costumes. I remember watching that when it went out, realising you hardly saw any of them and thinking, "Crikey, where are they all?"' Lucinda made a conscious decision to use red for the uniforms of the nurses on Floor 16, 'because it's not a colour you associate with safe hospitals and nurses'.

Simon Pegg prepares to editorialise on the merits of his employer's long game...

Above the Editor (Simon Pegg) is a huge green-screen ceiling onto which The Mill will position the Jagrafess.

Directed by BRIAN GRANT

CAST

Christopher Eccleston *The Doctor*
and Billie Piper *Rose Tyler*
with Bruno Langley *Adam*
Simon Pegg *The Editor*
Tamsin Greig *Nurse*
Christine Adams *Cathica*
Anna Maxwell-Martin *Suki*
Colin Prockter *Head Chef*
Judy Holt *Adam's Mum*

RECORDED AT

Q2 Studio, Newport
Old BT Building, Pendwyllt Road, Coryton

Millennium FX had comparatively little
to do on this story, apart from supplying a
few foam chunks of Jagrafess flesh, the
corpses Cathica finds in the upper Spike
Room (which were old props from other
series) and the little piece of brain tissue
seen in her and Adam's foreheads. The
Mill, though, were very busy on it. 'That
episode was supposed to be quite a light
one for us,' remembers Dave Houghton.
'Instead it's full of matte painting set
extensions – hardly a single set wasn't
extended or given more depth of field,
plus we had to do the little flaps opening
and closing in people's heads.' And then there was
the Jagrafess, a CG creation by The Mill artist JC Lee.
This was built in 3D to be 'as simple as possible for us
to animate. But we got carried away and made it more complicated than we
needed to.'

Suki and Cathica listen intently to the Doctor and Rose's plan to uncover the truth about Satellite Five.

The sound of the Jagrafess was a collaboration between soundsmith
Paul McFadden and actor Nicholas Briggs. 'I was busy on episodes nine
and ten when Nicholas recorded the voice, so I couldn't be there. No
disrespect to him, he did a top job, but it wasn't quite right. I think it was too
similar to the Nestene Consciousness voice and, as they looked similar, I
thought we needed to move away from that. Nick did some growling and I
went in afterwards and added a higher pitched growl, to make it sound a bit
more intelligent, as if it was reacting to Simon Pegg's dialogue. Then I laid
on some teeth gnashing noises and a bit of squelchy noise using wallpaper
paste. The only problem I had with the Jagrafess was that obviously the
dialogue was always going on and we had to keep the creature's voice
right down in the mix. It worked
best when the actors weren't
speaking because then the
Jagrafess cut through loudly,
which was good and shocking.'

Below: Adam Mitchell (Bruno Langley) prepares for the FX shot where he will receive his Chip Type Two upgrade. Below right: The crew wait to film scenes in the Mitchell family's living room.

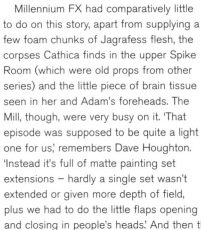

'I apologised to Billie Piper for *The Long Game*,' laughs Russell, 'because her dialogue was a bit naff, just asking questions. And, bless her, she said she was happy because it was less to learn. It's quite shocking, the small amount of Rose material, and I actually trimmed it back further in the editing!' The writer also feels that despite it being intended as a more contained episode to offset the high costs on stories such as *Dalek* and the *Empty Child* two-parter, 'people started to get ambitious, in a way that the budget couldn't always match.' One of the main reasons for this was the monster, the roof-mounted Jagrafess. 'It was meant to be a couple of shots of something much more static, a ceiling made of red, raw meat, that would have growled and screamed, and really to be a less lively Jagrafess. But Brian Grant loved the concept and The Mill wanted to really go for it, so we actually ended up with a very, very beautiful Jagrafess, although it couldn't actually do much.'

Directing the episode was the aforementioned Brian Grant, a director with a long pedigree in fast-paced television, as well as a CV stacked with ground-breaking pop promos for the likes of Kate Bush, Peter Gabriel, Duran Duran and the Thompson Twins. Julie Gardner describes Brian's work on *The Long Game* as 'beautiful and inspired'. After the strenuous first couple of blocks, plus the troubles that *Dalek* had caused in pre-production, everyone was ready for a slightly easier time. 'Maybe we were all tired by that point, and just needed an easy episode. And it was an easy episode, because Brian Grant was so meticulously organised, it kind of went by in the blink of an eye.'

Edward Thomas agrees. 'Brian came at it with that very "pop promo" feel in mind – everything was shot with long lenses with a lot of foreground action, superb visual imagery. His directing was more like a feature film, so we were able to go big on the sets, get a feeling of size and grandeur. I really enjoyed working with Brian. He was a gentleman.'

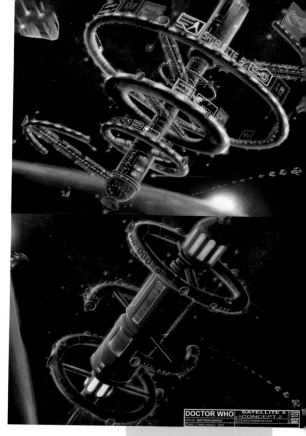

Two concept paintings of Satellite Five by Matthew Savage.

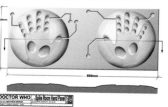

Left: Matthew Savage's detailed look at Floor 500 and (below) 'Engage safety' – concept art for some Spike Room equipment.

1.8 FATHER'S DAY

'I think Russell wanted me to do this particular story because of my *Doctor Who* novels in the *New Adventures* range. He wanted a tear-jerker and he had seen me jerking the tears in the books.' So says Paul Cornell, author of the HUGO-nominated *Father's Day*, the beginnings of which lie in the series bible. 'Despite not knowing which episode I was going to be asked to do, I noted the one that said it was along the lines of "no monsters, Rose sees her Dad die over and over while the Doctor finds out who Pete Tyler was by hearing the stories of those who knew him." I thought, "Oh that's mine, isn't it?" Just as I knew that the Dickens one was bound to be Mark Gatiss's.' Like Mark, Paul developed the brief, feeling that Pete Tyler dying over and over again quickly lost its impact and instead reversed Russell's idea so that Rose stops her dad dying and, when everything begins to go wrong as a result, they all end up in a pub. 'I was trying to keep everything low-budget, so they didn't go outside and there were various versions of the pub going back in time as time became split up. We endlessly talked about whether or not there should be some sort of barrier, to contain the Reapers in a certain area of the pub, but then it became clear the pub idea wasn't going to work.'

It was Russell T Davies's idea to move the story to a church, because it meant there could be a wedding and it was felt that a wedding would provide a set of characters that included loads of friends of the Tyler family. At this point, it was planned that older versions of many of those friends would already have been seen in *Aliens of London*, though that idea eventually came to nothing. But the wedding itself remained, because the Church location provided a big space for the story to take place in, and the 1980s setting was ideal: it meant Rose herself was a baby and would have no recollection of the events. Although the story loses the Doctor halfway through, it was originally going to have even less of him because production was being planned to allow the lead actors a holiday. As it transpired, that luxury became impractical.

Above: Christopher Eccleston rehearses the sequence where the Doctor discovers the TARDIS is an empty shell. Below: The Doctor and Rose hide from a yet-to-be-added Reaper.

'I believed this was going to be one of our most difficult challenges,' remembers production manager Edward Thomas. 'We were told it was set in the 1980s, which isn't a very visually pleasing idea anyway and then they tell you it's all set in a church and you wonder how you can make a church look interesting on Saturday night TV for forty-five minutes, and hold the audience's attention. Then I read the script and realised it could be set in a black box and it wouldn't matter what the visuals looked like because the story is just so emotional and so incredibly written that you know you're going to cry when you watch it.' Despite his reservations, Edward's team found the right church and dressed it up for an eighties-style wedding, all huge pastel bows and potted plants. They also had fun redesigning the Tyler's flat with 1980s wallpaper and colourings. 'We

even took some of Jackie's hairdressing equipment back to the 1980s. It was a nice episode to do after all the sci-fi ones.' Edward suggests that this is a good example of why the order of the episodes is important for everyone on the team. Coming after *Dalek* and *The Long Game* and before the Second World War story and the big Dalek finale, *Father's Day* provided a breather for the Art Department. 'It was a chance for everyone to slow down a little and allow the set-dressing team to run an episode. It was all very cleverly worked out by Russell and Phil Collinson.'

Russell's original series outline had described this episode as 'fx-less', but drama head Jane Tranter wanted lots of monsters throughout the series. So Russell suggested 'little, glimpsed, feral creatures like the things seen in *Dead Like Me*. And we developed it from there.' Paul Cornell describes the monsters in his first draft as 'these little dinosaur things'. Members of the production team recall that Paul wanted to use vampires and, although the writer has no recollection of this, he says that at one point the Reapers were nameless mouths on legs, with no other body parts. As the script was redrafted, he recalls, 'they became like the Grim Reaper, just a sort of cloak with a hand that shot out'. Neill Gorton drew some initial designs, but the production team swiftly rejected the idea of, in Russell's words, 'men walking about in hoods and prosthetics in broad daylight'. That quickly led everyone to the idea that they should fly, which, Paul considers, 'really makes them more dangerous than if they were just running about outside'. So The Mill were briefed on the CGI effects that would be needed to realise what were to become the Reapers.

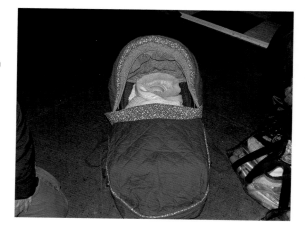

Alex Fort's designs for the Reapers and the finished CG creation by The Mill.

Dave Houghton of The Mill was pleased with the way the Reapers interacted with the live-action shooting although he would have preferred a bit more time to set things up on location. 'I think the Reapers look very good battering the church door, scratching at the wall and eating the priest. I did wish that there had been time on location to shoot a frame with the ground churned up; we put those Reaper claw-marks into the ground during the compositing stage of the CGI instead. I wasn't sure how convincing that was, but no one has ever said they thought it was an effect; they must just think it was real, which is how it should be.'

To create the sound of the Reapers' wings, sound editor Paul McFadden used a rapidly opening and closing umbrella. The screech was a mix of an animal growl from a library CD and Paul giving himself a sore throat! But the most interesting aspect of the sound was provided by the church, and the way director Joe Ahearne shot it. Rather than having microphones following the action, the church enabled sound recordist Ian Richardson to carefully position microphones out of shot. This meant that Joe could get lots of wide shots but the sound could still be used, so not much dubbing was needed. 'The ambience that the church possessed was still there,' Paul recalls, 'which gave it an echo and a depth that's both recognisable and exciting. It's the way feature films are made these days, and this actually felt like a forty-five-minute feature!'

'Although there are monsters in it, it was a more emotional story,' says Joe Ahearne, explaining why he liked *Father's Day* so much. 'The script was quite powerful, and I had to make sure that the emotion and passion was preserved right through the filming.' One of the most important emotional aspects to get right was the character of Pete Tyler, Rose's dad. Paul Cornell agreed with Russell that there would be no mileage in having him secretly be a brilliant man, or a brave undercover SAS-type. The tragedy comes out of him being just an ordinary bloke – so much so that among the production team it became referred to as the 'Daddy's got something in his eye' episode. 'So much of that is down to Shaun Dingwall – he can make the most ordinary man seem to be someone you want to love,' says script editor Helen Raynor. 'It takes real acting talent to make

Left: Pete and Jackie's wedding rehearsal. Below: The couple's signatures in the church's visitors' record.

someone seem so ordinary and yet so important.'

The location was important too – the use of a church was the series' first stab at religious iconography, and there were thoughts that this might raise a few eyebrows. 'I know that Paul's personal take on the series and on life in general is very strongly Christian,' notes Helen. 'The church as a place of sanctuary is a motif that's been with us for as long as we've been telling stories. I find redemption stories incredibly moving, and I think Paul wrote an extraordinary redemption story. That's not exclusively the province of Christianity – it is about having another opportunity but also about sacrifice and realising what you can and you can't have. All of the characters come out of it so changed. Yes, you can lay a sort of Christian template over that story, or take it as a Christian story and lay a redemption template over it, and it works beautifully. We didn't make anything explicitly Christian and I think it would diminish the story if we had, because it's not the job of *Doctor Who* to preach.'

Directed by JOE AHEARNE

CAST

Christopher Eccleston *The Doctor*
and Billie Piper *Rose Tyler*
with Camille Coduri *Jackie Tyler*
Shaun Dingwall *Pete Tyler*
Robert Barton *Registrar*
Christopher Llewellyn *Stuart*
Frank Rozelaar-Green *Sonny*
Natalie Jones *Sarah*
Eirlys Bellin *Bev*
Rhian James *Suzie*
Julie Joyce *Young Rose*
Casey Dyer *Young Mickey*
Colin Galton *Wino*
Ken Teale *Gardener*
Zoë Marie Morris *Teenage Mother*
Richard Glyn Hughes *Driver*
Lee Griffiths *Young Vicar*
Kaeleigh Beddoe *Bridesmaid*
Michael Wilson *Limousine Driver*
Abigail Nichols, Charlotte Nicols *Baby Rose*
Alex Varney, Jay Worley, Joshua Hughes, Gabriella Panfili, Wesley Nelson *Children in Playground*
Monique Ennis *Mickey's Mum*

RECORDED AT

Q2 Studio, Newport
St Paul's Church, Paget Street, Grangetown, Cardiff
Furniture Land Car Park, Cardiff Bay
St Fagans Street, Grangetown
Oakley Place, Grangetown
HTV, Culverhouse Cross
Hoel Trelai, Ely
Hoel Pennar, Ely
Loudoun Square, Butetown, Cardiff
Llanmales St, Grangetown
Grange Gardens, Pentrebane St, Grangetown

VISITORS RECORD

Date	Name	Company	Car

1.9/1.10 THE EMPTY CHILD and THE DOCTOR DANCES

London, the Blitz. It's 21 January 1941, and Captain Jack Harkness, an American volunteer working with the RAF's 133 Squadron, is about to vanish from history and join the Doctor and Rose aboard the TARDIS. Jack was outlined by Russell T Davies in his series bible, but it fell to writer Steven Moffat to flesh him out.

'I was given four hundred provisos,' laughs Steven. 'Jack, or Jax as he was then, had to be a military man, heroic and dashing, good with guns. And, although it wasn't a big part of the brief, he was pansexual. I also knew that he was on board specifically because there was going to be a grand battle in the last episode and they needed to have a soldier around to do the soldiery bits. The idea of him being this kind of intergalactic con-man pretending to be a Time Agent was mine — my story really needed him to be a human not an alien. We already have the Doctor, who is embarrassingly human for an alien, so I made Jack a human from the future. As I knew he was staying on, it made better story sense.

Above left: A supporting artist is fitted with his gas mask for the scenes set inside Albion Hospital. Above: Captain Jack Harkness flies to the rescue on his Schlechter Wolf bomb.

'I thought that any alien intervention couldn't be alien robots stomping around the place because, if the story is about alien robots, it doesn't really matter if it's set in 1940s London or 1970s London. You wouldn't be looking at London, you'd be looking at the robots. So whatever I wrote about had to be stitched into the visuals of the time. It's the Blitz and it's terrible with London being bombed, but Russell felt that there's an iconography and a terribly romantic mood to that period. And of course gas masks look creepy. I saw a little picture of a boy in a gas mask that looked so scary because there is nothing more symptomatic of a world gone wrong than a child in a gas mask.'

Shortly after filming wrapped, Steven flew out on holiday to Australia, but the old problem of under-running cropped up, and Steven awoke in his hotel one morning to find messages from script editor Helen Raynor asking him to get in touch. 'I woke to half a ton of emails and phone messages saying it was two minutes short. This was after I'd taken two minutes out of the last scene to ensure they could film it in time! Russell had made a stab at a scene, which was fine but wasn't quite creepy enough. So I wrote the sequence where the typewriter starts going off by itself. I remember talking with Helen: I asked what I could have and she said, "Just two speaking kids and Nancy. That's all we've got." I asked for a man in a gas mask. "No." "Couldn't Phil stand in a gas mask at the back of the scene?" "No." "Can I have a record player?" "No." "Can I have a typewriter?" "Yes!" It really was down to that. It's got a good kick to it, Florence Hoath is very good as Nancy, and it brings the kids into the second episode. In the original version the kids were all the way through it but only as gas mask people.'

This was James Hawes's *Doctor Who* directing debut, although his *Who* pedigree goes some way back – to an episode of BBC One's *The Mrs Bradley Mysteries*

(script edited by Julie Gardner) which starred the Fifth Doctor, Peter Davison, as the villain and a young unknown called David Tennant. James had been one of the potential directors interviewed for Block One and, when it came to doing a historical adventure, his was the name that Russell, Julie and Phil went for. On top of child actors, freezing January weather and period detail, one of James's biggest problems was making Cardiff look like war-torn London. That would be a problem in London but in Cardiff, which has gone through so much urban renewal in recent years, it proved difficult to find wastelands for the closing scenes, particularly wastelands with no contemporary light pollution – essential for a London in blackout. James's crew ended up on Barry Island – literally on the other side of the road from a long-gone holiday camp where *Doctor Who* was once filmed back in 1987.

'We had to find somewhere that was controllable, because we had massive explosions going off,' explains James. 'The script didn't suggest a railway station, but we found this little cutting with a station in it and a tunnel, which meant we didn't have to worry about sodium glow over the horizon. We had an area that we could keep the locals out of, while safely using special effects explosions to look like bombs falling from the *Luftwaffe*. There were even period railway carriages, which added value to the whole thing. It was problematic for Ernie Vincze, the director of photography, because the terrain made it terribly difficult to move his lights around for different set-ups. He initially solved this by having one huge arc-lamp illuminating the whole area. I didn't like it, it lit up like a football

Ben Austin's sketch for the World War Two bomb.

Directed by JAMES HAWES

CAST

Christopher Eccleston *The Doctor*
and Billie Piper *Rose Tyler*
with John Barrowman *Jack Harkness*
Richard Wilson *Dr Constantine*
Florence Hoath *Nancy*
Albert Valentine *The Child*
Noah Johnson *Voice of The Empty Child*
Cheryl Fergison *Mrs Lloyd*
Damian Samuels *Mr Lloyd*
Robert Hands *Algy*
Joseph Tremain *Jim*
Jordan Murphy *Ernie*
Brandon Miller *Alf*
Luke Perry *Timothy Lloyd*
Martin Hodgson *Jenkins*
Vilma Hollingbury *Mrs Harcourt*
Dian Perry *Computer Voice*
Kate Harvey *Nightclub Singer*
John Martin *Pianist*
Frazer Lawson *Drummer*
Colin Lewis *Double Bass Player*
Eric Clarke *Tenor Sax Player*
Paul Newbolt *Barman*
David Pursey, Laura Flook, Levi Cavelli, Jessica
Grey, Ryan Conway, Chris Conway *Kids*

RECORDED AT

Q2 Studio, Newport
Cardiff Royal Infirmary, Cardiff
Alley off Womanby Street, Cardiff
Headlands School, St Augustines Road, Penarth
RAF St Athan Aircraft Hangar
Vale of Glamorgan Railway Ltd, Plymouth Road,
Barry Island
Bargoed Street, Grangetown
Glamorgan House, College Road, Cardiff

Above left: Director James Hawes and Florence Hoath rehearse the sequence where Nancy is trapped in the house by the Child. Above: The model effects team prepares the barrage balloon which will carry Rose across London.

stadium, but he argued, very reasonably, that this was the only way we'd achieve our night-filming schedule. Then the complaints came in – trains arriving at Barry station couldn't see the platform and cars on the roads couldn't see the roundabout because of our bright light. Then the poor locals complained they couldn't sleep, so we supplied blackout curtains to them. Phil Collinson turned up, saying he'd seen the light several miles away. He decided this light had to go, so we used smaller lights. It was moodier for it – I was delighted.'

Every successful series has that important moment where suddenly the public and the national press know, without a doubt, the success of the show is no flash in the pan. For *Doctor Who*, it was when a four-year-old boy with a gas mask growing out of his face said 'Are you my mummy?' in a voice that was both scary and heart-rending. 'I thought the Empty Child – Albert Valentine – was brilliant,' says James. 'And, bless him, he had to be out there at three in the morning, when any self-respecting little boy would rather be fast asleep. We had to wake him up on a couple of occasions to bring him onto the set, but he hit his mark every time, he took direction, his consistency was fantastic, and it would have taken a lot longer without him. The only problem with Albert was that his voice was so sweet, it was a bit like a Kinder Egg ad, and so we decided to dub someone else over him.'

Left: A design drawing by Matthew Savage for Jack's watch. Right: The watch in action!

In voice work, girls will often play little boys, since their voices sound less masculine, so sound editor Paul McFadden asked Zoë Thorne, who had played the Gelth in *The Unquiet Dead*, to do it. After recording, however, Paul realised that Zoë still sounded too much like a girl and subsequently asked the son of a friend of his to do it. 'Noah Johnson came in, and we spent a whole day doing the lines. I would perform it, and then he would repeat it to me.'

Mike Tucker's model effects team's contributions began with the scenes where Jack and Rose are dancing on the wing of the spaceship. The huge backdrop of the clock face is a photographic blow-up of Mike's model for *Aliens of London*, which Edward Thomas's Art Department dirtied down because Big Ben in 1941 was significantly grimier than it is today. Then there was the barrage balloon that Rose hangs from. Although a majority of the air raid sequence was created by The Mill, the team wanted a real barrage balloon, to get the weight and movement right. When costs proved prohibitive, Mike was asked to create a model. 'We shot it against black, which allowed us to control the flickering firelight underneath it and searchlights going across it. We also shot a series of explosions against black and built a matte model, in this case of a ruined building; basically, it's a building shape, it's got windows cut in it, but it's painted black without surface detail, and it's filmed against black. We set fire to the building, giving us flames coming around the hard edges of windows and chimneys. The Mill took all those flame elements and dropped them into their matte paintings. It's a good example of putting several different techniques – live action, miniatures, real flames, matte paintings and 3D – into the mix.'

Millennium FX found that the gas masks weren't actually all that practical, partly because a real Second World War gas mask has much wider eye glasses, which would have revealed the secret of the eponymous Empty Child, but mostly because they were made from asbestos and are now illegal! With production beginning in late December, Rob Mayor began the search for a suitable replacement: 'How do you find twenty gas masks three days before Christmas? Eventually, Edward Thomas's people had to design one, and we made them from scratch. We took the eye glass out of Russian ones because it was a good shape, then we needed the metal rim. Neill nipped into the supermarket and bought up cans of baked beans and we used the raised rims from the tops and bottoms of those! It was all a bit last minute, but we pulled it out of the bag.'

Top: Jenny Bower's detailed Blitz poster.
Above: John Barrowman and Billie Piper rehearse the sequence when Rose first wakes up on Jack's ship.

1.11 BOOM TOWN

Joe Ahearne was preparing to shoot the Dalek two-parter at the end of the series, when he was asked at short notice if he'd also tackle the intermediary story, *Boom Town*. 'I wasn't initially in the game plan for that one, and it landed in my lap fairly late on. I loved the script, which wasn't as technically challenging as the others: a Slitheen on a toilet in Cardiff and an earthquake. It was more of a character piece, less about monsters. I loved the stuff with the Doctor and Margaret in the restaurant – it was originally going to be called "Dining with Monsters". Having been working on fantastic Dalek and Reaper episodes with wall-to-wall chasing down corridors and laser beams and explosions and monsters killing people for a few months, I was very happy to get something that was just people talking and looking each other in the eyes.'

With so much filming having taken place in and around the city over the previous months, *Boom Town* was the first story to actually make a point of being set in present-day Cardiff, and in the Bay and Millennium Centre specifically. The interest in *Doctor Who* was always going to be large, but filming in such a high-profile location can bring a few problems of its own. 'Wherever we went,' says Joe, 'there were always a few *Doctor Who* fans politely loitering around watching what was going on, but I don't remember there ever being an issue with it. When we were doing *Dalek* at the Millennium Stadium, the police were called a couple of times because of the gunfire – they thought there had been a terrorist attack. *Boom Town* was a lot easier, despite the fact that we used a lot of public locations around Cardiff Bay. We were filming in February, of course; if we had been trying to film in the Bay in June or July, it might have been a lot more difficult. It gets very crowded in the summer.'

Another contemporary local location was Cardiff University, which doubled for the interiors of the Town Hall where Margaret Blaine's offices were based. For Edward Thomas's team, as with *Father's Day*, this was what the production designer terms 'a lock-down episode – where Russell sets it in Cardiff, allowing us to all catch our breath and get as much prep as possible with the incoming director for the double episode at the end, which was very complicated. It allowed us to spend more money on Daleks and spaceships.'

However, the location of the Rift did create problems for Paul McFadden and the sound team as the constant running water down the Millennium Water Tower was very noisy. Most of the sequences shot there had to be redubbed in ADR sessions. And then there's a fully working restaurant to contend with... 'One of the most horrible dialogue scenes for me in the whole series,' Paul recalls, 'was the scene where the Doctor and Margaret Slitheen were having their steak and chips just before the earthquake happened. Joe Ahearne did a fantastic tracking shot of them walking, panning left to right on the scene, but on a wooden floor and all you could hear was the "clunk-

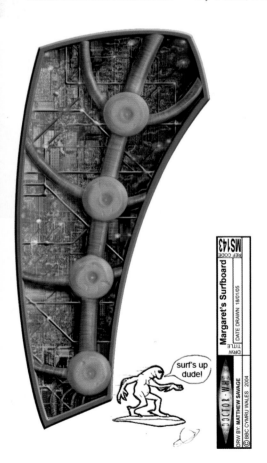

Matthew Savage's detailed concept art for the tribophysical waveform macro-kinetic extrapolator.

Margaret's Surfboard

REF CODE MS143
DATE DRAWN 18/01/05
DRW
DOCTOR · WHO
TITLE
DRW BY MATTHEW SAVAGE 2004
©BBC CYMRU WALES 2004

surf's up dude!

clunk-clunk" of the camera dolly all the way through their dialogue. So I had to load up every single take that was done for that scene, find out where the clunks didn't happen, and remake the whole scene from a variety of different sources. It took a day to do that two-minute scene, just to find all the different takes – a lot of searching and trying to make sure it was all in sync, and the performances were consistent. Then of course we had the earthquake, all the screams and yells, all the glass smashing and the hoverboard effects.'

These scenes feature lots of supporting artists eating, serving and then screaming when the quake strikes. For these scenes, Paul asked the assistant directors to ensure the extras mouthed words and screams, but never actually made any noise. He added these sounds in later, without them going over the unique sounds of breaking glass or falling plaster. 'Sometimes that can be a double-edged sword. There might be someone immediately behind the Doctor speaking silently but you need to know what they're saying so it can be put in later, so we do a lot of lip-reading and figuring out what they were actually saying.'

'I remember when we first discussed *Boom Town*,' says Julie Gardner, 'it was supposed to be utterly effects-less. It was going so well until Russell decided he wanted an earthquake in Cardiff! Beyond that, it's got some of the best work I've ever seen in those exchanges between Christopher Eccleston and Annette Badland's Margaret Slitheen. And it's huge fun because we had Captain Jack and Mickey, all on this mission together. They're blocking off entrances to where the mayor works, so it's a team show; it's one of the few gang shows that we did. Yet underneath that fun is the very dark undercurrent of what it means to execute someone.'

Millennium FX were very happy with this story because, working alongside The Mill, they could create a better Slitheen, using the prosthetic only for extreme close-up shots, and CG for full body shots. Neill Gorton feels that having a lot of rehearsal time helped too, because it meant Paul Kasey, inside the Slitheen costume, could watch Annette

60mm

Finished the same
as a slitheen claw

Left: Filming the café sequence in Cardiff Bay. Top: Matthew Savage's design idea for the Slitheen dart. Above and below: The unpainted model of the Blaidd Drwg nuclear power plant.

Badland's performance as the human Margaret and mimic her head movements and body language. 'The chaos of the first block got forgotten about; it all looked fantastic and, because we'd reached the sixth block, we'd all settled down. Everyone understood why we were asking for the time to get it right, because they saw for themselves how smoothly it was going.'

The eleventh episode had long been a bit of a blank slate, other than always needing to be reasonably budget-conscious. At one point, *Shameless* creator Paul Abbot was in discussions to write an episode and, if he had, it would probably have occupied this slot. Paul's commitments kept him away, and it quickly became a Russell T Davies story. In fact, *Boom Town* was written after *Aliens of London* had been made, making it the last script Russell actually had to plot out. Annette Badland wasn't booked for *Boom Town* when she made *Aliens of London/World War Three*, but Russell spoke to her during the filming to see if she would come back. 'I'd seen the Slitheen and loved them, and said to Phil Collinson that I loved Annette Badland as well and wanted to bring her back. She was, however, booked in for *Cutting It* – being shot in Manchester – and it was a nightmare, getting her. Bless them, both series had to break schedules in half to get her to do it, but of course she loved it. Chris Eccleston had enjoyed working with her as well. So the project came about without any forward planning. Of course, if we had planned it in advance, we probably would never have cast Annette, because we knew she was doing *Cutting It* in the winter – so it was all a big happy accident.'

Another change this time around was having Annette on hand to read

in her lines whenever Margaret was in her Slitheen form, another thing which hadn't happened in the earlier story. 'That's why the Slitheen in *Aliens of London* talk so slowly – the stage manager was off set, shouting all their lines quite slowly, and the lines were dubbed in by the actors later. It would have been better to have had the actors standing next to the person operating the mouth, and that's what we did for *Boom Town* – having Annette there meant that the whole thing came together wonderfully. Lot of lessons had been learnt, and it was all a lot more coordinated.'

The story also sets up the Torchwood scenario that plays such a part in the second series and has since spun off into its own series. 'All the visual imagery that we created, such as the Rift, was reused for *Torchwood*, because *Boom Town* links closely to that series,' notes Edward Thomas. 'That was why we chose to land the TARDIS at the Millennium Water Tower specifically – we had a rough idea of where it was all heading.' Russell T Davies had a very detailed idea, and on *Boom Town* he made a point of asking Edward's team to make notes of certain props and set-ups for future use.

'Although it's the little inconsequential throwaway episode, the whole of *Torchwood* is based on a lot of it,' Russell confirms. 'The look of it and the feel of it, and some of the detail of it – the TARDIS landing where it did – are a huge part of what *Torchwood* is now. The Water Tower is the location for the Torchwood base, because something extra-dimensional once happened there. That's where the Rift once opened. So, weirdly, that little, cheap thrown-away episode has become a whole series in itself. I like that.'

Directed by JOE AHEARNE

CAST
Christopher Eccleston *The Doctor*
and Billie Piper *Rose Tyler*
with Noel Clarke *Mickey*
John Barrowman *Jack Harkness*
Annette Badland *Margaret Blaine*
William Thomas *Mr Cleaver*
Mali Harries *Cathy*
Aled Pedrick *Idris Hopper*
Alan Ruscoe *Slitheen*
Lucy Allen *Tea Lady*
Janice Prydderch Lloyd *Cleaner*

RECORDED AT
Q2 Studio, Newport
Bistro 10, Mermaid Quay, Cardiff Bay
Mermaid Quay, Cardiff Bay
Glamorgan House, College Road, Cardiff
Cardiff Railway Station, Cardiff

The TARDIS prop awaits some action, watched over by Noel Clarke and Billie Piper.

1.12/1.13 BAD WOLF and THE PARTING OF THE WAYS

'My overriding memory of those last two episodes,' says director Joe Ahearne, 'was the cleverness of the concept, especially in *Bad Wolf*, where you've got these iconic reality TV characters, Trinny and Suzannah, Anne Robinson and Davina McCall, to do the voices. I thought that was remarkable. It was very funny and very witty and then, for the last fifteen minutes, it turns a lot darker, leading up to one of the greatest cliffhangers ever. I knew Chris was leaving so I knew a regeneration was coming up, but a lot of people had a script with a dummy scene at the end which had Rose being fatally damaged by the Time Vortex energy she had absorbed, so the cliffhanger of the first series was would Rose live or die? A small core of people knew that wasn't going to be the real ending, and that it was the Doctor who was going to be fatally damaged and have to regenerate.'

Coming to the end of the series meant that time was running out. In other stories, there was always the option to go back and re-shoot a scene, to get extra pick-up shots or special effects. This wasn't the case for Joe here, as the filming had to end on time

Below: The Doctor tries to convince Lynda (with a Y) to join his escape from the Big Brother House.

– by Monday 14 March, all the actors would be out of contract. 'In the last week of the shoot I was running two set-ups at once: filming in the TARDIS with Camille and Billie, and then running across Q2 to another set where they were simultaneously filming the Emperor Dalek bellowing at the Doctor, who had earlier been dealing with a Dalek back on the TARDIS set. That last week was quite intense!'

This time around the script required more than just one Dalek, so Barnaby Edwards, returning to operate the creature, was asked to recommend actors. He suggested Nicholas Pegg who, alongside Barnaby, had operated one in BBC One's 1993 documentary, *30 Years in the TARDIS*, and Nicholas suggested David Hankinson. As an extra bonus, David had to learn to operate his dome, as Nicholas and Barnaby had the only two remote-controlled heads. 'Despite what appears on-screen, there really were only three of us for those episodes,' confirms Barnaby. 'The BBC added another day to the schedule but David was unavailable, so Dan Barratt came up and did a day as a Dalek. David then resumed his role for the rest of the recording. I was the Dalek which the TARDIS materialised around, and also the one which floated in space and disposed of poor Lynda with a Y. Nicholas was given the special claw with the blowtorch in it but, for the actual shots of the flame being used, they whipped him out of the Dalek and put a technician in for health and safety reasons.'

One thing that probably didn't help Joe Ahearne was the need to shoot a regeneration scene that was, for obvious reasons, being kept as secret as possible. 'We did it with minimal crew in about three hours. It was fun, but it was also very strange, because we weren't just doing the regeneration – we also recorded the fake scene where Rose is supposedly dying from Time Vortex damage. The plan was to put that into the edit then replace it at the last moment before broadcast. It would have been great if the episode had gone out in the middle of June and all the press had reviewed the dummy ending. Then people would have been hit between the eyes with this regeneration. But, alas, It's impossible to keep secrets in television nowadays, but everyone tried their best.'

A rehearsal shot of Billie Piper telling the Dalek Emperor that 'everything must come to dust'.

Main filming finished in the middle of March. Then, while he was doing post-production work on the story, Joe and a skeleton crew re-entered Q2's TARDIS set one late-April lunchtime to record the final moments with David Tennant. 'It was odd,' remembers Doctor number ten, 'although, at least I had a couple of lines. Some Doctors have been introduced just lying on the floor and appearing, blinking or sitting up. At least I had a tiny bit of a scene to do, although without Billie – Rose was a strip of gaffer tape stuck on one of the TARDIS columns so I had an eyeline. They showed me the scenes with Chris and Billie in the TARDIS, but not the bit that led up to it, the kiss as he takes all the Vortex energy from her. So I knew what I was immediately following, but not the actual reason for the regeneration. That was probably right, because it's part of the joy of regeneration that the Doctor's slate gets wiped clean.'

Not surprisingly, the regeneration was the last sequence created for Series One. Russell's scripts had two requirements: that it was done with the Doctor standing up, and that it resembled a volcano. The Mill began work on the flame effects surrounding the Doctor in mid May, and completed work on the sequence on 27 May 2005. For the sound effects of this regeneration, sound editor Paul McFadden admits he simply followed The Mill's visual lead. 'We actually recorded a blowtorch and used that, with extra emphasis from myself and my fellow editor Paul Jefferies blowing into our hands.'

The regeneration came at the climax of a two-part story that had to tie up all the ongoing plot strands of the series. An important part of that – and one that no one, least of all Russell T Davies, had predicted – was the whole Bad Wolf theme that ran through the series and culminated in *The Parting of the Ways*. 'It was when articles about the Bad Wolf references started appearing in the broadsheet press that I thought things were out of control. You see, it doesn't stand up to that much scrutiny,' Russell confesses. 'I wrote that kid spray-painting "Bad Wolf" on the side of the TARDIS because it's the sort of thing I do to keep myself entertained when I'm writing a script. I remember wondering why he did it and where those words had come from. I always wanted something slightly linking things together, something for the keen-eyed fans to spot each week, but it had to be a bit insignificant, just a bit of fun. We didn't want a great big arc

Martha Cope is given some last-minute make-up adjustments as the Controller of the Game Station.

because it's Saturday night and your mainstream audience doesn't need to get bogged down in that sort of stuff, it's just too complicated. But it wasn't as subtle as I'd thought, and a lot of people started noticing. That was nice but it was just two random words, really, and I was surprised that it caught on as it did. I still think a lot of people were watching it in blissful ignorance. Of course the fans notice that sort of stuff, that's why they're fans – they like that sort of detail. It's the sort of thing I'd notice too. So it gets talked about online and suddenly we're in this loop where the programme was so

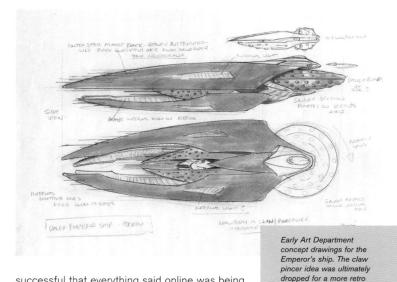

Early Art Department concept drawings for the Emperor's ship. The claw pincer idea was ultimately dropped for a more retro look based on 1960s TV Century 21 *comic strips.*

successful that everything said online was being reported in the newspapers. Stuff that perhaps the whole nation wasn't actually talking about. I don't think much school was cancelled or many factories came to a halt as people debated what Bad Wolf was. It kind of took on a life of its own.'

When Russell had discussed bringing the series back with BBC executive Laura Mackie back in 2001, his initial ideas had included using *The Weakest Link* in a *Doctor Who* story. 'The Anne Droid – how can you not call her the Anne Droid? It was just perfect. In fact, a *Weakest Link* parody was then used in one of the Big Finish audio adventures, because it was just crying out to be done. And so, when this series was commissioned, the idea was top of my list and I always knew that's where it would be heading. When the rights to the Daleks seemed to have fallen through, the worst thing for me was not that poor Robert Shearman was suffering, because I think we could have had any old caged-up monster in the sixth episode. The worst thing was thinking that I was building the series to a great big climax of – what? It probably would have been the Cybermen, to be honest. We would have done something like that. But Daleks give it that great big outer space opera feel. I remember being out in LA, with Julie Gardner and Mal Young,

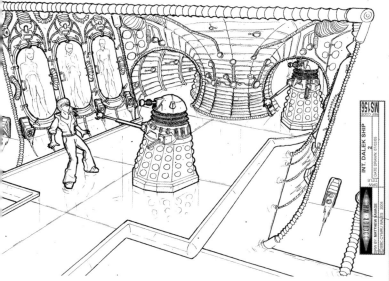

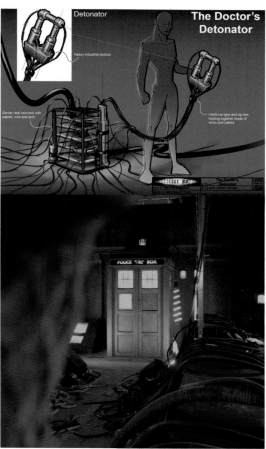

trying to sell the programme early in 2004. We had that great big book by Justin Richards, *Doctor Who: The Legend*. Best calling card you could possibly have — "Look, Hollywood, it's called a legend". Anyway that has a photo of the Emperor Dalek in it, and I told them I was dying to bring him back. And Julie and Mal said, "Ooh, he looks good; let's do that again"'.

With the return of the Emperor Dalek on the cards from the start, work on its design started quite early in production, right back when Dan Walker, Matthew Savage and the rest of the Art Department were experimenting with various Dalek designs for episode six. 'We've got Dalek designs that will never come to fruition on-screen,' explains Edward Thomas, 'but Dan Walker did some incredible Daleks climbing stairs and doing all these wonderful things, and he wanted to take it to the next level, how it keeps important bits encased within the actual shell itself.' Dan Walker looked at examples of military defence such as the Roman army who, when under attack, would crouch beneath their huge shields and tuck them tightly around themselves in a circular formation known as a "turtle manoeuvre". Dan adopted this idea for the Emperor: when it opened up, the shields moved in a similar way to protect the Emperor creature itself. 'We handed those designs over to Mike Tucker,' Edward confirms, 'who then created the model of the Emperor, and did a superb job.'

In Mike's view, Dan Walker's background in industrial and automotive design was crucial to the successful realisation of the Emperor. 'Dan draws things that he knows can actually be built, so we just took his design, and adapted one or two things. The claws underneath it were skinnier, but Edward wanted them to be a bit chunkier to echo the claw that they were adding to the full-size Dalek that would burn through doors on the space station. Because there was so much religious iconography to the Emperor, I had the arms put together, as if praying.' To work out how big it needed to be, Mike's team made the model in scale with the prototypes of the twelve-inch toy Daleks that were released commercially after the first series, so the Emperor stood nearly six feet tall — meaning that on-screen it looked thirty feet high. Mike is very pleased with the shots of the Emperor, not least because, once again, he feels it represents the best work of all the design teams coming together. 'It's got a digital matte painting, courtesy

Top left: An early concept idea by Matthew Savage showing Rose discovering the identity of her captors. Top: Matthew Savage's design for the detonator the Doctor rigs up. Above: The TARDIS returns to the devastation on Floor 500.

Above: Exhauasted crew and actors grab forty winks on a stunt mattress between takes. Right: The Dalek destroyed by Jack aboard the TARDIS.

of Alex Fort, in the background,' Mike says. 'Plus it's got Dave Houghton and Chris Petts's CG 3D Daleks flying around; it's got my miniature; it's got live action in the foreground; and inside it there's an animatronic creature, which is by Neill Gorton.' That creature was actually the prosthetic from *Dalek*. 'We were rather alarmed that it was going to be dropped into a water tank,' says Neill. 'Being made of silicone, the creature wouldn't be harmed, but its animatronics would rust very quickly and seize up.'

The Millennium FX team also created the three droids for the story. 'They had to look very robotic,' says Neill. 'Nobody wanted them to look like someone in a suit, so they were almost cartoon-y sorts of robot. The Anne-Droid was the hardest, because we couldn't get actor Alan Ruscoe for a fitting until the night before. He had a problem with the neck piece and the head join, which were restricting his circulation, so they trimmed a chunk out of the back on set, never what you want on the day of recording. The Trine-E and Zu-Zana droids went better. It was the last day of the shoot: we bolted Alan and Paul in, had a good day of shooting, blew them up and then went to the wrap party.'

Below: Alan Ruscoe, John Barrowman and Paul Kasey on the What Not To Wear *studio set. Below right: David Hankinson, Barnaby Edwards and Nicholas Pegg pose beside their carriages!*

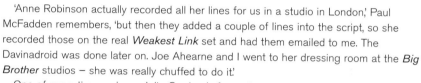

'Anne Robinson actually recorded all her lines for us in a studio in London,' Paul McFadden remembers, 'but then they added a couple of lines into the script, so she recorded those on the real *Weakest Link* set and had them emailed to me. The Davinadroid was done later on. Joe Ahearne and I went to her dressing room at the *Big Brother* studios – she was really chuffed to do it.'

One of executive producer Julie Gardner's favourite scenes of the first series was the Doctor as a hologram inside the TARDIS, as he sent Rose back to Earth. 'That final moment where he turns to her and says, "Have a fantastic life." I think that moment is at the heart of the whole series, full of emotion, passion, optimism and life, even when he's facing certain annihilation. I think it's wonderful storytelling.'

Once back on Earth, Rose's efforts to return to the Game Station would involve a big yellow truck being driven to the scene by her mother. Since Camille Coduri, playing Jackie, doesn't have an HGV licence, some innovative means were developed to allow 'her' to steer the vehicle into shot. 'I sat on this bloke's lap,' hoots Camille. 'Poor bloke, he was sweating like mad. First we tried it with him sitting in the seat and me in front of him so he did the pedals and gears and I steered. Not very well. At one point his hand suddenly came out and turned us right because I was going to crash us into this vehicle parked on the road.' After all that, it turned out that the driver sitting underneath Camille would be visible on-screen. 'So they covered him in a balaclava and got him to wear a black thing from Costume. He was really nervous every time I climbed into the cabin and climbed over him. But he was really professional, despite this great big blonde sitting on his lap.'

The next thing the viewers saw of Rose, she had been transformed by Vortex energy from the heart of the TARDIS. Although much of this transformation would be effected by The Mill, Davy Jones's make-up team was asked to 'do something unearthly' to give The Mill a starting point. 'We glammed her up like a huge big Hollywood eighties thing – I've never seen so much root lift on a girl,' remembers Davy. 'Because they were going to use a wind machine, it had to be very strong so it wouldn't get blown all over the place.'

But let's give the last word to the man who is ultimately responsible for the success of that first series of *Doctor Who*, the Ninth Doctor, Christopher Eccleston. '*Doctor Who* was my life for eight months. I loved playing him, and taking part in the basic essence and message of the series which is, it's a short life, seize it, and live it as fully as you can. Care for others. Be respectful of all other life forms, regardless of colour or creed. To be part of that was fantastic.'

Series Two

2.X THE CHRISTMAS INVASION

David Tennant's official debut came in *The Christmas Invasion* on Christmas Day, but over ten million viewers saw him in action a little sooner than that. *Doctor Who* has often played a big part in the BBC's annual *Children in Need* telethon, most notably in 1993 for the show's thirtieth anniversary, when a special story was created, made in 3D, and filmed with members of the BBC's other flagship programme, *EastEnders*. But that was not really intended as a real part of the *Doctor Who* mythology. This time around, Julie Gardner and Russell T Davies were keen not to do a 'sketch' – they wanted to contribute something special and unique.

Russell made some very important demands on the *Children in Need* producers – there would be no audience reaction for the duration of the scene, no rolling captions thanking Emma from Swindon for sitting in a bath full of baked beans, and, despite their pleas, no Pudsey Bear on the TARDIS console. Once this was all agreed, the scene was written and prepped. Filming was already under way on the third block of the new series, but director Graeme Harper was able to spare his two leads for one day and Euros Lyn was asked to direct an eight-minute piece set in the TARDIS. Julie had suggested that it should occur straight after the regeneration in *The Parting of the Ways*, so the scene acted as a prologue for the start of *The Christmas Invasion*. It starred just David Tennant and Billie Piper who, like everyone involved, gave their services for free.

Rose (Billie Piper) and a post-regenerative Doctor (David Tennant) pose outside the TARDIS.

'I was really pleased because, when you're asked to do little specials or little extra things, it's a nice affirmation that people think you're doing a good job,' says Euros Lyn. 'It was one set, just a couple of hours in a morning with a very well-written scene. Because it would now form David's first outing as the Doctor, it was bound to attract a lot of attention. When I first read it, it just seemed to be a standard two-handed dialogue scene without anything like an event going on – just two people discussing that he'd changed. But the more I read it, the more I realised that the subject of that conversation *was* the event. Yes, it was just two people talking but what they were talking about was something so special and important. Then I understood just how monumental this piece was going to be.'

'It was kind of weird getting back in the leather jacket again,' says David Tennant, who had not had to wear the Ninth Doctor's costume since filming for *The Christmas Invasion* during the summer. 'Apart from that, it was just coming to work, like any other day. There was an awareness that this was going to be the first bit to go out but by that stage Billie and I were very comfortable with each other, although I remember both of us expressing doubts that it was a good idea, whether it diffused the bigness of the moment that was *The Christmas Invasion* as the beginning for the Tenth Doctor; of course we were both proved completely wrong because it worked well. It was a nice little teaser for what was to come.'

The *Children in Need* scene went out on BBC One a few minutes after nine o'clock on Friday 18 November 2005. Five weeks later, David Tennant's first proper episode

was the sixty-minute Christmas special, transmitted on the most important day of the television year, Christmas Day, as the flagship of the BBC's schedules. Given the task of bringing Russell T Davies's latest script to life was James Hawes, who had directed Steven Moffat's two-part story *The Empty Child* and *The Doctor Dances* to huge acclaim for Series One. The story had started life, however, Christmas-less. Before the Christmas special was commissioned, Russell's initial idea for the story that would introduce the Tenth Doctor to the audience at the start of Series Two had been a straightforward forty-five-minutes of swashbuckling adventure against an alien invasion of Earth by the Sycorax.

'It took me a while to realise the BBC wanted fourteen episodes out of us,' Russell admits. 'I'd presumed it was going to be Christmas then a series of twelve. So that was hard for the hardest-working team in the world, but Phil juggled schedules. That's partly why Series Two included *Love & Monsters*, which was quite Doctor and Rose-less – that's the inheritance of *The Christmas Invasion*, and will always be the case; with Christmas specials we'll always have to factor that sort of story into each series now.'

When James Hawes saw the script for *The Christmas Invasion*, he had some initial reservations: 'I had considerable doubts about the length of time the Doctor was unconscious for. But what Russell had done brilliantly was left you waiting for the Doctor for so long that, when he woke up, it was so exciting and you were so willing to welcome him that somehow the transition no longer mattered. With due respect to Christopher Eccleston, by the time the Doctor and the Sycorax leader were having the sword fight, David *was* the Doctor. There were lines in that final scene in the snow, where Rose said, "I miss him," and David's Doctor said, "So do I," but we cut those in the final edit.'

The Doctor emerges from the TARDIS to confront the Sycorax Leader. The green screen behind him will allow The Mill to add the TARDIS interior later.

For Russell, *The Christmas Invasion* was a bit of a dream come true: 'I've always wanted to write a Christmas story, all my life. I seriously love them, and I think they should be Christmassy – there's nothing worse than going abroad to the Costa Brava and things like that.'

Everyone was agreed that this was a Christmas special that was going to *look* special. 'I didn't want that sort of slightly apologetic, tawdry British Christmas that you often see on television,' say James. 'We wanted it to be glitzy. Sod whether that was realistic or naturalistic or not. It needed to be wholeheartedly British. UNIT HQ was supposed to be in a very stylish but anonymous building outside the city somewhere but I suggested we might bury it under the Tower of London, as a British icon. Russell went for that idea and, phenomenally, the Tower of London were willing to give us permission to do that. It's a testament to the success of Series One that they had no doubt about how useful that would be for their public relations – to be seen on the TV screens on Christmas Day, a great piece of PR for the Palace. I often wonder if people are turning up and asking to see where UNIT is.'

'Russell absolutely understood what a Christmas special should be,' explains Julie Gardner. 'It's very brave, because the Doctor's off-screen for so long, but we needed to re-establish why he's important to the world, and to Rose. To balance that, there's that huge speech the Doctor has when he steps out of the TARDIS and we remember why we love him. In that last ten minutes you have everything – a sword fight on the wing of a spaceship over London; a terrible, deeply upsetting moment with the Prime Minister, where you reassess the character; the Doctor choosing his clothes to a very cheery song composed by Murray Gold, followed by Christmas lunch; and Rose and the Doctor in what should be snow but is actually Sycorax ash, which is quite horrible, but so brilliant because you've gone through this trauma and actually earned your Christmas.'

The cheery 'Song for Ten' was composed, as always, by Murray Gold. 'Some Phil Spector music had been used as a guide track on the edited episode. The minute I heard that, I realised they'd have to spend more to clear the rights for that than they would

Half a flying TARDIS suspended across the Powell Estate.

spend on the entire music budget, so it had to go. I asked James Hawes if it had been cleared and he said it hadn't been. I know how these things get costed: Phil Spector, anything American, in a drama for worldwide DVD distribution would have been exorbitant. I did a film, *Mojo*, where the producers wanted to use about ten seconds of "Jailhouse Rock" by Elvis Presley, which I think was priced at about thirty thousand pounds. I've always liked Phil Spector, so I thought I'd do a new song in that style. I already had a notebook full of lyrics. I made sure that the line "You followed your star, cos that's what you are" led into the moment when David Tennant enters the Tyler flat and looks across at Billie Piper. And then she smiles at him, on the line "I've had a merry time with you". I wrote the rest of the lyrics and recorded it with a singer called Tim Phillips – we worked very quickly, and I sent it off, assuming that it wouldn't make the final cut. I was delighted that they kept it in and that it's become to David Tennant what the "Bad Wolf" theme was to Christopher Eccleston.'

The last time he'd directed *Doctor Who*, James Hawes had filmed in the freezing cold of Barry Island at night, whereas *The Christmas Invasion* was filmed in the middle of summer, six months before the festive season it was depicting, which ought to have brought in a whole host of additional problems. Yet, in typically British fashion, it didn't. 'We came to London for the start of the shoot, from late July into the beginning of August, and it was like November. It got dark at about four o'clock, it rained and rained. We were supposed to be having snow and of course we got rain falling on snow. All around us there were green trees, and we had to choose locations to avoid seeing those. We couldn't shoot all the exteriors at the Tower of London when we wanted to, because we were waiting for the leaves to come off the trees. Then we had the mildest ever autumn and the leaves weren't falling off! The Mill had to put in bare trees where previously there had been trees with leaves on. And if you watch carefully you will see there are several places where you can clearly see green trees, especially around the Powell estate, because I couldn't avoid them.'

Creating the Sycorax ship was a case of serendipity as during the tone

Below left: The Sycorax Leader has his helmet fitted. Below centre: On the Sycorax spaceship. Below right: James Hawes directs a Robot Santa.

Directed by JAMES HAWES

CAST

David Tennant *The Doctor*
and Billie Piper *Rose Tyler*
with Camille Coduri *Jackie Tyler*
Noel Clarke *Mickey Smith*
Penelope Wilton *Harriet Jones*
Daniel Evans *Danny Llewelyn*
Adam Garcia *Alex*
Sean Gilder *Sycorax Leader*
Chu Omambala *Major Blake*
Anita Briem *Sally*
Sian McDowall *Sandra*
Paul Anderson *Jason*
Cathy Murphy *Mum*
Sean Carlsen *Policeman*
Jason Mohammed *Newsreader 1*
Sagar Arya *Newsreader 2*
Lachele Carl *Newsreader 3*
Johnie Cross *Luke Parsons*
Ian Hilditch *Geoffrey Baxter*
Kristian Hicks *Major*
Julia Bisby *Army Captain*
Anthony Molton *PC*
Dean Forster, Tony Gallagher, Richard Pullen, Andrew Mitchel, Alex Bennett, Alex Donald, Simon Lee *Robot Santas*
Lee Griffiths, Lloyd Everitt, Jamie Jones, Alun Cowles, Mike Freeman, Martin Thorne, Jonathan Thomas, Richard Harris, Greg Bennett, Geraint Jones, Paul Blackwell, Nick Gwyn Evans, Phil Kirk, Ian Richardson, Mark Griffiths, Andrew Mitchel, Paul Zeph Gould *Sycorax Warriors*

RECORDED AT

Q2 Studio, Newport
Tredegar House & Park, Newport
Wallis House, Great West Road, Brentford
Brandon Estate, Kennington, London
Tower of London, London
Loudoun Square, Butetown, Cardiff
HTV Studios, Culverhouse Cross, Cardiff
Baltic House, James Street, Cardiff Bay
British Gas Building, Churchill Way, Cardiff
The Hayes, Cardiff
Broadstairs Road, Leckwith (Suburban Street)
Clearwell Caves, nr Coleford, Gloucestershire
Brian Cox Motor Engineering, Elwood
Barry Docks, Atlantic Way, Barry
Millennium Stadium, Westgate Street, Cardiff
C2 News Studio, BBC Broadcasting House, Llandaff, Cardiff

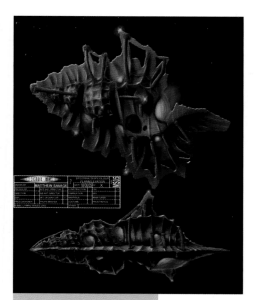

An early concept painting of a possible Sycorax ship by Matthew Savage.

meetings for this episode, lots of discussions went on between The Mill and the Art Department as to how to do it. At one point it was going to be industrial and metallic, but this was quickly changed to an organic feel, suggesting that the craft was more grown than constructed. 'Even though we hadn't designed the Sycorax by then, I knew that they were going to be bone-like,' recalls Edward Thomas, 'and I came up with the idea that it was a lump of molten rock. probably a meteorite, that was flying through space. The colour schemes then came from the location we'd chosen to film in, Clearwell Caves.'

Model unit supervisor Mike Tucker was asked back for the early stages of Series Two, ostensibly to see whether the shattering glass of London's Gherkin would work best as a model. 'I left that meeting thinking how marvellous it was that I'd be blowing up another London landmark but then I started looking at it and it's a spiral; it's all glass. What happens when the glass is gone? What's left? How big does it need to be for that glass to actually hold up? And as I started thinking it through, it was painfully apparent that there was no way on Earth we were ever going to be able to build a big enough model of the Gherkin on a TV budget to realistically blow out all the windows. So, we looked briefly at doing just a section of it, but James pointed out that the shot is far enough back to see the whole Gherkin. So we had to give that one to The Mill.' One piece that did require a model from Mike was the moment that the Sycorax ship passes above the Powell Estate and all the windows blow out. The majority of practical effects are handled by Any Effects, but James Hawes wanted to see more than just a couple of windows

Another of Matthew Savage's paintings, this time showing where the TARDIS materialises inside the Sycorax spaceship.

shatter – he wanted to see every window go. Obviously the residents of the real Brandon Estate in North Peckham were unlikely to be overly positive about losing every window in the block, so Mike made a one-sixth scale model of the top eight storeys. 'We included washing, Christmas decorations, things in the balcony. Edward sent us photographs of how they'd dressed the actual location, so we knew that it all had tinsel and tacky Christmas decorations.'

The Tenth Doctor's first story set up a thread that would run throughout Series Two, with the first mention of the Torchwood Institute by Prime Minister Harriet Jones. In Series One, the MP for Flydale North had been a heroic figure you wanted to see in charge, but here it is clear that the weight of leadership has taken a toll on her, and she approves the use of Torchwood to wipe out the Sycorax. Julie Gardner loves that twist in Russell's characters but remembers that Phil Collinson was alarmed and upset because he had so loved Harriet in *Aliens of London*. For Julie, 'This is what I imagine happens if you're Harriet Jones and you suddenly have all this responsibility. I don't believe she makes the wrong decision, but she doesn't necessarily make the

right decision – there's no simple answer, it's all shades of grey. I think the Doctor's been showing off a bit and he planted that seed in her head by talking about how many aliens there are out there and that the world is getting noticed. It's a complicated moment. In the end, I side with the Doctor, but you understand why she's done it. And the Doctor does take revenge in a way that I don't think the Ninth Doctor would have. That's a great moment in the Tenth Doctor's first story.'

For the show's new star, reading the script for the first time was a slightly peculiar experience. 'By page forty, I still hadn't done very much,' David points out. 'I thought that was bold, keeping the main character in a coma for most of it. Then he wakes up and you have five pages of sparkling Russell T Davies dialogue, and it works brilliantly. Obviously, it's daunting because when you wake up you have to justify the fact that you've been kept off-screen all this time by making an impact. So from an acting point of view that was the challenge. But it's a great script; it's got some fantastic gags in it; a wonderful kind of heroic swagger; and it has a slightly off-the-wall, mercurial anarchy, which I think is what defines what's extraordinary about the Doctor. I don't do very much, then I wake up. I talk for five pages; I press the button that nobody's allowed to press; I break the monster's staff; I haul away his whip. And then, just to top it all off, I have a sword fight with him on the wing of a spaceship – my hand is cut off; I grow it back, and then bring down the Prime Minister of Great Britain – all within ten minutes. You can't really ask for a better entrance than that.'

2.1 NEW EARTH

The first block of Series One had had some teething problems, and problems of a different kind cropped up in the first production block of Series Two, which comprised *The Christmas Invasion*, *School Reunion* and *New Earth*. The addition of the Christmas special put extra pressure on everyone. No matter how adept Phil Collinson was at juggling finances, even he couldn't invent extra weeks or months in which things could be shot – it was quickly realised that at least two blocks would have to be filmed simultaneously later in the series. James Hawes was already sensing a great deal of that pressure during the first block. Although it was recorded after *The Christmas Invasion* and *School Reunion*, it was on *New Earth* that he had the biggest hiccups.

'*New Earth* was a nightmare, honestly, where the ambition of the script burst the seams of the budget and the schedule. My first assistant director and I sat down with producer Phil Collinson and explained that there were days when we would not achieve everything that was scheduled. The Art Department said the same thing. The Millennium Centre was being used as the hospital atrium, which had been written for that specific location, but we could only have it for one day. There was no way we were going to get everything we needed – because of the effects, because of the make-up, because of the spaces we needed to light. Of all the episodes I've done, *New Earth* is by far my least favourite, although I do think that Billie and David's performances are stunning and the final scene with Zoë Wanamaker is incredibly moving.'

David Tennant also felt that the production was a tad more challenging than most. '*The Christmas Invasion* had overshot, *School Reunion* had overshot a bit too, so by the time we got to *New Earth* we were chasing our tails. So *New Earth* to me is just images of people running around Q2, screaming, "What are we going to shoot next?" It was a very complicated one to shoot, and a very fractured shoot, and Billie and I both felt we got a bit lost. We were still doing pick-up shots from *New Earth* while Graeme Harper was directing the Cybermen episodes at Christmas; James Hawes was still trailing back up to Cardiff and setting up some white medical screens at one end of the studio, and we'd race down from the Cybermen shoot and do scenes in the hospital. There are drop-in shots of Billie and me from the Duke of Manhattan scenes that were shot four months after the main scene – it was such a jigsaw to finally get it all done. I think James would concede that it was only when he started editing it together that we all got what it was really about. You can track my hair getting longer and shorter through that episode.'

The length of Rose's hair was also an issue, since Billie Piper had had her hair cut after Series One, not realising that *The Christmas Invasion* would follow straight on from *The Parting of the Ways*. For the Christmas special – and, later, for the *Children in Need* scene – she was given hair extensions. For *New Earth*, this was no longer a continuity problem, until it was realised that Zoë Wanamaker's availability meant that Cassandra's sole physical scene would have to be filmed in the middle of production of *The Christmas Invasion*. 'And that,' reveals Russell, 'is why Rose suddenly has her hair up in the nightclub – to hide the Christmas hair extensions!'

There were more problems for James Hawes on location at the Gower Penninsula. When he and his team had done the recce, it was bathed in glorious summer sunshine.

Top: Billie Piper rehearses in the TARDIS doorway at the start of New Earth.
Above: The Tenth Doctor looks angrily down on the thousands of humans being grown in the Intensive Care Unit on New Earth.

Bad weather had then delayed the start of filming there, so the cast and crew
were already a few days late when they finally turned up to film. The weather was
still absolutely terrible, but they had to shoot before their allotted schedule ran out
completely. 'It was so bad that, as they tried to build the TARDIS on the cliff top, they
were having to hold it down to prevent it being blown off,' James explains. 'In the end,
we had to lie the actors down, so we'd have any chance of recording the sound. There's
an out-take of David trying to talk to Billie, and all he could see was this face of hair. He
just laughed because she looked like the Dulux dog. As if that wasn't bad enough, at
about 3.30 night came in along with – I'm not exaggerating – a force eight or nine gale.
With rain. The director of photography, Ernie Vincze, did a fantastic job with a huge light,
which made it look like day.

'The next day, I got a phone call telling me that
they had changed the tapes after lunch, and nothing
was recorded. Everything from this really poignant
moment where the Doctor and Rose come out of
the TARDIS, they look at each other and she says
how much she loves travelling with him, all shot in
beautiful close-ups – all lost. There was a sequence
from the end of the episode where the Doctor and
Rose take Chip, now inhabited by Cassandra, out
of the hospital. They're outside, looking back at
the hospital, the sun's setting over New Earth; the
Doctor makes the decision to take Chip/Cassandra
to Cassandra in the past, and they walk off to the
TARDIS – none of that recorded. I assumed we'd
go back and redo it but it was too difficult to set
it up again: we'd have had to re-book the artists
and David and Billie's shooting schedule was so
hectic that getting them for another day was almost
impossible. So it was decided we could do without
the scene. As we drove away, in the pouring rain,

Left: The Face of Boe gets a look at the ceiling. Below: Matthew Savage's concept sketch of the Doctor wearing the cures.

Directed by JAMES HAWES

CAST

David Tennant *The Doctor*
and Billie Piper *Rose Tyler*
with Camille Coduri *Jackie Tyler*
Noel Clarke *Mickey Smith*
Zoë Wanamaker *Cassandra*
Sean Gallagher *Chip*
Dona Croll *Matron Casp*
Adjoa Andoh *Sister Jatt*
Anna Hope *Novice Hame*
Michael Fitzgerald *Duke of Manhattan*
Lucy Robinson *Frau Clovis*
Simon Ludders *Patient*
Struan Rodger *Voice of Boe*
Claire Saddler *Red Lady*
Mal Kearney *White Man*
Stuart Ashman *Butler*
Helen Irving *Posh Mum*
Dave Bremner *Posh Dad*
Liza Meggitt, Nia Collier, Hazel Beauchamp, Jade Kenning, Natalie Cuzner *Cat Nuns*
Dani Biernat, Dave Wong, Gareth Somers *NNYPD Cops*
Michael Tudor, Jitka Charyparova *Paramedics*

RECORDED AT

Q2 Studio, Newport
Bar Orient, Mermaid Quay, Cardiff Bay
Loudoun Square, Butetown, Cardiff
HTV Studios, Culverhouse Cross, Cardiff
Millennium Centre, Cardiff
The Paper Mill, Sanatorium Road, Cardiff
Tredegar House, Newport
Worm's Head, Rhossili, Gower

Billie said to me, "Oh my god, that was your last day, wasn't it?" And it felt like the most incredible anti-climax. It was a real soggy, gloomy, glum ending to the shoot.'

One aspect that James Hawes *was* immensely pleased with was the work put in by Millennium FX. 'The cat-nuns are bewitching to look at – you just can't take your eyes off those characters. I thought the scenes with Anna Hope as the novice looking after the Face of Boe were the strongest scenes in the episode; I just wanted more of her and the legend of Boe and the Doctor.'

'The cat-nuns were straightforward,' says Rob Mayor of Millennium FX, 'because James cast people who had extremely good eyes and good bone structure so you could picture them as cats beforehand. We didn't want to use contact lenses, just because you can't anchor lenses in the eye, they tend to twist around, so you'll have one wonky eye. Also the cats' faces were pieces of foam with actual hair glued onto them, and sometimes one or two bits can come loose. It would have been extremely uncomfortable if that had got into an actor's eye with a contact lens, so we couldn't risk it. We requested that they should not cast people with large noses, because there is that slope to a cat's face, so it was easier to hide smaller-shaped noses within the cat mask.'

For Louise Page, the costume design work was a nice challenge after Sycorax robes and the modernity of both *The Christmas Invasion* and *School Reunion*. 'Cassandra had obviously been this very glamorous woman and they wanted her to be in a gold or silver dress that would stand out. I thought it should have a 1930s glamorous Hollywood star feel to it. In the script, the Sisters of Plenitude were described as cat nurses and right from the beginning I told Russell that I saw them as nuns – I think it was because one of them was called Novice Hame. Russell said that, much as he loved big headdresses, he was worried they might distract people too much. The headdresses are made out of a paper-like fabric, heavily starched, all white and cream. I found some fantastic pebble necklaces in a high-street shop, and I used them like a rosary.'

The city of New New York and the hospital exterior were both matte paintings by Alex Fort, digitally added to James Hawes's shots at the Gower Peninsula. 'Then we built the cars as 3D models and animated them as if there were roads in the air,' explains The Mill's Dave Houghton. 'The difficulty there was making that look real – it is quite stylised. The basic elements are not complicated but the backgrounds we were shooting against don't naturally lend themselves to far-off matte paintings of buildings. That gives it a comic-book feel, we're in a natural environment and we're looking at an unnatural, man-made environment.'

Edward Thomas's team were hard at work at all the locations, but the first thing that needed designing was the exterior of the hospital, so that The Mill could begin their work on it. 'Russell's concern when we designed it was that it had to look as if it would get planning permission. That's a wise comment, because some science fiction designs just look ridiculous. This had to feel as if it had been built to withstand the weather and was part of the landscape. We used the Millennium Centre in Cardiff for the hospital reception with its timber and steelwork. We then built the ward set and the lifts in the studio with all those elements in mind, so hopefully there's a fluid flow right through the episode, and people will think it was all shot in one place.'

There was a lot of discussion between the executive producers and the BBC executives over the transmission order at the start of this new series: should the opening episode be *New Earth* or *Tooth and Claw*? 'At the beginning of *Tooth and Claw*,' says Russell, 'Rose is just changing her clothes. I added that detail, so that we would have the option of using *New Earth*'s pre-title sequence of Jackie and Mickey watching Rose get aboard the TARDIS bolted on to the front of *Tooth and Claw*. Jane Tranter decided in the end that *New Earth* was more fun, a livelier opening for the new Doctor. When you look at it now, it's daft to think we even considered that, because in *New Earth* the Doctor's talking about being new: it's a new Earth, it's a new Doctor, it's New New York. It all just makes sense like that.'

2.2 TOOTH AND CLAW

After a contemporary Christmas in SE15 and the far future on an alien world, it seemed right to dip back into Earth's history, in another of Russell T Davies's 'celebrity historicals', this time in the shape of the austere Queen Victoria, mourning the death of her beloved Albert whilst traversing the Highlands of Scotland.

'It was an irresistible idea really – Queen Victoria and a werewolf. Marvellous', is Russell's take on it. 'It was quite a late commission and it wasn't meant to be mine. I was swapping stories about and indeed Series Two existed without *Tooth and Claw* for quite a while. Because of *The Christmas Invasion* and the powers-that-be asking for another fourteen not thirteen episodes, we needed a new story. Another writer, a great writer in fact, started it off, but we couldn't get it to work. He very graciously pulled out, but by then it was too late to commission anyone else, so I picked it up and wrote it quite quickly. I decided to call the house Torchwood and started to include all that sort of stuff in it...'

'I read the script and, I must admit, I was dancing round my kitchen', laughs Euros Lyn, given the job of directing this story. 'I didn't have a single note on it, it was so perfectly paced. Every single event, every single prop, every single location is significant and pays off in some way at the end. Russell's most magnificently structured script.'

For Euros though, it wasn't just the script which excited him, but the opportunity to work with new Doctor David Tennant for the first time – although Euros also directed the *Children in Need* special, that was made a while after *Tooth and Claw*. 'The way David has fun with his language is just astonishing. And surprising. It was like working on a different show with a different actor, and yet the adventures he has are the same adventures. I tried to find some of the soulfulness that Christopher Eccleston had, and David can do it, but it's not where his instinct takes him. There's a tiny moment in *Tooth and Claw*, which I'm not sure anyone's ever noticed, but I notice it every time with pride: when Queen Victoria's talking about her grief for Albert, and we keep cutting back to the Doctor's reaction, and then she finishes off, saying something about waiting for an answer, which never comes. The camera goes to the Doctor, and there's David's reaction, where you think he's in his own

Josh Green stood in for the werewolf during filming of Tooth and Claw.

grief in that moment. That was something that Christopher had in his performance which David carried over.'

David Tennant reckons this was because the script had 'a wonderful sense of humour and brio and joy to it as only Russell can really do. I love the Doctor and Rose's relationship in that because they start to fall in love with each other again, as Rose begins to trust the new bloke, and I love the way that Russell pushes that so that they're almost enjoying themselves too much. I think it's quite nice that the Doctor and Rose are actually being flippant and Queen Victoria reprimands them for that in no small measure.'

One of the most striking things about *Tooth and Claw* was that Euros moved away from any hint of 'standard' directing styles and instead used a lot of low angles, hand-held cameras and at the start, memorably, the almost bullet-time effect of the monks beginning their fight with the staff of Torchwood House.

'Russell wrote something very impressionistic like, "Wailing guitars, flashing fighting". I took that style and expanded it to cover the whole episode. Writing a fight sequence involving monks who can do kung-fu and fly allows you to go to places stylistically that you couldn't for, say, the swordfight on the wing of the Sycorax ship. The Sycorax Leader couldn't fly over the Doctor, because that's not what he does, so the style just grows out of the content of the scene.'

Another important aspect of the story, not just because of its use here but because of the influence it would cast over the whole second series, was Torchwood House, the imposing Scottish home of Sir Robert MacLeish, ultimately taken over by Victoria. Edward Thomas had an idea of exactly where to shoot that the moment he saw the script. 'I remember as a child going to Craig-y-Nos castle in the Swansea Valley built by Adelina Patti, a renowned nineteenth-century soprano who sang regularly for Queen Victoria for twenty-five years. We fell in love with it because it was rugged enough, and rustic and we thought it was somewhere Queen Victoria wouldn't really want to go and spend the night but in a state of emergency she has to. It's cold and it's damp, and we actually used some of its interiors as well as building sets back at Q2. In fact, we went to five different locations to get the interiors, because of various staircase and tunnel elements. So that episode was a real jigsaw to put together.'

The impressive telescope at Torchwood House was a prop designed by Peter McKinstry. For on-screen views through the telescope, Mike Tucker and his team actually created a model of the telescope, which the camera could then shoot through. 'It was described as a CSI-style shot inside the telescope, as the light beam shoots down, past little reflectors and lenses and mirrors and out the other end. Nick Kool built an eight-foot-long section of telescope, riveted and made to look like brass and wood, similar to what Peter McKinstry had designed, but big enough to be able to get a film camera down the middle of it. It was fitted with mirrors and little crystals that glowed on cue. In the final show, however, those views were all cut out and they just used a static shot. That was the first thing we did for *Doctor Who* as the Model Unit rather than as the now-defunct BBC effects team.'

For Louise Page, the story threw up a number of unusual costume requirements. Firstly, she needed to provide a white leotard for the actor representing the werewolf, onto which she drew all the creature's muscles. This was a live-action guide for The Mill, who later digitally painted the werewolf over what had been filmed. Then there were the outfits for the Shaolin-like monks, which Euros asked to be the same red as Louise's

Top: Tom Smith awaits the cue to begin his transformation scene. Above: Shaun Williams's storyboards for the werewolf's emergence.

Directed by EUROS LYN

CAST

David Tennant *The Doctor*
and Billie Piper *Rose Tyler*
with Pauline Collins *Queen Victoria*
Ian Hanmore *Father Angelo*
Michelle Duncan *Lady Isobel*
Derek Riddell *Sir Robert*
Jamie Sives *Captain Reynolds*
Ron Donachie *Steward*
Tom Smith *The Host*
Ruthie Milne *Flora*
Suzanne Downs *Cook*
Debbie Reid, Jade Harris Cupit *Maids*
Ruari Mears, Marc Llewellyn-Thompson, Laurence
Chanon, Andrew Morgan Evans, Sam Stennett,
Alessandro Noble, Stephen Giffard, Dave Jennings,
Richard Carpenter, Rob Taylor, Levan Doran, Kai
Martin, Rick English *Monks*
Darryl Cross, Pete Newman, John Jones Snr, Glen
Foster, Tony Van Silva, Adam Sweet, Michael Barry,
John Mallon *Farm Hands*

RECORDED AT

Q2 Studio, Newport
Penllyn Castle, Penllyn, Cowbridge
Mountain Roads, Gelligaer Common, Mythyr
Craig-y-Nos, Brecon Road, Pen y Cae
Headlands School, St Augustines Road, Penarth
Llansannor Court, Llansannor, Vale of Glamorgan
Treowen Manor, Dingestow, Monmouth
HTV Studios, Culverhouse Cross, Cardiff
Dyffryn Gardens, St Nicholas, Vale of Glamorgan

Matthew Savage's design for the telescope atop Torchwood House.

own lipstick: 'I found the perfect red fabric, that matched my lipstick, that had weight to it, but was floppy enough for the flying harnesses and it wasn't transparent so they showed through.'

Louise's biggest task was dressing Queen Victoria, for two reasons. Firstly, the costume was a vast, layered one and was needed in at least two versions, since there had to be one for a stunt performer to wear for all the running scenes. A far bigger problem was that, less than a week before filming began, no one had confirmed to Louise who was actually playing Victoria. 'I'd bought all the fabric to make the dress, and I'd lined up a person to make it, but on the Friday morning of the week before we filmed, I still didn't have an actress. My lady was making the dress to fairly loose measurements but pointed out that if we didn't know by Monday, there wouldn't be time to adjust anything. Then I was told it was Pauline Collins, who I knew lived a mile or so up the road from me! I spoke to her but unfortunately she was going away for the weekend. She kindly got her husband, John Alderton, to measure her, and he rang me back and gave me her bust, waist and hips. In the end we made the dresses from those measurements and nipped round for a fitting on Tuesday afternoon when she was back. They were terribly heavy, because there were twenty metres of fabric in those dresses. But I needed to get the shape and bulk, and we didn't pad her out — we did it with fabric. I was very pleased — the dresses fitted perfectly and they looked brilliant.'

'I remember shaving a lot of men to get bald monks,' says make-up artist Sheelagh Wells. 'One gentleman had hair to his shoulders — that took quite a while. And of course, every day they filmed, their heads needed to be shaved again, but they were all very good about it. For Queen Victoria I needed a wig, but time was short and once I knew it was Pauline Collins I set about finding

HEIGHT: 1M 10CM
LENGTH: 6 FEET

the wig she'd just worn in the BBC's *Bleak House*. That wasn't owned by a wigmaker, it was actually the property of the make-up designer Daniel Phillips, who was halfway up a mountain in Scotland and slightly surprised to hear from me. He was helpful beyond belief and had the wig sent to me. I got it two days later, knowing it was going to fit her, so that was no problem.'

By far the most essential element of the story was the werewolf itself, created entirely in CG by The Mill, quite an achievement as fur and hair is still a tricky thing to pull off successfully in computer graphics. 'We would never have considered doing it if some of our team hadn't bitten off our arm for the opportunity to do it,' laughs Will Cohen. 'To be honest, it was a tough thing to achieve in the seven or eight weeks that we had to do it. We got it done just about in time, mainly because we limited the number of shots it was actually in. We rebuilt the actor in 3D – we had him cyber-scanned and made a model of him, so we then had a half-werewolf, half-guy model to morph to as well.' Dave Houghton was pleased that The Mill got to do all of the werewolf, rather than it being a meld of prosthetics, costume and make-up. 'It would have taken too much time to have gone through the process of dressing and re-dressing an actor's face for us to either morph between or cut from. This way it was harder work for us, but it paid off because everyone applauds the werewolf and wonders how it was done. Which is ideal because if they can see how it's done, we've not really done our job properly.'

The Host's cage, designed by Peter McKinstry.

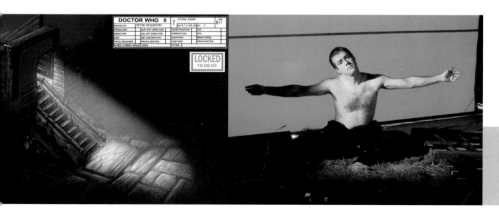

Far left: The ramp down to the cellar, painted by Peter McKinstry.
Left: Tom Smith against green screen for the climax where the Host is transfixed and then dissipated by the moonlight.

2.3 SCHOOL REUNION

The first story of the second series of *Doctor Who* not to be written by Russell T Davies was the story of an old friend of the Doctor's catching up with him many years after they had abruptly parted. Featuring the return of Sarah Jane Smith and K-9, *School Reunion* was the work of Toby Whithouse. 'They said they wanted me to bring back Sarah Jane and K-9 — aside from that I could do absolutely anything,' remembers Toby. 'So I came up with an idea for a story and they said no, it was completely wrong. You can do absolutely anything you want, as long as it's not that. A race of aliens wanted to get revenge on him for something he'd done hundreds of years earlier, but the format of the series is that the Doctor is the investigator and never the instigator; in my storyline he was the instigator, so that was out.'

Russell then suggested setting the story in an army camp and a village. Something strange was going on in the army base and all the villagers were being turned into incredibly skilled scientists/engineers and were building a bomb. 'I did a couple of treatments for that,' says Toby, 'and everyone said it was fantastic but let's set it in a

Top: Elisabeth Sladen, as Sarah Jane Smith, back on the set of Doctor Who *for the first time in over twenty years. Above: The Doctor waits to say a proper goodbye to his old friend.*

school! We kept the idea of an alien race doing something that enhances brain power for their own ends and Sarah's role changed over the course of the drafts — at first, she rather than the Doctor was the undercover teacher. The Krillitanes also changed over time — at first they were much more bat-like with their heads covered in blue fur. In earlier drafts, Mr Finch was completely Krillitane as well. In one version, there's a scene where Finch has wings but the rest of him is human, flying down the corridor. At the tone meeting they said that was impossible, they just couldn't do it.'

The Mill's Dave Houghton remembers this well. 'It's not easy building a 3D creature but, once you have, it's there and you can animate it. It is much more complicated to turn a real person into a creature because you have to somehow meld them into the creature. Eventually we came up with a way for the teachers to fragment and then coalesce into the shape of the Krillitanes.'

Bringing Sarah back into the series was always going to be popular with the fans, but would it work for the less committed audience? 'Well, she is the most widely and fondly remembered companion,' Russell points out. 'There's something very generic about Sarah Jane. I mean, if you brought Peri back you'd have to explain how she escaped from an alien planet. Or if you brought Ace back you'd get into terribly complicated decisions about which of her fates from the comics or from the audios or from the books is actually the correct one. Or if you brought Dodo back, no one would remember who she was. But we can find Sarah Jane exactly as we left her, so the story starts from there.'

Sarah Jane had last been seen on television accompanied by K-9 in the 1981 *Doctor Who* spin-off *K-9 and Company* and the twentieth-anniversary special *The Five Doctors* in 1983. 'Although I don't argue about *Doctor Who* canon much,' says Russell, 'I do believe that everything televised is canonical, so if we'd not had K-9, I would have

insisted on some dialogue explaining why he wasn't there. Plus, I love K-9. I really think he's funny and sweet, and when I see him in action – when he's fighting Krillitanes, I'm so happy. And, quite selfishly, I wanted something concrete, saying that David Tennant's Doctor is the same man who went to a pyramid on Mars with Sarah. And was in a junkyard in 1963. Let's examine his past, not by bringing on a poncey Time Lord in a great big collar, but via Sarah.'

One of the reasons for shooting this before *New Earth* was because *School Reunion* was largely set in a school, so shooting during the summer holiday was a must. 'As it was,' says James Hawes, 'I think we only finished one or two days before the teachers came back to prepare for the start of the new term. I'd made a conscious decision to stay away from anything that could be seen as a *Harry Potter*-type school, because this is about what could happen to you kids in school, on Monday. One of the great things about *Doctor Who* is that you don't have to be a member of the US Navy or be on the Starship Enterprise for cool stuff to happen to you. The TARDIS could land at the end of your street, so you can imagine it could just happen to you. I knew that kids would start checking out certain teachers to see if they might be an alien.

'It was a great shopping list of a story – zombie kids, unseen monsters and a robot dog that can't actually work, as far as I can tell, on any surface known to man or to any other alien beast. Plus Mickey, Sarah Jane and a demon headmaster. But it had a fantastic set of character dynamics: the old and new companions; two suitors for Rose's attention, in Mickey and the Doctor; and two champions for good and bad, in the Doctor and Finch. The moment David walked into that confrontation scene – which was originally written for the school gym, but I opted for the pool – it became rather like a 1970s British gangster movie where the Essex baddies meet at the posh mansion's swimming pool and size each other up from either side. It was a rich episode and showed how hungry an episode of *Doctor Who* is – how much plot and character and idiom and device one episode consumes.'

James also recalls that Elisabeth Sladen was nervous about returning as Sarah. 'However, in her very first scene she had to grab the Doctor's hand and run. As they did that, Elisabeth said, "Oh, I remember – running, hand in hand and screaming, that's me." Then, on the second day, she twisted her ankle, so we had to shoot a lot of scenes with

Above: The K-9 prop in Mike Tucker's workshop. Facing page: Sarah Jane and the Doctor set about repairing K-9.

DR WHO II "THE DOG!"

RECESSED PANEL R.H. SIDE 3"-4" (MAX DEEP - MAGNETS OR PUSH CLIP AT TOP - PIVOT AT BTM)

MIRROR INT? TO GIVE MORE DEPTH

Above: Lee Sullivan's designs for K-9's Gallifreyan inner workings. Right: K-9 in the workshop.

the second assistant director wigged up to look like her. I shot them running in shadow, shot just feet, and we dropped various scenes because Elisabeth couldn't run. It actually happened halfway through that attack in the dining hall. If you look carefully, you'll see that in some shoots she's moving, in others she's on all fours, because that was the only position she could get into.'

When Sarah and K-9 had last been seen together, John Leeson had been on set to provide the voice of the robot dog, but that wasn't the case here – John supplied it in post-production. One result of not having him there, remembers James Hawes, 'was that we flushed out of the woodwork all the people on set, notably the producer, who'd always wanted to be K-9. For the DVD there should be a version where John Leeson's voice is not heard, but you do get Phil Collinson! Phil was in seventh heaven!'

'K-9 needed to look battered and twenty years old,' notes Mike Tucker. 'I happen to have a K-9 that's battered and about twenty years old. When his first story had been made in 1977, a number of K-9s were produced from the mould, including the famous one that appeared in most stories, the full radio-controlled prop, though that had to be given a slightly bigger head because they'd forgotten to put the tickertape mechanism into it. That one lives with Mat Irvine, who used to operate him, and it is the prop used at

Directed by JAMES HAWES

CAST

David Tennant *The Doctor*
and Billie Piper *Rose Tyler*
with Noel Clarke *Mickey Smith*
Elisabeth Sladen *Sarah Jane Smith*
John Leeson *Voice of K-9*
Anthony Head *Mr Finch*
Rod Arthur *Mr Parsons*
Eugene Washington *Mr Wagner*
Heather Cameron *Nina*
Joe Pickley *Kenny*
Benjamin Smith *Luke*
Clem Tibber *Milo*
Lucinda Dryzek *Melissa*
Caroline Berry *Dinner Lady*
Suzanne Cazenove *Krillitane Nurse*
Moira Hunt, Laura Semmens, Ceri Clutterbuck
Dinner Ladies
Amanda Renate, Sharelle Hughes,
Verdun Rolands, Shane Morgan *Teachers*
Steve Darling, Carl Carew, Glen Jones,
Matthew John *Krillitane Teachers*

RECORDED AT

Q2 Studio, Newport
Fitzalan High School, Leckwith, Cardiff
Duffryn High School, Lighthouse Road, Newport
Belle View Car Park, Cardiff Road, Newport
Da Vinci's Coffee Shop, High Street, Newport

the end of *School Reunion*. When the story came up, I was able to say that I had one of the original K-9 body shells – it wasn't the fully radio-controlled one, and the head needed a bit of modification to make him look like the way he had on television, but basically we used one of the original 1977 props. We created a removable side panel to display all this Time Lord technology inside it, because this is K-9 Mark III, built by the Doctor and given to Sarah in *K-9 and Company*. It's got coral and that organic technology feel, to echo the TARDIS. I asked Edward Thomas if he had any thoughts about how he wanted the inside of K-9 to look but he said he didn't mind. So I phoned Lee Sullivan, an artist who'd done lots of *Doctor Who* comic strips, and asked what he would do if he had to design the inside of K-9. Lee sent me some nice design sketches, which were more elaborate than we had the time and budget to go with, but we incorporated a lot of his ideas into the overall look.'

Mike's Model Unit also blew up the school. 'We were given background shots of the school, and we took a set of measurements from those and built a series of matt-black shapes that matched the contours of the front of the school building. Then we let off a series of six fairly large gunpowder and petrol explosions to blow out the front. Since we'd lined it up to that plate shot, The Mill were then able to take the explosion and slap it straight back onto the front of the school.'

'If anything, the explosion was too big,' laughs The Mill's Will Cohen. 'We did have a line of schoolchildren running away from it, but once we put the shot together we realised that they'd have been fried, so we left them out, and put them into the shot a little later on when things had died down a bit.'

Explosions are always fun, not just for Mike's effects team and The Mill, but also for Paul McFadden and his sound editors. 'We used a lot of grenades. Obviously we couldn't blow up a school, but we have lots of sound effects on CD and we add to those. The best way to make a big crunchy explosion is to tape a plastic bag with a hole in it over the microphone. When you blow on it, and distort the sound, the air on the bag makes that wall of fire sound.'

2.4 THE GIRL IN THE FIREPLACE

'We decided to go for a baroque feel,' says Euros Lyn, director of Steven Moffat's hugely popular *The Girl in the Fireplace, Doctor Who*'s first ever real love story. 'The classic features of baroque art are symmetry and order and composition; we wanted to capture those features, visually and musically. There are lots of graceful camera movements and very formal wide-shot framings, and the set is quite theatrical. Versailles looked very warm and rich, and the spaceship seemed very cold. We tried to find a kind of inverse symmetry when the Doctor has jumped through the mirror on horseback and he finds himself trapped on the other side: the camera moves from the Doctor and Madame de Pompadour on one side, then we cut to a similar movement from Rose to Mickey; when we see Rose looking out on the stars, the cut is to the Doctor and Madame de Pompadour looking up at the stars. Throughout the episode we tried to find a symmetry and yet, stylistically, the two worlds are very different.'

The cast and crew prepare to shoot the climactic ballroom scene with the clockwork droid and (below) the Doctor riding Arthur – horse to be added later.

Creating those two worlds was a lot of fun for writer Steven Moffat, flushed from the success of *The Empty Child* and *The Doctor Dances* the year before. 'I came back from Australia and saw Russell's outline for Series Two – Cybermen, Satan Pits, werewolves… yes, please. And what did I get? Frocks! I mean what? What? The only way to do it really was to go for a love story and start it off on a fifty-first-century spaceship, just to prove I'd read the brief! There was part of me thinking that if I was a little boy I'd have been really hacked off if I'd heard, "Next week it's Madame de Pompadour and we're in eighteenth-century France." So I figured I'd get a spaceship in there! I read this book about Madame de Pompadour and the first thing that stuck in my mind was this man who discovers his wife is cheating on him because he discovers she's installed a revolving fireplace. Can you imagine that? I thought we had to have one of those. And if we have a revolving fireplace, it obviously has to be a time-and-space revolving fireplace, because this is *Doctor Who*, right? It's got to be stupid, it's just got to be more than you do in other shows and it's an irresistible visual, isn't it? You walk out into a spaceship, see a fireplace and through the fire you see Reinette and that's the start of the story.'

'I don't know if Steven Moffat was prepared for my big analysis of that episode,' says musician Murray Gold, 'but I really got into that story. It's about the temporal asymmetry – it's like Ovid, the Roman myth about love and how a man loves a woman in a day, and the woman loves the man across the entire span of her life. And the end of the man's day is the end of the woman's life. I felt that was just so touching and sad. I went and told Steven that, and he thought I was drunk.'

Steven claims Russell didn't really give him a storyline. He just mentioned Madame de Pompadour and asked if Steven knew that there had been a clockwork chess player around at the time? 'I liked the idea of the clockwork man but realised that if the story was about a clockwork man, it wouldn't be about Madame de Pompadour. There's only forty-five minutes, so I made the clockwork men just idiots really. They didn't even have a decent plan, just an intrinsically gruesome one.'

Realising these clockwork idiots began with their masks, designed by Neill Gorton. These were painted with acrylic crackle glaze, which gives a faux ageing effect by simulating the natural cracking that appears over time in oil paints and varnish. 'The

face masks were very striking, especially with the wigs that Sheelagh Wells's staff made, and Costume did a grand job on the robots' outfits.' Louise Page ensured that Millennium saw her costume designs as soon as possible, so that they could paint each mask to correspond with the colour scheme of the costume that the individual clockwork robots were wearing.' Sheelagh Wells admired the masks enormously: 'I thought it was an absolutely beautiful design. A very cruel mouth; if you put your hand over the mouth the rest of the mask wouldn't scare you, but once you see that grin it's a very nasty thing.' Underneath the masks was a beautiful domed glass head, made by Gustav Hogan at Millennium FX. 'This was his dream job,' explains Millennium FX's Rob Mayor. 'We told him to make it beautiful and intricate, we wanted to see the mechanics move. He loved doing it. It's not just a few cogs, the whole thing is connected. There's one motor to turn everything and it would click and make everything move up and down.'

Playing Reinette was Sophia Myles, best known at this point from her role in the movie version of *Thunderbirds*. 'My little boy absolutely loves *Thunderbirds*,' Steven Moffat comments, 'so I had seen it a hundred times every morning at 6 am and was so in love with Sophia as Lady Penelope – frankly the only good thing about that movie.

Top: Peter McKinstry's concept art for the SS Madame de Pompadour. *Below: Rob Mayor of Millennium FX operates the clockwork droid head they built for the episode.*

Directed by EUROS LYN

CAST

David Tennant *The Doctor*
and Billie Piper *Rose Tyler*
with Noel Clarke *Mickey Smith*
Sophia Myles *Reinette*
Ben Turner *King Louis*
Jessica Atkins *Young Reinette*
Angel Coulby *Katherine*
Gareth Wyn Griffiths *Manservant*
Gayle Anne Felton *Queen*
Paul Kasey *Clockwork Man*
Ellen Thomas *Clockwork Woman*
Jonathan Hart, Emily Joyce *Alien Voices*
Sean Palmer, Romina Chiappa, Marc Rees,
Neil Davies, Aga Blonska, Caroline Sabin,
Marega Palsar *Droids*

RECORDED AT

Q2 Studio, Newport
HTV Studios, Culverhouse Cross, Cardiff
Tredegar House and Park, Newport
Dyffryn Gardens, St Nicholas, Vale of Glamorgan
Ragley Hall, Alcester, Warwickshire
Mount Ballan Manor, Crick, Monmouthshire

There's not a lot to choose between Matthew Savage's original concept painting of the TARDIS arriving and the finished shot (above right).

She is wonderful, funny and dead sexy, so while I was writing Madame de Pompadour it was Sophia's voice I was writing for in my head. I never once mentioned it but they sent me the list of people that they were considering for the part and there she was. So I wrote back saying I thought she'd be fantastic. And she was.'

Steven was determined that Madame de Pompadour would be at the centre of the story and not just running up and down corridors. As he read up on her background, he discovered that 'she was very clever and witty and smart and actually trained to be the consort to a megalomaniac. So there you go, that's Doctor Who's girlfriend, that is. And the series is so much sexier now than it was, so it was believable to do a love story. Almost as believable as having a horse in the TARDIS. I wrote a draft, when we thought it was going to be impossible to do the horse-through-the-mirror sequence, where Arthur the horse winds up in the TARDIS stables. But Russell wouldn't have that. Why not? Why can't he have a horse – he's got a motorbike! In the shooting script, it was emphasised that Arthur was a sort of temporary companion. When the Doctor goes out and sees Reinette in the garden and hides, as he turns to go back to the time window, he meets the horse's rider who says, "Have you seen my bloody horse? I'm going to thrash it within an inch of it's life." The Doctor says, "Oh, I wish you hadn't said that," and walks back through the time window. Then he says to the horse, "Rule one is you don't wander off," which makes Arthur now officially a companion of the Doctor. There's a few more gags with the Doctor saying, "I keep humans, I keep horses, what the hell?"

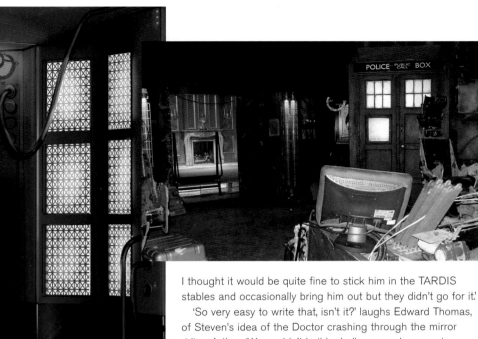

I thought it would be quite fine to stick him in the TARDIS stables and occasionally bring him out but they didn't go for it.'

'So very easy to write that, isn't it?' laughs Edward Thomas, of Steven's idea of the Doctor crashing through the mirror riding Arthur. 'We couldn't build a ballroom and no one in their right mind was going to allow us to make a horse jump over a hurdle onto their ballroom floor. So we storyboarded it: "Up to that point it can be real – David on horseback; from that point it's CGI – David's face superimposed over a real horse-rider's face, jumping through the shards of glass. The horse coming through an empty mirror frame is shot against green screen; after the jump, with David on the trotting horse, it's shot on the set." We broke it down like that and ended up with a sequence of shots that, by the time they were all edited together, told a total lie. But the audience, because of what they think they've seen, believe it.'

The palace was in fact a house just outside Cardiff called Dyffryn Gardens which was designed as a reproduction Parisian chateau. 'It's a derelict house,' says Edward Thomas. 'The façade is there and the gardens are kept very nicely; it has the pond. We reinstated the fountain and stuck Sophia Myles in the garden and all of a sudden we had Versailles.'

'One of my favourite shots in the whole series,' says Will Cohen of The Mill, 'is a shot you wouldn't even know we'd touched, with the Doctor and Louis looking out of the rainy window as Reinette's carriage leaves the gate at Versailles. We painted in the window and the rain, and it adds to the emotional ending of the scene. And it was much easier than shoving a horse through a mirror!'

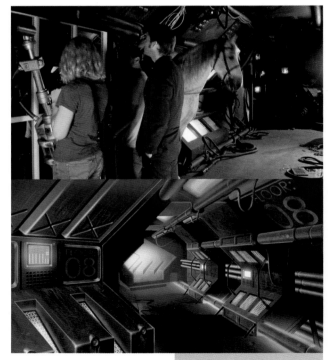

Top: Billie Piper, David Tennant and Arthur the Horse explore the ship. Above: Matthew Savage's concept art for the same set.

2.5/2.6 RISE OF THE CYBERMEN and THE AGE OF STEEL

Cybermen. Tall, silver giants, with the strength of ten men, they can live in the airless vacuum of space… so the classic series used to introduce the Cybermen. For the 2006 upgrade, the production took the central concept – humanity replacing itself with mechanical parts – and set their evolution on a parallel Earth where Cybermen had never been seen before.

'It took months to realise,' says Russell T Davies, 'but the hardest thing was getting a grip on what exactly is a Cyberman now, what does it mean and what consequences does it have? Because if you were really telling the stories of Cybermen now, away from the 1960s point of view of spare-part surgery, you'd be telling a story about genetics and DNA manipulation. You'd be telling a story about mice with ears on their backs. We were stuck with the problem that we wanted an army of tin soldiers; there's a great thriller, great dramas and great *Doctor Who* adventures to be written about genetics and genetic experimentation and research, but I wanted tin soldiers on the streets. So it took us ages to come up with the whole upgrading idea, to latch onto mobile phones and hard drives and technology and, as well as that, what we fear about technology. I speak as someone who feels out of his depth with an mp3 player – I'm scared of that, but equally inquisitive about it.'

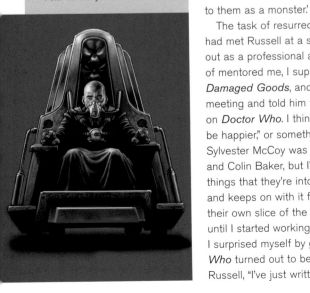

Above: A CG Cyber head by The Mill.
Below: An early concept for John Lumic's life support system by Peter McKinstry.

'If you bring back the Cybermen,' says Julie Gardner, 'you've got to have something to say about the world, about humanity's obsession with getting the latest gadget or upgrading or improving themselves, and the ultimate upgrade is turning yourself into a Cyberman. You don't have to feel emotion, you don't have to feel ill. I think that's why it feels very scary but in a recognisable way. There's a scale to them as a monster.'

The task of resurrecting them was offered to a young TV writer, Tom MacRae, who had met Russell at a signing for his *Queer As Folk* novel, just as Tom was starting out as a professional author. Russell had given him lots of help and advice. 'He sort of mentored me, I suppose. One day, he gave me a copy of his *Doctor Who* novel, *Damaged Goods*, and when I got the job on the *Doctor Who* series I took it to a meeting and told him to sign it. Which he did, and dated it on the very day I started on *Doctor Who*. I think he wrote, "I knew this would happen one day and I couldn't be happier," or something like that. I do remember watching *Doctor Who* as a kid, Sylvester McCoy was really my Doctor, although I can recall a bit of Peter Davison and Colin Baker, but I'm not a fan. Children can't really be fans; they just love the things that they're into at the time, whereas a fan is someone who doesn't let it go and keeps on with it for the rest of their life. I think a fan investigates more than just their own slice of the thing – I'd never seen a Tom Baker or Jon Pertwee episode until I started working on the show. The only thing I've been a fan of was *He-Man*. So I surprised myself by getting excited about writing for Cybermen; writing for *Doctor Who* turned out to be a dream come true, and every writer has said this. I texted Russell, "I've just written 'TARDIS'," and then found out later that actually everyone did that. He must have a standard response saved in his phone: "Hooray, marvellous."'

The parallel world was at the heart of the original idea for the story: police boxes stood on street corners, everything was steam-driven, the Cybermen were clockwork, and disease was killing off the human race. Tom remembers spending a lot of time exploring why this world was dying. 'Then Russell said, "What if they *weren't* dying; what if the Cybermen, instead of being dirty and greasy, were shiny and lovely." I never really explored at which point that world diverged from ours – it wasn't the Nazis, perhaps it was Cromwell defeating the monarchy – and it was Russell's suggestion that we shouldn't even address it. We also wanted to avoid taking the route where everyone's counterpart was evil; we even twisted that by implying that Pete's a bad guy by working for Lumic. In fact, he's Gemini, or Puck as I originally wrote it; then he was going to be Janus, the two-headed one.' As the scripts developed, the character of Mrs Moore gained a larger role, surviving a lot longer than originally intended. There were also ideas that didn't survive to the final script: an additional character called Esme, another of the Preachers, who was a kick-boxer; and the fact that Jake and Ricky were lovers. 'That was lost in the final edit,' Tom recalls, 'which is a shame as there was a fun scene when Mickey and Jake drive off and Mickey realises for the first time why Jake was so upset by Ricky's death and has to explain that not everything about them was the same!'

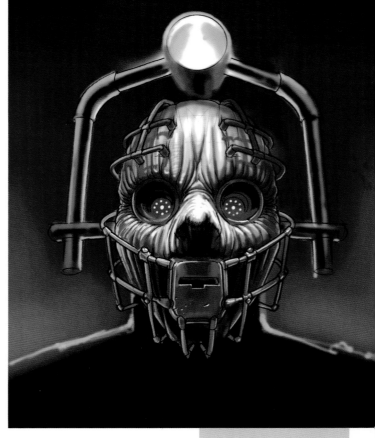

Above: Peter McKinstry's very early idea for a semi-converted Cyberman.
Below: Matthew Savage's variations on a theme.

CYBERMEN CONCEPTS

The Doctor's other great foes, the Daleks, were created by Davros, an injured scientist who lived his life in a wheelchair that doubled as a life-support machine. Though there might seem to be parallels with John Lumic, in fact Tom's lack of *Doctor Who* knowledge meant that he simply didn't know of Davros. 'The reason Lumic's in a wheelchair is that he's dying,' he says. 'It's not supposed to be a Davros parallel. Originally, Lumic was this young, strapping, heroic businessman out to cure humanity's sickness, and that was all he was bothered about. To do that, he experimented on himself, kept giving himself the sickness and injecting himself with anti-sickness things, which kept failing. Then he'd keep amputating parts of himself, so he ended up with a half-metal face and a Cyber arm. He cared so much he'd sacrificed his body to try to stop this thing, but gradually he was turning into a Cyberman. Then, once we dropped the sickness concept, he became a rather suave businessman, and I wondered why he was doing it? So I came up with this idea that his dad was dying, so his dad was the sickly old man in a wheelchair. Then it was decided that we didn't want two Lumics, so I combined them. Thus the businessman went into the wheelchair.'

These episodes were directed, alongside the series' concluding two-parter, by Graeme Harper. Graeme had directed two well-received *Doctor Who* stories in the mid 1980s, *The Caves of Androzani* and *Revelation of the Daleks*. 'Getting Graeme Harper in was a huge thrill for me,' says producer Phil Collinson. '*The Caves of Androzani* was my favourite classic *Doctor Who* ever. He has fabulous visual flare and a great sense of what can be achieved with a single camera. We wanted somebody who would appreciate how important it was, in the way Joe Ahearne had done with *Dalek*, that we were bringing back the Cybermen. He came on board and he directed the biggest production block we've ever done: four episodes shot at the same time in a nine-week shoot, from November to January, so Christmas kind of vanished. We'll never do four episodes together again – it was too much to get ready. Having said that, we made them; they look fabulous; we got there. It was really tough on Graeme because it is relentless yet, despite the age difference between all our other directors and Graeme, he has more energy, more enthusiasm than you see in anyone else. And he loves *Doctor Who*.'

Graeme was taken out to lunch by Phil and Russell, and the director enthused about Series One, which he had been watching avidly. At the end of the meal, they asked if he would direct a block for Series Two, and Graeme readily agreed. 'Then the scripts arrived and I'd got two double stories, and I couldn't believe it. Terrific. Then I got the news that I was going to have to shoot them back to back. That was going to be a killer. We got nearer and nearer to the dates of shooting and the scripts were being rewritten, re-sorted, re-chased, re-looked at and re-thought, and obviously getting better and better and better... I was getting a bit panicked but when we finally began, the warmth and the friendliness that I got and the freedom to do exactly what I wanted was unbeatable.

Matthew Savage's Cyber concept, with lots of electric blue, Russell T Davies's favourite colour where monsters are concerned.

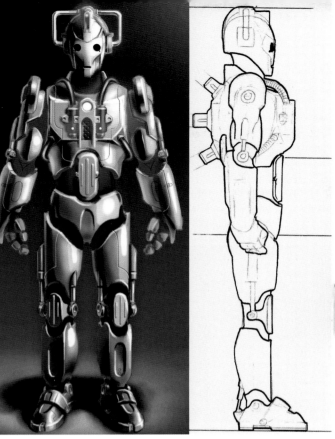

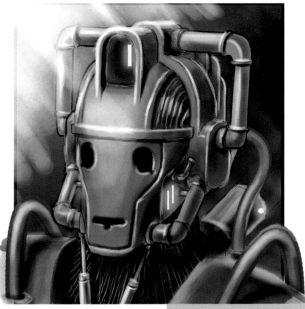

There was a fantastic atmosphere. So after the first day the fear faded and we began to realise everything was possible.' The next big question was what the new Cybermen would look like. Graeme remembers raising this question at the tone meeting in August. 'As soon as I said that, out came all these folders and brochures and paintings and pictures and God knows what.' 'Everyone and their dog had a bash, because it's the Cybermen,' laughs concept designer Matthew Savage. 'Peter McKinstry did the guns, I did the Cybus logo and Millennium FX contributed loads because they were designing as they sculpted.' Rob Mayor of Millennium FX states that the eventual look of the redesigned Cybermen developed out of the look of the new story: 'It was very industrial and had hints of both *Metropolis* and the Hoover Factory. Russell looked at everyone's designs, then the final general look was designed by the Art Department. We didn't change it, we just made it fit an actual person. Because we have to build the suits, we know what their constraints are and how we have to make stuff so the actors can move.'

'I love the art deco nature of them,' David Tennant enthuses. 'It gives them a timelessness, which is great. And I imagine in ten years' time this design will stand up rather well, whereas some of the earlier designs when you look back, were very much of their time.'

'We did all the Cybermen fittings on Paul Kasey,' says Neill Gorton of Millennium. 'People like Paul are great for giving you feedback, because they have to wear these costumes week in week out. If Paul says it's uncomfortable, it is uncomfortable; if Paul says it's fine, it is fine. We had one guy turn up for a Cyberman fitting who threw his hands up after we'd fitted

Directed by GRAEME HARPER

CAST

David Tennant *The Doctor*
and Billie Piper *Rose Tyler*
with Camille Coduri *Jackie Tyler*
Noel Clarke *Mickey/Ricky Smith*
Shaun Dingwall *Pete Tyler*
Andrew Hayden-Smith *Jake Simmonds*
Roger Lloyd Pack *John Lumic*
Don Warrington *The President*
Mona Hammond *Rita-Anne*
Helen Griffin *Mrs Moore*
Colin Spaull *Mr Crane*, Paul Antony-Barber *Dr Kendrick*
Adam Shaw *Morris*
Andrew Ufondo *Soldier*
Duncan Duff *Newsreader*
Paul Kasey *Cyber Leader*
Nicholas Briggs *Cyber Voice*
Paul Burke *Captain*
Mathew Gregory *Navigator*
Noel Fitzpatrick, Scott Price *Able Seamen*
John Mallon, William Adrian, Chris Ilston, Alan Bowen, Tim Warlock *Homeless*
Natascha Mortee, Sarah Vaughton *Waitresses*
Nick Madge, Joseph Lippiat *Waiters*
Tom Munro *Crane's Driver*
Ken Hosking, Kevin Hudson, Jon Davey, Joe White, Adam Sweet, Karl Greenwood, JJ Angell, Ruari Mears, Gethin Jones, Peter Symonds, Mathew Doman, Teilo Trimble, Paul Kennington, James O'Dee *Cybermen*
Tinkerbell *Rose*

RECORDED AT

Q2 Studio, Newport
Lambeth Pier, Lambeth Palace Road, London
Battersea Power Station, London
MI5, London
Tal-y-Garn Manor & Country House, Nr pontyclun
South-Side Roath Dock, Cardiff Docks
various roads, Cardiff Docks
Riverfront Arts Centre, Bristol Packet Wharf, Newport
Uskmouth Power Station, Newport
Veritair Limited, Cardiff Heliport, Cardiff Bay
The Paper Mill, Sanatorium Road, Cardiff
St Nicholas, nr Cardiff
Coedarhydyglyn
Unit G12, Bridge Road, Trefforest
Compton Street, Grangetown, Cardiff
Clarence Embankment, Cardiff Bay/Hamadrayad Hospital
Grangemore Park, off Cardiff Bay Retail Park, Cardiff Bay   >>

him into the body suit as soon as he saw the helmet. "I can't wear that! I'm terribly claustrophobic, can't even go on a tube train." We did wonder how he'd managed not to know what a Cyberman was before he came along for the fitting! Unbelievable.'

The series' resident choreographer, Ailsa Berk, had been working on the show since *Rose* and *The End of the World*, and her task here was to ensure that the Cybermen's movement was strictly controlled. Although the occupants of the Cyber suits were actors, headed once again by Paul Kasey, Graeme

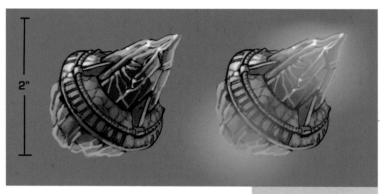

Peter McKinstry's pass at the energy crystal from the TARDIS.

Harper had initially suggested employing military men to play the Cybermen because they would understand precision and timing. 'The first thing I said to Ailsa was they have to be regimented; this is a killing machine – powerful individually and fantastically powerful as a group. I wanted them to have the precision of the cartoon hammers in Pink Floyd's *The Wall*, uniform and relentless. Given the limited vision from the Cyber helmets, Ailsa suggested putting elastic bands on their hands between their wrists: they would each hold their wrists together, which would keep them in line. I remember doing a shot looking down from a high roof as they came round a corner. It had the precision, but they looked like little girls in frou-frous, coming on to take their bow after a school pantomime. It just looked funny. So she used the elastic band idea when the Cybermen were marching in a straight line, but not on curves. Ailsa then suggested that, if they formed a V, they could see ahead and take their lead from one another. The person who can't see is the man in front, but that was okay because he was the one setting the pace and precision the rest had to follow.'

Another essential aspect of the Cybermen was the voice. 'We had one test session with Nicholas Briggs recording the voices,' explains sound editor Paul McFadden. 'He did about fourteen different versions, sent them to Russell, Julie and Phil and they decided on one. Nick then came back to Cardiff and we recorded them, and then gave them to the editor to cut in over what had been recorded by Nick on set. He had done it very slowly on set, and the pictures had to be cut to match the new delivery. We added a couple of lines in ADR with the Doctor and Mrs Moore running up the ladder away from the

Cybermen. That sequence was dialogue-free, but we had them do a bit of urging each other on, just to keep the pace going. Graeme also added a woman's voice under Nick's for the Cyber Bride as she died. Nick also did the Cyber Controller, but that was replaced in editing by Roger Lloyd Pack's voice. Nick tends to do the Cybermen with a marvellous monotone, but the Controller needed to be a bit more Lumic, a bit more emotive.'

'When I was sitting writing the Cybermen for the last two episodes,' says Russell T Davies, 'I kept hearing that buzz underneath the voice, that sort of flat, monotone vocoder buzz underneath it. The voices needed to be speeded up because we discovered in the edit that on set Nick was talking at a Dalek speed, so it didn't come alive until we got into the edit. I think we had an idea that it might not be working on set, which is why the blue light in the mouthpiece just comes on and goes off, rather than flashing in sync with the voice like a Dalek does. I had the most tedious day of my life – I mean, bless Nick, but when fourteen different voices arrived, all slightly different, I nearly died. If they'd been vastly different, that would have been fine, but they were only slightly different. Drove me bananas. You couldn't remember which one you liked, or why you liked it. But we got there in the end.'

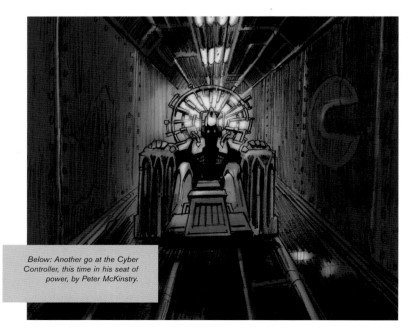

Below: Another go at the Cyber Controller, this time in his seat of power, by Peter McKinstry.

2.7 THE IDIOT'S LANTERN

Moving away from the very technological world of Lumic's Cybermen living on 'Pete's World', the TARDIS takes the Doctor and Rose back to North London in 1953. For writer Mark Gatiss, this touched on a lot of things he loves, with the birth of television and monochromatic nods to the likes of *Quatermass* and *Coronation Street*. The script might be about an alien presence draining people's faces and personalities away, but beneath the monster adventure is a really powerful human drama concerning the rite of passage: a boy grows up enough to stand up to his bullying father, and yet they come to terms with one another at the end. But it wasn't always like that, as Mark explains.

'The original story was 1950s, but it was rock 'n' roll. Then I had this Coronation idea, and they absolutely loved it, but I pointed out that it couldn't be rock 'n' roll any longer – the Coronation was too early. So it had now become austerity Britain. For a while we moved it later again, to 1957, and it became about Sputnik and a sound monster that was a sort of living tune. But that just wouldn't fit with the telly thing – we needed to be doing something visual not something aural. Eventually, Russell took us back to the Coronation. So it became firmly about television, and I immediately felt I was on strong ground: Ally Pally, Bakelite televisions, the Coronation broadcast itself. I suddenly had the idea of a 1950s continuity announcer being the monster throughout, and being very waspish! There were a few *Quatermass* parallels, most of which got cut, but the whole flavour of it, I felt, was my kind of story.

'I liked the family stuff best, because it was very real and very sad, but also very true. My dad wasn't any kind of tartar, but he was the head of the household, and I put a few

Above: The Wire in Bakelite.
Below: Tommy (Rory Jennings) helps invent the home video recorder.

things in that had chilled me when I was a kid. My mother wanted to leave her job because she said it was putting her in an early grave, so there was a worry that we wouldn't be able to manage without the two incomes, and there were lots of heated words heard from the top of the banisters. My dad finally relented and there was a family conference, with my dad saying, "Right, well, there's going to be some changes around here." And I thought I was going down the pit or something. So I wanted to get some of that "dadness" in, which I think works very well.'

In his early drafts of the episode, Mark put a lot more of himself into the character of Tommy than was to end up in the finished version. 'He was a lot geekier and gay and a bit older, around eighteen. I wrote the first couple of drafts halfway through the transmission of Series One, and I had an ending which I really loved but, when I saw what Captain Jack was doing, I thought my subtle gay suggestions had been blown out of the water. In those drafts, Tommy gets on very well with Rose – who doesn't lose her face in the first draft – and at the end he takes her to one side and says, "I know this is sudden, but..." Rose says, "Oh, I'm very flattered, love," but Tommy says, "No, not you." He fancies the Doctor. And she suggests he ask him. So she goes off to the TARDIS, smiling, and you see Tommy walking up to the Doctor, who's just got a

David Tennant and Billie Piper
enjoy getting used to the
scooter.

big smile on his face. Cut to the inside of the TARDIS, Rose waiting and then the Doctor comes in very quickly: "Hmm. Ah. So. Erm."'

Director Euros Lyn, responded strongly to Tommy's journey as well. 'I love the fact that this is a story of a teenage boy desperate to express his curiosity about the universe and science and the way forward. His happier, brighter future is in opposition to the figure of the oppressive father, who seems to be a British war hero. Mark's clever twists of historical context were inspired. Why didn't Tommy go off with Rose and the Doctor at the end? Rose actually sticks around in the story much later than written; we rejigged the story a bit to keep Rose around for longer. But she is still absent from much of the second half of the episode, and I think Billie was probably very pleased to get a little bit of time off. In *Fear Her*, it's the other way round – the Doctor gets trapped in the drawing, and Rose has to save the day – and it's nice to see them separately across the two stories. The Doctor and Rose don't always succeed as a team, sometimes they do have to go off and do things alone. It's a chance for us to do something a little different.' The decision to take Rose out of the second half of the episode was, says Mark, 'just to raise the stakes. The Doctor's frantic when he discovers what's happened and it's about him working suddenly without his best friend to actually save her.'

The story also has a marvellous, deliciously alien villain called the Wire, played by Maureen Lipman, someone Mark was overjoyed to see acting out his dialogue. 'Well, what can you say? Who else could it have been? Normally she would have gone to Cardiff and shot her bits at Q2, but she was doing *Glorious* in the West End and could only spare an afternoon. Maureen lives in Muswell Hill and she's a patron of Alexandra Palace, so we were able to shoot the scenes of her playing a 1950s continuity announcer in the studio where she would have done it if she'd been the real thing!'

Making Maureen Lipman up, giving her that 1950s homely look, was a pleasure for make-up designer Sheelagh Wells. 'Basically she would have been very prim and proper. Make-up for 1950s black and white TV was very different from make-up for black and white TV fifteen years later, and quite different from the quite natural make-up used for colour TV. Because the picture of the Wire was going to burst into colour for one or two minutes, we had to hit a middle line – she couldn't look too bizarre when the picture blossomed into colour. I once had to recreate the very first make-up that was ever seen on TV for the very first newscast, and the woman was painted in dark blue and yellow, which was the extreme. By the 1950s, it was more natural, but all the colours were a lot more ginger, with more orange in it. We tried to make Maureen look right for the period with things like the prissy red lips. We decided we could just about get away with using Maureen's own hair dressed in a 1950s style.'

Above: The design for Magpie's shop. Below: Billie Piper prepares to shoot the scene where the Doctor emerges from the TARDIS on the scooter.

'I'd worked with Maureen many, many years ago,' says costume designer Louise Page. 'I knew she had some 1950s clothes from when she did her Joyce Grenfell tribute show, but she said none of it would fit her now. I went round to her home and we had a chat and she pulled out the dresses, and some of them did still fit but weren't right. There was one outfit that I thought would work, but she was adamant she wouldn't get it on, so I suggested leaving it open at the back. I took a picture of it and showed Euros, and he said it would be perfect. I then bought all the accessories and earrings, although she wore her own brooch. I was very pleased with the way that the Wire turned out.' Louise also worked hard to get the post-war austerity of Tommy's family right, especially for the bullying father, played by Jamie Foreman. 'I had long discussions with Simon Winstone, the script editor, about the medals worn by Tommy's dad,' she adds. 'Eddie Connelly wears the Burma Star medal, but soldiers awarded the Burma Star during the Second World War would have received other medals before qualifying for that one. We didn't want to make him into a hero, so under no circumstances was he to wear any medals for gallantry.' Jamie Foreman wore his own watch, which his wife had bought him for Christmas, as it was an original 1950s one.

With the episode set in the 1950s, finding 'London' locations was, for once, not a problem for Edward Thomas's art department, as Cardiff offers a number of London-esque streets. 'We found a beautiful street in Cardiff, which gave us a really lovely long run of red-brick houses and felt as if it was somewhere in North London. I hadn't done the 1950s before, but it gave us lots of great props to make. We had to make all the televisions work to show the Wire but obviously 1950s televisions don't work with modern SCART plugs so we used normal, modern portable televisions and then surrounded them with Bakelite.'

Mark Gatiss was very satisfied with *The Idiot's Lantern*, and he managed to have a lot of fun during the writing process. 'I got a couple of nice in-jokes in there – we're watching the Coronation in Tommy's house in Florizel Street – a *Coronation Street* in-joke (it was the working title for the soap) that only Russell got. Simon Winstone, the script editor, had to come up with some other street names in case we needed them, one of which was Mafeking Street, which was so authentic – I wish I'd thought of it. Also, I got a nice *Quatermass* bit in with all the faceless people clenching and unclenching their hands. I had to lose Inspector Bishop referring to watching *Quatermass* live every week – Russell pointed out that as the writer and the star had both recently been in the *Quatermass* remake, it was a little self-indulgent. I thought, "Damn your eyes." He did initially let me have a *Doctor Who* reference: as they run into Alexandra Park and see the transmitter, Tommy's saying, "Come on, Doctor," and the Doctor replies, "I've just got this thing about transmitters. I fell off one once." But it was a specific reference to the Fourth Doctor falling from a radio telescope in Tom Baker's final story, and in the end it was cut.'

David Tennant chats to Rory Jennings between takes in the Connolly house.

Directed by EUROS LYN

CAST

David Tennant *The Doctor*
and Billie Piper *Rose Tyler*
with Maureen Lipman *The Wire*
Ron Cook *Magpie*
Jamie Foreman *Eddie Connolly*
Debra Gillett *Rita Connolly*
Rory Jennings *Tommy Connolly*
Margaret John *Grandma Connolly*
Sam Cox *Detective Inspector Bishop*
Ieuan Rhys *Crabtree*
Jean Challis *Auntie Betty*
Christopher Driscoll *Security Guard*
Marie Lewis *Mrs Gallagher*
John Jenner *Mr Gallagher*
Dom Kynaston *Bishop's Driver*
Liz Edney *Rita's Sister*
Dai Murphy *Rita's Brother-in-law*
Christian Byard *Rita's Nephew*
Simon Howells *Rita's Cousin*
Katy Fin Bar *Rita's Cousin's Wife*
Richard Randall *Uncle John*
Lara Phillipart, Conner Edwards *Children*
Gareth Long, Trevor Payne *Market Workers*

RECORDED AT

Q2 Studio, Newport
Alexandra Palace, Wood Green, London
Florentia Street, Cathays, Cardiff
Blenheim Road, Pen-y-lan, Cardiff
Cardiff Royal Infirmary, Longcross Street, Cardiff
Veritair Limited, Cardiff Heliport, Cardiff Bay
South Dock, Newport Dock, Newport

2.8/2.9 THE IMPOSSIBLE PLANET and THE SATAN PIT

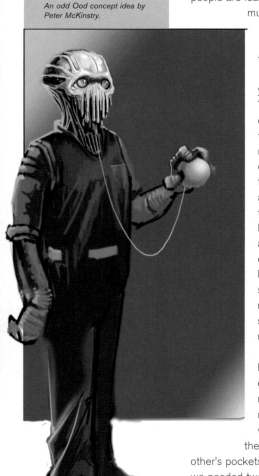

An odd Ood concept idea by Peter McKinstry.

'I've known James Strong for years,' says Russell T Davies of the director of this story. 'I knew him when he was a trainee researcher at Granada in the mid 1990s, when he came knocking on the door and I showed him round. I'd seen his name crop up on things but hadn't seen him for ten years. I confess I used to watch his work on *Holby City* three or four years ago and think, "Oh, shame, he's not very good." You forget that people are learning, it's so easy to get very judgmental. I kept watching him and saw so much improvement, he really started developing depth and foreground move-ment and good lens and colour work, using practical lights on set. He's a lovely man, and on this schedule you've got to be a nice bloke. That's a terrible thing to say, but it's true.'

'It's great to have done a two-parter,' enthuses James, 'because it means you're making a movie: it's a ninety-minute story when you put it together. To have that length of time to tell one fantastically exciting rollercoaster of a story is an amazing opportunity. And I got to do the pure science fiction one. I love Earth stories but there's always something in them you need to research to be accurate. On a planet orbiting a black hole we could do anything. Russell said at our very first meeting that it had to look tough and be very dark; the people had to be real. You watch *Star Trek* and it's like a library: very quiet, very calm, and technology has improved to the extent that no one gets ill. I wanted the Sanctuary Base to feel like it was an oil rig clinging to the bottom of the North Sea. These guys are clinging to this rock, it's a dangerous and precarious existence. It's crazy, they shouldn't be there; it defies all logic, and they've got a massive black hole, which could kill them at any second, but still they're there. My starting point was the first *Alien* film. We were showing space truckers; not soldiers, not astronauts; just guys that work on a commercial freight spaceship. That informed a lot of the very claustrophobic feel, the dark and metallic and steely greys, and the smoke and steam elements in the base.

'By contrast, there was the enormous underground cavern from a lost civilisation, and into that comes the devil. I was worried about some elements being very futuristic and sci-fi and some elements being mystical, so the challenge was to draw those together and make sure neither looked out of place. I wanted the people to have a reality, too. We were lucky to have rehearsal time so we could work out the dynamics of the crew and make it believable that they'd been there for two years, in each other's pockets. That rehearsal time is unheard of on new *Doctor Who* but I really felt we needed two days with the whole group of them to get to know one another and have a laugh. Phil Collinson was very supportive of that. Normally, there is a day's readthrough and the actors next meet on set. With an ensemble cast, I felt using the time in that way would be beneficial, which it truly was. It speeded the actual filming up, because everyone knew what they were doing in each scene.'

'It's pioneers,' says Russell. 'The story I always wanted to do was about a hardy bunch of pioneers, buffeted by the wind and frozen by the cold, on a rocky, desolate planet. And I like the Ood – I have to confess, we were running out of money, so it was going to be the Slitheen, just to save a bit of cash, but we looked at the sums and I emailed Millennium FX asking how many they could do for us if all the monsters' heads were identical. Neill Gorton said that if it was just heads, if the Ood were wearing clothes and gloves, they could do six. I showed him a picture of a Sensorite, from William Hartnell's time as the Doctor back in the 1960s; I've always loved that look, that uniformity and their expressionless faces, so we put a bit of that into the Ood. I think that's why the Ood hold those handballs which translate what they're saying – the Sensorites had a little thing that transmitted their telepathic thoughts and, in my head, they're from next-door planets. The Ood come from the Ood-Sphere, which is next door to the Sense-Sphere. The Ood are odd. That's how I came up with their name, I wanted them to sound odd.'

'The script described the Ood as albinos,' says Rob Mayor of Millennium FX. 'Albinos with red angry folds of skin coming down from their mouths, and I think it just took a natural evolution to a sort of squid creature. They weren't completely albino, because if you do anything too pale it creates problems for the camera. We ended up doing twelve of those – twice as many as we'd budgeted for – all made to fit Paul Kasey's head because, as always, he was going to be our lead monster. We made an animatronic version as well, which had some movement around the eyes and brow. We ended up doing the Ood balls as well, which had a little switch at the back so they could light up.'

For production designer Edward Thomas, both the station and the planet itself offered some nice new challenges, especially the latter. 'Obviously it wouldn't be *Doctor Who* without a quarry at some point, so we looked at white lime quarries and clay quarries, then settled for a vast limestone quarry. Ironically, we spent most of the time underground in it and only ventured out onto the planet's surface once or twice. We based the station interiors on *M*A*S*H*, the 1970s TV series set during the Korean War

'If you think there's going to be trouble, we could always get back inside and go somewhere else.'

– their mess tent, their medical tent, their living-in tents. Each room is very important, has its specific requirement, is differently designed and positioned around a central hub. We looked at things like *Alien* to see how dirty or distressed we wanted the base to be – and we chose not to let it be too run down, since these guys were actually working reasonably successfully. So that episode was set almost one hundred per cent in studio, bar the quarry and one old factory we went to.'

Originally, the base seen on the planet's surface was going to be a model, made by Mike Tucker, but during pre-production that changed and it ended up being entirely a CG build. Mike did contribute one thing, and it was his last work on Series Two: 'They wanted

Concept designs by Peter McKinstry. Above: The Sanctuary Base corridors. Right: The cave painting found by the Doctor at the bottom of the Pit. Far right: The entrance to the Beast's prison.

dust being blown past the base. The Mill couldn't achieve this easily, so I ended up shooting handfuls of dust blown against a black cloth for The Mill to overlay onto the model of the base and planet surface. I was disappointed as I think the base would have looked great as a model, and it was high on my list of things that I wanted to do in this show, but that's life.'

These episodes made up the final shooting block and were made in tandem with *Love & Monsters*, so there was very little preparation time on the story, particularly for costume designer Louise Page. After the cast readthrough for *The Idiot's Lantern*, Louise grabbed Russell to talk about spacesuits, which were going to be the most difficult costume of the story – they're the one thing you can't nip out and buy from high-street stores. 'I had reference material for NASA's white spacesuits, but Russell felt that they shouldn't be big, padded real spacesuits at all – as we were in the future, spacesuits would have moved on. He also said white wasn't a good idea, firstly because we were shooting on location in a quarry and secondly because it's uninteresting to look at. I researched reproduction spacesuits on some American websites, and Russell really liked orange, which he thought would stand out. Other than David, I had no idea

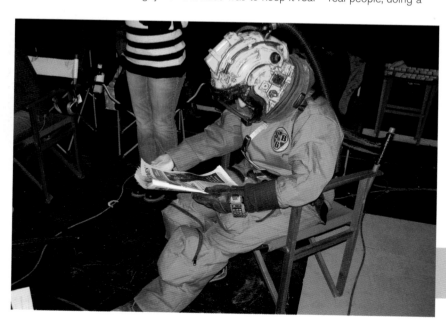

David Tennant abseils down into the Satan Pit.

which, or even how many, actors were going to be wearing them, which is a problem with custom-made clothing. We initially considered traditional space helmets, but Russell wanted something different there too – not a great big domed thing, so we needed to make those as well. That was beyond my capabilities, certainly within the time allotted. I spoke to Phil Collinson and we agreed that, since they would need microphones inside them, they were props, so they were an Art Department job. They were motorbike helmets, painted yellow; I wasn't sure about the yellow, but no one wanted black. Yellow tied in with what Edward Thomas was doing, because he had this Tonka-toy yellow all over the set. At that point, they hadn't cast anyone to play Ida, so I had to cross my fingers and order up her custom-made orange spacesuit thinking she was bound to be someone only about five-foot six. She wasn't, she was a completely different shape and I had to cut up the original prototype suit and adapt things to make it work. All of which we did on the day before we started filming with Claire Rushbrook.

'Russell's rule for those guys on the base was to keep it real – real people, doing a

David Tennant keeps up with the news between takes.

Directed by JAMES STRONG

CAST

David Tennant *The Doctor*
and Billie Piper *Rose Tyler*
with Danny Webb *Mr Jefferson*
Shaun Parkes *Zachary Cross Flame*
Claire Rushbrook *Ida Scott*
Will Thorp *Toby Zed*
Ronny Jhutti *Danny Bartock*
MyAnna Buring *Scooti*
Gabriel Woolf *The Voice of the Beast*
Silas Carson *The Voice of the Ood*
Lianna Stewart, Kristian Arthur *Base Guards*
Paul Kasey, Rauri Mears, Karl Greenwood, Joe White, Adam Sweet, Mark Llewellyn-Thompson, Lewis Drew, Stephen Reynolds, Scott Baker, Andy Jones, Claudio Laurini, Richard Tunesi *The Ood*
Ceres Doyle *Sanctuary Base Voice*

RECORDED AT

Q2 Studio, Newport
Wenvoe Quarry, Cemex UK Ltd, Wenvoe
HTV Studios, Culverhouse Cross, Cardiff
Clearwell Caves, nr Coleford, Gloucestershire
Enfys Television Studios, Unit 31, Portmanmoor Road, Cardiff
Johnsey Estates, Mamhilad Park Ind Estate South, Pontypool
Pinewood Studios, Iver Heath, Bucks

real job, aboard a real space station. That meant lots of pockets and pouches. I ordered piles of different ammunition pouches from a company that supplies the police force, then mixed up the styles and just managed to have the whole lot ready on the first day of shooting. It was horribly last minute, but it worked on screen. I also knew that at some point Scooti and Toby would be filmed underwater, in a water tank, but weren't meant to look wet because it was meant to be outer space. I had to weight the costumes down to make sure they didn't look like they were floating in water, because we wanted their hair to move, but not anything else, as they drifted through space.'

'Russell had always wanted to do somebody outside a space station with no oxygen,' notes James Strong. 'When we discussed Scooti being sucked to her death, we considered doing it on wires, but I suggested the best way was to do it underwater. So we went to the James Bond stage at Pinewood where they have this big underwater tank, and shot the deaths of Toby and Scooti there on thirty-five-millimetre film. It was fabulous and it looks amazing.'

While Louise Page's problems were time related, Sheelagh Wells's were equally as complicated but for wholly different reasons. Will Thorp, playing Toby Zed, needed to have his face and hands covered with symbols transferred from the pottery he'd found. 'The symbols were designed by the Art Department, but what works on a piece of pottery doesn't necessarily work on the face. I did a couple of tests, because it had to be either painted freehand or airbrushed on. We were a little short of

Above: An Ood getting dressed on set.
Right: MyAnna Buring gets in the mood for Scooti's final moments.

time by the point Will was cast, which meant I couldn't take the risk of applying it on set without tests first, but there was no time. I gave up on painting them on by hand, and contacted a very talented artist called Dave Stohlman, who had done similar things for *Harry Potter* and knew how to make them waterproof. He drew the symbols on a sheet which could be applied directly, like a tattoo. We also gave Will red contact lenses, but he hadn't used lenses before, so we had to go through a whole testing process with them. We took the colour out of his lips, his ears and his skin, and we turned his tongue a rather strange greeny-black colour, because Will had had some recent dental work so we weren't able to stain his teeth.'

Toby Zed (Will Thorp) with the inscriptions transferred to his face.

The Beast was the subject of a lot of discussion and emails between everyone involved over just how far they could go in depicting what would be seen by many viewers as the biblical devil if they weren't careful. 'The script cleverly avoids theological discussions,' says James Strong. 'I think the reason behind that is that this monster says he's the devil because that's what we recognise in our culture as the ultimate embodiment of evil. We wanted to avoid anything remotely clichéd with pitchforks. It had to have a very powerful, primeval and impressive body-like structure, but still retain certain devilish qualities – horn elements, red colours. It's much more akin to, say, Simon Bisley's comic-book art like *Slaine: The Horned God*, those intricate monsters with tongues of fire.

Gabriel Woolf provided the voice of the Beast once filming had been completed. 'What a voice!' enthuses sound editor Paul McFadden. 'I pitch-shifted him down slightly and added another little whispered delay, so every time he spoke there were little whispered repeats. When Silas Carson came in to do the Ood voices, we made sure their effect and the Beast's were totally different as they often spoke in unison.'

'The weird thing about the Beast,' says Dave Houghton from The Mill, 'is that it wasn't designed by one of our regular artists, but by a guy who works in our despatch department! We handed his ideas over to our modelling genius, Nicholas Hernandez, and it works particularly well, because it's so dark and moody in the caves and has a real sense of scale. When we first discussed it with Russell, he had this idea that the Doctor comes up to a wall and the wall is the creature's eyelids, so it would have been even bigger.' The Beast's scenes were created in six weeks by two of The Mill's animators, each doing the work of three, according to Will Cohen. But Will cites it as something that typifies The Mill's working relationship with the *Doctor Who* office. 'We get a lot of creative freedom given the amount of work involved, which you don't get necessarily working on movies. Here, we're dealing with Russell to get things approved and not seventeen people from Warner Bros. and five other producers, and because it's all planned and agreed up front, we can do it properly. And all our artists have enormous creative freedom to feel that they own the shots they work on and won't have to redo them time and again beyond reason.'

2.10 LOVE & MONSTERS

From the farthest reaches of outer space, it's back to contemporary Earth for one of the series' most unusual episodes. *Love & Monsters* features very little of the Doctor and Rose, focusing instead on a group of Doctor-hunting geeks and a monster originally created by young William Grantham for *Blue Peter*'s Design-a-Monster competition. The story was made simultaneously with the preceding two-parter, so David and Billie were rarely available and the story was deliberately structured to allow for that. For costume designer Louise Page, it looked on paper as though it would all be terribly easy...

'I could have killed Russell,' says Louise. 'Thirty-two costumes for Marc Warren and at least a dozen for everybody else in it. I needed glasses for Shirley Henderson, three pairs with non-reflective lenses – two for Shirley and one for Millennium FX to use in the paving slab. I found frames that worked but, of course, there was only one pair. So I had to ring opticians around the country to find them. One pair came from Derby, another from Brent Cross.'

When we see Ursula's face in a paving stone, what we're seeing is largely the prosthetics work of Millennium FX. Rob Mayor reveals that the process began with a latex sheet, 'which Shirley could push her face through to get the shape. We made an appliance from that and attached it to a lightweight foam paving slab, taken from a mould of the actual paving slab.' According to director Dan Zeff, Shirley Henderson was then filmed 'kneeling on the ground with her head in this fantastic prosthetic. The side-on shots have no CGI whatsoever; for the front-on angle, The Mill had to paint out Shirley's knees.'

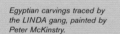

Egyptian carvings traced by the LINDA gang, painted by Peter McKinstry.

Whereas most episodes of *Doctor Who* have a linear narrative set within twenty-four to forty-eight hours, *Love & Monsters* is unusual in covering different days throughout Elton's life. Hence the various montage sequences during the episode, which Dan recalls could involve as many as forty costume changes in a single day's filming. 'We spent a whole week planning most of these costume changes and when they were going to happen, down to the exact minute,' says Louise Page. 'It was like a military operation. We had a little quick-change area at the side of the location, to make it quicker for Dan and his crew. At one point, they wanted to ask Russell and Phil if they could cut the montages but I put my foot down and explained that we had spent a frantic week working 24/7 to get it to work. Dan just looked at me – maybe I scared him – and nodded. Russell told me later how thrilled he was that we'd managed to do it because the episode was so much better with all the montages in it.'

Like Shirley Henderson, Peter Kay is not an off-the-peg suit shape, so he came to London to meet Louise for an afternoon. 'He came with his grandma because they were going to the theatre that night. Russell wanted him to look like an eccentric old actor/

manager type you get in local theatre so I suggested a 1930s coat, with this fur collar and stuff, plus the cane and the ring. We wanted him to look immaculate.' Peter Kay also provided a lot of fun for make-up designer Sheelagh Wells. 'Peter wanted a wig, so I decided to use some facial hair as well and give him a satanic look, so he's got a shock of light-coloured hair and a slightly devilish beard and moustache.'

Although David Tennant was barely in the episode, his presence was still felt. 'Billie and I had two days together, and then I did one little other bit at the end of a day; but I got to work with Lord Peter of Kay for one day, and with Marc Warren. I didn't get to work with Shirley Henderson, which was a great regret because I've sort of been in things with her twice now and we haven't actually worked together and I'm such a fan of hers. *Love & Monsters* was a sign that we were now a very confident show – we could've fallen flat on our faces with it obviously, but I doubted we would. Billie and I were a little bit jealous that there's this fantastic script that we hardly got to be in, but it was good for Camille and you can never have enough of Camille.'

Clearly the production team agreed, although, with the stories recorded out of order, Camille Coduri had assumed that her Jackie days were over after filming *Doomsday*. 'I got a call from Phil asking if I'd come back to do another one. Were they mad? I'd love to! Ironically, I didn't see David or Billie, although she came to the set for the filming with the pizza outside the flat, but I didn't get a chance to say hi. I spent my last day on *Doctor Who* watching Marc Warren's little bum bobbing up and down under a washing machine – nice way to go.'

'It was quite an unusual story,' says Dan Zeff, 'but it really suited my sensibilities. A dark fairy tale, sort of *Edward Scissorhands*-esque – that was the direction I took it in anyway, with Russell's blessing. I thought it was going to be this oddball episode they threw together and I'd end up doing the one everyone remembers as duff. Then I saw the script and loved it; it has such a pace and energy and the main characters are

Directed by DAN ZEFF

CAST

David Tennant *The Doctor*
and Billie Piper *Rose Tyler*
with Camille Coduri *Jackie Tyler*
Peter Kay *Victor Kennedy/Abzorbaloff*
Marc Warren *Elton Pope*
Shirley Henderson *Ursula Blake*
Simon Greenall *Mr Skinner*
Moya Brady *Bridget*
Kathryn Drysdale *Bliss*
Paul Kasey *The Hoix*
Bella Emberg *Mrs Croot*
Kimberley Carunana *Jackie's Mate*
Larmorna Chappell *Mrs Pope*
Thomas Coleman *4-year-old Elton*

RECORDED AT

Q2 Studio, Newport
Pop Factory, Jenkins Street, Porth
Llandaff Fields, Llandaff, Cardiff
Heol Pentwyn Road, Whitchurch, Cardiff
ABP Cardiff Docks, Cargo Road, Cardiff Bay
Glamorgan Buildings, King Edward VII Ave, Cardiff
Cardiff Fruit Market, Barrack Lane, Cardiff
Fredrick Street, The Hayes, Cardiff
St Peters Sports & Social Club, Minster Road, Cardiff
Wash Inn, Broadway, Splott, Cardiff
Maelfa Shopping Square, Llanederyn Drive, Llanederyn, Cardiff
Jacob's Antique Centre, West Canal Wharf, Cardiff
Taff Street/Garth Street, nr Adam Street, Cardiff
Impounding Station, Newport Docks, Newport
Burnell St, Pill adjacent to Newport Docks, Newport

so engaging that you don't notice the Doctor's not there. The tone was so delicate, and if you send it up too much, you lose the potency of the dark bits that come later. There are delicious moments – Elton dancing to 'Mr Blue Sky', and particularly having Peter Kay – but it's not pure farce. It's quite emotional and romantic, and deals with bereavement. Comedians bring a freshness and energy that lifts everybody; the flip side to that is keeping the focus, and I'm generally the one having to put my foot down and spoil the mood, trying to get some work done. I tend to do quite a few takes whereas Peter's more instinctive and will do things on the spur of the moment. Shirley and Marc helped to ground it all, but Peter did like to lark about.

'We found an amazing dockside location, with enormous, quite surreal structures, peeling old blue paint cranes, it was very striking. Edward Thomas loved it too. But the day before filming, a ship came in and unloaded some steel cable. It was about eight feet high and gleaming and looked completely wrong – suddenly our desolate, rusted location looked like a normal, working docks. So the first assistant director, Susie Liggat, looked round the other side and found a desolate pathway. We put the TARDIS down, threw a couple of newspapers on the ground – which rolled in front of the camera on cue so perfectly I told the props man he should change his job title to newspaper wrangler – and it felt absolutely perfect, like something out of a Sergio Leone movie. One of the lovely things about working on *Doctor Who* is you don't have to push people. With television's hectic schedules, you're so often trying to get people to be a bit more perfectionist, but they just want to get the job

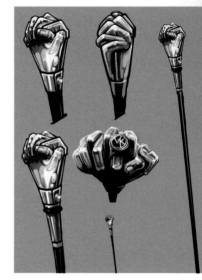

done and go home. On *Doctor Who*, everyone goes the extra mile. Remember when the cane snapped? In the script, it was just a snap across Elton's knee but someone in the Art Department came up with this idea that the cane should have clasped hands – as Victor Kennedy didn't like touching – and that the hands would open as the power leaves the Abzorbaloff. That dedication, that amount of thought is just lovely.'

Some more Art Department thought came from Edward Thomas himself, when he was designing the little cellar where LINDA meet. 'We start with a tight huddle of people, just having conversations and living their lives but, with the arrival of Victor Kennedy, everything starts to grow. We put forty coolie shades in the ceiling and illuminated them as the story progressed. It begins with just a couple lit, and on the floor was a carpet which contained the actors rather like an island. As the story progresses, the furniture starts spreading out, more lights go on, until eventually the whole place is illuminated and decorated in time for the arrival of the Abzorbaloff.'

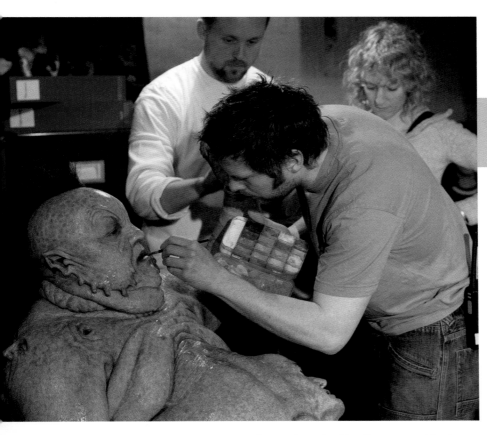

'I didn't know at first that the Abzorbaloff came from the *Blue Peter* competition,' adds Dan Zeff. 'Again it had a Tim Burton feel, a monster that absorbs people, absorbs souls – a lovely darkness to it; I think it's really quite a special monster. My four-year-old absolutely loved it.'

Handing over the creation of a big *Doctor Who* monster to a nine-year-old lad might have daunted some of his predecessors on the series, but for Russell T Davies, it was too great an opportunity to pass up. 'The editor of *Blue Peter*, Richard Marson, says doing the Design-a-Monster competition was my idea, but I think it was his. I had to be one of the judges because I needed to keep a close eye on what won. I couldn't get to the studio that day and David Tennant had to announce the winner live on air. He was phoning up, laughing, saying, "Shall I choose this football monster?" But it could only ever really have been the Abzorbaloff, which I loved. That drawing of the people sucked into its arm was brilliant, it was an easy choice. Hooray for William Grantham!'

For Millennium FX, creating the Abzorbaloff was a picnic. 'We had time,' says Rob Mayor, 'which was unusual. We already knew how to do big green monster suits because of the Slitheen – we even used the same three-fingered hand and a Slitheen tail. Peter Kay was extremely patient when he had the suit on, especially as we had to build servo mechanisms into it so the faces would move and the mouths could open and close. We did skin masks for Skinner and Ursula for the close-up shots, which were filmed using the monster's torso on a giant pole with the actors' faces pushing through it. Everything went very smoothly, which was ironic, really – we started the first series with the nightmare that was a big green monster and we finished the second series with a big green monster that was an absolute dream. Symbolic perhaps of the learning curve that everyone went through.'

2.11 FEAR HER

Staying on contemporary Earth, the Doctor and Rose touch down in London in 2012, the year of the Olympics in the delightfully named Kelly Holmes Drive, where children are mysteriously disappearing in front of their parents' eyes.

'The script came in as what we call an "over commission"', explains script editor Helen Raynor. 'That's when we commission in advance so that it's guaranteed for the next series but if something drops out for whatever reason, it's ready to go early. It would be utter folly when you've got thirteen slots, to commission just thirteen scripts, because anything can happen. What happens if Russell gets glandular fever or is run over by a bus? Also, to be brutally honest, if a first draft comes in and it is absolutely abysmal, if it's miles off target, and it's clear that, for whatever reason, it's just been a horrendous misfire, then alarm bells will start ringing and, if the second draft isn't any better, then something exists to replace it. The chances are you're only seven weeks away from filming, so asking someone else to come on board and start from scratch would be madness. This hasn't happened to us — though by the law of averages it's bound to one day.' That's not what happened here. Episode 11 was originally to be by Stephen Fry but he was simply too busy to even start in time for Series Two. 'As we had *Fear Her* ready,' recalls Helen, 'in it went. Originally I think it was set on an alien world, but Russell asked Matthew Graham to bring it down to Earth, literally.'

'Matthew's so brilliant,' says an admiring Russell T Davies. 'He took that bog-standard science fiction idea of a child drawing someone that becomes trapped in the picture, and

Rose Tyler (Billie Piper) discovers something terrible hiding in the wardrobe.

he took it to all its extremes. What if she draws the father who abused her? What if the drawings — and the dad — come back to life? And, brilliantly, what if she draws the Earth to make everyone disappear? Very clever. Abisola Agbaje is brilliant as Chloe; I always dread an episode that has a child at the centre of it but she was marvellous, just like Jessica Atkins in *The Girl in the Fireplace*. Euros casts children very well indeed.'

'It's so imaginatively written, not grand; it's careful and considered and small, and has the gag about the TARDIS — the Doctor arrives in the TARDIS and he's parked it the wrong way round. How come in all the years of *Doctor Who* nobody's played that gag before?' asks director Euros Lyn, to which writer Matthew Graham offers this reply: 'That came about because I can't parallel park, I hate parallel parking and men are supposed to be able to parallel park. And I thought, you know what, I'd love to see the Doctor messing up a piece of parallel parking with the TARDIS.'

According to Matthew, Russell's original brief to him was 'Ha, ha, ha, Matthew! You've got the cheap one. You've got episode 11.' Russell suggested the story could be set somewhere very self-contained, like a bunker. 'I really can't think of anything more boring than setting something in a bunker and said so,' smiles Matthew. 'The next thing he offered was what would happen if the Doctor comes down your street. And I loved that idea of the Doctor turning up in *Brookside*, basically. The 2012 Olympics places it nicely, and it's not as expensive as setting it in the eighteenth century or the fifty-first!'

When Euros read the script, he was worried that 'it would be small and wouldn't have the grandeur of some of the others, but that moment where the Doctor picks up the torch and starts to run, with this rousing music building up, and then a great crescendo as he runs up the red carpet and ignites the flame and the crowd roar, moves me.' Matthew recalls that he decided to place an entire stadium audience under threat 'just because I wanted the Doctor running about through the stadium, with the Olympic torch and lighting it. I pitched that to Russell, and he clapped. Once he claps, you know you're there – so that's what we did.'

Trish (Nina Sosanya), Rose (Billie Piper) and the Doctor (David Tennant) try to help Chloe Webber (Abisola Agbaje) cope with the alien child in her head.

'Russell's notes said *Edward Scissorhands* meets *Desperate Housewives*,' says costume designer Louise Page. 'Because it came soon after some very dark episodes, he wanted it to be really brightly coloured – summer, sunny, bright clothes and it's the Olympics. So I put everybody in summer clothes in the middle of winter and the freezing cold. I remember the first assistant asking me if the extras could put jackets and coats on and I had to say no because it was meant to look like a lovely hot summer's day. No one liked me that day, I can tell you.'

Chloe's unusual drawing ability originated in the bunker idea: 'Russell suggested doing something akin to *Dorian Gray*, the concept of scary pictures that take your soul,' says Matthew. 'I came up with what I thought was a very sophisticated sci-fi idea, but he felt it wouldn't really work for children: I suggested demonic or possessed children's drawings, pictures where people's eyes follow you round the room. Children's drawings always have big eyes and big hair and stick arms so what if they move? We really wanted to find something iconic that children would think was very scary. The best episodes of *Doctor Who*, going by my own kids' reactions, involved the gas mask people – Daleks scared them, but the Daleks were a concept, whereas the idea of a kid with a gas mask on saying, "Are you my mummy?" seemed to stick in a child's psyche. I wanted to find an image that did that – mainlined into a child's fears.'

Right: Concept artwork for the Isolus's pod, drawn by Peter McKinstry. Facing page: Peter McKinstry's concept sketches for the flower form of the Isolus alien.

'I'd got to a point halfway through the story where I was writing scenes where the Doctor and Rose were separated and wandering around gardens, but I was concerned that nothing scary was happening. Steven Moffat said to me, "When in doubt, have a door creaking, a sound that you can't identify, or a shadow on a wall." So I went for a noise behind a door, and put in a completely gratuitous bit of jeopardy where Rose gets attacked by the scribble monster. Funnily enough, once I'd had the idea of the scribble creature – because the scribble creature obviously is the manifestation of Chloe's fears coming out, the power coming out of the page – it spiralled off into a new bit of story. So necessity was the mother of invention, really, putting in something just for a blatant scare and then finding it taking the story on.'

Chloe's fear manifesting itself takes centre stage during the climax where the image of her father returns to threaten her, which could have been an utterly terrifying moment for young children. 'We had conversations about how bad the abuse against Chloe had been and decided to imply that he was a violent man and leave it there. I think kids now are very used to dealing with dramas about big issues and *Doctor Who* feels like a good delivery mechanism for those big issues, because children also know that the Doctor's going to sort it out, and so you can actually go into those darkish places. If you can't play with those big themes then it's not really science fiction, and I think *Doctor Who* is

The posters created by the BBC's Graphics Department. The Franz Ferdinand poster, showing the band aged up, went unused.

science fiction at its best. Originally it was more explicit that her father used to come into her room, but that might have suggested there was sexual abuse and that's a territory too extreme for *Doctor Who*.'

'I think *Fear Her* is brilliant,' says composer Murray Gold. 'What Matthew's done is address the subject of male anger in a episode which is principally about female characters, which makes an eloquent statement about how anger works in the world, because it is often perpetrated by men and released on women. It's a good summary of what a lot of *Doctor Who* is – you look at a Dalek and it's a little metal case of rage, isn't it? And *Fear Her* has that really potent image, the angry father. Whenever I think about what an angry father represents, I just think of God. In the Old Testament, God is

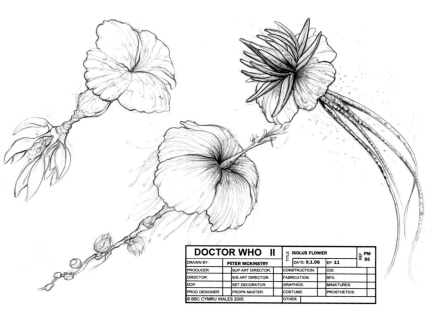

DOCTOR WHO II			TITLE	ISOLUS FLOWER		REF	PM 85
DRAWN BY:	PETER MCKINSTRY		DATE: 9.1.06	EP: 11			
PRODUCER:		SUP ART DIRECTOR:	CONSTRUCTION:		CGI:		
DIRECTOR:		S/B ART DIRECTOR:	FABRICATION:		SFX:		
DOP:		SET DECORATOR:	GRAPHICS:		MINIATURES:		
PROD DESIGNER:		PROPS MASTER:	COSTUME:		PROSTHETICS:		
© BBC CYMRU WALES 2005			OTHER:				

Directed by EUROS LYN

CAST

David Tennant *The Doctor*
and Billie Piper *Rose Tyler*
with Nina Sosanya *Trish*
Abisola Agbaje *Chloe*
Edna Doré *Maeve*
Tim Faraday *Tom's Dad*
Abdul Salis *Kel*
Richard Nichols *Driver*
Erica Eirian *Neighbour*
Stephen Marzella *Police Officer*
Huw Edwards *Commentator*
Jamie Roberts, Paul McFadden *Dad's Voice*
Jamie Roberts *Kel's Mate*
Becky Moore *Young Mum*
Karen Hulse *Weeping Mum*
Von Pearce *Postman*
Jaxon Hembry, *Dale*
Jack Palmer *Tom*
Leon Gregory *Danny Edwards*
Gabrielle Evans *Jane McKillen*
Gamala Daver *Bag Lady*
Ian Hilditch *Nervy Man*
Karl Yurkwich, Scott Simpson *Torch Runners*
Bob Currell, Bob Davies *Policemen*

RECORDED AT

Q2 Studio, Newport
Page Drive, off Pallet Way, Tremorfa, Cardiff
Cardiff Streets around City Hall
Millennium Stadium, Cardiff
Chapman's Removals & Storage Yard, Rhymney
River Bridge Road, Cardiff
St Albans Rugby Club, Tremorfa Park, Cardiff
Blenheim Road, Pen-y-lan, Cardiff

a completely capricious, bitter, wrathful, jealous and unpredictable force, who consistently demands obedience and consistently punishes his people.'

The major design element of *Fear Her* is Chloe's drawings. Edward Thomas reckons you can be the cleverest concept artist in the world but there is nothing easy about catching the naivety of a twelve-year-old's drawings and how they think. 'Joelle Rumbelow, one of our production buyers, has a twelve-year-old sister, Indigo, who's an incredible artist for her age. We sent her the script and she did us some drawings, sitting with our storyboard artist, Shaun Williams. She was doing fabulous pictures of the TARDIS and our characters from the photographs on the wall behind Shaun. He guided her, and would do very simple cartoon sketches of someone with their mouth open or closed, and then she'd look at the photograph of the person and sketch it with the mouth open or closed. Shaun then took Indigo's drawings and copied various ones in different stages of completion so that Abisola could literally just be finishing them off by following really loose and almost invisible pencil lines. We did enough bits of progression that if she didn't get one right, it didn't matter because we had the next one there straight away. It was almost like stop-frame animation.'

'I was so scared, I got as far as writing, "Interior TARDIS," and then I stopped,' laughs Matthew Graham. 'I emailed Mark Gatiss and said I was really scared. He emailed back saying, "Yep, that's right – and it doesn't go away!" So for a moment it felt as if I had been given this beautiful, valuable, historical object that everyone had heard of, and told it was mine to look after, polish, and then pass on. When *Fear Her* went out, that was my moment of holding that precious object in my hands for a few moments, and then passing it on. They'll never take that away from me. On my deathbed, I can say, "I wrote for *Doctor Who*," and then die.'

2.12/2.13 ARMY OF GHOSTS and DOOMSDAY

The end of the second series; the end of Rose Tyler and her family; the first showcase of the Torchwood Institute. If all that wasn't enough, Russell T Davies's scripts throw a couple of other ingredients into the mix, namely Daleks versus Cybermen. Every fan's dream or every fan's nightmare?

'I think it's a great idea,' the writer explains. 'Frankly, you've had the Daleks in a hugely popular series; you've had the Cybermen. It's irresistible to put them together; it's begging to be done. Watching the programme as a kid, I used to wonder vaguely whether they bumped into each other and had skirmishes off-screen… But this didn't come from that – this was just about using two great big icons. Bronze and steel – they're just meant to clash. You've got to keep raising the stakes (and believe me in Series Three the stakes will get even higher for planet Earth, let me tell you now). I wanted to create battleground Earth, where the human race is trapped in the middle of two giants scrapping. I always think that, in the mythology of the programme, they're like gods, and it's nice to give things this status in a godless universe. These are two great big creatures from hell and they're sent into hell at the end. At the end of Series One, God is Rose; Bad Wolf/God appears as a nineteen-year-old shop girl. Later, they meet the devil, but it's a thing on a planet underneath a black hole. It's a very Humanist approach to it all – an atheist approach, really – to say that all these things exist, but they're ordinary people, they're ordinary things. So, for there to be hell on Earth, it means Daleks versus Cybermen, and the stakes have got to be that high for the Doctor to lose Rose at the end. If it had just been a monster called the Zogs coming along for that episode, I think you'd end up feeling slightly disappointed. You'd think, "What, the Zogs separated the Doctor and Rose forever? The Daleks didn't? The Cybermen didn't? That doesn't work." The Daleks and the Cybermen together means the stakes are raised high enough for the ending to be truly cataclysmic.'

'We specifically designed the Dalek in the first series in relation to Billie's height,' explains production designer Edward Thomas. 'When Billie looks at the Dalek they are eye-to-eye, which is why the Dalek ended up being slightly taller than it had been in the classic series. In *Doomsday*, we have the same thing except, this time, Rose is in charge, and against a Black Dalek. Funnily enough, the toy Dalek that was produced after the first series came in very handy. The toy company sent us gifts of Daleks, which we sprayed with various colours, matts and glosses when we were working out the colour scheme for the new Dalek. We kept on coming back to black, it just seemed the most evil. We added bits of silver, took them off; added bits of gold, took them off.'

'The Dalek boys were absolutely brilliant at the movement,' Graeme Harper recalls. 'There was one moment – Scene 35, it's burnt into my memory – just before the Doctor makes his entrance into the Sphere Room. Rose and Mickey are to the left of the Genesis Ark and they're being backed off by the Daleks, who are doing this wonderful ballet, spreading round the Ark so they're ending up at quarters to it – it was a lovely pirouette, beautiful. A movement which is so balletic and yet absolutely monstrous. It might not seem to be a big deal, but when you know how difficult it is to move a Dalek, it's brilliant.'

13.68.18   DALEKS GET SUCKED TO THE LEFT. PAN WITH THEM.

13.68.19   DALEKS GET SUCKED IN THROUGH WINDOW.

13.68.19   DALEKS GET SUCKED TOWARDS BOTTOM LEFT OF FRAME.

13.74.01.01   DALEK "EMERGENCY TEMPORAL SHIFT"

13.74.01   GENESIS SUCKED UP INTO TORCHWOOD TOWERS.

Shaun Williams's storyboards of the Daleks being drawn violently back into the Void. Facing page: Daleks versus Cybermen in the Sphere Room. Battle of the century!

Inside the Daleks were the same team from the climax to Series One, led by Barnaby Edwards. 'Nicholas Pegg played Sec, the Black Dalek (which was actually my original Dalek from Series One repainted), while I operated one of the gold Daleks, as did David Hankinson and Dan Barratt. Stuart Crossman was hired to be the Genesis Arc, and we had a few days' rehearsal so we could get used to moving around one another but, as it turned out, Stuart never actually did anything other than sit in it to stop it falling over when Mickey crashed into it during the fight sequence. Stuart was meant to move it during the other big battle in the Torchwood set but an FX man had to operate it for those scenes because it had dry ice pumping out of it. I was already contracted for panto when the BBC contacted me about *Doomsday*, so I couldn't make the first block which was all the Sphere Room stuff. Flatteringly, they were keen to have me for whatever dates I could manage, so Anthony Spargo replaced me for the dates I couldn't make. When Dalek Thay is ordered to go and confront the two Cybermen, it's Anthony who goes out, but it's me, weeks later, on another set facing them.' This was, in fact, the last Dalek scene to be shot, and all the other operators had gone home the previous day. 'It was just Nick Briggs and me in a corridor – which is pretty much how we began with *Dalek* the year before.'

'I'm so proud that when you ask someone about *Doctor Who*,' laughs Dalek voice artiste Nicholas Briggs, 'the first thing they say is "Ex-ter-min-ate!" and now it's me providing that. It also brings with it heaps of peripheral stuff, like doing voices for toys and press launches, the *Blue Peter Prom*, BAFTA, endless radio interviews and such like but, when all's said and done, it's being on set with the Doctor and the Daleks that's the best part of it!'

Directed by GRAEME HARPER

CAST

David Tennant *The Doctor*
and Billie Piper *Rose Tyler*
with Camille Coduri *Jackie Tyler*
Noel Clarke *Mickey Smith*
Shaun Dingwall *Pete Tyler*
Andrew Hayden-Smith *Jake Simmonds*
Tracy-Ann Oberman *Yvonne Hartman*
Raji James *Dr Rajesh Singh*
Freema Agyeman *Adeola*
Hadley Fraser *Gareth*
Oliver Mellor *Matt*
Barbara Windsor *Peggy Mitchell*
Hajaz Akram *Indian Newsreader*
Anthony Debaeck *French Newsreader*
Takako Akashi *Japanese Newsreader*
Paul Fields *Weatherman*
David Warwick *Police Commissioner*
Rachel Webster *Eileen*
Kyoko Morita, Eriko Kurasawa,
Mari Yoshida *Japanese Girls*
Maddi Cryer *Housewife in Advert*
Derek Acorah *Himself*
Alistair Appleton *Himself*
Trisha Goddard *Herself*
Paul Kasey *Cyber Leader*
Nicholas Briggs *Dalek/Cybermen Voices*
Barnaby Edwards, Nicholas Pegg, Anthony Spargo,
Dan Barratt, Dave Hankinson *Dalek Operators*
Stuart Crossman *Genesis Ark Operator*
Jon Davey, Adam Sweet, JJ Angel, Kristian Arthur,
Matthew Gregory, Claudio Laurini, Scott Price,
Joe White, Pete Symmonds, Matt Doman *Ghosts*
Ian Wilson, Nick Wade, Sabrina Morris *Ghost Shift Suits*
Yolaris Khan, Marc Bradley, Peter Crebbin *Ghost Shift White Coats*
Brian Morgan *Sphere Room Technician*
Liz Edne *Mum*
Simon Cornish *Dad*
Finnian Cohen-Ennis *Son*
Ciara Cohen-Ennis *Daughter*
Marcus Hobbs *Captain*
Luke Parsons, Jason Ingram, Sarah Emerson
Thomas, Shane Davis, Eddie Martin, Jon William,
Elfed Price, Adeola Akande, Brett Postians,
Mike Freeman *Torchwood Soldiers*
Nicky Valentine *Exterminated Lady*
Andrew Michell, Phil Kirk *Sergeants*
Jeff Jones, Steve Cooper *Policemen*
Ken Hoskings, Ruari Mears, Karl Greenwood,
Pete Symmonds, Mat Doman, Jon Davy,
Kevin Hudson, Adam Sweet, Joe White, >>

This story is another showcase for the CG work of The Mill. 'Flying Daleks, easy,' says Dave Houghton. 'Cybermen were harder, because it was touch and go whether we were going to have time to do any Cybermen at all. We wanted to make it feel like there were hundreds walking through the streets of London in formation. I think you'd be hard-pressed to spot the difference between our Cybermen and the real ones.'

'The ghosts were the tough thing,' says Will Cohen. 'We filmed the shot that they were to go into and then we shot lots of men in black skintight bodysuits with hoods, just walking around in front of green screens. We then blended those with the Cybermen. When we composited it all, we used the men in black suits as a mask, warped the backgrounds, added key flaring highlights – it looks quite effective and, when they change into Cybermen, it's a nice reveal. The Dalek Sphere was meant to have a reflective surface, but because of time constraints – and the fact that you'd have to film every shot from two angles to get the reflection to wrap around it – we didn't really have time. So we ended up with a burnished steel sphere.'

Two important elements drew to a conclusion in these episodes. Something called 'Torchwood' had been mentioned fleetingly in *Bad Wolf* in Series One, then in *The Christmas Invasion* and in seven episodes of the second series. 'The Torchwood stuff,' confirms Russell, 'was meant to be just those fleeting mentions, culminating with seeing the Torchwood Institute in episodes twelve and thirteen. It was only when I was writing *Tooth and Claw* that I thought I could show the foundation of Torchwood, but that wasn't the original plan at all. By showing Queen Victoria

Matthew Savage's concept drawings of (below) a Dalek in relation to the Genesis Ark and (above) the Daleks emerging from the Void Ship.

JJ Angel, Peter McKinstry, Teilo Trimble, Jimmy O'Dee *Cybermen*
and introducing Catherine Tate as *Donna Noble*

RECORDED AT
Q2 Studio, Newport
Brandon Estate, Kennington, London
Westminster Bridge, London
Tredegar House & Park, Newport
St Nicholas, nr Cardiff
Hoel Spencer, Brynceithyn, Bridgend
Brackla Bunkers, Brackla, Bridgend
Mount Stuart Square, Bute Street, Cardiff Bay
HTV Studios, Culverhouse Cross, Cardiff
Unit 878 Picketston Site, RAF St Athan, Barry
RAF St Athan
Loudoun Square, Butetown, Cardiff
Cardiff Dockside, Cargo Rd, Cardiff
Basement, Capital Arcade, Churchill Way, Cardiff
Southerndown Beach, Ogmore Vale, nr Bridgend
Broadstairs Road, Canton, Cardiff
The Hayes, Cardiff
Teddington Studios, London
Enfys Television Studios, Unit 31, Portmanmoor Road, Cardiff
BBC Elstree Studios
News Studio C2, BBC Broadcasting House, Llandaff, Cardiff

deciding upon Torchwood House, I could then say that she had set everything in motion, but it was just one of those on-the-hoof things.'

'I didn't know anything about Torchwood, other than what I read in my stories,' says director Graeme Harper. 'I then read *Tooth and Claw* and understood the connection. Russell explained that the Torchwood that I was dealing with is very different to Queen Victoria's Torchwood. It's now become much more politicised and working with the secret information side of government. And the Torchwood of the spin-off series is different again – different building, different environment, different set-up. It's moved on. So I didn't have to worry about all that.'

The second element, and the biggest event of the story, indeed of the whole second series, was the departure of Rose Tyler from the Doctor's life, forever safe in 'Pete's World', the parallel world first seen earlier in the year in *Rise of the Cybermen* and *The Age of Steel*.

'Russell and I had a conversation late one night at The Mill, talking about his vision and dreams for each scene,' says Graeme Harper. 'Not how I was to shoot it, but the emotion that he wanted to convey and consolidate. Of course, most of it I'd got from the scripts, but there were little tricks, little details, tiny moments that I hadn't picked up on that were really important. Thank goodness we had that conversation, because they were the icing on the cake: details of characterisation; little looks and reactions. If we hadn't had those moments, I still think it would have been great television, because they're good scripts, but the little nuances that he gave me made the overall story richer. I could then pass that on to the actors, so if you watch Rose, for example,

whenever we cut to her, she's always reacting, caring, no matter what else is going on. So, when it comes to editing, you see little quick looks between Rose and the Doctor, between Rose and her father, between Rose and Mickey. It's absolutely magical – their eyes are darting, they're playing, they're listening, they're really reacting.

'Our duty is to tell a good story well, and they're all good stories. They're all so different, so you can't just take the money and run. I would never do that in any job, because I want to make the best I can with what I've got. A lot of the time that's easy; sometimes it's hard. But *Doctor Who* is an absolute joy, because it's such fun. The hard part can be making sure it's plausible and you cover the cracks so that people believe the story, get wrapped up in it, and don't ask too many silly questions.'

Above: Didn't we have a lovely time the day we went to Bad Wolf Bay! Mickey (Noel Clarke), Rose (Billie Piper), Jackie (Camille Coduri) and Pete (Shaun Dingwall). Below: Rose following Mickey into the Sphere Room, psychic paper in hand…

'The parallel worlds story was domestic, and therefore a much more real story,' Russell suggests. 'Although it involved a sci-fi parallel world, it's actually about a mum and dad and their daughter; about a family brought together by the Doctor across time and space, and across parallel worlds. And so that was how we wrote out Rose: there's no other way you could do it. She was so fundamental to the series that I was never going to kill her. I had to seal the walls between different universes and say they can never be transgressed. And I had to leave her happy, that's the only ending that I could possibly have been satisfied with. So I took the whole history, going all the way back to *Father's Day*, as a big set-up for the only thing that could separate her from the Doctor. We knew Billie was leaving at the end of Series Two, right from the end of production on Series One; so we could really plan it all in advance.'

'Those last two episodes are so beautifully paced,' thinks star David Tennant. 'Again, it's that whole Rose journey, which has been seeded throughout the series; the Mickey journey, the Jackie journey, the Pete Tyler journey, all of these chickens coming home to roost. When I first read the scripts, I just cried my eyes out. Billie and I were two of only five people to have the Bad Wolf Bay pages, which were kept secret from everyone else. Even the crew didn't know what they were filming that day. They just had to turn up. To this day, I don't even know how many of them knew what they had filmed, because we were on a very windy beach. The sound man will have heard it, and they'd all have seen what was going on, but beyond that I don't know how much people were aware of. I use the sonic screwdriver at one point and, because nobody had been given scripts or briefed, Phil Shellard, our standby props man, didn't even know it was needed. But Phil is known as the Grand Master, so of course he had brought everything just in case.

And then there was the Catherine Tate scene, which even fewer people knew about. That was filmed with five people. We wrapped the final day's shoot for Series Two, which was for *The Satan Pit*, and everyone said, "Cheerio". We came back a couple of hours later, once the studio had cleared. Graeme Harper came down and we filmed the Donna scene for the very, very end of *Doomsday* in top, top secret. Then we all went off to the wrap party as if nothing had happened. It was the last thing done and, nicely, it was on the TARDIS set , at Q2. After that, everything was shifted to Upper Boat.'

'When I got the script, it broke my heart,' says Graeme Harper. 'Worse, I realised I had to guide this really difficult, tender moment on the beach. Talk about pressure. Talk about iconic moments – we'd been building our whole story up to that one scene. My problem with that scene was how many times could I shoot this scene favouring Billie? How many times do I have to shoot it with her doing the dialogue for David and ask her to get emotional? On the morning we were doing the scene, I met Billie and David in the make-up caravan, and I asked how they wanted to do it. I explained the shots I wanted to get, so they would know how many times I needed to do the scene. But who was I going to shoot in close-up first? I was worried for Billie, to be honest. They'd obviously discussed it, because there was a little look between them, and then David told me to

Above: David Hankinson getting into his Dalek. Below: The Doctor stands amidst the legendary Cult of Skaro.

Above right: David Tennant
prepares for the climactic loss
of Rose from his life.
Below: Cameras roll on the
tragic farewell.

do Billie first. Billie said she'd probably got two takes in her and then the tears would be all dried up. Well, the first take was magnificent, you couldn't top it. She gave it everything and it was brilliant. Unfortunately, her nose looked very cold – it was a freezing January day on the coldest, most open to the wind beach anywhere, and there was something running down her nose. I felt that I couldn't cut it because she was right in the middle of it, so I allowed her to get to the end of the scene, then went over and told her it was the best scene I'd ever directed in my life. Which it was, no argument. Then I had to explain that during the latter part something had come down her face. I asked her if she would do it again, and I know she was upset, she wasn't rude or aggressive to me, but she was clearly upset because she'd given it so much. We did it again and it was even better but, this time, her hair was blown all over her face. In the end I used most of the second take and covered any moment that the hair was in the way by using bits from the first take. And what you see is a fantastic performance. And then David's performance is fantastic too. It's her scene and he gives her the moment. He wasn't going to let her down in any way and between them, they create a fantastic ending.'

Also making her final appearance was Jackie Tyler. 'She got back with Pete, well, *a* Pete,' grins Camille Coduri. 'I never expected that, I thought she was going to be

obliterated or eaten by something, in a comic but sad moment. I was so thrilled we were going to be a family again, Jackie could have her daughter back, and Mickey was a hero, and we were going to go off and live in the other universe – how fantastic. I got shivers when I read it, I thought this was so wonderful. And Jackie was pregnant! Billie, Shaun and I decided it was a boy, and we'd call him Billy!'

'At the beginning of *Army of Ghosts*, we had to make Billie look slightly younger,' puts in make-up designer Sheelagh Wells. 'Putting her in a ponytail and taking away the sophisticated bob immediately makes her look young. We didn't have to do any particular work on her face, because she's just gorgeous anyway. At the end of *Doomsday*, there's a very small amount of ageing – just a discreet bit of hair work to help and to let her talent do the rest, really.

The end of an era.

But the final word on Rose Tyler has to go to the man who created her and guided her right through to these final traumatic moments – Russell T Davies.

'I do have a good antenna for a spin-off too far, and "Rose Tyler: Earth Defence" was commissioned by BBC One. They wanted a ninety-minute special for a bank holiday about the adventures of Rose working for Torchwood in the parallel world. That was commissioned for about two months until I said we'd gone too far. It had a huge budget for a bank holiday film. Was I mad to turn that down? No, because the whole point of losing her is that we miss her but she's gone. Like the Doctor, we can never see what she gets up to in that parallel world. It would have spoilt the heart of the whole franchise actually, and we'd know too much and it would water down that climax. And I like the fact you don't find out everything… On that beach at the end, we had some dialogue where the Doctor asks if she's back with Mickey, but we removed that and Rose's reply. I doubt that she is, but we didn't want any concrete answers – her life is too big and too exciting. She's never going to settle down; her mind is too wide to ever do that. That's why I love the fact that it's her mother who runs towards her in the end. It's not her dad, not her boyfriend; it's her lovely mother. It's the only ending you could give Rose Tyler.'

INTER-ACTIVITY

Following the phenomenal success of Series One, Julie Gardner was keen to see how else the programme could be made available to today's modern children and teenagers. Back in the heyday of the show in the 1970s and 1980s, the most the average fan could do was look through the fledgling *Doctor Who Magazine*, or read a novelisation of a story that had already been seen on television. Throw in a few toys and a couple of jigsaw puzzles and that was about as interactive as it got.

But this is a whole new millennium and, as the highly popular *Doctor Who* website (bbc.co.uk/doctorwho) has shown, there's always a thirst for what is loosely termed 'new media' where this show is concerned. The *Doctor Who* site, overseen by senior content producer James Goss and his team at BBC Online's Interactive Drama and

Merry Christmas! The Graske wants to add you to his alien collection!

Entertainment Department, has wonderfully supported both new series of *Doctor Who*. Offering both factual information and some amazing fictional sites, the website is the flagship of the BBC's commitment to using new media to enable the *Doctor Who* viewer to keep up with everything about the show.

ATTACK OF THE GRASKE

When the decision was taken to make *The Christmas Invasion*, the BBC's New Media arm got onboard and a decision was made to increase the interactive output even further…

Straight after *The Christmas Invasion* was transmitted on Christmas Day 2005, viewers on digital platforms – and, subsequently, Internet users – could access a wholly interactive *Doctor Who* adventure in which the Doctor, played of course by David Tennant, invited viewers to take part, via their TV remote control handsets, in his hunt for the time-travelling Graske. The participants were set a series of puzzles and observational games that would help the Doctor reach the Graske's lair. A number of alternative outcomes were shot, so that one pre-recorded sequence was shown if viewers solved a puzzle successfully and, if they got it wrong, a different outcome was seen.

Andrew Whitehouse and Jo Pearce of BBC New Media's Interactive team were the instigators of this project, originally entitled 'Changeling World', before they settled on the more child-friendly *Attack of the Graske*. They reasoned that there was an opening for an interactive experience that younger viewers would relish. Russell T Davies suggested Gareth Roberts as a writer; Gareth believes this was thanks to his Ninth Doctor novel *Only Human*. 'Shortly after they'd read that, I got a call from script editor Simon Winstone asking me if I'd have a crack at a treatment for an interactive challenge episode. Nobody had done anything like it before!' For Jo Pearce it was a nice challenge as well: new media is rapidly becoming an integral part of television production. 'It's still fairly new,' she explains, 'but, as technology changes constantly, who knows what we will be producing in five years.' It also gave Gareth the chance to create a new monster for the Doctor to defeat, although he's not seeking a rematch in his television episode for Series Three. 'The Graske was reverse-engineered from the requirements of the interactive challenge; I'm not sure how it could work in another story. But you never know – if the story was right…'

Work on *Attack of the Graske* took four days, in four different locations. The first was a house in the Penarth area of Cardiff and featured all the scenes involving the family in their home, featuring Nicholas Beveney as the Dad, with Lisa Palfrey as the Mum, James Harris and Mollie Kabia as the two children, and Robin Meredith and Gwenyth Petty as the grandparents, whilst Jimmy Vee was inside the Graske prosthetics. This was useful for Neill Gorton at Millennium

Anna Hope and Sophie Higgs prepare for the morning's shoot on the first Tardisode.

FX, since Jimmy's previous appearances as the Moxx of Balhoon and the Space Pig meant a body cast was already available. 'I read the script and saw the Graske as a little mischievous jester, with a three-pronged hat,' Neill recalls. 'I did a doodle, sent it off to everyone and they approved it quickly. So we handed it over to Martin Rezard, who did the sculpt – his first one for *Doctor Who* in fact – and then they shot it.'

The second day was all the stuff aboard the Graske's ship, recorded at Enfys Studios, with The Mill's fully computer-generated Slitheen. Then it was onto the Victorian streets, shot around Butetown in Cardiff. Joining the Graske, Mum and Dad were Ben Holland as the unfortunate Urchin, with Catherine Olding as the woman and Roger Nott as the man. The last day was on the TARDIS set at Q2, and comprised all the linking material with David Tennant as the new Doctor, providing viewers with their first opportunity to see the newly clothed Doctor in action after his trademark suit's brief appearance at the end of *The Christmas Invasion*.

TARDISODES

'The *Tardisodes* and *Attack of the Graske* were commissioned at the same time,' says producer Jo Pearce. 'Initially called "Vortexts", the *Tardisodes* were designed as a treat for the audience and to use as a testing ground for mobile television.'

Brought in to script each of these was Gareth Roberts. 'When Jo and Ashley Way, the director of *Attack of the Graske*, got the green light to make *Tardisodes*, I was in the right place,' says Gareth. 'Writing *Graske* had proved I could handle the strangeness and newness of it all.'

For executive producer Julie Gardner, the various new media platforms, as they are called, are very important. 'I absolutely love the idea of these one-minute mini-episodes that you can have on your phone or on your PC – it's just a little bit of extra fun. I love Pixar films, and the joy for me in going to see one is not only how well the stories are told, how beautiful the animation is, how extraordinary that experience is, but all the extras you get, like the shorts at the beginning or the outtakes during the credits. You feel like you're part of this world, and that they really care about you. And I think doing the *Tardisodes*, doing *Attack of the Graske*, doing the websites, doing all the things that tie in with the show – you can really immerse yourself in additional *Doctor Who*, but it's being done in a coherent way that benefits the actual episodes.'

The *Tardisodes* were available to download to mobile telephones and PCs a week before transmission of each episode of Series Two. The first to be made was for *Fear Her*, shot whilst the main crew were filming on the housing estate in Tremorfa. Daniel Roachford was the presenter of a *Crimewatch*-style programme, asking for help locating the missing children, Dale and Jane. The next day, the *Tardisode* crew started off shooting the one for *New Earth*, which was available a fortnight before any of the series had been transmitted. It showed Novice Hame (played again by Anna Hope), a patient (Sophie Higgs) and two cat-nuns (Kim Wyld and Natalie Cuzner) demonstrating the benefits of the New New York hospital. This was recorded alongside the *Tardisodes* for *The Girl in the Fireplace* and *School Reunion* – the clock shattering and the human crew of the *Madame de Pompadour* (Liz Armon-Lloyd and David Martin) coming to a grisly end, and Noel Clarke as Mickey researching strange lights in the sky over Deffry Vale school. All of these were recorded at Enfys Studios in Cardiff rather than on the original locations or sets at Q2.

Liz Armon-Lloyd, before the droids find a use for her body...

The third day of recording was for two other episodes, *Tooth and Claw* and *Rise of the Cybermen*, this time on location. The first of these was shot in the Cefn-y-crib moors at Hafod yr Ynrs, where a Crofter (Alan Dorrington) meets his death at the teeth and claws of the werewolf. The Mill later added in both the meteorite crash and the CG werewolf, expressing a certain amount of curiosity that the full beast was actually going to be seen a whole week before the episode was transmitted. 'That said,' says Dave Houghton, 'it's such a quick glimpse, and shot really nicely, so you barely have time to register it.' Also done that day was the shot of Ricky, again requiring Noel Clarke, in an alleyway off the Newport Road in Cardiff, shutting off his Cybus Industries mobile phone for *Tardisode* no. 5.

The *Tardisode* for *The Age of Steel* was a simple voiceover by Robert Booth, who did the same for *Rise of the Cybermen*. 'We wanted a lot of variety,' explains Gareth Roberts, 'so you'd never be able to predict what you'd be getting on your phone. And the tone could be quite different to that of the actual episode, just to spice things up and not be formulaic. *Tooth and Claw*'s *Tardisode* was very a "old-school" prologue, whereas the ones for *New Earth* and *Rise of the Cybermen* were clearly media snippets from the particular fictional universe of each episode.'

It was back to a drama clip for *The Idiot's Lantern*, once again featuring a member of the actual cast, this time Margaret John as Tommy Connolly's Gran as the Wire removes her face. This was the first *Tardisode* shot at the Q2 studios in February, during recording of the episode itself, which enabled the use of the actual Connolly house set. This was also true of *The Satan Pit*: that *Tardisode*, shot in April on the Sanctuary Base set, showed Curt (played by Kenon Mann) receiving the late Captain Walker's effects from an Ood (Carl Greenwood) and becoming infected by the hieroglyphs on the book, before being discovered by Chenna (Alys Thomas). Later the same afternoon, the production team moved to BBC Wales's main Broadcasting House in Llandaff to shoot the discussion between Captain Walker (Jason May) and McMillan (Ri Richards) for *The Impossible Planet* in the staff canteen! 'It was pretty much left up to me what went into each script,' says Gareth Roberts. 'That said, Simon Winstone sometimes had far better ideas, so we often went with his notes and I fleshed it all out. But I was always encouraged not to worry about budgets and things and just let my imagination go.'

The final day of *Tardisode* shooting took place on New Media's own doorstep, using their Presentation Studio for the *Tardisode* sequence for *Doomsday* where the news presenter (Adrienne O'Sullivan) alerts the public to the invasion. This was followed by the *Tardisode* for *Army of Ghosts* featuring investigative reporter Artif (Shane Zaza), having been given top secret documents by his anonymous source (Catherine Harris), being betrayed by his editor (Nicky Rainsford) to the Torchwood Agent (Dafydd Emyr) and scientists (Gerard Cooke and Angus Brown).

The day ended with the *Tardisode* for *Love & Monsters*, shot at Insole Court, a Function House in Llandaff with the tea lady (Olwen Rees) coming to an absorbing end with Victor Kennedy (played here by Dean Harris).

Whether the *Tardisode* experiment will continue for Series Three has yet to be decided but, whatever happens, it seems that the New Media team will have something out there to support the series again. 'Although we are overjoyed by the success of the *Tardisodes*,' explains Jo Pearce, 'mobile television is still very much in its infancy. We'll continue to focus on the website because the *Tardisodes* performed exceptionally well there as well, and so we are hoping to make the various platform content more cohesive during the coming year.'

Top: Mickey uncovers a mystery at Deffry Vale and contacts Rose. Above: The Connolly's new television has a nasty surprise in store for Gran.

Anna Hope watches as work progresses on the New Earth Tardisode.

Christmas 2006... and Beyond

At the outset of production on Series Three, the year's stories have been broken down into eight blocks:

Block One directed by Euros Lyn
    3.X *The Runaway Bride* by Russell T Davies
Block Two directed by Charles Palmer
    3.1 *Smith and Jones* by Russell T Davies
    3.2 by Gareth Roberts
Block Three directed by Richard Clarke
    3.3 by Russell T Davies
    3.6 by Stephen Greenhorn
Block Four directed by James Strong
    3.4 & 3.5 by Helen Raynor
Block Five directed by Graeme Harper
    3.8 & 3.9 by Paul Cornell
Block Six
    3.7 by Chris Chibnall
    3.10 by Steven Moffat
Block Seven
    3.11 (to be shot simultaneously with 3.10)
Block Eight
    3.12 & 3.13 by Russell T Davies

CHRISTMAS 2006... AND BEYOND

It's Tuesday 6 June 2006. A huge meeting room at the new Upper Boat studios on one of the hottest days during the hottest summer in the lifetime of a majority of the people in the room. Euros Lyn has brought together his team for Block One of Series Three, which consists of this year's one-hour Christmas special, *The Runaway Bride*: Edward Thomas and his art department; Louise Page for costume, with newcomer Barbara Southcott overseeing make-up; Neill Gorton and Rob Mayor are there from Millennium FX; Mike Tucker from the Model Unit and Will Cohen and Dave Houghton from The Mill are back as well. Add to this script editors, location managers, assistant directors, production manager Tracie Simpson's production staff, executive producers Russell and Julie, and producer Phil, who is being trailed by Susie Liggat because Phil's taking some well-deserved R & R midway through Series Three, and you have a large number of people gathered together at the first tone meeting for the first script of the 2007 series.

And what a script it is. As seen at the end of *Doomsday*, bride-to-be Donna Noble has found herself aboard the TARDIS, and is understandably distressed. What follows is a rollercoaster ride of a script involving everything from car chases on the Chiswick flyover with one of the Robot Santas last seen in *The Christmas Invasion* (Euros uses toy cars to demonstrate how this will work, while a salt shaker doubles for the TARDIS) to a confrontation with the Empress of the Racnoss.

During the course of the tone meeting a number of points are raised, ranging from Louise's choice of grey or black suits at the wedding to how big Mike Tucker's models need to be. (In fact, Mike's other work commitments will ultimately preclude him working on *The Runaway Bride* but, like a true pro, he recommends one of his former BBC Visual Effects Workshop associates to take the job on.) 'Can we use the *Torchwood* helicopter to get visual shots of the road?' asks location manager Patrick Schweitzer, whilst there's a lot of discussion between The Mill and Edward Thomas's people about the best way to hang Donna from the ceiling.

Then there's the Empress of the Racnoss herself, to be played by Sarah Parish – how will she be achieved? The art department's Peter McKinstry has produced some beautiful concept art; Neill Gorton of Millennium FX points out a possible drawback in the design but Russell just grins: 'And that's a problem because?' Millennium meanwhile will be making some changes to the Pilot Fish – the Robot Santas – because, this year, their faces must be full head masks, made to fit over the robot heads beneath. 'They were just face masks for *The Christmas Invasion*,' recalls Millennium's Rob Mayor, 'but this time we've made the droid mask to fit on a stuntman while he's driving. That was quite a process – we needed to know who the stuntman was so we could make the droid mask to fit him and then cast the Santa mask that goes on top. We also sculpted the Santa mask with a beard on, so it was recognisably a Santa as soon as it came out of the mould.'

One sequence requires filming in a Cardiff office building and, if possible, the real workers will feature in the background. 'But we can't film on a Friday,' explains first assistant director Peter Bennett 'because we want to see suits and ties and for them it's dress-down Friday!'

LOCKED 07.06.06

DOCTOR WHO III		TITLE	BURNT OUT SONIC		PM 26
DRAWN BY:	PETER MCKINSTRY		DATE: 07.06.06	EP: 1	
PRODUCER:		DIRECTOR:		PROP MASTER:	
PROD DESIGNER:		ASSOC DESIGNER:	DOP:	CONSTRUCTION:	
SUP ART DIR:		CHIEF SUP ART DIR:	SFX:	CGI:	
S/B ART DIR:		SET DECORATOR:	COSTUME:	GRAPHICS:	
©BBC CYMRU/WALES 2006/2007			OTHER:		

One victim of the Judoon's plans during the first episode of the third series appears to be the Doctor's trusty sonic screwdriver, going by this concept picture by Peter McKinstry.

COFFEE AND TV

Many hours, cups of coffee and chocolate cakes later, everyone retired back to their offices or homes to mull over the day's discussions. Russell headed home to do some rewriting, while Euros prepared for his first day of shooting. This would be Tuesday 4 July, when a series of what are called plate shots were taken. These are background shots of London locations that The Mill is then able to add elements to. A solitary office worker was needed for this day, played by supporting artist Samantha Bennett. The next day, still in London, the cameras rolled for the first time on some action sequences – the car chase. A stunt driver, George Cottle, became a Robot Santa for the day, with Corinna McShane replacing Catherine Tate as Donna for a number of tricky and dangerous shots involving swerves and near-misses.

On Thursday 6 July, David Tennant and Catherine Tate met up again at the helipad atop the IPC Building in the City of London and filming began in earnest for *The Runaway Bride*. It all wrapped up exactly four weeks later, on Thursday 3 August, with David Tennant shot against a green-screen background for scenes of the Doctor standing in the TARDIS doorway.

But there was no rest – four days later it all started up again. This time, it was Charles Palmer directing *Smith and Jones*, the episode that introduces Freema Agyeman as Martha Jones. Freema's first day of shooting, Tuesday 8 August, was on location at the University of Glamorgan, doubling as the Royal Hope Hospital, alongside fellow actors Roy Marsden, Anne Reid, Ben Righton and Vineeta Rishi. The next day, she was joined for the first time by David Tennant, as Martha learns how many hearts the Doctor has.

Within moments, the Doctor has found his new soul mate. Rose Tyler will never be forgotten, nor replaced but, for the last of the Time Lords, Martha is a wonderful alternative. Before long they'll be such firm friends that the viewers of *Doctor Who* will care about Martha as much as they did for Rose.

Above: Peter McKinstry's early designs for the Empress of the Racnoss, seen in The Runaway Bride.
Right: A translator device, used by the leader of the alien Judoon, drawn by Peter McKinstry.

For Russell and his team, creating a new companion is never an easy task. 'I did consider a companion from the past – a nineteenth-century girl, like one of those maids that Rose was always bumping into. I carried that around in my head for a couple of months but started to have more and more reservations about it… it just felt too obvious and had really all been done in *Doctor Who*.'

Enter then lovely twenty-three-year-old medical student Martha Jones, who works at the Royal Hope Hospital in London. Script editor and, for Series Three, script writer Helen Raynor explains that the new companion is evolving from the scripts and the performances, rather than from a checklist of character attributes. 'Script editors tend to sit in a room and talk till they're blue in the face about how she's this character, she's warm, she's adventurous, she's all these character qualities – little labels on a post-it note stuck all over a cut-out character. But it's only when you actually see characters in a script doing things – how they behave, how adventurous they are, the decisions they make – that, all of a sudden, you really see the character. It's all very well saying a character's "warm" but that doesn't actually mean anything – does it mean that they're warm and maternal with a big bosom and a cup of tea always on the go? Or they're "tough but with a heart of gold" – it doesn't really mean anything.

'It's true that the companion role changes with each character, but they're always just a few degrees away from that basic companion character. You couldn't, for example, have a companion in our show who hated travelling in the TARDIS, because then you'd just want to kill her. She's going to have to enjoy it in a different way from Rose, and there are lots of small things that will come out in the writing, but essentially they are still a Doctor and a human travelling through time and space. Although, because there was always a childlike quality about Rose, I don't think that's going to be there as much in Martha.'

'A true twenty-first-century girl,' agrees Russell. 'But we're not sitting down with a great big list of adjectives – we won't give her an allergy to bananas. The character has to develop organically, she has to be a true person rather than ticks on a list. She'll have a family, but they're very different from Rose's because there are lots of different ways of approaching it.'

KEEPING UP WITH THE JONES

'Freema's hit the ground running, thank God!' is Russell's satisfied reaction. 'I was watching a scene of Martha in the TARDIS – her very first TARDIS scene, in fact, for both the actor and the character – and, I swear, I got this strange sensation. Literally, like a tingling at the back of my neck. Took me a few minutes to work it out. And then I realised – I was remembering. I could feel that memory again, of being ten years old, and watching Sarah Jane Smith replace Jo Grant. Exactly the same, after all those years. You're trying to resist the newcomer, just slightly, because someone you love has gone but, at the same time, there's the Doctor, and the TARDIS, and the adventure and, best of all, the chance to see all that through a newcomer's eyes. The format of the programme takes over, and the format wins. That's when I really knew that Martha fitted in.'

During her first few episodes, Martha will meet William Shakespeare in seventeenth-century London. She'll encounter an evil Plasmavore. She'll take a trip to a very different side of New New York which will reunite the Doctor with the Face of Boe – will he reveal the secret he hinted at in *New Earth*? And Martha will also get to see old New York, in the 1930s to be precise, before heading home. After that? Surely the Daleks can't be too far away? 'They are always going to be part of the Doctor's life, whether he likes it or not,' says Russell. 'But in Series Three? Well, we'll have to wait and see…'

We don't want to know everything, but Steven Moffat will be back. Exactly what his story will be remains shrouded in secrecy, but he says he has ideas. 'It's a one-part story, which will have to get cheaper and cheaper as I deliver later and later. No horses, no mirrors, no Blitz. And I'm probably less inclined to bring back old foes than some – once you've had the two iconic ones back, that's it, I think. If you've got brand new villains each week it's creepy and scary. You don't know what they're up to and you've got to find that out. I like stories where the Doctor and his companion walk out of the doors and encounter fear, horror and screaming women, as they always do.'

THE RUNAWAY BRIDE

Directed by EUROS LYN

CAST

David Tennant *The Doctor*
and Catherine Tate *Donna Noble*
with Sarah Parish *The Empress*
Don Gilet *Lance Bennett*
Howard Attfield *Geoff Noble*
Jacqueline King *Sylvia Noble*
Trevor Georges *Vicar*
Rhodri Meiler *Rhodri*
Krystal Archer *Nerys*
Glen Wilson *Taxi Driver*
Zafirah Boateng *Little Girl*
Paul Kasey, George Cottle *Robot Santas*

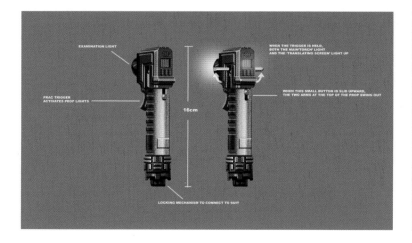

Cauldrons in Shakespeare's England – concept art by Peter McKinstry.

There is also at least one more adventure in store for former companion Sarah Jane Smith, played by Elisabeth Sladen. BBC Wales are producing a sixty-minute special written by Gareth Roberts, to be broadcast on BBC One in the New Year. 'Children's BBC approached us,' Russell explains. 'They wanted to do a drama based around the idea of a young Doctor Who, but I said no to that. Somehow the idea of a fourteen-year-old Doctor, on Gallifrey inventing sonic screwdrivers, takes away from the mystery and intrigue of who he is and where he came from. So instead I suggested doing a series with Sarah Jane Smith, because she'd been so popular in *School Reunion*. Truth be told, if they'd said no to that, I'd have found a way to bring her back in Series Three, but this is much better. At the end of *School Reunion*, she and K-9 left together but I was concerned she'd just go back to her same old life, which she might have to have done to justify a new story with the Doctor. This way, we can see that meeting the Tenth Doctor really did change her, moved her life on and indeed she's better for it. This special sees her with new friends, a new team, and so it really is the new life the Doctor promised she'd have. And who knows, maybe one day, we might have a whole series of Sarah Jane's adventures. Hooray!' *The Sarah Jane Adventures* will be directed by Colin Teague and produced by Susie Liggat, ahead of her production duties during Series Three of *Doctor Who*.

In its current incarnation, *Doctor Who* has managed that rarest of things in television – it has combined critical acclaim with popular success. Across the two series, the show has been watched by an average of eight million viewers on BBC One. In fact, not only did Series Two match Series One, in the end it managed to outperform it: both *Army of Ghosts* and *Doomsday* were seen by 1.3m more viewers than had spent the hot summer Saturday evenings of June 2005 in front of the first year's climax. The show was a constant feature of television's top twenty right from episode one, but *The Christmas Invasion* heralded a second series that would frequently break into the top ten, and in the end the adventures of the Doctor and Rose were proving more popular than the previously unbeatable soaps. Under-sixteens made up about twenty per cent of the programme's total audience, with around 1.2m children regularly watching, making *Doctor Who* by far that age group's most-watched programme. CBBC's children's magazine show *Totally Doctor Who* was able to boast a peak audience of 1.5m, and throughout its run gained audiences at least as high as those for other children's television flagships. On digital channel BBC Three, repeated episodes could attract audiences of up to 0.8m, frequently outdoing opposition from the likes of *The Simpsons* to take the top spot in the charts for non-terrestrial television. The same channel's *Doctor Who Confidential* broke another significant barrier when it achieved ratings of 1.0m for the final edition of its second series. Add to all this statistics showing some of television's best results for how much the audiences were actually enjoying what they were watching, and it would be quite usual to find the press queuing up to knock this sort of success story…

Instead, reviewers from *The Times* to *The Sun* to the *New Statesman* have devoted ever-increasing column inches to singing the show's praises. Meanwhile, the series has been a hit around the world, increasing audience numbers for the Sci-Fi channel in America and for CBC in Canada, being subtitled or dubbed into French, Hungarian (under the title 'Ki Vagy, Doki') and a dozen other languages, breaking into the Korean TV market, and even being shown as in-flight entertainment on some airlines. Back in the UK, an ongoing range of print adventures for the Ninth and Tenth Doctors from BBC Books has seen *Doctor Who* novels in the fiction charts throughout 2005 and 2006, with industry figures putting total sales at more than half a million copies. The toy market has been similarly captured, with retailers reporting huge demand for Daleks, TARDISes and Cybermen of all shapes and sizes – the top-selling toy of 2005, and the recipient of an industry award, was a remote-controlled Dalek.

Which brings us to the awards collected by the series itself. No show will win every award that it's nominated for – and *Doctor Who* was nominated for an awful lot of awards following its return. A lengthy run of success in awards voted for by the public was launched when Christopher Eccleston was named best actor in the *TV Quick/TV Choice Awards*, while in October 2005 Christopher, Billie Piper and *Doctor Who* itself were selected as Most Popular Actor, Most Popular Actress and Most Popular Drama, in a huge public poll for the 2005 *National Television Awards*. Similar success followed at the 2005 *TV Moments* – where the show not only won in its category but actually took the top award for 'Golden TV Moment' of 2005 – as well as at the *South Bank Show Awards*, the *What Satellite and Digital TV Awards*, the *Glamour Magazine Awards* (for Billie, naturally) and, in America, the top three places at the prestigious *Hugo Awards* for episodes by Steven Moffat, Robert Shearman and Paul Cornell. Series Two again received several nominations for the 2006 *National Television Awards*, the results of which were announced after this book went to press, as well as picking up awards from *TV Quick* for the second year running, again for Best Drama, and Best Actress and Actor – the latter this year for David Tennant of course. There were also plenty of accolades from the television industry, with *Doctor Who* recognised by the judging panels of the 2006 *Broadcast Awards*, *BAFTA Cymru* (for Best Drama Series, Best Drama Director, Best Costume Design, Best Make-up Design and Best Photography Direction, and the Sian Phillips Award for Outstanding Contribution to Network Television for Russell), 'Industry Player of the Year' for Russell at the Edinburgh Television Festival and, most prestigious of all, the *BAFTAs* themselves. The show was selected as the year's Best Drama Series by the British Academy and, in an audience vote, as best television programme, with Russell also being presented with the Dennis Potter Award for outstanding writing for television.

However Series Three shapes up (and we know Captain Jack Harkness is in there at the finale, and hopefully other friends and enemies, old and new will materialise as the series progresses), no one can claim that Jane Tranter and Lorraine Heggessey's belief in *Doctor Who* was misplaced. With Russell T Davies, Julie Gardner, Phil Collinson in the production hot seats, BBC Television has the most popular drama series on British television today. Who could ever have predicted, way back in 1963 when Verity Lambert, Sydney Newman, Waris Hussein and William Hartnell started it all off in a fogbound junkyard, that the show would still be here forty-four years later, more popular than ever before and showing no signs of fading away.

Because *Doctor Who* is a programme driven by the fertile imaginations of those who write and produce it. And imagination is one thing we can never run out of.

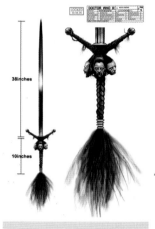

Lilith's sword, designed by Peter McKinstry.

AFTERWORD BY RUSSELL T DAVIES

Sometimes I think this must be the most documented programme in the world. You can stand on set and watch the official crew being filmed by *Doctor Who Confidential*, who are taping an item for *Totally Doctor Who*, while being followed by a *Blue Peter* crew and a Website Video Diary team, all of which is being captured on David Tennant's camcorder. If something funny happens — ooh, a Slitheen fell over! — then I catch myself thinking, at the back of my mind, where to tell that story? On the DVD commentary, the podcast, in *Doctor Who Magazine*, on *Wales Today* or in a BBC Four 'History of Monsters'…?

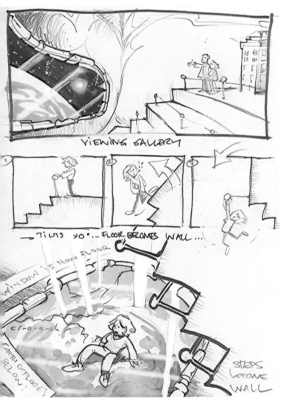

YIEWING GALLERY

TILTS >0°… FLOOR BECOMES WALL…

WINDOW'S NOW FLOOR

STEPS BECOME WALL

Truth is, I like all that coverage. I think it opens up TV, it demystifies and democratises the process, and it says to a watching eight-year-old — look, anyone can do this job! In a decade or so, this could be you! These aren't special TV People, born on a mountainside in a storm; they're ordinary folk, working hard, just doing their jobs and doing them well. Most of them Welsh! When I grew up in Swansea, and yearned to work in telly, I thought the only place to go was London or Manchester, those distant cities with big TV traditions. Now, the equivalent of me could just get the bus to Upper Boat! That's why we wanted this book, to continue that open access and to celebrate it.

But despite appearances, the documentary cameras aren't always there. In fact, the most crucial decisions — the stories, the style, the monsters — take place in private. Often in emails at three in the morning. And that's where this book really comes into its own.

If *The Inside Story* has taught me one thing, it's that there's no such thing as history. There's just people. All with different voices, all talking and remembering. And that's why I love this book, because Gary Russell has slaved like an Ood in a mineshaft, capturing so many different voices, each one colouring the history of *Doctor Who* with their own personality. This could've been a list of dry old facts, dates, and the inside leg measurement of Clockwork Droid 3 (32", if you're wondering). But instead, Gary has opted for an oral history. He's captured memories and opinions and anecdotes, a few good laughs and a couple of snarls. And that's been instructive for me; there's been a few times, reading these chapters, that I've paused over a sentence, wondered, and found myself thinking, 'It didn't happen like that!' Or 'I didn't say that, Julie/Phil/Ed/Dalek Sec did.' But then I realised, their version of the truth is just as real as mine. If that's how they remember it, then that's how it happened. If 400 people have worked on the new *Doctor Who*, then there are 400 different *Inside Stories* waiting to be told.

And alongside the stories, there are the pictures. We've got so many design teams working alongside each other — Ed Thomas's empire, Neill Gorton's Millennium FX, the computer wizards of The Mill, costume and make-up, the model-makers, let alone the directors – that it's genuinely a hothouse of creativity. Sometimes they're all battling away in splendid competition – whose version of the Judoon spaceship is best? Fight!! – and sometimes not; I vividly remember the final tone meeting for *The End of the World*, just days before filming, when we realised that every department had assumed that the Face of Boe was being built by someone else (is it a prop? A costume? CGI?). Poor old Boe didn't exist! Cue frantic scribbling, hammering, carving…

But every day I'm astonished by what these departments produce. When I was a lad, no bigger than a Space Pig, I worked briefly for BBC Wales Graphics, illustrating *Jackanory*-style Welsh-language stories for children's TV. *Y Robin Goch*, that was one of mine. Oh, a classic! (What d'you mean, you never saw it?!) But I was just a doodler, and I look with envy and wonder at anyone who can pick up a pen, a mouse or a swathe of fabric and create a world, a spaceship, a dress, a prosthetic nose. Every day, my rushes arrive – that's a DVD containing everything that was filmed the day before – and, I swear, *Doctor Who* is the only programme whose rushes make me laugh out loud. The sheer audacity of what those designers have created! There's a nun falling down a lift shaft! Penelope Wilton running away from Slitheen! Through Downing Street! Raffalo! The 1860s, the 1950s, 1599, 2012! And I promise, when the first footage of the Empress of the Racnoss arrived, from the Christmas Special 2006 – oh, the best day's rushes on any programme ever!

It's a joy to watch, a joy to work on – and such a joy to work with Gary that we promptly signed him up to join the team. And if the shifting memories of those involved prove one thing, it's that *Doctor Who* is a different thing to every person watching. If you love it, then you love it in your own individual way. We just make it. You own it. So enjoy!

Russell T Davies

WINDOWS CRACK…
–
THE CRACKS SHINE…
–
STREAMS OF LIGHT PIERCE THROUGH…

This page and opposite: At the very start of production, Russell T Davies did these concept sketches for the dropped sequence where Rose falls onto the glass window in the Viewing Gallery as the sunlight breaks through.

INDEX